Black Wine

Black Wine

▼

Candas Jane Dorsey

A Tom Doherty Associates Book
New York

BLACK WINE

Copyright © 1997 by Candas Jane Dorsey

Edited by David G. Hartwell

A Tor Book
Published by Tom Doherty Associates, Inc.
175 Fifth Avenue
New York, NY 10010

Tor Books on the World Wide Web:
http://www.tor.com

Tor® is a registered trademark of Tom Doherty Associates, Inc.

Library of Congress Cataloging-in-Publication Data

Dorsey, Candas Jane.
    Black wine / Candas Jane Dorsey.—1st ed.
      p. cm.
    "A Tom Doherty Associates book."
    ISBN 0-312-86578-3 (pb)
    I. Title.
    PR9199.3.D56B57   1997
    813'.54—dc20   96-33021
                                    CIP

First hardcover edition: January 1997
First trade paperback edition: January 1998

Printed in the United States of America

0 9 8 7 6 5 4 3 2 1

To all those who taught me how to listen to the children
—and when to speak for the voiceless

Acknowledgments

I am grateful, for financial support and a supportive writing environment variously, to the Canada Council; the Alberta Foundation for the Arts; the Leighton Colony at the Banff Centre for the Arts; the Strawberry Creek Lodge retreat of the Writers Guild of Alberta; David Greer's Pender Island retreat; Amber and Perry Hayward's Black Cat Ranch, and Wooden Door. Thank you to those who read various drafts, including but not limited to: Timothy Anderson, Jane Bisbee, Beverley Estock, Betty Gibbs, Amber Hayward, Michael Skeet, Lorna Toolis, Elisabeth Vonarburg (whose cats all had the same name), and Mary Woodbury. Thanks to the ghosts and hedgehogs who caused it to be and/or were there for the process; thanks to Kim Stanley Robinson for a powerful image; to David Hartwell for buying and editing it, and to Marie Jakober for telling me it was a novel in the first place. Thanks to the dream world.

Contents

(1) Ea & Annalise
(2) Essa
(3) Essa / Fierce-Frightened
(4) Essa telling own story, passing on book
(5) Ehta wrap up (6) Essa, Ea, & Despot

Black Wine

Life in the zone of control (1)

There is a scarred, twisted old madwoman in a cage in the courtyard. The nurse throws a crust at her as he passes, therefore so does the girl. Others bring a can of water, or a trencher of meat cut up small, to stuff through the bars. The woman shoves the food into her mouth, dribbling and drooling and muttering.

"Why do they keep her?" says the girl. "She is useless. She is crazy. She eats too much."

"So do you," says the nurse offhandedly.

"But I work," says the girl. "I am a slave."

"She is not a slave."

"She is in a cage."

"It doesn't matter."

The old woman babbles in a language the waif understands but the others don't. She calls names, she recites recipes, she counts things. Sometimes she talks of hanging, and carrion crows. The girl thinks she calls like a crow herself, and the voice makes her shiver with an atavistic fear she hardly notices, so like the rest of her life it is.

The waif grows used to her hoarse, angry voice raving; does her bit to feed the caged beast, and hopes the evil is never released.

She begins to dream: that the madwoman cradles her, sings lullabies in her birdlike voice, bends over her with eyes like cloudy fire and pecks out her heart. She wakes whimpering and her nurse, in whose bed she now lies, wakes too and fucks her for comfort, lying beside her after saying, "There now. You'll sleep now. Sleep."

But the girl never sleeps, only dreams some more, of sun she scarcely remembers, of hills gleaming white and impossibly large, of a giant crow who nurses her with a bitter milk, then flies away. Flies away and turns silver, and is shot by arrows from an evil god, and bleeds, head exploding and the feel of cobblestone underfoot.

She learns to dream silently and never to turn for comfort to the nurse because he will always fuck her then, and to save a bit of every meal to propitiate the madwoman.

One day she stops by the cage, her heart screaming with fear, her face flushed with it, her hands full of sweets she has stolen from the kitchen.

"You must stop them," she says desperately, in the secret language. "You must stop sending me the dreams. I don't know what to do with them. Here. I will steal you anything. Just stop them."

She is thrusting the sticky stuff through the bars. The old woman backs away, silent for a change and, the girl thinks oddly, horrified.

"Who are you?" says the woman. "Are you me? Have you come to kill me, at last? To carry me up the Remarkable Mountains?"

"I don't know," says the girl.

"Tell me who you are, before I go mad again. How do you know this language?"

"I don't know. I don't know anything. Just take the dreams away. Give me back my heart."

"Your name, girl, your name first."

"I don't own a name yet. They found me, they fixed my head. I belong to them."

"You should have a name," the old woman insists, scrabbling among the sweet buns, tearing one open, then licks out the filling with a greedy swiping tongue.

"I can't afford one. I can't even afford to be free. Please, leave me alone. Eat the heart of someone with a name. Please, please."

"You are the only one who speaks my language. Do you know that?"

"I will stop. Honestly. I can't help it. It's in my head from before. I can't help it."

"When is before? Where is before?" The woman comes closer, crawling across the food, her hands and knees mashing it to useless paste. The girl thinks how hard it was to steal the food, how she could have eaten it herself. The eyes paralyze her. They are the eyes in her dreams, but there is no fire. They are cloudy and almost blind, but yet she knows they see her.

"When? Where?" insists the hag.

"I don't know. I don't know anything before I was here. They say I fell out of a cloud. I was all broken, and my head still hurts. It's flat here, see? And it hurts if I touch it."

"Should be trepanned," says the woman, and reaches out to the girl, who stands paralyzed like a snake.

"What is a snake?" says the girl.

"An animal," says the woman absently. "Why?"

"I thought of it. Sometimes I think of things and I don't know what they are."

"I could tell you. Lessons, now that's an idea. Pass the time."

"You don't sound mad anymore."

"I'm only mad when the wind's from . . . oh, what's the quote? North-north-east? I'm never mad in this language. I could teach you about snakes, and silver clouds—"

"How did you know it was silver?"

"How did you?"

"A man saw it. He told my nurse, who told me when he was fucking me."

"Oh, he touches you?"

"No. Just at night."

"Why?"

"He took care of me when they found me. Now I belong to him, so he fucks me. And his master. Because they put all that time into saving me. So I have to pay it back. They explained."

"Don't you get lonely?"

"What's that mean?"

"For someone you like to touch you."

The girl realizes that the woman is not mad, she is a pervert. But the idea of touch has never repelled her as it does the others and she draws closer. "Is that why they put you here?"

"They put me here because I refused to be owned. I wouldn't take enough from any one person. So they all have to give me a bit, and they think I belong to all of them, and so no-one can kill me alone, or the others will want reparations. But I belong to no-one."

"No-one?"

"Except myself. Nor do you. Nor does anyone, really. You are lucky you speak this language. In theirs, I couldn't say this. There are no words for it."

The girl realizes this is true. She steps even closer, and the sticky, scarred hand darts further out to touch her head. She turns so that the woman cannot reach the tender spot on the skull, still afraid enough to be that careful. The touch is only seconds long, yet in the girl awakes such a wave of warmth and then of terror and illness that she thinks she will fall. She grabs at the cage bars, and begins to cry.

"I hate crying," says the woman. "Go away. You've had your first lesson. Steal me some more goodies, and I'll give you another." And she hitches herself away to huddle, back to the girl, in the other corner of the cage, spoiling her pose somewhat by furtively half-turning to snatch some squashed scraps of the new food. In the shadow, the girl hears her slobbery munching and all her previous despair returns.

She has stolen food, and risked coming out here, and let that scabrous hand touch her, and all for nothing. Instead of taking her dreams away, the madwoman has given her more to know, more than she needed to know to survive, more than she wanted to know, and all in the shadowy secret language of her dreams. As soon as she can stand, she runs away to the showers, where she knows no-one will be, and washes her hair, and if she cries, no-one will notice under the flowing water, she thinks, and lets it run and run until it runs cold and gives her a reason for shivering.

A dream:

> *In childhood it seems there are easy answers. Later in life the curriculum will spiral and all the easy things will be re-evaluated, but for the child running in the dusty track of a mountain summer the world was simple.*
>
> *She was safe. She ran from her father to her mother down a dusty path. Roots gnarling across the track just under the ground made a kind of gentle staircase for her feet, and she ran downhill accelerating, her plump feet finding the safe places. Below her on the path the woman, her mother, had turned, laughing, and was holding out her arms. She wore bright colors and her hair was loose and tangling in the wind. Behind her the giant trees rose straight and fragrant into the sun.*
>
> *As the child ran into the haven of arms her mother picked her up and swung her dizzyingly into the sky and back to her hip, then turned and ran down the path herself, her feet as sure as the child's had been. The man, her father, came behind, calling to them through laughter. They were all laughing. The world seemed to the child to be wheeling by in*

*great forward-and-back arcs as the path twisted down the
mountain, into the shade of the trees then out, through the
meadow of flowers and then onto the strip of dusty moraine
again, then back toward the trees, then into the sun . . .*

*After they had run down and down they came out
suddenly on a great gray-tan talus slope and the woman
stopped and set the child down, let the man catch up. They
went across the slope hand in hand in hand, the child between the adults, all of them slipping and sliding and
laughing more.*

It was a long way down the slope.

*"The beach of an ocean feels like this to walk on," said
the woman. "The dunes at Avanue are steep like this, and
climbing them is slippery. Can you imagine going up this?"*

The man snorted.

*"Then imagine all the bits of rock are little grains of
sand. It's amazing. It's like some kind of hard water. It flows.
And if the wind blows . . . "*

*The child imagined the wind slipping and sliding down
the dunes at Avanue. She imagined the dunes as some kind
of geometrical slope, at thirty-five degrees, like this one, but
the mother kept talking and the mind picture changed with
each sentence, like the shape of the wind.*

*"It is an amazing landscape there. It is all billowy and
soft, like a puffy quilt. Or maybe like the body of some great
voluptuous fat person turning over in bed, the covers falling
off, the mounds of flesh shifting gently and sensually. You
know, you can memorize the patterns and then a big wind-
storm comes and when you go out the next day everything is
different. The skyline is different. The shoreline is different.
The sand has turned over in its sleep. While you slept."*

*They arrived at the bottom of the slope, where the grasses
began to grow again. There were tiny flowers scattered
through the grass. Vetch, broom, clover stood tall, and win-
tergreen, bedstraw, strawberry flowers—no berries yet, the
child noted with regret—nestled in at their bases. The heat
sat heavier here, and the buzz of the honey-gathering bees
mixed with the clatter of grasshoppers. The plain was not easy
walking—under the grasses and wildflowers the ground was
uneven. Duster-pods popped underfoot.*

They moved slowly, meandering across the open and toward the trees. Here, there were some deciduous trees with the evergreens. The white trunks flashed in the dappled sunlight through their rounded, shivering leaves. Swallows had swooped low over the field, diving on insects, but once the trees surrounded the family, they could hear birds all around but see hardly any.

There was a tangle of berry-bushes and rose-prickles all around them, but they followed a path clear of all but grasses and the occasional thistle. The child tugged at her father's hand, wanting to be carried; when he picked her up, she leaned her head back until she could see the blue, clear, slightly hazy sky above the trees. There, so high that it was almost invisible, some kind of raptor—hawk, maybe even eagle—was circling slowly in and out of the open stripe of sky above the path. She saw it suddenly stoop and dive, but its rapid fall took it out of sight, and she straightened up and turned to a close scrutiny of the bushes unrolling into the past behind her father's shoulder.

The path was well used, and it was cut down into the clay to make a little dry-mud bank on each side, where some kind of animal or bird had tunneled out a riddle of holes. Like little caves, she thought with satisfaction, and imagined living in a cave. She imagined that her mother would know about caves; her mother knew about everything.

"Little mother," she said, "did you ever live in a cave?"

"Like a squirrel?" her mother said. "Not a cave like a squirrel or a swallow. But I went exploring once in the caves of Denamona. They are big limestone caves with icicles in them, but the icicles are made of rock, not water. They form the same way though, but slowly as these mountains."

"Not fast like the doomes."

"Dunes, you mean."

"Yes, dunes. Not fast like fat people dreaming."

"No, slow, like icicles but one drip in a person's lifetime. Maybe. Or maybe a mother and her daughter both have their lives in the time it takes one drop to freeze into rock in the caves of Denamona."

The child shivered with joy. She loved her mother's stories. She loved the pictures her mother put into her mind.

"When can we go?" she said.

"Go, little one?"

"Go to the caves. To see the sleeping fat people. Everywhere."

"When you are older."

"Next year, when I'm four?"

"No, a little later than that. When you are old enough to carry your own pack, and walk all day, then the three of us will go somewhere."

"Promise?"

The father hugged her. "Promise," he said. His voice sounded a little wistful.

"Do you want to see the pictures too, little father?" It was a new idea for the child. She knew her mother was telling the stories to her father too, but it was the first time in her small life that she imagined that her father might feel as she did, might not know everything. It made her shiver a little with another kind of shiver.

"Yes," he said. "I want to see it all too."

She was watching his face, and so she saw then the look that passed between her parents, a gentle look but much too deep for a three-and-a-half year old. You would have to swim a long way down in that look; the mountains had no pools that deep, not in the places she was allowed to go.

Then she thought about the sea. "Can you swim in the sea?" she asked her mother.

"Yes, if you are strong," said her mother.

"And it's big down, right?"

"Deep. Yes."

"Big down." The child liked bigness. "I want to go big down, and big up, and big across."

"Deep, wide and far," said her father and mother, accidentally together, in that parent tone that's so patient and knows everything. Their collision of voices made everybody laugh again. The child thought nothing of that. They were all always laughing.

The waif awakens sweating from a dream forgotten but for the language and the terror.

* * *

"I don't like you," she practices saying to the madwoman. "I don't want you in my head."

But when she says it, the old woman just laughs. "Why not? What else is in there?"

To that, the girl has no answer. The bizarre logic has caught her.

"So we'll fill it up. What kind of food did you bring?"

She hasn't any, except a bread-roll she'd stolen for herself. Trapped, she thrusts it sullenly at the bars.

"We'll share," says the old woman. "You keep half." The waif looks at her. "Go on, you break it—I'm sure you wouldn't want it after I'd touched it!" And she laughs.

The girl breaks the roll, dividing it as fairly as she can, keeping the sticky meat filling inside from dropping out. She holds out the two halves.

The old woman reaches through the bars and takes the smaller half. "Eat," she says. "Then we'll talk."

"No." But she has to say it in the dream language. The nurse's language doesn't seem to have a word like that. So she's broken her resolve. Tears form, and she sniffs and blinks them back.

"Never mind," says the old woman. "It won't hurt for long. You'll go crazy, or they'll hang you. Easy as that, really."

The girl knows that is true, and so, comforted, she stays for a while. That is the second lesson.

And so it goes.

"Looks like it's going to clear."

The old woman in the cage harrumphs. She is soaking wet despite the bits of wood and tin the girl has over time stolen for a makeshift roof to the cage. The storm has blown in hard and horizontal.

She and the girl crouch on either side of the bars, as far leeward as she can go, as close to her as the girl can get. A little warmth is shared.

The doors were locked when the storm came, of course, so the girl has been trapped in the courtyard.

"It's because of the demons in the lightning who'll get you if you're out in a storm."

"Nonsense," says the old woman. "Lightning is dangerous for a much more prosaic reason."

So the storm is devoted to a learning session on electricity. The girl is cold but whenever her attention wanders the old woman shouts at her, grabs her through the bars and shakes her, or turns a ragged back to her in silence. The latter is most effective: soon the girl is begging for her to speak, and promising to listen.

The girl would have thought that both the storm and the old woman at such close quarters would be frightening, but it seems that over the past months she has grown less and less afraid of the madwoman, so much so that she would rather be here, cold and wet, huddled close to her, than locked in the warm, safe corridors. Especially considering what her nurse and owner might think a suitable way to pass the idle hours of the storm-confinement.

The lesson is over and the rain has slowed to a tranquil drip. The woman is silent. The girl hums to herself a little.

"Tell me a story," she says, "about your Othertime."

The old woman starts. "Story? What do you want?"

"A story. You know. About before you were in the cage. Before nobody owned you. Somebody must have owned you once, or you owned somebody. Or—"remembering some of her lessons "—you did something else. What was it?"

The old woman laughs. "You think I can remember that?"

"You can remember everything else. Electricity and how genetics work and how to plant trees in the mountains."

"Do you have any idea what it was like?" the old woman demands shrilly.

"Of course I don't; why do you think I asked?" snaps the girl, then hears in her voice the echo of the old woman and begins to laugh. So does the old woman.

"Learned your lessons well, girl, eh? Eh?"

Then the nurse comes out into the eaves-dripping calm and shouts for her, and she has to run away before he sees her. No stories that day.

In the afternoons, now, the girl is to go over to the hairdresser for some lessons in makeup and deportment. Her nurse must have paid for it, or his master, because she is not required to serve the woman, or her assistant who teaches about makeup. The assistant is an impeccably turned-out boy with skin as pale as hers. He is the one who knew which makeup suits her coloring, and gives her lessons until she masters the elaborate eye paint and cheek contouring which is the fashion in the Land of the Dark Isles.

"Why there?" the girl asks her nurse.

"That's where you're sold," says the nurse, and it is thus she finds out she is to leave the place.

That evening she hurries to the cage with her gift of food. She has long since stopped stealing sweets and gone instead for meat and vegetables; she has begun to take the life of the old woman more seriously, and has developed a peculiar desire to nourish her properly. The madwoman always grumbles.

This day, the girl still wears the face paint when she comes up to the cage in the evening light.

"They are selling me north!" she whispers.

The madwoman turns around and sees her face. She begins to cry and backs into the corner of the cage.

"Don't fuck the old woman!" she says. "Don't fuck the regent. Don't let anybody in."

"What?"

"I know, I saw in the mirror. I saw through the wall. I know what they will do to you. To me, I mean. You are me, aren't you?"

"Talk sense, old woman. I won't be here much longer. Who will take care of you then?"

"You will die," says the old woman, "if you go there without a brain in your head like this. You know you shouldn't go there."

"I have no choice. You know that; I keep telling you. And anywhere is better than here."

"Here, at least, the cages have real bars and when they kill someone, they stay dead. There the corpses walk around for years after they're dead inside."

The girl shivers even though she doesn't believe the old woman. "Have you been there?"

"Been there! I was born there, that cursed citadel looking out to the Dark Isles. I saw the weather blow from the north for eighteen years before I ran away. I know everything about that place—but it doesn't help, you know. It didn't help us."

"Us?" She gives the old woman a potato.

"Us, yes, us, don't think I'll tell you anything."

"You have to. You were the one that made me come back and back for these lessons, as you call them, but you never tell me anything. You know things that would help."

"Can't talk to you in that face. Go take it off. Put your other one back." The woman throws the potato at the girl; she darts away, angry, and almost eats the rest herself and doesn't come back. But the shower does feel good, and her face feels better without all the greasepaint on it. It is almost dark by now.

"Here's your meat," she says. "Tell me!"

"What I've told you a thousand times before," says the woman. "You aren't a prisoner. You just take their word for everything. Do you know it is possible to live in the mountains with everyone taking care of everyone else, and no debt at all? I did it, yes, we both did it, long enough for our cells to replace and then some, but I'm the one alive to tell. I'm not hanging for the flies and birds to eat. No, no, don't be thinking of that. Ee-yah! What a fool you are."

"How would I be free? I don't have anything."

"Steal it. You steal my food. You think you can do that. Steal away. Steal away to the east, or across the sea. That's where you should go. Find my family, that's it. That's it. Here, here."

And she scrabbles in the filthy nest at the other end of the cage. Under the rags and scraps there is a small box; the girl has always wondered what was in it. The woman shakes it open impatiently. Out falls a peculiar tablet, all bound together on one side, with a metal hook holding the other side together.

"What is it?" says the girl.

"It's a book, my book. Everything is in here. You should take it and send it to my daughter. She lives in the mountains, across the sea. She must be my age now, my age when I went there, I mean, she must be old enough to live her life. She was supposed to have it. Look, I wrote in it." The woman shows how the clasp unhooks, the pages spread open. There are marks on the pages and with familiar horror the girl realizes she knows what they mean. They are flat, silent words. She knows how they are made, with a stylus, like the marks on a kitchen tablet or a laundry count but more complicated, and every sound and word has its own shape. She even knows the words for the stylus, and the medium it spreads.

"Pen," she says. "Ink." Her head hurts to think of it.

"Didn't have ink," says the hag. "But I'm not stupid!" She cackles loudly.

"Shhh!" The girl huddles against the cage. It is almost completely dark in the courtyard now except for the weak light above the page. She is grateful for that; the individual words are hard to see, and maybe that will protect her. This old woman always catches me with some kind of magic, she thinks angrily.

"I figured it out pretty quick! Helped to remember her blood dripping down on me, from where they put the spear in her. There's lots of blood in a woman, you know. Lots of blood. Dippers and dippers full. And if you aren't dead, you make more every day. So there's plenty to write with. Here, see?"

The pages all look the same, dark marks shadowy against them in the dimness. In the daylight, many months later, she will see the writing in blood clearly for the first time. But now, she believes the woman.

"Here, I'll write the name and the place in it," and taking from the edge of the open side of the binding a thin sharp pen, the old woman drives it into her arm. The waif jumps and cries out a little, as if she were struck. The swelling drop of blood looks black. With bizarre care, the old woman dips her nib in it, opens the cover, and gently scratches a few words, bringing the pen back and back to the swelling drop to load it again.

"Pretty good, eh? Pretty tidy, don't you think? One thing I've learned in the last few years, to be tidy." The woman looks at her keenly through the bars; if not for the grotesque shadows of her rag-pile bed, the smells of half-rotted food and unwashed flesh and clothing, her careful, serious expression would look credible. "Otherwise," she says confidentially, "you can't find a thing when you need it. Keep tidy, that's what I say."

She beckons the girl closer. "Take this," she whispers. "Put it on a black ship north if you aren't going there yourself. She was supposed to have it when I left. Keep it with the abacus. It'll be safe."

"How do you know about that?" blurts the girl. It is her only possession, her only secret. She had remembered its name first, though her own still remains a mystery. "It's mine!"

"Yes, certainly, it's yours. It was a gift. A person doesn't take back a gift. But sometimes a gift gets lost and it has to be sent back. You'll send it, won't you?" And she grabbed the girl's arm in her filthy, sharp-clawed fingers.

"You said you wouldn't touch me any more!" says the girl, angrily pulling away. She has the book in her hand now, though. The woman looks at her steadily. The girl looks into the shadowed eyes and something stirs from the dream world, something from the nights she has tried to forget. "Yes, I'll send it," she promises, and tucks it into her shirt. The hag rummages, comes up with a thin light rag.

"This'll be fine when it's washed," she says. "It's all of hers I have left. Take it. My daughter should give it to her children. They should have something back, too, since their mother is dead." And she begins to weep, great heaving sobs too loud for the girl's taste. She is afraid of the curfew guard, if the hag isn't.

She begins to steal away. The old woman stops crying suddenly, and "Hsst!" she whispers. The girl stops, looks back.

"You will remember," says the old woman. "You won't like it, but you will remember. Remember this too. It will be important."

"Why?" the girl says, half-angry, half-believing.

"We all remember," says the old woman. "It's our curse. It is our freedom. I think sometimes this cage will drive me mad, but memory takes me out of it. Of course," she goes on reasonably, "then the memories drive me mad instead, but a person in these circumstances can't have everything."

The girl can't help it. She begins to laugh. "You are crazy," she says, "and I think you are the most frightening dream I have ever had, but I like you."

These are words she didn't learn in the south, and they come out of her in the madwoman's secret language. She stands still, shocked. The hag doesn't laugh.

"That's fine," she says. "That's all I can expect, these days. Where's that meat, anyway; I put it down somewhere and do you think I can find it?" She begins to rummage in her cage, throwing out old crusts and rags. The girl runs.

She finds that the nurse, luckily, is not yet in the room, so she washes the scarf—for it is that, an oblong silk scarf—and hangs it up under her other set of clothes, where he will not see it. In the morning, while he is out pissing, she unties the ragged end of the long strip of cotton cloth which is the turban she was found in, and there is the abacus. She wraps the little book and the abacus in the silk and ties them again in the end of the cotton strip.

She sits for a second fingering the strip, which is longer than she is tall, but only as wide as two spread hands. It was once a bright saffron color, but it is faded from washing, and there are stains now where her blood did not come out, even in cold water: by the time she had been well enough to wash the clothes in which she had been found, the stains had set.

The reflex, when she found the abacus, had been to trade it for safety, but she had realized that while she could have sold it for some nights free of sex, it would not buy her autonomy, so she hid it instead. Its colors echo her dreams.

She folds the turban strip, thinking for the first time that it had probably saved her life, cushioning her head on landing. Then she goes out to do her morning ablutions. It is the hag who has taught her to wash morning and night, and the habit is pleasant—now that she is used to the abuse others give her for it.

She is returning to the room, her hair dripping, when the nurse comes running. "There you are, little bitch. Should have known—you're always washing. Get your things together. Your new owner has sent for you."

And this is how it is that the girl, instead of running away, goes north in a guarded caravan, with her little bundle, to the home of her new master, the prince of the Land of the Dark Isles. She thinks often on the way of the madwoman's stories, and shivers even in the sunlight, even as she sweats her way the long walk, the long road north. And at night, once, the hag's words ring in a dream, and wake her sweating: "Don't fuck the regent," she had said. The girl's terror abates quickly with the foolishness of it. What choice would she have? The richest man in the world, for so her nurse had called him, won't trade her abacus for celibacy.

She shivers again. There are dreams where she likes sex, but in her short life since awakening, there has not been one awake-time she has not hated it: the pain, the roughness, the perfunctory nature of her nurse's pleasure, and the mess. She is only glad that the nurse had never made her pregnant, to bear a child belonging to him. As she walked, her courses had come again, so she is sure. But if the regent ever sees her and ever wants her, she will have no chance.

For the first time, also, in her short sentience, she has begun to think about how she can run away. And although she has come up with no idea of how, still, the thinking itself has made her feel different, as if she were changing, or as if at least she can see now the bars of which her cage is made.

Essa

Morning. The clear air was soft to breathe, in the town at the side of the sea, in the yard at the top of the town. Essa stood on the low, wide graystone wall of the house, shaking her bright-red blanket out in the new sunlight. There were dark sails on the horizon, silver dirigibles above them; this town was a freeport. Essa had been working in the houses, and watching for a sign.

From here, it looked as if the trader town spills down over the edge of the low, flat shelf of rich farmland between the foothills and the sea. But it was the other way, really: around the natural harbor, where the town was founded, it had climbed the hill until it filled the amphitheater-shaped bowl and overflowed back onto the flatland. From her corner room upstairs in this house, Essa could see the ocean from one window and, from the other, back onto the flat, where prosperous farms checker the landscape. She missed the feel of mountains surrounding her, and the taste of the ozone-rich air of the heights, but there was a freedom to be gained from a low horizon devoid of the massy bulk of surrounding rock. As if anything could happen.

"Hey!" Unfair of her heart to leap like a teenager's heart, unfair of her to expect a response from the world to her wishful thoughts. It was only a merchant's helper, coming from the cheap hotels on the hill, calling to her from the base of the wall. Towheaded, stocky, acne-cheeked and much younger than her own twenty-one years.

"I hear you," she said.

"What's to do in this town?" came the answer. "Just in from last night's barquentine; surely a stranger here."

"Aye, so am I," said Essa, smiling. "Can't you tell by my gear?"

"Everyone in these towns has gear traded from the ships. Makes them all look like strangers. Can't even tell the decent folks from the sailors any more. Hear that in towns like this they can walk together and not a soul even cares, should they notice."

"Spoken like a true international; where are you from?"

"South. Above the Dark Isles. You?"

"The mountains. Lake Eslyn. By the Fjord of Tears."

Face screwed against the sunlight, he squinted at her wisely. "I know that place. We had envoys up there last month. Nothing came of it, though. How long since came you here?"

Essa knew several languages. "Since I came here, you mean. Six months. Waiting for a berth east."

"East? Across the water?"

"Do you go there?" Essa played innocent.

"Surely not; are you mad? I'm a merchanter!"

"So?"

"To set foot on the eastern sail-ships is exile from the guild. Don't you know how they have taken our commerce from us? We don't trade."

"In Eslyn, we trade with everyone."

Essa had taken the name of her town with her, to go out in the world. What was she looking for? She knew, now, so might as well not keep it a secret. It was said her mother came from east over the water. Dressed like a sky sailor, and said she came—or left—in a sky-ship blown off course. She swaggered through seven cold winters of Essa's life, and one before her birth of course, before she went again, angry at leaving and yet, Essa assumed, driven to go home.

What a cliché, Essa thought as she shook the blanket after the departing merchanter-kid. When the kid's my age, she thought, nothing will be as simple as sailors and merchanters again. It was a game they played in Fjord of Tears, sailors one crew of ruffian children, merchanters another, dousing each other with water and running home after a damp day's play to parents who laughed or scolded, depending on the crispness of the weather.

No use thinking of Eslyn; her father's dead, her life there become hollow, more clichés. She wished she were an assassin or another kind of romantic fanatic.

But it was morning, and time for her to work. She folded her blanket quickly, took it back to her room. Her mug from breakfast stood on the bedside table, the tea cold.

She took the mug, and her calculator, and went down into the office of the house. The woman who had hired her was a merchanter who wholesaled goods into the interior. Essa knew the mountain towns; she had become assistant to this woman's trade programmer.

The trader she assisted was a pleasant man in his early thirties, as black-haired as any sailor but ivory-skinned and with a different accent and his hair was straight and sleek; he also was unfettered with either sailor or merchanter prejudices. He was from the nameless clan which lives upcoast above Avanue, a long way north. As a supervisor he suited Essa very well. She could even talk her own dialect, for he had often been to the mountains, and knew Lake Eslyn, it seemed, as well as any devoted tourist, which was well enough to please Essa.

As a lover he would have suited her even better, but far up the coast they are kindly and cheerful, but careful who they befriend. And she knew furthermore that he worried about being her boss, the ethics of it. She was gently approaching him, seeing that for the one of lesser power to approach is the way to do it right; she entertained herself by imagining that someday soon they would eat together in taverns, walk by the waterfront when they were not working, and maybe he would give her a name of his on which to hang her knowledge of him as they turned into each other's bodies one warm night in the summer to come.

The calculator was a rectangle frame of wires strung with opal beads. She got it from her mother, when she was the age to start counting. The beads felt cold at first under her fingers, then warmed suddenly to her touch, in the way of semiprecious stones, every time she used it. She thought little of it any more, except on days like this when the sun's rays through the window slats drew green and red fire from the heart of the oval white counters.

The office was warm with the heat of spring sun, and a fly wakened from hibernation was crawling sluggishly on the sill near where Essa set her mug. Soon she too was sluggish with stuffy warmth, and the numbers blurred, and her fingers slowed their counting and lost their place.

The trader came in from the sun-filled yard, a clipboard under his arm. He had been checking the manifests of a small shipment of decorative arts which had come down the trails from Elphender. Dust from the opened bales had marked his cheek and brow with pale streaks, and packing-cotton tufted his long straight hair. The thong with which he tied his ponytail had pulled loose so he held its wayward strands back with one long, knotty-knuckled hand.

He was yawning too.

"Minh," he said, "these spring days take away the brain. Let's do something better with our lives."

Essa jumped up to swab the dust off his face with her hand-
kerchief dipped in tea. As he shook the litter out of his hair and
bound it roughly back she grinned at him. "How about going east?"
she said lightly, but he looked sly down at her, so she felt she should
check for breakfast stains on her shirt or spinach in her teeth. His
eyes were light like an animal's. He released her from the look with
a laugh.

"Why not east?" he cried, left the room in a rush, as always, on
the way snatching their coats from the hooks in the hall. "Come on,"
he said. "Don't be slow." He tossed Essa her jacket.

Essa was laughing too as they went down the hill to the warehouses, laughing and clicking the beads of her calculator like a
gourd full of sand, a rhythm instrument, and he was humming a
trader song, his accent making the snatches of words sound strange,
like the wind in the trees of home.

Essa didn't know his language but she felt she could, felt the
rules of it were simple and expressive, knew how to parse a sentence
already but had no nouns to put into such a sentence, no adjectives,
no participles. On such a day, though, she could not be impatient.

They turned not toward the sea but along one of the parallel streets
that circled the hill like necklaces. The trader had not put on his coat,
was trying to reach the center of his itchy back.

"That stuff gets down my shirt every time," he said.

"Let me," said Essa, greatly daring, and scratched through his
shirt down his spine. She felt his back arch as if he shivered, but he
smiled at her.

They were going, it appeared, to his house. She had never been
there before. He had a narrow house in a row of connected bur-
rows along a close with no street sign. Essa gestured at the naked
lamppost. "Yes," he said. "My street. Northerner district. Nobody
needs a sign here." And they laughed.

The door was a deep magenta purple, set with a golden knocker
and a pattern in gold-headed studs: a coiled sand-snake, she thought,
familiar with the symbol, or perhaps a firedrake, but that would be
mountain mythology, and he was from up-coast—a long way up-
coast, past the dunes at Avanue and north again, where the warm
ocean currents sweep past the Nogard Archipelago. The door swung
wide into a cool, light, open interior.

A cat watched them from a low couch. Another turned from the windowsill. A third had run to meet them. She heard the thump of small paws in the kitchen she saw through an archway. And from under a chair near the door, as she stepped past it into the house, Essa heard a feline growl.

"Ah, Minh!" said the trader to one of the cats, the brown one.

"You have a lot of cats," said Essa.

"Seven," he said, grinning. "I think. A couple of them are out catting around, I guess. Minh is always out this time of day and Minh likes to sleep upstairs in the sun from the skylight."

He picked up the kitten who stood at the kitchen door. "Minh, Minh, Minh!" he said. "What have you been into?"

Essa stood in the center of the first room. She looked at cats. They looked at her. Even a small nose poked out from under the safe draperies of the entryway chair, as the white cat there decided it was safe to check out the stranger.

The kitten was black-and-orange, and climbed to the trader's shoulder. "I named this one for you," he said. "Minh."

She stepped carefully over the brown cat, who was sitting before her, grooming, and went into the kitchen. The trader handed her the kitten.

"Minh," she said tentatively. The kitten growled and tried to bite her nose.

"I have to get out of this shirt," the trader said. He ran up the spiral staircase into the upper room from which sunlight streamed down to make a bright patch near the kitchen door. A brown tabby lay down and rolled in the light, then arranged itself like a naked person on a lounge in an erotic photograph. "Minh?" she said. It turned an ear to her without moving. The kitten miaowed. The white cat scuttled around the edge of the kitchen door and hid behind the stove. Essa put the kitten aside and went to crouch near the stove where the white cat could see her, but not too close. The cat shrank back into the very corner.

"Minh, Minh, Minh," Essa said experimentally, holding out her hand. She said it with all the different inflexions she had heard in the trader's voice, until she struck one which relaxed it a little. Then she went back to her chair.

She was popular. The kitten swarmed up the leg of her trousers, the brown tabby rubbed against her leg then leapt into her lap. The two had a little fight there and Essa pushed them off, laughing.

Down the staircase came a big orange tiger-tom, slow and senten-
tious, and when she scooped him up he lay in her arms like a pillow,
inert and unworried.

"Minh," she said, and he started to purr.

Essa thought she was getting the hang of this. She put the big
cat down in the patch of sunlight. The brown cat jumped on it and
it retired to the couch while the brown cat sat in the sun, washing
its face again.

The trader came down the stairs at the same breakneck pace,
his torso bare, a shirt in one hand, a towel in the other drying wet
hair. "Cotton," he said. "So good in towels, so bad in bales. What
do you think of the guys?"

Essa pointed to the five she could see. "Minh, Minh, Minh,
Minh and Minh," she said.

"Pretty good," he said, then pointed to two and corrected her.
"Minh. Minh."

"Minh. Minh," she practiced dutifully. One of the indicated cats
spoke to the sound of its name.

"I had a cat for a while in the mountains," she said. "But I was
pretty young, I guess. I can't remember it being there after my
mother left."

He was standing in the patch of sunlight combing his hair. He
was burnished and lovely. Which one of them stepped first? She
thought it was her. She felt the teeth of the comb against her back,
his other fist still holding the shirt pulled her waist to him, and she
had her fingers tangled in his wet hair. It was a satisfying kiss, but
its unexpectedness shocked them apart.

"Oh!" he said. Her hand was over her breath. They looked at
each other. He started to comb his hair again. She bent and handed
him the shirt, which he had dropped. "Thanks," he said, and turned
away to the cupboard, pulling his shirt over his head.

"Something to drink? I have juice, I have red and black
wine . . ."

"Black wine," she said, seeing he had his hand on the bottle already. He reached down two goblets, then put one back. It was another unexpected intimacy, a graceful gesture in deference to the
mountain habit of sharing, another step beyond work. He poured
the wine and gave her the goblet. Then he walked away into the
other room.

She sat again at the table, trying to steady herself. She could
see on the rich dark surface of the wine the shimmers caused by her

hand shaking. She put the goblet down, put her hands in her pockets, and tried to breathe. The trader came back with a small square bundle in his hands. He reached for the goblet, drank a deep draught of the black wine, and she saw he smiled as he licked it from his lips.

He unwrapped the silk from a deck of northern cards, the game which is also a divining tool. He said nothing as he shuffled and fanned them, held them out to her to choose. She knew to take seven. He put the other cards aside, took the cards from her hands. As their hands touched he smiled, a secretive and sexual smile, and they both shivered slightly. She took the wine then, pulled a mouthful of its spiky smoothness into herself, savored it, swallowed.

He squared the cards in front of him and covered them with his hands. "I know your wish," he said. His voice was a little rough; he cleared his throat. "I know your wish and I ask, what say the cards?" He looked down at his hands.

She smiled. The sunlight was coming down behind his hair, which was tangled, half-combed and voluptuous. He looked up to catch her look, lifted one hand and placed its forefinger in the center of her forehead. "Concentrate," he said, "on your desire. I will still be here when the cards have been read." His finger traced her cheek and neck before he pulled his hand back to the fortuneteller pose he was affecting.

Or maybe not affecting. She looked aside from his serious face, and saw that there were seven cats sitting in a row behind him, an even, graduated row with the large orange cat in the center and the others symmetrical around it. The kitten was fidgeting like a child at its first ritual, but held the line. Now Essa shivered for certain.

The trader turned the cards, and made a semicircle in front of him which echoed the shape he could not see behind him. As he laid down each card, the cat in the mirror-image position to it lay down. Essa breathed, and her hands relaxed.

"The cloud, the hand, the pit, the tower, the mother, the heart, the new wood," he said, slowly, and looked up at her. His face looked serious, troubled. Essa wanted to take him on the couch in the room behind, she wanted to rumple his hair more, she wanted to escape the semicircle of fear which had gripped the back of her neck. She swept the cards off the table. Startled, the cats scattered. He was startled too.

"Don't . . . " he said, and threw his hands up for protection, but not from her.

"I can't bear it," she said. "Tell my future later. Tell the present now."

"Not now," he said, taking her hands. "Later. There is plenty of time tonight, after we finish the inventory."

"Oh, yes! The inventory!" Laughing, she stood up, and he did too, still joined to her by the grasp of hands. She pulled away, leaned down and gathered the cards from the floor. "I didn't mean to do it," she said. "I got afraid for a minute. I don't know why. Maybe . . . "

He took the cards gently, put them with the others but, she saw, with their faces toward the others' faces to keep them distinct. "Later for that too," he said. "Let's go." The goblet stood alone on the table, the black wine half-drunk.

As they left the house he held back the kitten, but one of the cats bounded out with them and he didn't seem to mind. She didn't look back or name them, and the one outside climbed a drainpipe and vanished across a roof. The trader put his hand on her back to turn her toward the street, and the touch was sensuous and unnerving. She pulled away. "Too fast," she said, "too sweet," and with his smile around her she swung away down the street at his side.

Down on the docks they made short work of the inventory in the warehouses, finishing in the largest one which blocked the street to the water. They came out its dockside door into the sunlight at the water's edge and Essa blinked at the dazzle. The wind was off the water and despite the sun her coat was now not warm enough to blunt its cutting edge. There was a silver shadow suddenly, intensifying the chill, the trader drew breath, and Essa's vision clouded and cleared. The ship from the east was gliding into a berth in front of them.

Essa too was shocked, at the sudden coming of her dreams into the real world. She stood blinking, wondering why the day seemed hardly to have changed. On the deck of the ship, sailors dressed like her mother was dressed on that last night worked rigging and tossed out mooring cables. The trader was closest; he jumped forward to hitch a cable around the bollard. The ship gently drifted down to rest.

Essa stood staring.

The trader stood beside her to watch the gangplank lowered,

the sailors preparing to disembark, waiting for their leader to give the word. Essa could understand their shouting. She thought the trader could not.

"Essa," the trader said, "I have in mind to send you east. There's trade to come from across the sea, and your face is turned to the rising sun."

Her face was turned to him in wonder, and he laughed at her wide-eyed shock.

"You wanted to go east," he said. "I have been getting you ready." The sea was behind his head, half-blinding her with its sparkle, hiding his expression.

The terror in her heart was the sudden doubt of anyone who gets what she wants unexpectedly, improbably and simply. She waited for the other foot to fall. The ship was real. Its shadow on the boards of the dock was as sharp as her own. It was her mother who was the ghost, standing beside her. Perhaps word of her death had been greatly exaggerated. Essa's hand clenched around the calculator frame until it hurt her palm. Then she released the hand, and her fear, with a great laugh. She pulled the frame into the sunlight where the opals caught the light and responded with their fire.

"Isn't it beautiful?" she said to the trader. "My mother gave it to me."

"Yes," he said, "I know," and turned so she could see his quick smile, his gentle look bent on her. You leave what you love, she thought; my mother taught me that. They walked forward into the shadow of the great eastern ship until it loomed above them, silver-sided and smooth.

On their way back home through the town, Essa and the trader passed through the alleys surrounding the square, and heard a great murmuring noise. There were scores of people, most of them young and curiously intent, but among them old folks and families, and single parents with little children in carry-harnesses and older others handheld and herded, all hurrying toward the center of the town. The two of them turned and followed the crowd, unurgent and idly curious.

"It is the students again, I imagine," said Essa.

"Yes," said the trader. "Did you read the proclamation against this yesterday?"

"Public order, indeed," said Essa by way of answer, and as they turned another corner the noise intensified and resolved into near-words.

"I hope they don't try to enforce it," said the trader.

"I hear the guards refused," said Essa, and they rounded another wynd and came out onto the main square. Immediately tumult erased the end of their quiet-voiced conversation. The trader took Essa's hand almost involuntarily, and she felt his pulse beat against her wrist, speeding up as they looked out from the top of a short flight of steps over the heads of a massive, humming crowd. There were banners held aloft by pairs of youths, all in green tunics. There was chanting. There was a sense of raw power there, seething.

"Let's get out of here," shouted the trader, pulling against Essa's hand, but her mood had sharpened, and she tugged him back to her side, strong hand on his wiry arm, then stepped forward instead, pushing down the cobble stairs between tightening groups of people, turning her head back to talk to him as they snaked, still hand-joined, through.

"No way," she said. "This is history. I go from here tomorrow. You think I want to miss this?"

There was a banner which read: CLIMB THE REMARKABLE MOUNTAINS; another: SAIL AND SOAR. Essa understood the latter but not the former; she asked her boss. "You should know," he said; she cocked her head at him. "You are from there," he said.

"What?"

"The Remarkable Mountains rise from the plain behind the Fjord of Tears."

"You mean The Range."

"Most people here don't know that name. Those would be sailors, under that banner. Probably from the Black Ship, from their skin color. They want the freedom of the trails too."

"They come up."

"Not very often, and they meet much resistance."

"So it's all economics, then?"

"Not at all. Who keeps the sailors and merchanters apart? Figure it out. Who do we work for?"

For whom do we work, thought Essa idly as she looked out over the crowd. It seemed simple. Almost all were students or sailors, but there were merchanters among them, some singly among disparately composed groups, others in groups of their own, looking angry. Among these she was surprised to see the raw-faced young merchanter-kid she'd talked with that morning; he was shouting some slogan in company with his mates, his face contorted with effort and dislike.

Somehow this shocked her. Not that he was angry or on the edge of violence, but that she so recently had talked with him, that she knew him. Alerted, she searched the crowd for other familiar faces and found two: a student who had worked for the same company as Essa during university break and a sailor she had met only two hours ago on the sleek ship she was to board tomorrow.

This too shocked her: that she had no one to favor among the factions. She had been here long enough; she should have known who had something sensible to say. Yet she stood at the edge of the crowd feeling every inch a foreigner.

The shouting seemed louder suddenly, and the almost-static groups she had been scanning suddenly broke and swirled. A banner was down, and another, as factions overwhelmed each other. The temperature in the square seemed to rise, and the air to thicken.

Essa felt the pull of the crowd as if her throat were in its grip. She could have thrown herself into the mêlée and been lost, and found. But she was a foreigner, suddenly with its weight of danger, so she backed slowly sideways up the stairs until her back was against the red pumice wall of the White Hotel. Above the moan of the crowd there was a deep humming, a crackle like duster-pods popping on a hot day in an alpine meadow.

The trader was still holding her hand, and she realized with a sudden adrenaline start that he was shouting at her, and she could not hear him. The noise had become so loud that she could not hear it any more, yet it blanketed all intimate sound. She tried to call out but could not even hear herself. The effect was shouting underwater, panicky and ineffective. Around them, the pushing of the crowd intensified. Essa felt rough coats, smelled sweat and dust and urgency from the people around. A woman with a baby on her back slipped by, her baby-sling of silk, trailing the incongruous smell of milk and talc, which Essa remembered from her auntie's house of perpetual new cousins.

The woman was swept back into the turmoil in the square, though Essa was sure she had been pushing away. If she and the trader had not had their backs against the wall, there would have been no choice for them either. Or was the pressure away, into the side streets? She saw a current like that, several feet away, and hoped the woman, too short to see it herself, had happened upon it and taken her baby away. But even if she had, down which side street would she have been able to move? They were full too.

The trader was pulling on her arm, and she saw that he had stepped back and up into a window niche in the building. She scrambled up beside him, awkward but unwilling to let go of him. An older man tried to join them but there was no room; Essa saw him groping along the side of the hotel toward the next window, but the crowd thickened and she lost sight of him. She looked back out across the square. From this vantage point, she could see the battle.

Battle. The word was another small shock to her. The demonstration had indeed become a battle, it seemed. From above the crowd level now, she could see the bulky shapes in the square and suddenly knew them for what they were: armored vehicles, giant trucks, pressing into the crowd without regard. Now the pressure made sense. The crowd was trying to get out of the square, and the streets were too small. The vehicles were pressing inexorably on the mass of people.

But it was not a mass of people, Essa thought. It was one plus one plus one, all of them like me, all of them there for simple petty reasons . . . and now she feared for herself for the first time.

The crackling noise was the percussive fire of weapons. The only other sound that pierced the blanket of noise-no-noise was a new, high screaming which was taken up by more and more mouths. Essa might have been screaming herself, though everything around her seemed silent and slow.

Textures intensified, smell and sound became a blur which someday she would realize she remembered, but which now seemed only insensible and overwhelming. The window niche was safe, but intimate to the turmoil in a way she could not analyze, so massive the assault on her senses.

She and the trader stayed there until the square was empty except for the bodies. There were a lot of bodies, lying crumpled and unreal on the flagstones. Essa was still holding the trader's hand. They clambered down out of their embrasure together, and went toward the bodies still hand-in-hand, terrified children in a tale no parent would tell. The nearest fallen were clearly dead, though now in the real silence there were moans coming from somewhere.

Essa saw that others were emerging like broken toys from their hiding and huddling places. She saw too that there were soldiers there, patrolling in couples and groups. One of the pairs came toward them as they crouched on the street beside one of the bodies.

The two soldiers did not have the uniform of the guard.

"They are from up the river," said the trader. "Why it took so long. They had to send for them."

"We'd better get out of here," said Essa, surprised that she sounded no different. Maybe a little hoarse. She cleared her throat.

But the soldiers had seen them, and unslung their weapons as they approached. Essa stood up.

"I am a visitor," she said, feeling like a fool; "I was not involved. Please tell me how to get back to a safe street."

One of the soldiers answered. His voice cracked. Why, he is young! she thought. Younger than she was. His face was livid and terrified.

"I didn't kill anyone," he said. "I am not a bad person."

"I know," she said. "I can see that. That is why I asked you to help us."

"Go down that street," he said, pointing with his weapon. His partner was as young as he was, and her hair was kept out of her face by a bandanna tied around her head. She looked like she had been reading fantasies and had tried to dress up like a soldier in a book. So did he.

Near them two students in green tunics were struggling with a fallen bicycle, trying to straighten the handlebars. Essa saw that they needed it because one student was wounded in the leg and could not walk. She averted her eyes as if from an intimate act.

Essa pulled the hand of the trader, whose palm was slimy with hot sweat. If the smell of death, something she thought was a cliché which is not, had not been filling the square his and her fear would have been palpable. Essa could only be grateful for the camouflage as they started to run.

She heard a ragged, officious shout behind them. They turned, still running but ready to dodge, thinking they were the target. The two young soldiers were beating the two students. The boy who had given Essa directions raised the club he had unhooked from his belt and brought it down on the skull of the wounded student. Her long hair seemed to shatter into a spray of black and glittering red.

Essa had no time for the vomit in her mouth. She was running.

*   *   *

The trader put her on the ship within the hour. Returning to Essa's room, rolling her belongings up, and making their way back to the docks had not taken long. Essa traveled light, and it was a small town. He stopped her in the shadow at the door of the big warehouse, where they crouched scanning the silent dock.

"It's all right; there's no-one there," said Essa.

"I want to talk to you," said the trader.

His face was in shadow. Essa made light, sketching its limits in a tight envelope around their heads.

"This is not the farewell I wanted," he said. "There was a whole night and a morning until you would go. Things I wanted you to do. I made notes in my notebook; you will have to take it and figure it out yourself." He pressed the little book on her, a handbound compact thing wrapped in a cloth. "And things I wanted to say to you. Personal."

"Come with me. It can't be safe here. You can brief me on the flight."

"Someone must take care of my mother's business," he said.

"She is your mother?"

"It's an idiom. Not like the mother you seek. But she shaped. She is who she is. And because of her, I am who I am."

"And who are you?" She knew she bordered on rudeness, but she had seen worse than bad manners this day.

He touched her face. His hands were cool. Her hands were never that cool, and especially not after this day. "You make such a fire against the sun," he said. "Now I see you make light in the darkness too. If the night had gone on as we thought, I would have told you my name."

"You know mine."

"But that is your custom." He sounded weary and tentative.

"Even if I were of your people," she said, "I would have told you tonight." Earlier, she had tried to give him her calculator but he had refused. Now she said, "I tried to give you a gift as good as my name."

"But a name can be given and kept. You have only one gift from your mother. You will need it."

"I know your name," she said suddenly. "Aren't you Minh too, like everyone, like everything?"

He smiled broadly. "Yes, you know," he said. "What names are. I have given you that, anyway. You know me, now, Minh. Essa."

"Thank you for naming everything." It sounded stupid to her, but he hugged her then, so maybe he heard that she meant it.

"Take care of your name," he said. "It is good to know something about yourself."

All she knew was that she had seen death and still disbelieved it. Who was she herself, then? She popped the bubble of light, and they stood holding each other for a moment, as their eyes readjusted to the dark. Then he took her hand again, and one of her packs with the other hand, and they ran, outrigger bundles making them clumsy, across the moonlit strip of dock. There were shadows waiting for their shadows.

"It seems the moon is always full here," said Essa.

"It shines in the east as well, they say," he said. "Remember, you are doing my job. You are my child as I am my mother's, now."

"I do not want to be your child," she protested irritably.

"It is an idiom. For business. The rest—it is too late for the rest."

She nodded and hugged him again, they held each other tightly for a minuscule tranquillity. Then they pulled away into an opposingly large silence. "I will do well for you," she said finally. "And remember."

"Come back carefully. No-one can know where this all will lead." She remembered the bodies, and shivered. The shadowy sailors pulled her bundles and her arm. She had to move.

"Careful—you too," she said. He nodded. She ran up the steep gangplank. The sailors cast off. As the ship rose, she saw him standing in the bright moonlight, looking up. When he was small enough—when the ship was high enough—that the detail was lost in his face, she saw him run back into the warehouse shadow, his dark cape swirling. Down the dock, she saw a patrol. She thought they were the guard, which meant safety, but they were too far away to be sure; maybe they were the militia, soldiers, more young murderers like today. And thinking of the square, the merchanter-kid's hate, the sailor, the students, the soldier, she started to shake. She couldn't move.

She spent her first night aboard puking into a barrel until she vomited blood. After they saw that, they gave her a sedative, but she slept only enough for terrifying dreams where a red mist glittering in the late afternoon sun spread until it caught her, was an acid which ate to her bones, and she heard her mother's voice saying, "Climb the Remarkable Mountains, sail and soar," but her mother was not there.

The sailor she had seen in the crowd was not on the ship.

The Remarkable Mountains (1)

Only today as I sat in my bath did I realize that my whole life has been spent in the search for safety. I first became aware of the fragility of my existence at a very young age. In my parents' garden there was a little birdhouse designed for finches. One day I came upon a sparrow with its head caught in the entry hole. It was struggling unsuccessfully to free itself. I thought I would help it, save it. I took it firmly, ignoring the thrill of fear I felt when my hand closed around its feathered body, and pulled.

After that it did not struggle, even though its body was still as warm, its feathers as stiff and soft. Horrified at what my intervention had done, I ran away, and never wanted to go near that tree again, though it was near the path and difficult to avoid.

As a child and youth in my parents' house I was surrounded by things, each in its place, and each named in family memory. The provenance of each treasured thing was part of the skein of history which bound not only that object but all of us into our particular niches.

That seemed like safety at the time, and I treasured it as I treasured each thing I added to the hoard as I joined the family tradition of acquisition.

I suppose that every wanderer started in a garden somewhere. So few of us are born into motion.

When I left my parents' home, however, I took with me only what I could carry. I thought I was coming back, you see. I thought it would be that simple—to cross the sea and to go up the Fjord of Tears in the back of the Remarkable Mountains seemed a worthy picaresque sort of goal, one that would occupy me for the few years until I attained my majority and the dangers at home diminished.

But I didn't know where I was going when I left and I had been gone only a few months when I knew, with my gift—or is it a curse?—of being bound to those I love, that my family had been killed. Later I discovered it was in the fire which burned their house down, but then I merely felt the thread break, snap, to release me.

Even now I can only say it so boldly. I cannot reproduce (although I feel it again almost as strongly as the first time, whenever I think of it) the terror and relief I felt in that moment. Their death was my death, but I knew, knew with a fateful clarity, that I alone could escape it.

And I would escape it.

I turned with no more feeling on my face than I have now, and resumed my walk toward the Remarkable Mountains, thinking of things, things, things with every step, thinking how I was torn loose from all history, not just my own. Thinking of how to escape being murdered in my turn, and filled with a freedom I had never known before.

I say I have been looking for safety all my life, since I played in my mother's garden, and so of course my path has taken me away from all that is safe, into countries where I lost everything, including, I sometimes think, my soul, for otherwise how could I carry on after what has happened to me, after so many have died, after I left my child without a backward glance, after all that, and not feel guilty, not mourn, not feel?

When I came to the Fjord of Tears in the Remarkable Mountains, I was much older than when I left home. I had been traveling for almost five years, a fugitive for four of those. I had only the knapsack, two sets of clothes and boots; my notebooks, maps and navigating equipment, and a little abacus my grandmother had given me, with a frame of ebony and opal counter beads. And Annalise, of course, walked beside me.

The Fjord of Tears cuts the sea deeply into the heart of the Remarkable Mountains, but it was not from the sea I came. The cliffs of the Fjord are too steep to allow access to the sea anyway, except by a great flight of thousands of stairs at one place I did not yet know. We came up from the plains. I never kept a journal until I first saw the mountains cut jagged into the sky of the world. Then I began to write, as Annalise always wanted me to do, the story of our lives.

FORTY-SECOND DAY FROM AVANUE:
DAY ONE OF THIS RECORD

This morning we came in sight of the Remarkable Mountains.

The people here call them the Range. To them the skyline is commonplace. To us, born and raised with the

long views of the sea, come fresh from another seacoast,
and having walked for over forty days under the big skies
of the prairie, they are an astonishment. My navigator was
stunned with success and later confessed to me that she had
not believed for a minute, not a minute, that they would
look like that.

What did you expect? I said. You had the maps.

Hills, she said. Like at the edge of the sea by Avanue.

At Avanue the dunes, it is true, are very high, and inland they have become permanent, fleshed over with a thin
soil and a subsequent layer of green growth; but the dunes
of Avanue are comprehensible to the mind, while these
great massifs must, if our maps are correct about the distance we have to travel, be unthinkably large when one is
among them.

I confess privily that I cannot extend my imagination
that far. I will have to wait and see.

DAY TEN

We have had no recurrence of yesterday's trouble, though
the man is sulky today, and I expect that I have not heard
the last of these objections. This morning I told him that
if he obstructed the expedition further I would leave him
behind. We have managed very well with the people of this
country but he has never cast aside his prejudices and now
he seems terrified. From his place in line I can see him
glancing around at me even now, and it makes him more
nervous to see me making these notes. Just as well. If he
only knew it, I would have difficulty leaving him, both because I am not so hard as I pretend and because I would
hesitate to impose him on these tolerant and pleasant people who have given us, strangers, nothing but help and
kindness. I fear he would abuse their trust viciously.

All of this taking place in the shadow of the most as-
tounding rocks that must be in the world. No wonder on
our maps they are called Remarkable. If I am angry at him

for anything it is for depriving me of the chance to think of nothing but mountains.

Mountains. The word said at a distance of hundreds of miles, as I heard it last spring in the lowlands, or tens of miles, as a tenday ago I saw them on the horizon, can hardly begin to convey what they really are. My navigator thinks they loom and she is frankly terrified whenever we pass through any gap narrower than the widest valley, but I am exhilarated with them. Mountains.

Maybe tomorrow I will have the words for it.

Of course, that is what I have been thinking, and saying, for the last ten days. That is why I began this record in the first place: simply to write that sentence: this morning we came in sight of the Remarkable Mountains. And then to try to make sense of it. It may be an effort which takes my whole life.

DAY ELEVEN

Just when I think I get used to this I come around another corner. And what is it that is taking my words away? I must try, for when I look back on these notes years hence, I will see only the shadows of these peaks, not their substance. I wish I had brought more recording media, but even what I have used will give no real idea, cramped as the views from inside viewfinders must perforce be.

Mostly the rock is gray, but such a range of colors that subsumes as to make a whole rainbow. They are all more than five thousand meters above the level of the sea, by our instruments and calculations, and some are twice that. They look like some giant parody of a jumble of earth and rocks thrust up by a bulldozing tractor, with some broken and jagged, some bent and folded over themselves. The more folded ones have the look of some fantastic pastry, like the thousand-layers cakes my grandmother's cook used to take days to make. The edges of the layers even flake off the same way.

In one narrow defile where we walked, these flaky edges were close to hand, and I reached out and broke a piece from one. How could these mountains endure so long if a mere human could break a piece away? I thought, but then, later, there was a jumble of stone full of multi-colored flecks, so hard that even the horses' sharp-shod hooves could not chip it away, but struck sparks.

All this is on such a gigantic scale, it is like the homes of the northerners' god-myths, where such giants as Ayam and Arasmas might have coupled or fought while they were making the moons and the stars.

But they are not bare and new, these gigantic upthrust tumbles of stone. They have been here for such a long time that generations of moss and underbrush and trees have grown and died and made soil for other generations to grow in. There are many here of that kind of spiky tree which is green all year, except for one variety which the native people tell me turns color and sheds in Autumn like our leafy trees. I would have found that hard to credit had I heard it at home at my parents' hearth, but here it seems only reasonable, surrounded by such strangeness.

DAY TWELVE

Sent the guides and horses back this morning. We go back to walking. I can't say I'm sorry, though we'll be slower. I found clambering up and down these rocks on horseback tense and sometimes terrifying, though the horses certainly knew what they were doing. It was just us who weren't sure. My legs were always cramped with trying to hold on tighter, and my feet with trying to grip a phantom ground. Annalise says it was the same with her.

DAY THIRTEEN

Today we heard a roaring like a raging river, but saw nothing except a mild, flat creek. We decided to cut across the rocks to save some time, and the roaring became louder. The four Avanue people were curious and unflappable, but that merchanter scum has been getting more obnoxious every day. I wish I didn't feel so responsible for him. He was the one who became superstitious and frightened. The others went ahead with me, while I asked Annalise to guard him.

I could hear the roaring fill the air but I could not find a source. A waterfall around the bend, I thought, across these rocks. Ahead, I could see a small crack in the rock. I went forward prepared to leap it. As I took the step nearest it, I glanced down.

And nearly fell, two hundred feet I'm sure, into a boiling cauldron of water trapped in a deep, narrow chasm of stone so curled and convoluted by erosion that it seemed like some fantastic cloth. I can record all this now but at the time I had to fling myself back, and the navigator grabbed me and prevented me from sliding in. We both fell backward, and I lay there panting and sweating.

"What?" she said. "What?" I gestured, and she crawled ahead. When she returned, her face was white, but she was laughing.

"I can die now," she said, that Avanue phrase Annalise has read in books but I had never heard spoken before. The navigator lay beside me laughing until she calmed, while the others, including the merchanter, took their turn. He alone seemed unmoved.

When we jumped across the chasm (so narrow there was no effort to it)—and there is no easy way to say it— she jumped not across but in. I did not see it. No-one saw it but the merchanter. I only heard her falling laughter.

DAY SEVENTEEN

Camped here for four days now. The navigator's body was impossible to find, so we went on to a campsite with water we could reach. But her brother, the morning after, lay in his sleepsack dead. How can a man cut his own artery and let the blood, such a lot of blood, spurt away in such silence and without a gesture of regret? How can grief take him, who the day before was laughing? The other Avanue people say he was wrong, that if his sister chose to die he should respect that. I asked them: did he not have the same choice? But he did not say so first, they said, and went away weeping to sit on the gravel bar at the foot of the waterfall. Not the same stream, another, this country seems to grow them every mile, these profligate beauties in the midst of beauty, but I do not think I can see rushing water again without a zero of horror in my gut. The merchanter was smiling; I nearly beat him, but I was horrified at the desire, as if I felt my grandmother take over my hands, and so I turned away and struggled within instead, until I had warded her off.

Annalise tells me that if a northerner says that phrase "I can die now," it means great joy, but they mean it truly. Not many of them choose to actually die, but they do not grieve for those who do.

Still, I cannot see it. She was so happy, and she was happy because every day she saw something new. Why would she choose to miss that? And he, why would he stop, if he believed she did it in joy? It goes around in circles, over and over.

They came to me to say they would take their brother home. I did not know they were all one family. "Everyone is one family," the older said.

"You weep for us," said the younger. "Minh and Minh would love you for it."

They went away to pack their things and the things of their brother and sister. They left by noon.

Leaving me with Annalise and the merchanter. I conferred with the older Avanuen before they left, but the merchanter, in the end, would not go with them, and swore he'd behave better if I just did not send him with those—he actually said *heathen*, I think, if I understood his

accent. But it might have been *perverts.* So my sister and
I have lost our friends, and had only this fool with us when
the sickness took me. I am feeling a little better today, but
I am still weak, and the tension in camp is strong. Why
does he stay? He does little but fight with Annalise, resent
me, complain and sulk.

DAY EIGHTEEN

Annalise went out to scout. An hour later, found the merchanter in my pack, scrabbling, this book in his hand.
Tackled him but he got away, and he turned like a wild
thing then and tried to tackle me. "You're mad!" I gasped
out.

"Not mad," he panted. "You're . . . worth more . . .
alive . . . " He pinned me and bound my wrists in front of
me.

The only person who would buy me is my husband.
A spy?

"You're a merchanter!"

"Good cover. They hired me to come up here among
the pigs and the brownhairs. Worth my while to wear rags
for a while, speak my birth tongue. Got rid of two of the
scum, at least."

I heard Annalise then, shouting, "A town! There's a
town on the next slope!"

He saw me ready to shout back a warning and
punched me in the solar plexus. While I gasped, paralyzed,
he secured my feet, then before I could recover breath,
gagged me. I couldn't breathe through my nose yet, and
began to choke. He ripped the gag off, swearing. I curled
upward with my whole body, thrusting my head into his
face, and tried again to shout. It was a ragged sound, but
I heard Annalise reply, and running steps—but toward us.

"Run away!" I yelled, but it came out a whisper.

"Her, I can kill, no problem," he said furiously, wiping blood from his nose. "And they don't care what kind

of shape they get you back in. Except alive." He kicked me in the side, so I was gasping again, and then rolled me into the water.

The cold convulsed me. I choked on water, tried to rise. I heard shouting, felt a splash, and when I turned he was running after Annalise up the steep path to the top of the waterfall. I was half-out of the water, still bound. I doubled up, pulled at the wet knots on my feet with frozen hands already numb from the cold and the tight ropes. I was coughing so hard I could hardly keep my eyes open. The loosing of the ropes was a surprise; I couldn't see anything for my streaming eyes. I dragged myself up from the stream, began to stumble up the path, trying without avail to twist my hands free.

I fell often on the way up. Finally I was leaving bloody handprints.

When I struggled to the top of the path, Annalise and the spy were grappling at the edge of the canyon, right where the quiet mossy stream dived suddenly into hundred-foot falls. He swayed back as if to pull her toward the brink. She was half a foot shorter than him, but she was holding her own. I cried out and he turned his head in surprise; that gave her a chance to twist away from him and throw herself away from the edge. Off balance, he tried to right himself, but he was too close to the edge.

He went over in slow motion. His windmilling arms looked almost ludicrous. All he said was "Oh, shit!" in a heartfelt way, in a more honest tone of voice than I ever heard from him before, and with less accent.

Then he fell. We heard him hit the rock below, a few moments after.

I ran to Annalise, knelt by her. She tugged at the knots holding my wrists and the rope finally fell away. She began to straighten it frantically. "We must get more rope!" she said. Her fervency almost convinced me.

I crawled to the edge and looked over, sick from vertigo and horrified surprise. He sprawled broken on the rock below, a sack of old clothes. There was no question of a rope, a rescue, a return.

I crawled back to Annalise, too frightened of the edge to stand. She tried to struggle up.

"He is dead," I said. "There's no hurry."

"I killed him?" she cried in horror.

"He fell," I said. "It was after you were clear. He would have sent you down there, and come for me. Don't sweat."

"If I hadn't shoved him as I got clear—"

"If he hadn't fought you . . . shut up now, and get up. I can't carry you."

I began to cough again, and Annalise seemed to snap into different focus, looking at my wet clothes.

"You must be freezing! You'll catch your death of damned foolishness!"

"Quite the . . . little sailor," I gasped, referring to her idiom, but in fact she was right. If I had been sick before, the dumping in the slush-cold water and the subsequent run up the mountain path had pushed me somewhere much further. Going down the mountain was much slower, and we leaned on each other and rested often. I coughed if I had to breathe deeply. She was scraped and scratched from the street-fighting battle she'd just had, and my hands left dirty blood-prints on her jacket. We were quite a pair.

At the bottom, in our solitary camp, we crawled into our linked-together night bags and I slept almost instantly. When I awoke, as she had obviously done much earlier, she had found mountain people from somewhere, and they were taking down the tent around me. She said, "Get up. We are going to a village. I told them about the accident, how Noh fell and you fell in the water. They will help us."

Annalise was a survivor. Though later she would cry in my arms many times for the man she felt she had killed (no matter that he fell himself, no matter he was a spy of my husband, no matter that Annalise had rescued us from discovery and return to that foul country), still now she was able to find help, take charge yet again, and seem everything she needed to be to convince the mountain people that we were innocent travelers waylaid by misadventure.

They gave me some kind of medicinal tisane, then put me on a litter and pulled a soft blanket tight around me. I felt straps tighten around my shoulders, hips and feet but I felt no claustrophobia, only security. They carried me down the path to the road where a four-wheeled cart waited. Annalise got in beside me and the stretcher-bearers got up in front and one drove the cart. It had some kind of engine but was almost silent, so I could hear them talking. One of the last thoughts I had before the drug took effect was "Dammit, another language to learn." I must have muttered it aloud because I heard Annalise's laughter, high and surprisedly clear, before the dark took me entirely.

On the Black Ship

She had been everywhere on the ship that she was welcome, and the young sailor was not there. She almost made herself sick again with the effort of not asking about him, but finally she chose someone who seemed to have some authority and stammered out the question.

"And who are you to him?"

"Essa, I came on at the trader town, you know. I saw him in the square . . . "

"You were in the square?"

"Yes."

"He never came back. You must have been the last one to see him, then. Come with me."

And they went through a hatch marked *Staff Only,* into a large room where Essa told her story once and then again to an ever-growing group of people, all of them serious-faced and half of them looking away most of the time as she told it, so that later she couldn't say what they looked like, only that they frightened her with their silence.

The one who took her there introduced herself as Gata, and three of the serious folk were Naio, Pewhim, and Cabroca. Or so it sounded when they were finally introduced, though by then Essa was swaying with tranquilized fatigue.

"Do you think he could get out of there?" she was asked three times, and she could not by the third time answer.

"We couldn't wait without the soldiers coming for us too. The only airship in port," said Cabroca. Not to her, but the others.

"He is my son," said Pewhim to Cabroca. "And mine," said Naio to Essa. As they were both men, she supposed that they meant *son* like her trader friend had meant *mother.*

"I remember the day he was born," said Naio.

"Don't," said Naio, putting a hand to his belly like a woman.

They seemed like her own parents at that moment. Essa looked at them, confused, thinking thoughts of magic and thinking about her mother, and thinking about what she herself remembered of the day of her own birth. There was nothing much more to say to the council of elders (as she thought of them) and her belly was so sore from vomiting and bleeding that she could hardly stand.

It was Gata who saw this and took her out, took her to the cabin they had given her earlier. It looked like someone had had to move out of it to give her room, much as when she went to her auntie's farther up the Range her younger cousin Ana had had to move in with his older brother so she could be accommodated, the only girl, in a private room.

"That was after I was twelve, of course," she said conversationally to Gata. The sedative was still strong in her. Gata smiled.

"This is my cabin," she said, "but I'm sharing with a friend. We don't take too many passengers. Most of us are family."

"How can two men have a son; is it magic?"

"Well, would you expect them to have a daughter? That would be magic indeed."

Essa let herself be tucked into bed, another parallel with visiting her father's sister, a relentlessly parental auntie of a woman, for all her craggy resemblance to her brother. It was all rather impressionistic by this time. Had she really witnessed murders that day? Had she felt anything? She didn't now; she didn't know.

As she drifted to sleep she thought that if she had done as she wanted she would have slept with the trader that night. He would have warmed her all right. Gata looked warm too, as Essa shivered under the puffy quilt. She must have made a sound, for the woman came to sit on the bed, stroked her hair back from her feverish face.

"Traders make friends slow," Essa said blurrily.

"Aircrew make friends fast," said Gata, seemingly to comfort her.

"It's your bed, after all," said Essa.

Geta smiled. "Go to sleep now. We'll talk about it sometime."

Essa was so eager to be alive that she stayed awake seconds longer, hoping to change Gata's mind, before she slid away again into her second dream-filled sleep of the night.

Essa woke exhausted and with her belly aching, but embarrassment was her first emotion. So grateful to that sailor woman for attention to her pain, it seemed, that she'd tried to proposition her. She didn't know enough about sailors, despite her mother and her mother's friend, to know if she had committed a breach of manners or how serious it might be. For all she knew she had proposed marriage, or offended some deep propriety.

The dreams had been of blood and screaming, of course, and Essa noted in passing that she was already editing the events in the square, so she could hear the screaming, so she saw more killing being done, so that the student she saw murdered begged for mercy or made a threat or did anything but just be there.

She tried to erase the edits but remembering was making the bile rise again, so she drank from the glass of stale water beside the bed, got up, tried to arrange her crumpled, slept-in clothes to look tidier, gave up, rummaged in her bag for a clean shirt, changed, hung her other shirt carefully across the chair, and went out of the dim cabin into a busy corridor.

Following the mainstream of people brought her out on deck, and she saw that it was just before or just after midday, depending on the direction they were traveling. Most of the deck was fully shadowed by the air bag of the dirigible.

At the rail, she looked below but there was nothing but ocean a long way down. She looked to the latitudinal horizons but saw nothing either way. She looked to the stern and then walked down until she could see past the curve of the ship's belly to one of the starboard propellers.

The vanes of the propeller were invisible with speed. She made a fan of her fingers, agitated her flat hand rapidly before her face, and saw with satisfaction that the trick made the propeller fleetingly seem still. It was something her mother taught her, though she had only ever done it with wheels before, to see the spokes.

She looked past the propellers and saw the shadow of the ship on the sea, tiny and following. So it was not yet noon, if they really were going east.

She straightened up and looked forward. The horizon was hazy and they were sailing into a scattered coverlet of almost invisible cloud. She could tell only by looking at the sea ahead, seeing it dappled slightly with bare shadow.

Slowly she worked her way forward along the rail, still looking outward, having to detour around lines and parachute lockers and cleats on the deck. About a third of the way aft from the bow, there was a section where there was no rail but only three lines of stout rope threaded through purpose-built stanchions and knotted at either end. There was a length of this about three times her height before the rail resumed. The gangplank went here when the ship was docked.

For the first time at this false rail she felt fear, vertigo, was conscious that they sailed thousands of feet above the sea. She backed away, colliding with a sailor.

"Sorry," she gasped, and turned away from the view, struggling with her nausea again.

"Here, now," he said, "don't be afraid of that rope. Stronger than the rail, really, and safer. Used to be we were all hedged about with rope only, in the old days."

And to her horror he hurled himself upright at the rope section, turning his back and bending in the middle at the last moment.

The rope, of course, bounced him back, and he straightened and ran a couple of steps to stop beside her again, laughing at her shock.

"Sailors," he said. "Never trust 'em." And he went off still laughing.

Essa lay on the deck, watching the stars out the sides between the rail and the air bag. She could see the same constellations as at home but much higher above the horizon, so she deduced that they were traveling south as well as east.

She looked at the Evening Star, behind them and ready to set in the last glow of the sunset. She imagined the worlds which could swing around it as they swung around their sun. The moon was rising and she saw that its waning face was showing, the one the traders call the Death's Head. She once had heard one of her teachers say that if the moon did not rotate, scientists would never have discovered that the earth was round and circled the sun. Or at least not until they had been misled for many centuries, even millennia. He had said this to her mother, who had replied, "But sailors and merchanters would know, because they see the earth curving all the time. Their business is with the horizon."

Her business tonight was beyond the horizon. She remembered how at home as a child, she would lie out on the roof in the summer and star-gaze, making wishes on the first star of evening, making shapes out of the accidental arrangement of the galaxy.

Sometimes her mother lay beside her, and taught her the sailor names for the stars. She would talk to Essa about traveling, and Essa would tell long rambling childish stories about visiting other worlds.

Now, indeed, she was traveling, and the ship was indeed another world, floating like a tiny moon above the water. A silver moon. From below it must have been more the size of a star. She wondered if the people on the islands could see, would wish on this moving star, at sunset when the sea was already in darkness but the sun still lit the tiny, to them pinpoint, silver ovoid which hung gleaming high above.

"There are people on the ship who want to throw you out," Gata said.

"What, here?" she said, and laughed, looking drolly out the porthole at thousands of feet of nothing but air.

Gata was not laughing. "If you're lucky, here," she said. "More likely over land, where the landing's not as soft."

Essa, who couldn't imagine diving into the ocean, missed the joke, and was too worried besides. "But I am a passenger. I've booked on to a destination."

"You have got a very familiar profile," said Gata, "and anywhere we go it will get you in trouble. Get all of us in trouble. Pewhim and Naio—" already Essa was getting tired of the singleminded way their joined names seem to arise "—are warning people. They were on the first of the Black Ships, fifteen years ago, you know."

This meant nothing to Essa. "What do you mean, profile? I'm just a trader's helper," she said. "And what's a Black Ship anyway, with that strange emphasis? All these ships are silver."

"This is a Black Ship," said Gata. Seeing Essa's puzzlement, she went on: "A Black Ship trades in places sailors are not welcome. A sort of first contact. The first Black Ship was really black, and it went far south, to the Dark Isles where the merchanters hold sway, and then further and further south until it got cold again. On the mainland overlooking the Dark Isles, they found these." And Gata twisted a coin out of the knotted end of her turban and tossed it to Essa.

Essa looked at it: the image of a strange tower with a bolt of lightning at its apex. She turned it over, and her mother's face shone up, in profile as she remembered it, as her mother had so often looked into the distance.

"She looks like my mother."

"She must be your mother, then," said Gata roughly. "And you look just like her, you little fool, but for the color of your hair."

"Why are you so angry? What have I done?"

"I am not angry at you, ninny." Gata looked at her fingers, tangling in her lap, and seemed to still them with effort. "Before they went south, they had been up the Fjord of Tears, almost to where you come from, I think. Do you know a place where the Fjord kinks like a cat's back leg, and there is a little town there, and steps down to the water, thousands of steps?"

"Yes, that's where you can cross the Fjord and go down the Range to Hasfeld. Nagroma, I think it's called. Yes, Nagroma."

"They, that first Black Ship, took on two passengers at Nagroma. She wanted to go—the leader of the two—south and east. To the Dark Isles? She was reluctant, but finally said that would do. When she found out they were going inland she said even better, we will go south and south until the ice closes over us. The other one was quiet, a sunny sort of woman, and cheerful, but she became upset and argued with her leader."

Gata had the sound of a storyteller now, telling a polished tale. Essa remembered that in the Fjord of Tears there are some stories not told after Spring thaw or before Autumn frost. If told out of season, they brought evil. Was this story to be like that? She already felt fear.

Gata went on, oblivious to Essa's shiver, to her pulling the quilt up around her shoulders. Gata was watching something a long time ago, reading the tale from some book in midair, or repeating it from some unknown voice only she could hear.

"The smaller woman said that they should have crossed over as they planned and gone down by—what did you call it? Hasfeld."

"Hasfeld."

"Yes. And the other woman said no, they must leave the Remarkable Mountains as they found them, free of murderous taint. If he was to follow, let him follow them south, where lived only slavers and gender pirates. Let him deal with the wrath of barbarians instead of the welcoming smiles at Eslyn.

"That seemed to quiet the other woman suddenly, and after that they were model passengers—like yourself—and nothing happened until the Dark Isles, when we changed our money for those." She jerked her chin at the coin Essa still held.

"We?" said Essa.

"Sailors. Shh. Her face was the face of the coin, and the crew began to gossip. The committee asked her companion, who said to ask her. The committee asked her if she was the queen of that unpleasant country, and she said no, I was never the queen. But her face on the money, they said. That is the evil fancy of an evil man, she said, and worthy of no intelligent person's concern. However, she said, if it will be more comforting to you, I will remain below the deck while you are docked in that country, in case others have the same misunderstanding. We agreed, and she kept her promise, and her companion stayed with her."

"We?"

"Sailors. However, spies from the coastal despot came on board, and though the committee decided to leave the women in the far south, in a forest far from any but the smallest village, we had in some way been found to have carried her, and the flaming arrows of the soldiers fired the ship's gasbag. When we drifted down on our parachutes, they killed all of us they could find."

"What happened to my mother?" cried Essa. "Where did they leave her? Why did anyone want to kill her? And how on earth or sea or sky did anyone learn this story if all were killed?"

"She was left in the south, in a forest. That's all. And three fought their way home: Naio, Pewhim and one of my mothers. The other mother, my lost one, was on the committee that had decided to throw your mother out."

Gata was looking at her hands again, and they were restless hands.

"What do you mean, throw her out?"

"Naio and Pewhim were the youngest on the committee. My oldest mother, and two others. The other two would not agree."

Now it was no story but a quiet, anguished confession.

"But they went down and left them in a forest by a village. You said!"

"They went down to the tops of the trees. Any further was dangerous to the bag. In those days we didn't have the strong silver fiber."

"You mean they were killed."

"No. My other mother saw them later, from where she hid and slid through the forest. They were alive. One was hurt, but would live, she thought. It helped with the guilt."

"Sailors; never trust 'em. I heard that on this ship."

"Why do you think they were always called Black Ships from

then on, with, as you so neatly put it, a strange emphasis? By all of us since then who sail into the southland? We trade with them now, you know."

"But wouldn't the village have helped them? I could trace them."

"In the south, we say, obligation is slavery. It isn't just a figure of speech, though it's a tidy phrase. Naio invented it, I think. He probably said it to your mother and her friend. Down there, they are full of avarice. They give nothing away, and if you have nothing to buy with, you buy with your life—with your own soul."

"And we go there again and again. We are full of avarice too, on the Black Ships."

"Didn't anyone do anything about the ship that was destroyed? What happened after? When the three came home with their story?"

"We started using helium in the air bags."

"And kept trading with the people who killed your people."

"Yes."

"And we are going there now."

"Yes."

"And I have my mother's face."

"Yes."

"Will I live to see the sea again?" said Essa sarcastically.

"If you are careful, and they are clumsy, and I am near you when they move."

Then she was sorry for sarcasm, changed the subject. "What is this committee? Does this ship have one? Could they help me?"

"You met them. When you told Naio and Pewhim their son was probably dead. Another reason to kill you."

"Kill the messenger? I thought you sailors were civilized with your medicine and magic and your far traveling."

"No more than anyone outside the Fjord of Tears."

"Oh, we are famous for our meekness, are we?"

Gata was silent. Essa was silent. After a while, Essa said, "I always thought my mother was a sailor."

"Well, she wasn't," said Gata.

Life in the zone of control (2)

The mute slave who greets them separates the waif smoothly from her keeper. She knows from the air of authority that the mute exudes that she will not see the keeper man again. She cannot help giving him a look of triumph over her shoulder as she is led away, the mute's hand firmly around her wrist, the first touch she has felt outside function and fucking, except for the old madwoman's occasional contact, since she woke into her life.

The mute takes her to a room. His hands move in the same pattern, over and over, then he points to the room. After a moment, the waif realizes that this is another language. She puts her hands up in front of herself and tries to imitate the birdlike flutter of his fingers. He laughs suddenly, and the booming, raucous noise frightens her. She backs away, pulling her hands against her.

"Shhh, shhh," he says, a strange, empty sound. She shakes her head; she is shaking. He opens his mouth. He has no tongue.

He puts his hands up, open and out toward her, a gesture of—peace?

"What is 'peace'?" she says absently, then moves idly around the room, her fear forgotten. It is a big room. Behind her, he grunts but she ignores him, is startled when he takes her shoulder, but he only turns her so she can see him.

He points to her, then the room.

"This is mine?" He nods. "All of it? It's big." He nods again, then opens a cupboard. Sheets. Towels. For her? He nods.

She puts her hands up again, flutters her fingers randomly. When he laughs again it is not as loud, and she is not as frightened. He makes several signs, carefully, clearly, and repeats them: a fist, a swoop of the opening hand, a lift of the open palm upward. Then he gestures to himself. She imitates the signs, and points to him. His name. He nods. She repeats them, silent. Then she tries to make up her own signs for her questions.

He laughs again, this a short, bitter sound of the throat. He puts his hand to her throat, to her mouth. He puts a finger inside her teeth, not invasively but impatiently. Oh, she suddenly thinks, I can talk. I have a tongue. He pulls his cupped hand toward himself sharply, and makes another grunt with a glottal stop at the end. Talk! he is saying. Talk!

"I will talk," she says. "But I don't know the sounds for your name." And her hand makes the sign: fist opening to fly to rest, float away. "Escape from bondage?" He nods, smiling, then covers her mouth with his hand and shakes his head.

"But don't say it out loud?" He nods.

She thinks: if the old woman hadn't told me, if I hadn't thought all the way here about freedom, I would never have understood his name. And the thought is so much more frightening than any other that she feels the tears fill her eyes. Angrily she wipes them away with her two fists. He touches her again, makes a mime: you are tired; sleep. She shakes her head again.

"That's not it. That's not it. Why do you touch down here, are slaves all perverts here? Up there they don't, do they? Like proper."

He shakes his head. He makes two levels in the air. Above the line, his hands walk about stiff and upright, and he makes a disgusted face: these are the perverts? Below the line, the hands flow, attracting each other's attention by grunts and touches, speaking to each other. He shows her the empty mouth again, and puts it below the line. He makes a second line in the below-stairs air: above it, there is noise and stiff touch; below it, there is silence and flowing touch.

She shows him she understands. Which servants and slaves still have their speech and thus belong in some subtle way more to the world above the line than below; which have lost their language and been forced outside the boundaries, to make another language in which touch is the currency.

Then he makes another line, this one vertical, dividing the lowest level into two side-by-side areas. He shows her his ears. His hand flutters from her throat to his ears and he nods, then puts himself into one of the areas. The other, he gestures, then covers his ears. She shakes her head another way: I don't understand. He takes his eating sticks out of his sleeve-pocket. Their ends are blunt, which has always seemed wrong to her: she sharpened hers long ago. He points one into each ear, makes a gesture of stabbing, then mimes covering his ears and sinking down into silence. Some of the slaves are made deaf as well as mute. There, his hands show her, there is more touch needed, attracting each other's attention especially.

The waif thought it was bad enough to have her past missing, her mind. Now she imagines all the languages going, which she has just understood keep her free. But looking at his flowing hands, she sees that there, too, is freedom, perhaps even more than she can imagine now, having only begun to think of the idea.

She puts her hands up to the top level. "Up here, do they know how to speak with hands?"

He shakes his head, smiles, puts his hands over his own mouth with a satisfied look. It is a secret. How can someone with no tongue tell a secret? They laugh together. Already his harsh throat noises sound familiar, comfortable.

The idea of comfort both reminds her of the madwoman and makes her deeply suspicious. She backs away to the bed he has called hers. He nods and turns away, then back, and opens the other cabinet. Clothing. His hands say: big, small, take what you need. She nods. He goes. She sinks down onto the bed. Her hands slowly cover her mouth. She forgot to ask him. When will her tongue be cut out?

There are flat windows on the wall that don't show what's on the other side of the wall. A slave who can talk calls them screens. Every screen is two-way; still, down in the bottom of the palace it is possible to achieve a measure of privacy, of autonomy. Everywhere else, it seems, is monitored.

The old man is the only one who doesn't seem to care. It's as if he has earned the right to some action of his own. He took her hand immediately that she reported to him, and holds it often, even when his other servants are there.

She is frightened and deeply embarrassed. In the south, she had been taught that touching was improper in front of any third party, even a baby. And likewise, babies were taught very young to stand alone, not to need comforting in crowds.

But that was then. Now, the old man tells her to sit near him. Despite the old woman making her head ache with thoughts about freedom, it was restful to do as one was told. It didn't hurt nearly as much.

The people gather in a circle in the greater kitchen. The waif does not know whether to join them or not, but Escape-from-bondage motions her in. The circle joins hands briefly, then they all let go so that the people can sign.

They all know the chant except her. She tries to follow along but her signs are halting. Still, the people on either side of her smile at her. The silence in the room is overwhelming, broken as it is by nothing but the involuntary sounds of the deaf and the rustling of the sleeves of the signing people. The girl is about to start to cry when she hears around her a muted chuckling sound. Who's laughing, she thinks furiously, only to realize that the sound was the sniffling of other people already weeping. At the realization, she is hard-put to suppress giggles instead. She thinks: maybe all ritual has mystery and absurdity, and maybe that is what it is for. It is a curious and complex thought and like most of her legacy from the madwoman it makes her head hurt. She concentrates then on her signing.

At the end of the chant, the people raise their arms and reach up, shouting a ragged, raucous single cry into the ceiling. Which must, she thinks, symbolize the sky, or maybe their oppressors. Then they drop their arms, assume normalcy, and walk quietly away down the many halls and out the many doors. Soon she stands alone, only then recalling that she too has tasks.

When she had first seen the man she had thought he was very old, and the palsy which spasmed his body shocked her, though she didn't know why. The room reeked sharply of sweat and urine.

"Come here," he had said, and when she did, he grabbed her arm and stroked it, then held her hand. She had thought of Escape-from-bondage's rules and she thought, this one must be either powerful or very stupid. If he is rich enough to have this much, stupid is unlikely.

She was to be his nurse, he had told her. That doesn't mean the same thing as in the south. Here, it means cleaning bedpans, wiping his ass, cleaning under his foreskin, giving him sponge baths, changing the sheets, and sometimes feeding him. He seems very weak, but everyone jumps to his command. No, not stupid.

Some things are the same. The screens are just a better way of ensuring observation and consequences. In the first week she had been sent to the market for fish (a bewildering and almost overwhelming journey) and found no fish, then had come back to the vendor unloading on the step, warned of their need by the network monitors. Nothing different from the south except in style. She had for one second wondered if the rules were different here, but she saw that in the market no-one touched, just as at home. This makes her judge his bold and dangerous action to be as revolutionary and inexplicable as she had first thought.

Her keeper on the road north had said her new owner was the regent, but she did not think this old man was the regent himself. He must have given her to someone else, a powerful priest perhaps, since he had so many lines on his face. When she says this to the mute Escape-from-bondage, he laughs like a seal's bark. (What is a seal? There was no-one any more to ask.) But she doesn't know the signs he makes, except to understand that she had indeed been bought by the regent himself, after he had seen her in the market.

She does not remember anyone from the slave markets: the frequent trips to stand in the little booths with their one-way glass had been a part of her routine, yes, but nothing ever seemed to come of it except time to herself. Now, it appears, more had happened among the shadowy figures on the other side of the glass than she had thought.

She learns to enjoy (without seeming to gloat) the pleasure of the power his touch bestows on her. But one day when his hands, which are firm and free of the spasming which arches his neck and curves his spine, reach for hers, and for her waist, and he turns her to him, she sees in the dim room that his face is not so old after all, just battered by pain and informed by a kind of cunning no different from that of her old nurse and his master, except in degree. Don't fuck the regent, the old woman had said. She knows suddenly she has been fooling herself with slave fantasies, and she wishes with all her frail heart that he would let her go.

He laughs, and lets her go. She sways back with relief, then continues the rub of his legs which he interrupted.

In the small dim room where he lay when she met him, there were often one or two attendants like herself, but there was no screen, so she felt safe. But he has become interested in motion, stronger, slower, and has begun to walk about the room, and she knows they will soon go out. He will soon be well and able to do anything. Anything he wants.

There is a portrait on the wall of the Great Hall, which makes the waif shiver and she doesn't know why. It is of a regal and rather

benign-looking woman posed in a conservatory with a garden showing behind through open doors. She asks Escape-from-bondage
who the woman is.

=The old mother,= he says. =What a power she was. I used to
have to service her when I was a boy. See these lines of scars? She
used to sharpen her fingernails and strengthen them with metallic
lacquer so they were as sharp as razor blades. When I got too old
she sent me down the chute and I ended up with my tongue out.=

"Who is she?"

=Oh, she's dead now. She was the old queen. Then her daughter took over in a coup—a bloodbath—and put the old woman away
in a tower. That's when I was her body slave. Didn't last long,
though. The daughter and her husband had made the regent their
second heir, after *their* daughter, the one who vanished. Left this
regent in charge. They were always lazy. The old woman had him
in her pocket of course. She had them killed. She walled them off
in their tower and burned it. The deaf slaves were the lucky ones. I
heard the screaming. Now that I think of it, it was after that when
the old woman had me tongue-snipped. She didn't last long, either,
of course—= (a shrug for "of course") =—he had her out of the way
within the year, I think.=

"How did she die?"

=Fucking, the story says. Nobody really knew. He saw to the
body himself.= He pauses. =He was always creative.=

"Don't fuck the regent," says the waif, thinking.

=What?=

"Something someone said to me. Don't fuck the regent."

=He wants you prepared to be a hostess now. He's having a
party. He wants you to be one of the table women. At his table. You
might have to fuck him there. Or someone else.=

"I figured I wouldn't have much choice."

=It's strange. He usually just uses a slave up. This hostess thing
is odd—he doesn't follow the fashion of the city and keep a chate-
laine.=

He has finger-spelled the last word, which means "keeper of the
keys." It's not a word the waif recognizes in any of her languages.
He mimes a stuck-up, fussy person with high standards and tastes.
She laughs.

=Maybe he's getting old.=

"He looked pretty old when I was first there nursing him, but
he's getting younger. He seems to do everything on purpose,

though. Maybe he just has to work off the leftover gratitude-guilt. After all that touch."

=Don't forget you're a slave. He doesn't have to treat you well.=

"Forget? That's stupid. It's all I have, am. How could I forget?"

=You forgot everything else, once before. At least once that we know.=

"But that wasn't my fault. I fell on my head."

=You could fall on your head again anytime. Be careful.=

She goes away laughing derisively, but her head aches all evening and when she sleeps, she dreams about the portrait of the old woman. She lies awake in the middle of the night, trying to imagine the razor edges on the nails of those hands in the painting, which are composed so calmly in the woman's lap. She decides that she is glad she never knew her. Far easier to know mutes and mad-women in cages than to know truly dangerous people.

=Fierce-frightened,= Escape-from-bondage says to her.

"What?"

=A name for you. My name for you, in my thoughts.=

"I have never had a name. Even the crazy old woman never gave me a name. She didn't have any names to spare, I guess."

=She didn't need to name you. You were the only one she had. But I know many. And I call you who you seem to me, fierce and frightened.=

"Is that who I am?"

=I don't know who you are. Only who you seem to me.=

The difference makes her head start to ache. That has been happening a lot lately. She holds it together with her hands, sinks down on the edge of the bed. He sits beside her, signs for her to lie down; obediently she stretches out, arms down by her sides, and he puts his large warm hands on her head. He strokes her forehead, her temples, holds the back of her head gently and rolls it a bit to loosen her neck muscles. He lies down beside her, not touching her but for the hand still stroking her head. After a while the pain starts to abate and the tears stop rolling down her cheeks.

Then he suddenly sits up. She rolls her head slowly to look at him.

=There is something to do,= he says. =Something we could do if you want it.=

"What?" Her voice comes out logy and sleepy.

He makes a sign.

"I don't understand."

He touches her belly, just above the pubic bone, touches his own belly. Then he puts one hand on his breastbone, palm over his heart and index finger in the hollow of his throat, and the other hand on her chest in the same place.

"It's about . . . " but there isn't a word for it in a language he knows.

He makes the sign again, two hands intertwined.

"Fucking?"

His face darkens. He makes the sign for fucking. It is different. He pushes his hands away and apart. Then he says, =Not fucking. That we have to do for them. Something we do for ourselves. Because we—= and he makes a strange sign, which she does not understand, then spells it out, *love,* repeating afterward his hands-on-heart sign.

=Do we 'love'?= she signs back, because she doesn't know a word for it in the spoken language he knows.

=Do we?= he repeats the interrogative sign.

"Maybe. It makes my head ache again." But it doesn't ache much. "But not much," she says hurriedly, and he laughs. He sits there cross-legged, hands in his lap, watching her.

"I don't know what to do," she says.

=You have to tell me you want it,= he says, =or I can't move. This has to be nothing like what they do to us.=

She thinks he is brilliant to think these thoughts. "Did you invent this?" she says.

=I invented myself entirely,= he replies arrogantly.

"Yes," she says. "But I still don't know what to do. They don't want you to do much when you fuck them. Unless they order you. I've never done anything with my body for me. I haven't been awake long enough." Alive, she means, since she awoke amnesiac.

=I have learned some things, over the years.=

"Show me."

He stands suddenly, smoothly, towering above her on the bed, and takes off his clothes quickly. She laughs suddenly at his serious, businesslike look.

"Is this a 'slave rebellion?' " she says.

=Why?= He reseats himself in another smooth motion.

"The old woman was always muttering that some day there

would be a slave rebellion. She seemed to think it was a good idea. This seems to me to be a good idea."

=Then I think it must be a 'slave rebellion'!=

She pulls off her shift and sits naked before him. He puts a hand up, halfway. Her hand meets his. Later she is not sure who first pulled the other closer, even though it all happens very slowly. She is small compared with him, and his hands are so big they cover large areas of her skin. She is very pale, also, compared with him, and this seems extremely strange to her, unfamiliar, as if it should be another way. But she forgets that soon enough.

His hands go inside her, and hers inside him. After a while it is time to put his wide cock into her, but he waits until she wants it, asks him shyly if perhaps that is what they should do. It is not as good for her as his hands and his mouth, so he turns her around so that he can reach around her to the bud they have found at the front of her cunt, which seems to give such pleasure when stroked and sucked. He rubs it while he moves inside her. Suddenly, an unfamiliar and terrifying feeling mounts through her belly to the top of her head. It seems to spread in circles, like the concentric circles at the servants' ritual, but spreads and spreads. She cries out, "What is it?" but her voice is wild and she doesn't know what language she has used. Suddenly she cannot bear his hand any more: she clasps it to her belly and pushes against him and he comes into her harder, comes with a ragged shout of his own which he later tells her would have been words if he hadn't, so many years ago, had his words stolen away.

They lie down then, touching over more surface than she has touched anyone in her short life, and sleep entangled like his fingers were when he made the sign for this, for whatever this has been, this that they have done together.

The Remarkable Mountains (2)

When I woke up. How many stories have that in them? Annalise has been laughing, here, at all my jokes, with the kind of hysterical edge I have heard seldom in her voice, often in my own. I tell her it was not her fault. I tell her he killed the others and he would have killed her. It doesn't seem to matter. At least the language proves easy: a variation of trader tongue, not too hard to learn, just add a hiss—and ask when a word strikes strange to the ear.

Annalise had almost forgotten what home was like, we'd been gone so long. Almost thought we were free, she says. I admit I think a lot of it too. Only knowing that the spy had no communication since Avanue gives me hope. We journeyed a long way from there. And this place seems a long way from anywhere, the people are so kind. Like no place on the earth I've known so far.

Now that I am on my feet a little, walking around, I begin to appreciate the full strangeness of this place. It is attractive, the way that households are open here in the mountains, but it has also been a shock to both Annalise and me. Despite thinking ourselves well beyond our frame, we have a lot left over, we both realize, from what we were taught at home.

What first makes impact is the physical shape of the houses. They looked to me like a sprawl of village buildings had all been lumped together. Every time a family needed a new area they seem to have built one. It has a crazy and positive aesthetic, because the materials are in harmony and each family's idea of roofs and walls is different from each other family's, but similar to each of their own other additions.

The second learning has been what a family is, who lives in these houses. At home, families are strictly structured, for the purpose of controlling lineage. Property must be handed down in an orderly fashion, after all, as my grandmother would have said. Since then, the sailors, with their hands of five, and the nameless ones at Avanue, with their privacy and good manners.

Here, everything seems to happen in the open. One family may be a couple with their grown children and their children in turn, or it may be a group of friends with their partners—and I notice that there are same-sex couples almost as often as mixed-gender—or combinations of friends and blood kin in untidy, contented tumbles—though it seems the couples have rooms of their own. Some houses are neat, some messy, but all are nicely appointed—and they are all kept unlocked.

I have been staying in the house of a couple with an adult son. I would have thought him old enough for a home of his own, since he already has a bit of white in his hair, despite a young face, but no, he lives in some far corner of his parents' rabbit-warren of a house. At first I thought quite a lot of other people lived here too, but I discovered after a few days that most of the people who make free use of the place are visitors.

One morning I was wakened—I was still sleeping on a cotton mattress on the gathering-room floor at that time—by a short, stocky, cheerful woman who walked in the unlocked door, took a bag of fresh-baked (by the smell) bread through to the kitchen area, then came back to plop down in a chair and pick up the news broadsheet.

"Go back to sleep," she said. "I'll just read until people wake up." I thought it powerful presumptuous of her, but I turned over obediently and to my surprise I did sleep. I woke again to voices: the woman of the house was hugging this woman and making private jokes and they were both laughing.

When they saw me turn over the woman of the house said: "Oh, we woke you, I'm sorry. We'll go into the library!" but the sun was high and I told them I was getting up. The man of the house was in the kitchen area (there seem to be few full walls anywhere in the main house, though the extremities are portioned into private rooms and rooms which seem to be workrooms) slicing the bread and grilling it over an electric fire.

"Haven't you ever had toast? Here," he said, and gave me a piece of this grilled bread spread with a kind of butter, I guess, and some honey. The taste was strange but delicious.

Before the day was out, three other people came in. Two visited with everyone and were introduced to me, but one went directly to the library.

"Oh, he's working on something and comes here to use the books," she said when I looked at his retreating back. "He's kind of preoccupied right now. His thesis is due."

"Thesis?"

"He went east to the university and they gave him five years to work on something. Of course his time's almost up now—who ever starts a thesis until the last possible minute?—so he doesn't do much but research and write."

By the time I would have started to worry about wearing out my welcome (remember the old adage about dead rats and visitors?) I had begun to realize I couldn't do it. After some thinking one day, the woman showed me a room which wasn't much used and said I could sleep in there if I didn't mind her sewing there in the day-time, come the fall. "But by then," she said, "you'll probably want to be building your own room. And we'll know if it should be here or somewhere else."

There is a hierarchy of friendship, I slowly perceive; not every-one is as welcome, not everyone has the freedom of the house. And most people seem to know their place in it, though one day, after a rather brassy young woman left, I saw the son roll his eyes in an un-mistakable message and we all laughed.

Annalise is staying next door. She has started doing some chores for her keep, though they don't seem to be expected; I am still coughing too much to do more than sit most of the day. We meet and walk slowly around the village in midafternoon. One day we went as far as the bench that sits on a slight rise above the main street.

"I feel like I am in one giant expository lump," she said. I laughed until I coughed, knowing just what she meant.

"What a literary critic you are!" I said.

"If you had read more of those foul romantic novels you would know what I mean. They have them here, too, you know."

"Really? I can't read their alphabet well enough yet to know what the books are. In my house there are about a dozen books of our language but they are mostly dull as dishwater."

"That bad, huh? Well, I've hit a fatherlode of adventure sto-ries. Some of them are for teenagers, I think. They seem to be full of kids with two problems and just enough skills to solve it and get kissed too, or kids taking the old metaphoric journey to adulthood and managing to find the magic ring and sword and suchlike on the way."

"Same old stuff only softer, eh?" I laughed.

But the idiom made her thoughtful. "It is softer, you know," she said. "Ee-yah, when I think of where we came from . . . Doesn't it ever strike you how lucky we are to see this?" and she flapped her hand at the village around us.

"Lucky? I still think too much about death and escape."

"So do I. But if it weren't for that husband of yours, that grandmother of ours for that matter, and all the petty and gigantic losses and punishments over the years, we would never have been able to live like this."

We were silent for a while.

"I really like it here," she said.

After a while more I said, "Yes, so do I."

"I like the son of your house," she said.

"Yes," said I.

"There are things to do here."

"Yes."

We looked at each other and laughed, but until now I didn't dare say anything like the word "home," though when I saw this valley, I thought I must stay here. It is too perilous to hope for something as impossible as a home, and we both know it. We tabulate the facts about the place, and grow to like the people, but there will come a time when it is all shattered—by something we find out that makes us realise we are living in fool's heaven, or by something—or someone—from outside, bringing our past along to catch us. It's bound to happen. It's only a matter of time.

The children run in and out of the houses in the autumn sun and everyone takes on a little of their care. So far I have seen cross words but no punishment. Maybe I am missing it. Yesterday, walking right down the street, I began to cry: no genteel tears but sobs and screaming breaths. I thought I was going crazy. There was a man walking the other way; he stopped and took care of me. I kept apologizing. He kept saying don't apologize. For a few minutes, after the worst was over, we almost argued. Finally he said, "Don't they have any sensible people where you come from?" I started to laugh but not from humor. He had to slap me to get me to stop. Then I laughed a different way and said: "I thought you people didn't know how to hit. You wonderful mountaineers."

In the end he brought me back here and I had to offer him

tea—which he made himself. He stayed for hours, not talking, just watching me rest. Finally I fell asleep, though it was only afternoon, and slept until this morning. His name is F.

Spent the day in bed. Can't seem to get up. Overwhelmed with memories of home. Except when I think it is home I feel more like vomiting. Can't seem to forget the time when I was a child that I had my nanny beaten because she—I can't remember. She never came back. I thought she died of it. She was old. All I remember is my triumph. This was my world and I knew how to manage it. My grandmother gave me a present then—an abacus made of opal beads. I have it with me still. Brought it to remind myself that I am what I despise. Or have been. That kind of blood doesn't wash off.

I have wondered why I stay alive. I ran away. I stayed away. I told myself there was nothing I could do. I just survive to spite them, to make them fear something at least. Certainly not because I love myself as they seem to do here, without lives and torture on their conscience. What does it mean to be good? Everywhere I go there is a different answer.

I am tired of the pain of this. There are people all around me in these mountain towns who have not had a life of such pain. I am starting to hate on account of it. Hate them for their happiness. Hate my family, even my parents, for the kind of world they made and live in. Hate myself, I suppose, too, for being trapped here. In these mountains, in this body, in this life.

I cannot imagine, right now, why I stay alive. I never questioned it in the years of struggle: life justified itself. But now that I am safe and sitting in these gardens, living in these easy households, playing with these carefree children, I cannot bear to live like this. I am a twisted creature without merit. Oh, Annalise, how did you manage to give me such hope when I was hopeless? How did I give myself hope? I must find the source and unblock it, or I will not be able to stay here. I am so close to giving up that only the scratching of the nib on the page distracts me; only the mechanical formation of rounded, even letters and words, in careful array, keeps me from falling.

* * *

Today I feel I am skittering off my life like the heroes who tried to climb the glass mountain in the faery tale. These Remarkable Mountains are far from glass, but it's possible to skate off them just as easily. The Range, the people here call them, as if there were no other mountains. I suppose there are no other mountains like these.

I'm so tired of everything good about this village. I can't remember anything good about my childhood. Everything I write down is shadowed and dark. I tried to tell the story of the glass mountain to Rosalka. She was horrified. "They sacrificed their child to the spirit of the mountain?"

"Don't you have any faery tales with gruesome bits?"

"Oh, sure, I guess so, but sacrificing your children? That's awful!" I imagined myself spread flat across the mirror like Little Dancer in the tale, ready for the knife. I know what symbolism is, even if Rose doesn't. Cut away the past, cut away what shaped you, as a sacrifice to the mountain spirit. Or maybe I was sacrificed to some other jealous godlet who insists that I cannot sleep now that I have abandoned my destiny.

Annalise is comforting as always. "Don't fancy yourself. I've read the family histories. You'll just be a footnote when the time comes."

"Well, that's encouraging. My whole life and all this misery and all I'll get is a footnote?" But I know what she means. I've read those books too, even had to memorize some of the texts during one of the periodic fitness evaluations Grandmother engineered. To see if I was fit to rule, what a joke:

> In the Autumn of that year they went down from the high ground where the ship lay into the valley where the stream ran. Gallien it was who thought they should build a road for the ship to be brought down, so that it might float. This was done, and it was found that the ship could not be made into a river vessel, for having too much draught on its fin-keel. So it was changed, and Gallien determined to take it to the sea. He was made chief that year and the first ten years of his reign were spent taking the ship to the sea. In the end the Ship on the Mountaintop sailed from Dexter to Ruyay seven times a year and back, with provender and stuffs. So the people from Ruyay and Dexter and Gal-

lienda turned to Gallien and made him king of all of them. He had another name before that but no-one remembers it. There was a sister, too, who ruled in Dexter and Ruyay before him, but she is not much mentioned except to say, she died of a lead surplus, and laugh. She was called Dushla and nothing more is known of her.

That sort of thing. Deadly dull.

Little birds. What are they called? They are colored like rocks and sky. How can they live through these winters? Their feet are bare. I can hardly go out. Wrapped in sweaters, I shiver by the heaters, look-ing out the windows at the birds. I don't know why I'm here. I ran away, that's why. Years of running are catching up with me. Annalise is down the valley with Jed. F. tries to wake me up. I'm so tired, I can barely write. I can't think of anything to say, anyway. All the old stories can't save me. He wants to take me to his bed. It might be warm there.

I have decided to start writing this in the mountain language. I know enough by now. I cannot keep thinking in the language of cruelty in which I was born, and sailor talk doesn't have space for what I want to learn, even if there were a sailor here to teach me the rest of the words. But here in the mountains they have names for the things I want to become: happy, secure, gentle, kind, good. I will learn the subtle words, the nuances of meaning, and I will be able to think thoughts I never thought before, dream dreams I never dreamed before.

All this winter of sleep—of hibernation, they call it here when animals wrap up and go to ground—it has brought me a fragile peace, a little healing. If I am to keep it, I must have new words. New ways. New waves in a new sea.

They don't understand the sea here, but they have stone, sky, water, wind, and trees. So many beautiful trees. Among them the people live like animals, and by that I mean natural and happy. It's a myth too, I'm sure: one of their poets wrote something about "na-ture red in tooth and claw." But I would rather live in their myth than the one I was groomed to take on. I would rather tell moun-tain stories. Or live them.

Can someone so hurt—here they call it "abused"—be good? I would like to have a child. Isn't that strange? F. and I talk about it. I know the risks, but I still long for a family life, a mountain family. Can I remake everything? Speak a new life-language as well?

If I have a child I will teach him or her to speak sailor tongue and trader tongue, but will I teach my birth language? I hope not, though perhaps, when she or he is old enough not to be changed so much by it, I will teach it for survival's sake. I don't know. Is it better to be warned about evil and have bad dreams, or to be ignorant of its existence and meet it bolstered with that innocence?

They make a kind of nepenthe drink here and take it during festivals: I found this out last night at the storytelling. It's a nasty greenish decoction and everyone made great jokes about its foul taste as they had their ritual sip. I could barely swallow it; it seemed to make my throat close up on contact, which I didn't realize was not its taste but a premonition of anaphylactic shock. Shortly thereafter I was having antihistamines of some sort blown into my nose with a straw by my hostess, serious-faced until she saw I could breathe again, then laughing and imitating herself, caricature of sputtery-lipped healer where before she had been efficient and sure.

She was going to bustle me home to bed but I convinced her I'd be fine in a comfortable chair in the corner of the meeting hall, wrapped in a blanket and with a big tankard of water to hand. She was just as glad: she was getting stoned by then, she said, using a strange term I thought, but I suppose it's fitting; the drug certainly hit me like a ton of rocks.

It took the others differently, though; they were mellow, slow-talking, and relaxed, but they stayed up all night, talking and listening, laughing and sometimes crying.

Some of the stories were obviously familiar: people chanted their favorite lines along with the teller. Others were new and were greeted with spellbound silence, or gusts of surprised laughter, or a combination of both.

One was about me, though I didn't realize it until I saw the others were trying to stifle their laughter. I listened more carefully. " . . . then the woman went down to the outhouse behind the main building," the teller was saying, "and she said, 'What's this for?' The people told her it was for shit. 'So small?' she said. 'Where I am from there is too much shit to fit in such a small house. My family had to build a big house to put it all in.' 'Well, that is the difference between your people and us,' the people said. 'We give our shit away.' "

It broke me up. I laughed so hard I coughed and my healer had to come by and check on me. Annalise came in just then and asked me, "What's everybody laughing at?" I couldn't repeat the tale, I was laughing so hard, and I told her you just had to be there.

When the laughter had subsided, another voice began to speak, quite quietly. Soon the hall was hushed and absorbed, so silent that I couldn't whisper questions to anyone, though I wanted to, for I hardly understood a thing. Oh, the words made sense all right: it was just the organization of them which bewildered me.

"You go down a long road," said the voice. Husky, a little gravelly, an old person, sitting in shadows and out of my direct line of sight. Could have been any one of the old people over there by the back wall.

Best as I remember it, here's the story: "You go down a long road, and you look for a sign. You were here once, and you will be here again. It really doesn't matter. There are people with you: a blind cat, a strong fighter, a parent who complains about the food. No-one wants to talk much—you know how it is. It is always this way.

"The blind cat turns into a blind crow, and scouts the road ahead. Then a blind horse, to carry you where you're going. Then a blind dog, to lie loyal and smelly beside you in the night. Then a blind cat again, to tell you what it all means, traveling in time and through space like this.

"The strong fighter is afraid of the dark. Do you have anything to say? A leaf turns on the night trees and everyone looks at the moon. The moon spins and spins its windlass. Nothing is drawn up in the bucket of the sky. All night long.

"Your parent becomes your child, your rib, your trial, your dwelling place. Change the words a little, and you have a chant, a robber, a trail in the wilderness. You recognize the road you're on. But you have nothing to take with you, and so there is nothing to be stolen. The robber sits down with you and the fighter serves breakfast. In the end you are all following a blind cat who walks with her tail high down the road that spirals through the beautiful morning. Soon it will be time to sleep. You have loved another night to pieces. You walk through her eyes, find the place of rest, lick your fur smooth and sleep under the silent sun."

The rest were even less clear. I can't remember them all: a darkened doorway, a singing vine, a rocking chair, a tall tree. The blind cat was in several, but only those told by the raspy-voiced person. I can't remember them all, but I wish I could: if I could, I would know more about this place and my chances here than I could ever find out by living here in the everyday.

After a while they asked me to tell a story, if I wanted, and if my throat was better. I begged off. I had already had some private reaction to my stories, and somehow I could not imagine Little Dancer of the Mirror would be comfortable here.

The sun was about to rise when we all left the hall. Everyone stood out in the village street until it was full day, gossiping and watching the rabbits bolt through the dewy grass. Cats emerged yawning from houses to greet us. I asked my hostess if there was a blind cat, but she only looked at me as if she were blind herself, her eyes blank, round and ambiguous of expression. The shortest night of the year was over.

"It does me no good to fall in love," I said to Annalise.

"Is that what this is?" she said, but not in her bantering tone. I looked at her. She was silent, looking down, chewing the corner of her lip. She was trying to hide behind her hair.

"Aha!" I said. "The fair Annalise falls at last."

She blushed angrily. "Leave me alone!"

"Come on, little sister, you know I meant no harm."

"I can't feel like this. It ruins everything!"

"Everything?"

"Us traveling. Us being together. Us."

Looking at her I was suddenly vested with a vision of such calmness as I could hardly imagine. "Do you think we are less us here than somewhere else? You have been taking care of me too long. I release you from that, little sister. Love me as you like, but you do not have to sacrifice for me. Love doesn't demand that, does it?"

She looked up. "I'm the wise one. Shut up!" she said. Then we both laughed and laughed.

It seems this mountain place gives us strange and terrifying gifts. I gave her the right to love, but I can't give it to myself. Yet. Maybe never. I can't forget what I bring into this quiet place.

Dark-headed F. walks in my dreams. When I wake up, I can imagine for a moment I am still there, still safe in a world where my cousin cannot find me. Annalise and I have been running for so many years. My parents are dead. My grandmother is dead. When can I rest? I want a life of my own, apart from the destiny they twisted for me.

Talked with F. all morning. Finally he said I should move into his place since we seem to need more time for talk. That's not all we need time for. I can't get used to these households' idea of privacy. Can't make love in public. He lives alone.

Afternoon I was offered citizenship. Or something like that. I'm sure F. set it all up to happen on the same day. Probably went bouncing out of here after I said yes and ran off to the council of elders, as they call them, though some are not very old, with a proposal. They just happened to be sitting today. Big coincidence. He's a sly sweetmeat. So I said what did I have to do and they said pull your weight. Seems like the best deal I've been offered in my life. I said I'd let them know. Have to talk with Annalise. Are we really safe here? Promises are not to be made lightly, even here.

Annalise and I walked out to the end of the town today. It was the first really warm day since the late mountain spring began. I like sitting on the cliffs looking out over the Fjord. She doesn't like heights much any more so we sat back from the edge, in the shade of some trees, on a blanket I spread. After a while we lay back and looked at the sky.

"They have a game here where they say what the shapes of the clouds are. Animals, trees, landscapes," said Annalise.

"What do you think they look like?"

"Clouds," she said comfortably, and we laughed.

"You're the only one here who doesn't make me think I'm crazy," I said.

"I know what you mean," she said. "All my habits are wrong. It makes me feel rotten most of the time. I mean really rotten, like I'm going to be eaten by maggots."

"Maybe we should just give up and live together."

"Do you want to?"

"Yes and no. I miss sleeping with you. The only time I felt normal was when we were . . . lovers." The word we never used. There it was.

But there was no earthquake. We didn't fall thousands of feet into the Fjord.

"I know," said Annalise quietly. "Until now, but it's like a shadow. What could be. I wish we could live together and with them."

"F. can't stand Jed," I said. "Silly fuckwit."

"Jed gets all defensive. I hate them both sometimes. And the mountain customs. So bloody nice."

"Yes." I put my arm out and she rolled into my embrace, her head in the hollow below my shoulder. I turned my head into her hair. It smelled like Annalise, with a floral overlay. "What are you washing your hair with?"

"Chamomile."

"Nice."

Slowly her hand came up to lie on my breast, then to form to my breast, then to stroke gently. Slowly I turned toward her, and after a while we were making love. So relaxed and familiar. Maybe the last time. These mountain people were full of household love, but would they tumble in groups together in the same big bed like the sailors? I envied those dark people their handfastings at this moment, holding my friend, my sister, my lover, so fragile she seemed now, no longer my strength. So fragile we both seemed.

At different times that afternoon, each of us cried. Finally the sun came around to shine under our trees and we put our clothes on and got up. We folded the blanket, one at each side like laundry servants. When we brought our ends together, our hands tangled and clasped. The blanket fell in a tumble at our feet as I held her desperately.

"I don't know how I'm going to get through this," I said. "I feel like the monster that ate Trebora's children."

"I'm pregnant," she said.

"So am I," I said. "I think."

"Our children will be sisters," she said.

"No, they won't," I said. "Not like we are. Not in the mountains. They'll run up and down the meadows playing at fantasies, like these others, and they'll probably hate us for even expecting them to be friends. And in the mountains, cousins don't marry. So no romantic endings."

"It's fine," she said, "no matter how it ends up. Because the cliff we look over doesn't look over the Dark Isles. Everything else is better. And . . . " She looked at me like I could finish her sentence—and I could.

"And we're not monsters."

"No. Just alive and stuck with it, like that mountain poet wrote."

"These people have a mean sense of humor."

"Not mean; that's what I like about it."

"Yes. Not mean. Just acute. Maybe with a few years and a lot of acting talent, I can get used to the difference."

"I think you can," Annalise said gently. "After all, it's what you wanted."

"Be careful what you ask for—you might get it," I said. She laughed at the proverb she had found in the old sailor book. We folded the blanket again and went home, each to our homes.

It wouldn't be the last time we made love, but it was one of the best. I often remember how my orgasm that day went through me in waves, how I held her, thinking how small she was, something I so seldom noticed.

Today I told F. who I really am. (Who am I?—rhetorical question.) I told him about the death of my parents and I told him about my husband who must now be the regent. Except I had to find a new word for husband because in this language husband is the word for my relationship with F. So I tried "stakeholder" and "indenture holder"—but he didn't understand indenture, only the sailors know about that—before I got to "master," which is actually a foreign word, but one that has been adapted enough into the language that they use it to describe a strange and repellent ritual done by people far away: "master" and "servant."

"But you were not a 'servant,' " said F.

"No, I was a princess," I replied.

"But a 'princess' is the 'master' of 'servants,' " he said.

"Yes, but a princess has a price and can be bought and sold too. The price is just higher."

"What did he pay for you?"

"Well, loyalty, the conquest of the south, and sexual services to his aunt. As far as I could see."

"Sexual services?"

"Yes, the only time I saw him, he had his sword in her up to the hilt." F. probably thinks I spoke metaphorically.

"Why didn't you stay, become queen, get rid of him?"

"Politics. He killed my parents. He had a lot of doctors and herbalists in his service. And of course my grandmother. She was really the queen. She had to give it up when my mother married but she was not willing to give it up forever."

"If you were married, weren't you the queen then?"

"Not until the marriage was consummated. We were married when I was an infant, after all. Even his tastes, and hers, did not run to infants. They preferred their victims old enough to be terrified."

"I really don't get it. She was a criminal. So was he. They should have been locked up."

"Who would lock them up? They had a lot of family money. They could buy as many soldiers as they wanted. And many of the court saw my mother and father as weaklings who had destroyed the warrior-class tradition."

"Warrior-class?"

"Soldiers of the nobility. Special status. My father did not beat his servants, or fight duels, or initiate his children sexually, and he took baths and dressed in clean clothes. That made him an oddity. And my mother drank, of course. Not festival nepenthe either. A kind of distilled drink with drugs dissolved in it. Distilled forgetfulness. The court found her intolerable, after a while. She had made my father king, though, and was beyond their reach. And there were some of the warrior aristos on their side. The ones who embraced complex culture. They thought they'd rather be clean sometimes too than sweaty from weapons practice all the time." I looked at him, smiling grimly. "It was the dawn of a golden age."

He laughed, but with anger not humor. "It sounds like Hell."

"Which level?"

"How can you joke?"

"Annalise once said to me, you can laugh or you can cry, and I'd rather laugh. I thought it was a good philosophy. When I stop laughing is if I'm ever traced here. Pray to your pantheon of universal forces that it never happens."

"Why would he chase you? Doesn't he have what he wants, the power?"

"But not the way he wants it. There, the queen is the powerful one. She must make the king. If I had been there, he could have forced me to make him king after the death of my parents, and then he could have displayed my head on a pole for all the people cared. But as long as I am their heir, and lost in lands away, and my death is not proven, he is simply regent, and there are powers he cannot take."

"By now wouldn't he have the rest of the . . . court, as you call it . . . on his side?"

"Not all. Some recall the law. The law binds the regents, the queens and the kings strongly. There are provisions in it: the people could tear him apart in the marketplace if he took what was mine. They take their responsibilities very seriously, the people. The marketplace is the center of justice for the rulers, even though it is the center of injustice for the common people."

"Couldn't he claim you are dead, pretend to find your remains?" I could see F. reaching for solutions that ended any danger to me, even though I could also see that he still had no idea what the danger really was. I will have to start telling him stories of my childhood. Maybe if he knows enough of them he will begin to "get it," as he says.

"We have borrowed genetic printing from the sailor people. My print is on record at the Hall of Mirrors. Unless he had a real sample of my tissue, he could prove nothing."

"Even so . . . " he began to argue in his earnest fashion.

"There is one thing more you forget." He looked at me. "Succession is through the women of our line," I said. "And now we have a daughter."

Then I watched him begin to understand.

In the sailor town (1)

Essa was not involved in the decision which sent the ship back to its own port, but Gata came back from the crew meeting with a satisfied look on her dark face.

"We are going home," she said. "You are safe now."

"Home?"

"Our home. My home. If you'll come with me to my home."

Essa felt a rush of such pleasure she was shocked. This woman had become—what?—to her. Important? Central?

It's cabin syndrome, she thought. Holiday fever. Bonding during crisis. Whatever.

But she didn't care what. She was going home with Gata. She remembered what going home felt like: to a home she didn't have any more.

Nostalgic, she thought of a day she climbed a mountain with her parents. Everybody laughed then. Gata never laughed quite like that, but now she was smiling, the white of her teeth flashing against her tanned, brown face.

"Going home," she said, and her voice reflected the comfort Essa felt from the word.

The rest of the journey was short. Soon the sailors saw a stripe of land on the edge of the eastern sky, and it grew into a continent, and the continent grew until it had a coastline, and the coastline widened until its crenellations were sharp against the surf-edged sea, and one of the crenellations became a harbor bounded by cliffs, and on the cliffs, and below the cliffs by the beach, there were houses, and Gata looked over the edge of the deck, at the bow, and smiled again, and said again, "Home."

Essa felt a wave of such profound strangeness cross her that for a moment she was short of breath. I know how my mother felt, she thought for the first time. This must be how she felt, sometimes.

* * *

As they sank down to the dock, Essa learned what it was like to be on a falling moon which eclipses the bright sunlight of those waiting on land. The silver ship loomed for them as it loomed for her these many weeks ago. Looking down on this clean landscape she could almost forget the rest of her leaving, how as the ship rose she could see the moonlit town, with shadows heavy on the square, and how the shadows heavy on her mind and her heart woke and tore out of her belly in blood.

Here, in this sunny place, there was no shadow.

"Look!" Gata cried out, pointing. "It's Lowlyn; he always wears red to meet me."

"Lowlyn?"

"My companion. Isn't he tall? He is marvelous, an artist in clay. There, there in the red," she went on impatiently, waiting for Essa to see him.

Essa was looking for a red shirt but she saw finally a red turban on a tall, pale, smiling man. Few of them here in the east were pale, she saw. She had a little pang of jealousy, not sure if it was because she wished Gata would be as excited about her—a revelation—or because she wished she were coming home. To here? Another surprising thought.

They drifted to a halt, the mooring ropes went out, the rail-ropes were loosed from their cleats and knots, and the gangplank went down. A crowd of welcoming people swelled toward the ship. Last time Essa had seen a crowd, murder had been done; she shrank back. The tall man in the red turban pushed through, his shouting drowned in the crowd's valedictory shouts. He stopped at the gangway.

Essa didn't need Gata's surge of welcome to alert her that this was a friend: she had already recognized this man with a shock and a thrill which both exhilarated her and took her aback. How was it that this total stranger was already familiar? As if she had dreamed him. She had heard that this could happen but had never believed it. Now it picked her up and chastised her like a cat shakes a kitten, briskly and lovingly.

He was staring and smiling, held in this motionless moment which was not nearly as long as it seemed. Gata ran to meet him, Essa followed slowly, he reached out to hug Gata, and over her head he looked at Essa more.

"Lowlyn, this is my friend," Gata said. "Essa. I know you'll like her."

"I expect so," said his deep voice, filling her with certainty.

She had sailed away from darkness into light. It was right that it should be so. She threw her arms wide, and laughed at her new friends.

"Let's go home," Gata said. "I can hardly wait to see the shop."

"What about me? I thought I was the main action," Lowlyn said.

"Oh, you," Gata said. "You!"

"She takes me for granted," Lowlyn said in an easy aside to Essa. "You must never do that."

"Oh, I never shall," said Essa foolishly. "I never shall. I promise."

With her bundles and Gata's trunk on a kind of handcart Lowlyn had brought with him, they trundled through sunlit confusing streets. Essa was dizzy with newness and acceptance. The house had blue-stained plaster walls and a blue-painted door; that's all she noticed. The sun was hot on her uncovered head.

They showed her to a cool shady room and she threw herself upon the ample bed, meaning to examine her delight, but instead she fell into a deep, dreamless, satisfying sleep.

The sailor town was neat and white with red tile roofs and cobbled streets. Essa thought she had read about such towns in every romance of the sea and air which she had read back home in Eslyn. She found the type so familiar that she felt peculiarly at home despite her constant sense of discovery.

There was only one difference: Gata and Lowlyn were her friends, and they lived in one of the houses. Their walls were dyed with indigo. Essa was astonished that they were not white until she started walking around the town and she saw indigo, terra-cotta, whitewashed plaster, colored plaster, painted stone, raw stone of rose and white and gray, and so many different colors she could not imagine why she thought they should not exist here.

Yet at sunset or in the early morning when she walked out to the point, along the breakfront, or clambered up the bluffs behind the town, and looked back on the jumble of habitation she had momentarily left behind, she saw a white town with red tile roofs. An eastern magic, subtle and painterly. She loved it as she loved the town.

Even knowing that she could not find her mother there, she loved the place.

"This is where I should live," she said to Gata, "if I were not from the Fjord of Tears."

"Even if you are, would you live here?"

Everyone here wore the turban, and often at midday they pulled over it a kind of veil. If they had been as pale as Lowlyn, she could have understood them trying to prevent their skins from sunburn, but they were almost all as dark as Essa or darker. Gata was much darker, and her face was hidden, so Essa could not see her eyes, only the shadow of her cheek against the gauzy cloth.

Essa didn't wear sunscreens: she tanned easily and might have approached Gata's color by the end of the summer, going as she did without the veil, though she had taken to wearing the turban. "Yes, perhaps," she said. "If I find my mother, and come home." She imagined sailing into the harbor in triumph, the ship looming down to dock with colored streamers flying, bringing her semi-royal mother home to a magically-white indigo house in this storybook town. "Yes, I can imagine it," she said.

"Good," Gata said, and reached out to clasp her hand quickly before swinging off down the street, market string-bag in hand.

When she had been in the sailor town for three days, she unwound the scarf she had wrapped around her mother's abacus, and the trader's notebook fell out. She had been looking for it but not very hard. She was struck then by memory: the moonlit dock, the shadow of the warehouse, his whisper, the dark shadows that hid his expression. She could hardly bear to think of it, the day which had begun sunny and ended in flight, in loss yet again. She put the notebook away and went to bed.

The next morning, however, she took the notebook in her pocket as she went out to walk around, exploring the town. That day she found a path leading up the hill to a low cliff which the locals called the bluffs. To someone who had walked the seven thousand steps down to the sea at Nagroma, who had clambered about on the rocks thousands of meters above the Fjord of Tears, it was hardly a cliff at all, but it reminded Essa a little of home, and she sat down in the shelter of a large rock, sun shining to warm her.

There, in comfort, she opened the notebook.

The first thing she saw was that the front section was full of quantities and deals. Enough to keep her busy here for months. But on the last marked page of the trader's notebook, he had written her a letter:

Essa,
No time to write. I will be here if you need me. If I am not here I am home. Home is: the road past Avanue until you reach Hamurbai. Ask for the weaver's guild, ask for my father whose weaver name is Linmat. He will know his oldest son's house. If I am not here and I am not there and six months go by after that, I am dead. Until you can return, send me a message in trade. If you come back, you may ask me any question then.

No signature, of course, just the mark for Minh.

She began to seek out the traders, do her work according to the notes. Each night she reported her progress in the blank pages of the notebook. She wrote no letter of her own. She did not know what to say. She lived in Gata and Lowlyn's house, and had nightmares some nights. She had a life. She hoped he still did.

It is a harder world than I ever thought, she thought as she looked down on the darkening town in the harbor curve of coast. People are shot or beaten, and they die. Mothers go away, fathers die. Or the other way 'round. Babies are sold south from cities like this— and men and women in some countries divide their lives like hair partings down an inflexible line, never quite meeting.

It was Lowlyn who knew enough to come up here sometimes, find her, talk with her until she was calm, care for her. That sunny man seemed to know her darkness well enough to know how it hurt. No-one had died before his eyes; his parents were alive and young and warm, his family full of love. His town was perfect, his art was good without painful self-questioning—and yet he understood, while Gata, who had traveled, whose own mother was a murderer, was brisk and brusque and preferred Essa to be happy. To help Gata stay calm, Essa supposed, but at times like this that was not useful.

*   *   *

One morning she went to a different shop than usual. The owner was darker-skinned than anyone Essa had met so far, and as she waited for service, Essa enjoyed watching the play of teeth and palms and eyes against dark brown. After a while she noticed that the people being served had come in after her.

"Excuse me," she said to the man beside her, "is there a serving order I don't know about?"

"First come, first served," he said, shrugging.

"Is there a lineup I didn't notice?"

"Not unless I didn't either. Hey, shoppie!" he called. The dark woman looked at him, smiling. "This little chip been here a while. Her turn, eh?"

The woman's smile vanished, and the noise level in the store diminished. Essa saw other shuttered faces. She moved to the counter with her champion beside her.

"Don't be shy," he said. "Foreign is as foreign does." He grinned.

"Should have a saying like that," she grinned back. "Sounds like a proverb."

"Thanks much," he said. "Always a pleasure to meet a good-looking young woman."

There was silence in the store as Essa ordered. The dark woman was curt as she added the amount, and Essa had to draw her attention to a mistake in her change. Her champion turned away to look at fruit, and as the woman put the vegetables into the string-bag she muttered something Essa did not understand.

It is chance that it's Lowlyn she asked, when she got home, to explain: "Lowl, what's 'blankie' mean?"

His face looked like those of the people in the shop. "Where'd you hear that?"

"Veggie shop lady down in the low town. She had a hard time noticing me, so a fellow there called her attention to me. She liked him fine but when he showed her me, she went all cold-faced—like you are now, I might add—and gave me the wrong change, so I told her and she muttered at me."

Lowlyn wiped the clay off his hands into the heap on the wheel, and then meticulously washed his hands twice, first in the clay-stained water in the pail by the wheel and then in the sink by the wall, silent the whole time. She waited, not very patient, but learning his rhythms enough to follow with a silence of her own.

Then he put his hand on her arm, pale and gentle against her summer tan. "They call me that too," he said. "It's because we're pale. The darker the better here, some say. There was quite a fuss when Gata and I partnered, among some of the cousins. And her mother, of course."

"It's an epithet?"

"Fancy name for an insult, isn't it?"

"Blankie because . . . ?"

"Our faces aren't there. Blank out in the sun. So they treat us as if we weren't there."

"But I'm almost as dark as Gata! Darker than a lot of them!" She thrust her arm into the bar of sun from the window, pushing up the blue cotton sleeve to show muscle and tan, and light brown hairs glinting in the sun.

"It's seasonal. They only like a full-time brownie."

"Brownie?"

"Me being like them, calling names."

Essa had never seen Lowlyn angry and certainly not in this cold, tense way. "This isn't like you—" she said nervously.

"Yes, it is," he cut in roughly. "I was born here, you know. I grew up with it. Got beat up by kids every school rotation. Three times a year, had to prove to some kid I wasn't a floor rag. Lucky I was big. And you ever wonder why Salliann keeps the store? Because they'll buy from each other. Bad enough a blankie makes it, for some, but to have to be polite while they buy it . . . too much."

Hotly Essa said, "Then you don't need their business! There must be enough reasonable people who need these things. Your work is wonderful!"

"No," he said. "There aren't enough, wonderful work or not. People get into habits. Most of them don't know if the habit of not coming here is because I'm a blankie. They just do it automatically."

"That's crazy!"

"Is it?" He went into the other room, the storeroom, and came back with a chip of pottery with a stripe of glaze across it. "See this glaze?" he said. "What color is it?"

"Brown," she said.

"No, the name of the color," he said.

"Brown," she said, puzzled. "In Eslyn I think a potter might call it something like Rich Earth. I think."

"Here it's called 'flesh,' " he said shortly.

"Oh," she said.

He went back to work. She hiked herself up on the bench by the sunny window, let the sun warm her arm. She watched him turn the wheel with one foot, while he shaped the vessel from the pale clay. Pale as his hands.

"Why don't you use a power wheel?" she said.

"I like the control," he said. "And the individual variations. It's warmer."

She nodded, and watched more.

"Is that why the Gruesome Twosome hates me?" she ventured after he had thrown two more hand-vessels.

"Oh, Nai and Pee? Probably that's part of it."

"But they trade with the mainland and even up to Eslyn! Most everyone is our colors there!"

"It's probably easier to trade with people you despise. Don't have to be as scrupulous about your bargains then."

She thought, as she often did, of her trader boss, the sweet man who insisted every deal go fair for everyone. And he traded with the Black Ship, with a smile and an open face, and he was almost the same skin color as she, though his hair was straight and dark.

No-one she had ever met was quite as pale as Lowlyn, with his reddish-blond hair and alabaster-white skin.

Her trader's notebook talked of trusting the sailors. Which ones? Her nemeses Naio and Pewhim (names she was heartily sick of repeating in chorus, even in thought) and their like (the shop-keeper that day, for example), or others like Gata, who married a blankie and brought another home as friend?

An unpromising train of thought, but she couldn't shake it.

"So Gata has two of us," she said suddenly to him. His hands tensed and the clay vessel went awry as he looked up at her. His gaze made her too warm; she moved out of the sun and turned from his eyes. He concentrated on straightening his clay form.

"Yes," he said finally. "That is correct."

Later, she wondered what they had each said, really, in that last exchange. Whatever it was, it disturbed her enough that she went out of the workshop and up along the bluffs to sit until dinnertime.

Essa sitting at the edge of the cliffs, as usual. Thinking. Too many things happen in the world, she thought as she looked down the now-familiar town curled into its harbor crescent. People were shot or beaten and they died. People died of heart failure, like her father had, heart failure such a metaphor she shivered every time she thought of it.

She picked at the loose edge of her sandal sole. These were her favorite shoes, and she'd had them since two years before she left Eslyn, and now they were wearing out, even though she only wore them occasionally any more.

When she thought about it, her main problem overall was entropy.

Long ago her mother had told her like a faery tale about the two extremes of process, building up and breaking down: information and entropy, they are called. She could cope perfectly well with learning new things, watching change and growth in progress, but the challenge of breakdown was beyond her. She resisted it blindly and angrily.

Shoes wore out, cats died, mothers went away, fathers died, people were abandoned into slavery in the south because traders feared losing business, young people became storybook soldiers only to shatter their dreams with death. It always came back to what was personal, what she had seen. She had buried the brown cat herself, she now remembered, when it died that terrible winter after her mother left, and even then she knew she didn't understand it. She was with her father when his heart first shook him, and now she understood that she ran away from his death even though it had already happened despite her. Telling herself it wasn't personal. And it wasn't personal. None of it.

Her mother though. That was personal. That *is* personal.

The Remarkable Mountains (3)

Ah, my dearest F., you still don't understand. She was my grandmother on both sides. She sent her son down south to be fostered out. When my mother met her brother she didn't know, thought he was the son of the southern lord, but it wouldn't have mattered anyhow. My grandmother fucked everyone in her family, I suppose, and she learned the habit from her parents and older brother, by demonstration, and she tried to teach her descendants the same tricks.

Here in the mountains you are so gentle. You have no idea what it means. My father was expected to teach me the rudiments. My grandmother would have tried me if she hadn't been so out of favor that my parents protected me.

It wasn't only sex. You listen to that part with horror. It wasn't sex at all. I told you how she beat me. When I set my slaves free, when I was older, she left these scars, that time. But she demonstrated the right way to flog a servant when I was very young.

We were in the garden, my nurse and me. She was an old slave who had wet-nursed me and stayed on. Later I heard someone say that my grandmother had killed her baby to make sure I had enough milk. Maybe that wasn't true.

She was old, I thought, but I don't know how old she really was. Everyone looks old at that age. I wanted to play some game and she was too slow, down on her hands and knees. I think she was supposed to be a riding horse or something. I had started to shout at her to go faster, and she was panting a little and saying she couldn't. I told her horses can't talk. She said, "Young mistress, please . . . " and I yelled at her to shut up, took off my little leather belt and tried to whip her.

My grandmother's voice cracked from behind me: "If you're going to put the effort out at all, do it right." She took the belt, held it by the tail so the buckle delivered the blow, and stood over the nurse, beating and beating. After the blood was soaking through the woman's shift, she gave the belt to me.

"Go on, little weakling. Hit!" And I did, as hard as I could. I felt proud and powerful.

Then I heard my mother's voice from the window, shouting, "Stop that at once! Stop that!"

The nurse never returned, though I cried for her. I was kept to my room for a week, and my mother sat with me. After her first angry tirade, when she brought me in from the garden, she did not speak. I cried for her to speak. I cried for Nurse to return. My mother shook her head.

After a week my father came in, and said to my mother, "Hasn't she been punished enough?"

"I swore to that woman she would never be hurt," said my mother, and began to cry. They went out and left me alone, astonished, and afraid of myself.

Even then, my parents never beat me; my grandmother disapproved but apparently could do nothing. I found out later that she was out of fashion at the time. There had been a shift in the household as a number of the older people died and younger, progressive-thinking people inherited their places. My father had been brought from the far south in the hope he would be a conservative influence but it turned out that the family compound where he had been fostered had been a rebellious and utopian one, and had an entirely different family style from most southerners, affectionate and warm, though sometimes awkward with unaccustomed behaviors. The match had been disappointing to everyone except my mother, who had loved him almost from the start, and who in any case had had her factions engineer the whole thing.

But I didn't know this when I was young. All I knew was that the only time I had bruises was when I came upon my grandmother, and I feared her deadly hands more than anything I had ever seen to date.

More even than Annalise feared the guardian of the library, for she had a defiant sense that she had a right, he would not recognize, while I knew I was the heir and yet there was nothing I could do to prevent my grandmother's assaults.

When I came up to the Fjord of Tears, one of the reasons I stayed was the way you treat your children.

* * *

Annalise was reading a book the first time I saw her. I had crept into my grandmother's library to read and so had she; for that reason, we became allies in that silent instant.

"Ee-yah!" she used to say, later. "How tired I am! And how my back hurts!" She meant from the beatings, not from bending over books.

"Stop reading, then," I would always say, but with a grin because I wanted to make her grin, and because I knew she would never stop. She would read the words on the gallows before she was hanged, she used to say, but I would shiver and tell her to be quiet. "That's true," she said once. "One never knows what one is asking for."

We were both very young. Now, it seems too young, too terribly young. But we thought we were getting quite accomplished at one thing and another.

I learned something that summer. I learned how to disobey my grandmother and not get caught. For years, since the time of the nurse, I had been refusing to have servants flogged, but that summer I had gone to the logical end point and had freed all my own slaves. As a result, I'd been beaten myself, by my grandmother of course, who made a special trip across the compound to do so. My parents had rewarded me, but unfortunately they were out inspecting the farms the day she came. So Annalise and I had been together in my bed, moaning.

"You could pretend," said Annalise, as always more protective of my delicate skin than her own.

"I don't think that's the point," I said. "I think the point is that sooner or later I was going to feel it myself. Isn't that what your books say the world is like? Certainly the ones I've read."

"Oh, that's so romantic," she said. "There has to be a way to catch her in her own snares." In the books, people got turned into animals a lot, to teach them things. We had been thinking of ourselves as rabbits for some time now.

"Maybe we're being the wrong animal," I said.

"What would you rather be, a fish?"

"So I could swim away? Yes!"

"So you could be grilled and served to her at supper, more like!" But she was not grinning very hard. She grabbed the pot of ointment and started to rub it on my back and legs. "Does this hurt?"

"Of course it hurts, you idiot! But don't stop." The ointment's coolness distracted my nerves for a while; I don't think it did much else, but it didn't matter.

"Look," I said. "We're going about this all wrong. In that book I read, the economics one, the scribe said that every person is a product of their time, so true solutions are hard because they're prevented by people's hidebound ideas. Well, here we are. After my parents, I am the first person in my line since that guy in the other book to ever refuse to hurt someone. Why is that bad? He got killed, and people like Grandmother won. Why is that good?"

"Oh, expository lump!" said Annalise. "We've been talking about it too long. When you write your book about it, this is the part that is going to sound really boring."

Notice it was me who had to write the book. For all her reading.

Safety. The thing about it is that wanting it has nothing to do with who one is or what is real. I am the daughter of my grandmother's daughter and thus the heir to the throne. My cousin, the son of my grandmother's brother, thought he had as strong a claim, so my grandmother, thinking to draw his teeth while making use of his fealty, made him my husband. Then, however, he persuaded my parents, by presenting himself as a kindly man, and in the absence of children—of a daughter—of mine, to make him my heir as well, their second heir as it is called. And thus my safety removed for all time, thus my deepest wish never to be granted.

Life in my parents' house was easier after Annalise came. For one thing, she loved to read even more than I, so she got the brunt of the attention and punishment for it. That meant I could read almost unnoticed, and strangely that made reading less attractive than it was. Annalise, however, did not have the heritage of my rebellion to spur her; it was love of what is in the books which drew her.

"I know something you don't know," said Annalise.

"What?"

"How to fuck."

All that year we had been talking about sex. Every day in the garden we would meet and walk back and forth along the diagonal path farthest from the palace, swapping the things we thought we

didn't know—you can't get pregnant from sitting on a man's knee—
and the things we thought we did know—you can get diseases from
a toilet seat; if a servant with the clap touches you, you can die. It
seems strange that we knew so little, but who ever talked to us? And
my parents had protected me more than usual from the rutting of
slaves, the excesses of household animals. I had seen my cat go at it
with a tom once, but my grandmother came down, saying the yowl-
ing had awakened her, and strangled the cats. I had no idea what
they would have done uninterrupted. There were books of erotic
engravings and photographs but they seemed improbable to us.
The naked male servants and slaves we had seen didn't have big fat
cocks sticking up like that, with knobs on the end instead of little
puckered buds.

"You do not," I said.

"Do too. I followed your granny's catamite last night, and
found a place to look."

This was typical: I was terribly afraid for her all the time: finally
I hardly noticed. "What did they do?"

"The maid interrupted with a message. I didn't see it all. I saw
his cock, though!"

"So you don't know. Told you so."

"Well, I know how to find out. Let's go tonight and look."

I hated my grandmother's foul smell, and never went near her
wing unless I had to. "She never has them two nights in a row."

"She didn't have him, I told you. There was a message and they
stopped."

"Was it fat?"

"Not yet. I think it doesn't look like that until they do it."

She talked me into it eventually. I was used to being afraid of
my grandmother, and Annalise was showing me how fear shouldn't
stop me. I peed just before we went, though, in case we were caught
and I lost my bladder with fright. I didn't want to show all my feelings.

There was a crack in the corner of the wall between my grandmother's closet and her bedroom. We huddled there, only not giggling because we knew how dangerous this was, and watched her
greet the catamite. She was wearing a white robe and in her hand
she twisted some kind of thin black rubber ring.

Take off your robe, she ordered him, and he did. His cock hung
long and flaccid, the sac of balls askew. She reached out to him and
took his cock in her fingers, took the black ring and twisted it

around the base. In a moment the cock was blowing up like a thin balloon until it bobbed red and swollen, and it did have a knob, pushing out from the puckered skin at the end.

Look in the mirror, she said, and he did, looking fascinated like a snake while she stood behind him and stroked his back with her nails. Tiny little lines of blood appeared but he didn't notice. Her nails were always that sharp.

She let her own robe drop and walked across to the bed, lay down with her legs spread. She had a jar of creamy stuff that she swiped with two fingers into her cunt. It creamed the hair around it, which looked like old, worn-out hair, and I could see why, when he walked over, transferring his hypnotized gaze to the mirror above the bed, and put his swollen cock into her cunt. She reached up and broke some kind of vial under his nose, and he began to move back and forth dreamily.

I had peed, but my own cunt felt wet, and I felt uncomfortably heavy in my gut. Annalise was kneeling in front of me so we could both see through the narrow crack. My hands clenched on her shoulders, and one of her hands, wet with sweat I thought, came up to hold mine. The other pressed flat into her crotch. I tried that too and it seemed to help.

The slave was moving faster, and my grandmother's face was as flaccid and slack as his cock had been at first. Then suddenly her legs and her arms went around him and she started to talk to him, too quietly at first for us to hear. Then her voice rose in volume.

"You are filthy," she said, "a slut, you are diseased, you disgust me. You are worthless, you fuck pigs, you fuck cows, you fuck raw meat, you fuck your father."

Her nails raked his back, and blood began to flow in earnest. She raked again and again, with the same hands that killed my kitten. The agreeable heaviness was gone. I began to feel ill. I put my hand back on Annalise's shoulder and she took it too, pressing it to caution me to silence. The slave began to scream, and my grandmother's curses suddenly became a shriek too. As suddenly as she had shrieked, she pushed him down to the floor, and reaching behind her, snapped a belt forward and began to beat him. The rubber ring still held his cock erect and the belt struck it. He arched his back in agony and then fainted. She stood above him, still beating him, the other hand at her cunt. There was a little blood there too but I think it was his from her nails. In a moment she went tense, then threw the belt down on him. The buckle struck his cheek and drew more blood.

She still straddled him. She reached down and took up one of the discarded robes, then pissed on him, wiped herself with the robe and threw it on him, and lay down again, her outstretched arm hitting the light control.

Annalise didn't catch up to me until we were back in my rooms and I was already vomiting into the toilet. When I was done she wiped my face, put her arms around me. I was shuddering and sobbing and the taste of bile mixed with the remembered smell of blood.

"You are not her," said Annalise, cutting to the root of it.

"Blood will tell?" I said, afraid to make it a statement.

"You are not her," she said. "How many times in your life do I have to tell you?"

"Until I die, if it helps make it so," I gasped out. "You don't know. She's not your monster."

"No?" Her voice was choked. I looked at her. She was crying too. We never cried. It was a rule.

"What is it?"

"Don't you ever wonder where I came from?" she said angrily. "I'm your father's bastard, don't you know that? I'm your half-sister, you pie-face. Don't you think I hate her too? My mother was a slave he fucked when your mother was so sick. That old bitch is my blood too. But you are not her and I am not her and we will never be. Now quit crying, I hate crying. Go to sleep."

"Why didn't you tell me before?"

"My mother made me promise. She thought if you knew you'd kill both of us."

"Me? I never would!"

"How would she know that? She's afraid of every woman in this family. Even me, now that I live here."

I went to piss again, and wiped my slimy cunt with disgust. "If that's what it's like I never want to do it," I said.

"It must be different," she said. "In the books it's different. And your mother doesn't have any scars, does she? My mother doesn't, and your father fucked her for years. It must be different."

We didn't talk much more. We were too exhausted. We finally went to sleep, me into mean dreams, still holding each other.

*   *   *

The next day, closeted in my shady room, everything seemed unreal. I woke up in Annalise's arms, and looked at her, and thought
of that deep recognition I always felt with her, and wondered if it
was because we were sisters. But I thought not. Rather, it was because we could sleep in each other's arms. Did that make sense? I
didn't care.

She wakened when I slipped out from under her arm to go to
the toilet. On her way back from the same errand, Annalise giggled
and played the catamite, swinging his hips across the room. "He likes
boys the rest of the time. Cook said," she said, and pulled off her
clothes, pulled a bedsheet around herself like his robe. So I was to
be my grandmother. Ignoring my shivers, I undressed quickly, giggling, and lay cruciform on the bed, naked. Annalise bent her head
down into my crotch. I was embarrassed, wet there but not from
peeing, I wiped well, I don't understand, it happened last night too,
at first, when we watched the boy with his stiff cock, when we
watched him put it in grandmother's cunt, before she started to
scratch his back and the blood started flowing. When she began to
swear and threaten him I forgot the feeling, fear replaced it, but now
I felt it again.

"You smell nice," said Annalise, "like raw fish from lunch." She
put her hand on my cunt. A hard bump at the front started to hurt
but not like pain. She slid her fingers inside. They went smoothly.
She put her mouth on the bump, began to move her lips and tongue.
The pain was not pain, it was such acute pleasure that it went up inside and tore me open. I gasped.

"What's the matter?" she said, raising her head.

"Nothing," I said, and I pushed her head back down. This
couldn't be what they were doing. An image like a photograph of
my grandmother's face slack and concentrating. But she whipped
the slave to get herself that way. I could not imagine making Annalise bleed. She was my only friend. The warmth she was pouring
into me from her mouth. Images flashed across my open eyes. Everything strobed blue. My belly strobed blue, in waves like the sea,
waves, I murmured, and she raised her head laughing.

"That's right, isn't it?" she said. The waves subsided and she
took her wet fingers out of my cunt and my ass. Aftershocks. "I knew
I could do it right."

"Where did you learn how?" I gasped.

"Out of a book," she said. "Now you do it to me."

She was dripping wet around my hand. She lost herself. Was

this what I looked like? It was terrifying but nothing like them, yesterday. It came to me that we must love each other. But in a different way than in the romantic books. Maybe trust was the word. How could you do this if you didn't trust, anyway, whatever love is?

"Shhh," she said. "Deeper. Harder."

How did she know?

But I did the same to her that she did to me. I learned in a second how to hold my mouth a little sideways, take the little knob in my lips and rub. She held my hair hard enough to pull. I could hardly breathe, except to inhale the strange and exciting smell that was like mine, but new. I used to rub myself, but nothing like this had come of it. She arched her back and called out something. What? I thought, but I couldn't stop, I was giving back to her what she had given me. Image of the blood flowing down the slave's back, his doomed screaming later. A sob tore through the same place the pleasure went. It hurt together there, the grief, the fear, the trust, the moment. She crested and my wrist was wet with her gush of fluid. The sheets were wet under us. My cunt throbbed with the need for more. So this was what they did in their beds, the real parents, the real adults. They must some of them do it like this, not like her. Not everybody could afford to use up so many slaves. My parents have no scars, I thought suddenly, do they? They must have done this, to make me. To make Annalise my father did it with someone else. Were they taken apart like this? But they seemed to be able to function after, though I couldn't imagine how we would. We clung to each other. After a while I started to cry. Annalise held me.

"In the book," she said, "they say that after fucking one is omnivorously sad."

"It's not that."

"What then?"

"It's so easy for you."

"Easy?" She looked at me and her grin slipped off, right off into nowhere. "Easy? We could die of this. Don't you feel it? Right now, we could be dying of each other. How do you think that feels, when I could be thrown out like garbage any day? And you, you are the heir to everything."

She had never talked about it before. Now I was so far into my own fear that it took me time to realize they were the same fears. We lay in silence, holding each other tight, until I caught up to it and passed ahead.

"How can she hurt them?" I said finally. "What if . . . ?"

"You are not her," said Annalise, which she had said before, but now, she took my shoulders fiercely and held me so she could look into my face. "You are not hers," she said. The difference was immense, and she struck my fear away easily. I was washed with gratitude, relief. "Stop it," she said. "You never cry."

"I never knew stuff before," I said. "How this changes everything. How it's full of fear. In the books I read, it's full of joy. In the books you read, it shows you how to put your hands into me and pull my heart out."

"Poor princess," she said. "And what have you done with mine heart? You have eaten it all up."

After that we were shy and had to start to make stupid jokes, though I could not imagine ever seeing the light of day again, I felt so different.

"I do it to myself all the time," said Annalise, "but it never felt like that before. Maybe because I didn't know what would happen next. Maybe because it's you."

Later, before sleep, I thought of menstrual blood, different, clean somehow. "If there's ever blood," I said, "let it be womanblood."

"I could make handprints on you," she said.

"And it wouldn't hurt anyone," I said.

Later we found out doing it cured cramps, but that day we just went to sleep and didn't wake up in our tumbled bed until suppertime.

Nobody noticed us differently, or different. Maybe that was the greatest marvel of it, I thought after.

My mother called me to her rooms the next morning. That was strange enough. When I got there she was drinking from her silver bottle. I sat silent and watched the familiar motion of her hands—undoing the screw-cap, tipping the bottle up for a sip, screwing on the lid, and a moment later repeating the ritual sequence. Between sips, she stared out the tower window at the horizon where the land curved away south. Turn, sip, turn, stare. Turn, sip, turn. We sat for a long time like that.

Finally she said, without turning, "You must be careful how loud you and Annalise play certain games."

I blushed all over, I'm sure, and said nothing.

"I heard you," she said, "through the window." My suite was two floors below hers.

"I'm sorry," I said.

"I'm not," she said. "It was the closest I can come to remembering that."

She stood and turned. She was wearing a long robe. She put the flask down and with one hand pulled the robe up. Under it she was naked.

"I have to show you what she did," she said. The *"she"* was the tone we all used for my grandmother; I shivered.

My mother sat down on her dressing-table stool and spread her legs. For an irrational, terrible minute I thought she meant me to serve her like my grandmother had ordered the boy. I looked up at her face. She was weeping silently. "Look," she said, and spread the lips of her cunt. Where Annalise and I, and my grandmother too, had a tightly knotted curl of flesh, my mother had a deep V-shaped scar. Something sharp had excised the knob in two strokes, the shape echoing the shape of her cunt.

"It's called your clit," she said. "When your father and I came back from the south, and your grandmother was still in favor, she said we disturbed her sleep too much. She sent her assassins, but they didn't kill me. They just cut out the heart of my love. They left me bleeding. He—" (gentle tone: my father) "—bandaged me and nursed me in secret. The servants never knew. You were born already."

I tried to imagine life without the amazing ability Annalise and I had found yesterday.

"Never let her hear you happy," said my mother. "She will kill what you love, and she will kill your ability to love."

I pulled her robe from her shaking hand and covered her again, then knelt beside her and held her. Then I knew something I had never known before.

"And you love me, don't you?" I said.

"Yes," she said, "but with my other heart. The one I still have." We both laughed, a little shakily.

"And my father loves me. That's why you both protect me."

"She must never know. Don't even tell Annalise."

"But I have to tell her about that." I gestured at my mother's lap.

"Yes."

"And Annalise would never betray me."

"Annalise is human," said my mother, "and we humans are weak. I had a chance to kill your grandmother. She lay at my feet. She was my mother. I couldn't do it. Now she threatens you. Someday I will kill her, I thought. But now you have that husband, I cannot. He will do her work for her when she is gone."

I heard the servant coming with the tea. Very daring, I kissed my mother's cheek, and to my surprise she stroked mine. Then I ran to the other chair and sat demurely. The slave came in and set the clanking tray down.

"That will do," said my mother. The slave sulked, but left. It was the boy the old woman had abused two nights before. I laughed because he was not dead, and because I had suddenly had a thought. When he was gone I ran to the door to see he wasn't listening, then said, "When I call her the old woman, in my thoughts, she goes far away!"

My mother's gaze sharpened indulgently. "Where do you get your wisdom?" she said, chuckling a little.

"Out of Annalise's books," I said.

"Is that where you learned to kiss my cheek, too?"

"Annalise reads them, and teaches me what I need to know."

"Annalise is your friend," she said. Outside the rooms where Annalise and I talked freely, it was the first time I can remember hearing that word spoken.

"She will stay my friend," I said.

"You could do no better," said my mother. "Now go back to her, and be quieter. The air is still here and sound is fast-moving. I would have you live with both your hearts intact. Both hearts, both of you."

I meant to ask her what it was like, what it had been like before. I imagined that maybe there was some world where a daughter could ask her mother something like that, both of them women together. But it was not the world we lived in.

She was moving as in a dream back to the window seat, and the distance between us widened to the vastness of the southland vista.

She leaned over to take up her flask again. I bowed to her, though she seemed insensible of me again, and went out.

Annalise and I were silent in our passions and our other play, after that. When I came up here to the Remarkable Mountains, that is why I never cried out under you, though I dreamed of it sometimes, asleep. You asked me why. Now you have heard it.

I must tell you I went back to watch my grandmother many more times, though I hated myself for it. Sometimes the slave tied her to the bed and pissed on her. Sometimes she had a girl there, and she made him fuck the girl's ass. I learned a lot. Annalise had a lot to do, keeping me sane there. You are an innocent. You do not know what it is like, to live like that.

The first day I saw my husband. You don't have the same thing here in Eslyn; when I translate the word "husband" it says what you are to me. Not the web of ritual and restriction the word means at home. I was still young. Annalise and I had only been lovers for a few years.

Perhaps it was a secret that he was coming, but Annalise and I had been hiding in the closet, watching my grandmother's room, hoping for diversion, when the messenger came.

"Bring him here," said the old woman.

And shortly he came following the servant, his face imperious and heavy. I knew him at once. This was the man my grandmother had married me to, when I was a baby and he was . . .

He looked as old as my father, though I was old enough by then to know that my father was not so old, except in experience. This man was about thirty-five, then, and I repeated the word "heavy" to myself. Not fat, but solid. Not jowly, but square of face. Strong and arrogant, I thought of the face I could see reflected in her boudoir mirror.

My grandmother's face was visible too. She looked at him with a curl in her lip that mirrored his, though I suppose neither of them knew they were imitating the other.

The servant was waved away, and scampered rather than walked out. The tapestries over the door swung shut, and behind them the lock clicked.

"You took long enough," she said.

"How lovely to see you, too," he said. Insolence was usually punished; my fingers dug into Annalise's poor shoulder: if I'd had better knees she would not have always been in front of me, kneeling. She prized my grip away, and we silently traded places while the old woman and the square-bodied man traded looks.

They were smiling slightly in that way I hated to see on my grandmother's face; multiplied by two it was even more frightening. This time it was Annalise gripping me by the back of the neck as I bent to adjust a folded robe under my knees. She took her hand away before I could twist loose, substituted a gentler grip, leaning on both my shoulders lightly, as if for balance. We had a complex system of supports, Annalise and I.

"Take off your clothes," said the old woman.

"You first," he said. She laughed, and they began to undress.

"It still works, does it, old man?" she said. He took one stride forward and grabbed her by the hair, pulling her head back. She laughed again, and he did too. He turned her around, and bent her over at the end of the bed.

I turned my head away and got up slowly, quietly, hung the robe on which I'd been kneeling back on its hook, and pushed past Annalise and out. I barely remembered to check for the servant, who was supposed to be waiting outside her door. But that one, also, seemed to have known enough to bolt. Annalise came after me, silent until we got to the garden.

And silent for a few minutes, until we'd regained our breath, sitting on a bench in the shade against the wall.

"We could climb this wall and be gone," she said. I leaned my head back and saw how the slanting sunlight put the stones into bas-relief, showed every knob and ledge clearly. The young nobles of the court often put on tight clothes and rubber-soled shoes, tied up their long hair and chalked their hands, and climbed on the cliff below the palace tower with handholds half as solid as these, and it was a long way down to the ocean-washed stones below. Annalise and I both had taken our turns, Annalise as daring as any of them, and me competent enough not to die.

"All right," I said.

Another long pause. It would be effective in drama, I thought idly; most of the plays I knew about I'd read at Annalise's recommendation, but it seemed timing was important.

"Timing is important," I said.

"I thought you would want to watch," she said. "After all, you have to know what you're getting into."

"I don't want to know in advance," I said. "Speaking of scripts."

"Eh?"

"If I don't know, I won't do what they expect."

"They expect you to be his. He will walk behind you at all the processions. You will be old enough soon. Nineteen. The last prime number before fingers and toes are used up counting, did you know that?"

"Yes, I knew that. Is that why it's the age?"

"Nah, I think it's the age when the first queen of the Dark Isles menstruated or something."

"Took her long enough."

"She was the child of a sister and brother who were the child of a father and daughter. She was probably a mutant too, like the old woman."

"If she's a mutant, what does that make us?" I said, laughing.

"Refugees," said Annalise. "Fugitives."

They were two good words. It was the first time I considered escape.

"My parents are still alive," I said. "They will win."

"With him back from the south? With both of them here? For how long?"

A chill propelled me into the sun to pace the path, Annalise catching up again. I was going to my mother.

Since the time almost four years ago when she showed me her clitoridectomy scar, I had become close to my mother in a strange and wonderful way. She still drank too much, but she left it until evening now so that in the daytime, while my father was at court and my grandmother still sleeping, I could come and talk with her. She told me a good deal about her life, and why she had made the choices she had. She could have been queen after my grandmother, of course; that she had let the land go to a king—her brother, it is true, but still a king—measured the success of her opposition to the old woman.

"Name," I said, suddenly. "She must have a name. The old woman. My mother too. Everyone in the chronicles has a name."

Annalise said, "Your name, of course. Where do you think you got it?"

We were at the door. The sun was low and cast the garden suddenly into shadow, while it shone rusty sideways rays into my mother's south-facing window. She stood leaning on the window frame. Momentarily my father's shadowy form appeared behind her, the sun glancing off his bracelets as he put his arms quickly around her, then glinting off his hair as he bent his head for a quick kiss to the angle between her neck and shoulder. Then, like a dream image, he was gone, and only my momentary attention had captured it. Annalise, looking over her shoulder for people in the garden, had not seen anything.

We went up to the top, instead of stopping at our rooms. Annalise wanted to let me go alone but I would not let her stay back.

We came into the room unannounced, avoiding the servant who was fossicking around in the linen room.

My parents were still standing close, my mother looking south as usual and my father a few steps behind her. He turned his head angrily as we came in, but when he saw it was us, a little smile came and went before his face was impassive again.

My mother hadn't moved.

"It's a cruel land, you know," she said.

"Yes," he said. "Pray none of our children ever have to go there."

"If not there, somewhere else," I said.

Annalise said nothing.

"Where?" said my mother. "Why?" said my father.

"He is here," I said. "He is with my grandmother." My mother turned then, panic in her quickening breath. "They will be some time," I reassured her, but her face was pale. She sat down swiftly in the chair by the window, and my father dropped to the window seat.

"If you had sent me on a journey," I said, "before he came. He did not announce himself. It is traditional, after all. Tef-a went to the south pole to prove she was strong enough to be queen. When Albyon was to be king after his sister went mad, he sailed all the way north and came back with tales of the nameless ones who weave cloth there. If I am to be queen, you can send me."

"And if," said Annalise, who knew me, "there is a terrible accident, and the princess never returns, her grieving regent will have what he wants, and may leave the rest of us alone."

"She will not go unless you go," said my father to Annalise. When I looked at him I was surprised at his look of gentle knowledge, after what sounded like an ultimatum.

"Who will protect you?" said Annalise.

"Not you," he said, not laughing at her sixteen-year-old cockiness. "You forget you are our blood too. Who do you think will take his thrusts if she is not here?"

Annalise too paled.

"You will die," I said to them.

"We have our friends in court," said my mother. "I will go to court again. I can do that. She will die before I do. I swear it."

My father barred the door, and we could safely hug then, and cry the tears we felt, and then make our plans. I expected to see them again, after our faction won, after my husband and my grandmother were sent south. It seemed the best way, to stay out of her reach until then.

I was young anyway, and Annalise and I had talked so much of the east and the north.

Sailor town first, in the trappings of a merchanter. Then, as we knew the language, a change of clothes, and west on a dirigible, to lose ourselves in the wilds of the western mountains.

I had not estimated him well, but it is hard to do that of a man one sees with his cock in the cunt, or maybe the ass, of someone one hates. One assumes he is nothing but lust. I assumed that. I forgot only a little, but it was this: he was trained by my grandmother. She had hold of him for years before I was born, and yet she smiled at him. She had not yet used him up. I forgot that.

In the sailor town (2)

Lowlyn started it, making mock embraces when he came back from working in the studio, and one noontime pulling the two women together, one under each arm, and playing at trying to kiss them both. Essa liked this a lot, and Gata laughed. Later Gata stroked Essa's hair as they sat relaxing at the end of the afternoon, shutters closed to keep out the heat.

Essa leaned her head back into the strong, long-fingered hand and felt it cradle her head, then felt fingertips gently rub the tension out of her scalp. She rolled her head sideways enough to smile at Gata.

"Lowlyn wants you to join us," Gata said.

"In bed?" Her heart suddenly racing.

"In our family."

"For good?"

"Yes." She was so precise in her "yes." Does she say "yes" in bed, Essa wondered idly, in just that crisp authoritative way?

"Lowlyn wants it. And you?"

"I tell you what Lowlyn wants, and Lowlyn tells you what I want. It is the way."

"Our way, where I come from, is for you to tell me what you want, and Lowlyn to tell me what he wants."

Gata laughed. "Oh, no question of that. But for family proposals, there is a ritual . . . not that I'm a traditionalist . . . "

Essa laughed. "But still!"

"And what do you paragons in the Fjord of Tears do?" Gata asked.

"We kiss," said Essa, "and hug, and make love to see if we like it, and after a while someone moves their stuff into someone else's little hovel, and our anthropologists double up in the spare room. Only in civilized places like the eastern continent do people actually do nothing but talk. I understand that in bed, all you do is talk too, not anything else."

"How would you know?" said Gata. "Since you are the soul of purity, aside from some brief indiscreet suggestions on a sail-ship, under the influence of drugs I am sure you would protest!"

"Oh, I hear stories. A good anthropologist doesn't ignore mating habits, you know. You can tell a lot about a culture by its mating habits. . . . "

But Gata had jumped on her, tickling and tumbling her to the floor where they wrestled, giggling, until they rolled against the legs of Lowlyn, just coming into the house.

Lowlyn, blinking at the change from bright sunlight, said, "What's going on?"

"As far as this anthropologist can tell," said Essa, breathless, through giggles, "that one just proposed marriage."

He hauled them both up by a hand, and they ended up one on either side of him, each nestled under a hugging arm. They were suddenly silent as Essa reached out to touch Gata's cheek. Lowlyn hugged them closer and they kissed below his chin.

"Hey, me too," he said, and there was more giggling as they experimented with a three-way kiss, intentionally this time.

"I think we have to take turns," he said. "Oh, this may be redundant, but Gata wonders if you'd like to join our family."

Essa laughed, Gata grinned, across his chest where he couldn't see them.

There were several more jokes to make but Essa the false anthropologist realized that this kind of joking was partly to relieve tension, and further that if she told her grandchildren about this, she would rather remember some serious words, so: "Thank you," she said quietly. "I would be honored to accept. As long as you are asking me understanding that I have journeys to make, and a home far away which I have not quite left."

"I think we understand you well enough," said Lowlyn. "Now, perhaps you'd like to seal the bargain?" And he gestured with his chin, a gesture like Gata's—Essa thought she might have to start practicing it, if it was a family trait—toward the bedroom.

He got no arguments. But Gata stopped them at the door. She was very serious.

"You must understand, Essa," she said, and with a shock Essa realized it was the first time Gata had used her name, and she thought fleetingly of her trader, "that we mean what we say. This will seal the bargain."

"It isn't that we are traditional . . . " said Lowlyn. They all stifled the giggle this little pattern provoked.

"Unless there is a lot I don't know about the east," said Essa, "I accept. How are you about extramarital affairs?"

"What does that mean?" said Gata, truly taken aback.

"Doing this—no, I mean making love—with someone else."

"That has nothing to do with this, does it?"

"I was hoping not," said Essa, and they went into the bedroom in a happy tumble.

"It's the best bonding ceremony this anthropologist can imagine," Essa said sleepily later, after they had loved the evening away, and eaten picnic-style amid the rumpled sheets, and made love again.

"It's the real one," said Gata, "no matter what is done by anthropologists, or in other countries." Essa chuckled. Lowlyn was, typically for his phlegmatic nature, already asleep, as Gata indicated with a jerk of her chin.

"Good idea," said Essa, more than halfway there herself. But Gata stayed awake, and if the coin with the face of her lover on it was in her hand part of the night, and if she looked upon it with a troubled look amid her companions' crumpled sleep, it was not for long, before she slid smiling into her own sleep in their embrace, and anyway Essa did not see her.

"So," said Essa, sly, "Naio and Pewhim, joined at the hip, didn't kill me after all."

"Yet," said Gata coldly. "Be careful if you ship south. Theirs is the only Black Ship that goes there in this season. See if I take ship with you, only to lose you."

"Take that worry off the drying line if it rains."

"Damned fjord homespun proverbs." Gata got angry instead of crying.

"Don't worry. Maybe I can live without my mother. Queen of a southern land, indeed. Our faces are like some southern type is all."

"Yes, yes, and your eyebrow curls to type. Fine, you'll stay home, or scribe on ships with me, trading to east and north where it's proper, no Black journeys. Right?"

"Oh, yes," said Essa, and believed it, at the time.

* * *

Essa had her own money in her pocket for the first time since her arrival. Her first trade commission. She stopped at a dockside tavern to write it up in the trader's notebook. The tavern had a clutch of outdoor tables, under an awning to shade them, set along the walkway right at the street, so the dust raised by the passing wagons and other vehicles settled gritty on the chairs and tables. But it was shady and they sold black wine.

It was an exorbitant price here, but Essa ordered a whole flagon. She sat with her single goblet, staring into the inscrutable surface of the wine. It wasn't the best black wine; it's a little bitter, she thought. She flipped the pages of the notebook, looking at the trader's neat handwriting. She left it lying open at his short letter to her while she drank another tumblerful.

I got married, Minh, she thought. Handfasted they call it here. It wasn't what I thought would happen.

Black wine is sudden. She felt the world tilt and right itself but nothing was the same. She remembered the day of her departure, how it began so golden and ended in blood. She stubbornly concentrated on the golden. She saw the trader in his kitchen laying out the cards. What had they been? She had swept them from the table and the cats had scattered. Had she and he kissed after that? She couldn't remember if it was before or after. Feeling disloyal to Gata and Lowlyn even as she began to cry.

The flagon was empty. That was fast. Another, please! The server brought an order of deep-fried seafood with it, but Essa could hardly eat it. She pushed aside the half-full bowl and concentrated on the wine.

Expensive wine. She should take her money home, shouldn't she? Pour it into the household like this black velvet into this goblet. Here they called them "glasses" because they were made of glass, so much sand on the beaches to melt into this transparent stuff which held its shape but no secrets, no mystery. Glass was cheap and black wine was dear, brought over the sea in the Black Ships: everything was reversed here. Essa was on a journey, so she had immediately settled down, now had a home into which to pour herself, her profits, her life. Well, her mother had done the same thing, after all.

For a while.

The second flagon took much longer to drink. Halfway through it, Essa was troubled by another customer bringing flagon and glass over to her table.

"May I join you?"

Essa looked intently at this swarthy stranger. "No. No, I don't think so. I have enough baggage, thank you. I don't need any more. Besides, you're drunk."

"So are you."

"That's a different story."

"Tell me all about it." And the stranger pulled out the chair opposite and sat, settled flagon and glass on the table opposite hers.

"Black wine is expensive here," said Essa. She took her glass and drained it, then carefully lifted her flagon to the ground an arm's length away from her chair. The stranger leaned forward, smiling.

"I have a room just above."

"My, my. Direct, aren't we? Yes, we. I am also direct." Essa picked up the edge of the table and flipped glasses and flagon and table into the lap of the stranger. The glasses fell and shattered around the other chair. The stranger's flagon had been full of some thick white liquor that looked suspicious, sticky and slow rolling down that dark face. Essa picked up her flagon and walked out.

The watch pair found her on the edge of the dock, drinking the last drops from the flagon, about to throw it into the ocean. The two came up on either side of her, and one took the flagon.

"Message," she said. "Inna bottle."

"It belongs to the inn," said the woman on her left.

"True. Forgot that."

"Where do you live, blankie?" said the man on her right.

"Nowhere," said Essa. But they took her back to Lowlyn's studio anyway. There she poured her coin onto the table, raged and cried on Gata's shoulder, vomited black-wine bile into the head, with Lowlyn holding her forehead and wiping her face after, and passed out exhausted.

The next day, the last of her trade commission went for her fine for being drunk and disorderly; she walked down to the laws office and paid it herself. The wine must not have been too bad after all: she had no headache.

What she did have was an anger, a great and, before this, unsuspected anger, which surprised her as much as it colored the day, surprised and frightened her with its depth. That night she stared into the mirror. "I look the same," she said to herself.

"What saying?" said Gata from the other room.

"Nothing," said Essa.

"Come to bed, little disturber of the peace," said Lowlyn. She went in to them laughing: "Teach you to call me little," she said, tickling him. But she did not forget, and she did not lose her anger. Something else to carry.

"Heavier the older I get," she muttered once as she was brushing her teeth. "Nonsense! If anything, you've lost weight," said Gata, coming up behind her and kissing her shoulder, surprised when Essa laughed. Surprised but not unhappy: laughter meant they would make love again, and they did, all these months, take each other often to that place so far beyond black wine and commerce.

"Where's Essa?" said Gata when she came in one night.

"Doing dishes," said Lowlyn.

"For a change."

"What's eating you?"

"Spends all her time kiting around making trade deals. We have to work too. She should share the chores."

"She does. You just never see it because you're off early. She does her work in the morning, and then she goes out."

"Yeah, yeah."

Essa listening through the wall, her hands carrying on with their task. Lowlyn's calm voice and Gata's even but angry tones both penetrated more, obviously, than the sound of dishes tinking together, cutlery rattling.

There was silence for long enough for Essa to be scouring the last pot when the silence was broken.

"She's going away, isn't she, Lowl?" asked Gata.

"I think she is, yes. Trade . . . " Gata's snort interrupted him " . . . and her search for her mother . . . "

"She promised me she wouldn't, that we'd be sailors and traders together!" She sounded petulant and childish.

"Oh, Gata," said Lowlyn, exasperatedly. "You didn't make her promise like that, did you?" Silence, then his voice again. "How could you?"

"I had to. It's been just the two of us for so long, and so hard to fight with every family. Even our friends, so wary of you, and of me for choosing you. And there she is, beautiful and free of it all. And loves us. How could I bear it if she went again?"

"You could."

"Why would I want to?"

You could come with me, Essa thought angrily.

"You could go with her," Lowlyn said after a moment.

"I have thought of that, but I can't. If I do, my mother will make sure every hand is against her. Mother lost a partner that way once, and she blames Essa's mom. Easy to blame Essa in turn if she also loses a daughter. And besides—"

"What?"

"How could I leave you? Fingers cannot leave a hand and live."

It sounded like a proverb to Essa. She was part of this hand now. Was that to say she would die if she went, or that Lowl and Gata would? And why on earth couldn't Lowlyn travel too? Was he land-bound like the far-western people in the myth? She was still holding the frying pan handle in a clenched fist. Without thinking, she took it with her, dripping greasy water on the rug, as she stormed into the other room.

"Why don't you ever say these things to me?" she demanded. "Do you talk about me all the time? Or only when you know I can hear you through the wall?"

"Ess . . . " Lowlyn began placatingly. She rounded on him.

"You're just as bad. Trying to make peace. Keeping all your anger inside. Saint Lowlyn."

"Saint" was a foreign word, in her father's language. Lowlyn said, "What?" as Essa turned back to Gata.

"You want me to stay. I told you when I married you both that I was still remembering my journey, and now you want me to forget it."

"Will you for goodness's sake quit calling it marriage? That's what you foreigners do. It's handfasting. It's different."

"You can say that again. Different. Never in my life have I seen anyone try to protect her family like you. No, maybe Auntie up the fjord, always tucking us in. And what happened to them? The mountain avalanched, and they were all killed. Nobody can protect anybody."

"Your mother thought different," Gata said furiously. "Ever wonder why she left, while you were so busy feeling sorry for yourself? She was making sure the same people that got her didn't get you, you ninny, and you've never figured it out. Why not give her that at least? Stay here where it's safe, or go home to your precious Fjord and quit complaining. But let us off the hook one way or the other. I'm going crazy worrying about you!"

The wind fell away from Essa's back: becalmed by surprise, she sat slowly, the pan still dripping in her hands. Lowlyn pulled it away, took it back to the dishwater, got a rag to soak the drips from the carpet, working silently as Essa and Gata spoke on.

"You're right, I have never really thought . . . " Essa said slowly. "Leaving. That's all I thought. Didn't want us any more."

"Now you have another idea, you selfish shellfish."

Essa laughed at the rhyme. Gata didn't know why.

"Is that an idiom here?" Essa said.

"What? Yes, it is. Bloody little turnip, are you even listening?"

"Yes, yes," Essa said absently. "Protection. Why wouldn't she face it with us? We would have stood by her, done anything."

"These are people who burned a whole ship to kill one woman. They don't care about sacrifices."

"But they didn't kill her."

"You sound like a parrot."

"What's a parrot?"

"Oh, never mind! It's a bird. Your mind is like a bird mind." Essa giggled. Gata was even more furious: "What? What?"

"It's an insult at home. Birdbrain."

Gata had to laugh despite herself. "It's an insult here too, birdbrain!"

"Yeah, yeah, I get it."

"Now listen to me," Gata said, calmer. "You're obsessed by this search. What do you expect to find? If she lived then, she could have died since, and either way, you can bet she tried her best to disappear. You get yourself into trouble and you probably don't even find her. And if you do, what then? The Gruesome Twosome, as you call them, are watching you. They go where you go. You think the spies won't follow and find her then? You could be leading her enemies right to her."

Essa walked over to the window. Dusk was falling over the white town. Their house had a glimpse of the harbor. The previous owner had charged more for that. From this window, she could barely see the ocean, red with the last of the day's sun reflected from the clouds.

"You don't understand because you never met her," she said. "What she was like . . . she was like a story in a book, come to life. She had such power to enthrall. We were her family, and we felt like it. So much power and strength, but she was good. She helped people. You could count on her, always. I had a brother and sister once, for a day or so. They died. They were too early. Annalise came to help. My mother was angry. If only we had been in the east, she said, they could have lived. It was the only time I ever saw her like that. Then she damned her husband. I thought she meant my father and I was going to jump up and defend him, but Annalise said, 'You have a good partner now.' My mother went to bed and she wouldn't get up for three days. But then there was a forest fire too near the town, and people out of their homes. Annalise went to the library, where people were helping keep it safe. Father was up in the hills, but I was left home to take care of my mother. She woke up and turned over in bed and said, 'Where's Annalise?' 'Fighting the big fire,' I told her. 'Where's your father?' 'Fighting the big fire.' So she got up and went down to fight it herself, and stayed until the town was safe and the people had food and shelter.

"After that they elected her to the council of elders. She almost refused but they insisted. Then she was a leader. Then the airship came, and she left on it. Annalise too. I couldn't believe it. An elder came to the house to ask for her. She had missed the meeting about the trading with the Ship. That was when I found out she was gone. All she left me was her abacus. Not even a note. Didn't even say goodbye. Left us both. But she took Annalise. I was so jealous, I had a fight with Annalise's kids for years. I never thought until later that they must have been feeling like I did. It was a relief to fight. Such a change from crying."

Gata was silent. Lowlyn made a little noise and Essa turned. "I made promises," she said. "I'm sorry. I don't know what to do."

"If you . . . " Gata started, then stopped. "Look now," she managed. "Go if you must. I'm being a fool about it. Spent too much time being my mother's daughter. She wants to hold onto everything."

"I really don't know," said Essa. "It's like a fool's quest. I know it. I've lost everything so far for it, and now I'm messing things up with you two. But something pushes me, pushes me. I can't bear it." And she started to cry.

It was Gata first, not Lowlyn, who comforted, but they were both there eventually. Essa felt she was the only one who was missing. Was she what this language called a psychopath, someone who could feel nothing? She was just so tired of being flayed, constantly, by love and pain and the need to do the right thing. The need to understand, the need to feel. She wanted to take a break, feel nothing, remember nothing, and be comforted. Their love was not comforting. She felt it around her like a too-tight sweater, making her neck itchy, her arms constricted and her heart heavy. Yet if she pulled it off, she would be naked and alone.

She had no idea how to solve the paradox. Later, when they were sleeping, she cried silently until she was too tired, and then fell asleep.

When she awakened her face was stiff with the salt of dried tears. She wished she had dreamed an answer but in fact she was no closer to clarity, and she had to take a leak. She climbed over one of her partners and padded to the toilet in the early morning light.

When she had relieved herself she went outside into the walled yard, walked naked to Lowlyn's studio. The sunrise was starting to pour glowing light into the east-facing skylights. The one un-screened window looked out over the roofs to the harbor. The shadow of the town was obscuring the ocean but she could see the silver airships floating at their berths. From this distance she could not see which was the Black Ship; the ship of (it seemed, though the idea was still strange after all this time) her enemies, of Naio and Pewhim and the rest of their hand; the ship which would sail south at the end of the season.

Gata would never have hand enough to sail her own ship, be-cause she had chosen first a blankie from home, then a foreigner. So she crewed on everyone else's ships, and kept her anger for her fam-ily. She didn't want to crew with that ship again; she hated being beholden to the ones who had betrayed a guest, hated it before she met Essa.

Consider Lowlyn. He had never even imagined he could come with Essa himself; was he used to thinking of himself as outside pos-sibilities like that? Would they let him on that Black Ship anyway, as second passenger after Essa?

And would she want them with her, on what was essentially her quest, her irrational and passionate search to understand? Ashamedly, she realized that she wouldn't. They would get in the way. They made her adult, they took her away from the child who quested.

In this dawn light she was hardest on herself. She forgave them for everything, except perhaps loving her—no, even that. If only she were as kind to her mother and herself. She could not imagine how she could lay these ghosts to rest when one of them was herself.

"Essa." It was Lowlyn. He always seemed to know. "Come back to bed."

"No, I can't. I'm too warm in there right now."

He walked to the window and looked down at the view, the ships. "Home or onward?"

"This is as much home as I have. It's here or onward, you know that."

"No, I didn't, really. I hoped we would have at least that much place in your heart."

"Oh, Lowlyn, this is all such a cliché. Why can't I just do one thing and do it well?"

"You know the answers to that."

"Oh, yes, I'm sure. But you and Gata in there—" jerking her chin unconsciously in their gesture "—make it more than just my own life. I shouldn't have involved you both but it happened. Now it's all going to hurt, no matter what I do."

His arms were around her, his chin on the top of her head, a bit sharp against her as he talked: "I like living here, Ess. I like it even with all the difficulty. I liked Gata and I before, and now I like you with us. I can live with whatever you decide, you know."

"Oh, that makes it worse. Then it doesn't matter either way. I'm dispensable. No-one really cares. That's even worse."

"You're a mess, kid," he said, his voice grinning.

"I look like my mother and now I consider acting like her. Go away leaving others to cry. Chip off the old rock."

"What?" A common word in their family, with all these languages and cross-purposes.

"Never mind. Idiom again. It's all talk. Blah-blah-blah."

"Let's go to bed, my cynical love. Maybe we'll have some nice dreams."

But they didn't, really. And they woke tired.

my soul is sore
I leave my mountain home
walk the long roads to the sea
no-one remembers me
except the dead
no-one remembers the dead

The cheap tavern ballad brought tears to Essa's eyes. She wiped them on her napkin as surreptitiously as possible, though she saw at least one person notice. Well, let them all think her sentimental. It didn't matter.

Salliann had organized the party for all the workers at the shop and the pottery, their hands, and any friends they cared to invite. The result was more people in one place than Essa had imagined when she heard about the event. There were even some children of a couple of the hands: the baby cried, and the toddlers ran around the tavern's round tables, indulged by all in a way that reminded Essa of the mountains. The food, however, was northern food, considered exotic here: recipes from the land of her trader; the tavern specialized in it. Essa was the only one who knew how much these recipes were changed from the real thing, but she said nothing, and ate the hybrid cuisine silently.

The party was also a farewell for two of Gata's friends on the aircrew, who would be leaving on the Black Ship soon. Gata was definitely not going, she had declared, and Essa thought the decision had made her grumpy. But Essa also believed Gata was trying to control Essa's behavior with her own by staying home; it made sense, and it infuriated Essa. She picked at the food, listened to the song about leaving, and the cries of the children quickly ceased being nostalgic and became intensely irritating.

Finally she ordered a large flagon of the strong black wine and found a dark pottery goblet to drink it from, so no-one could see its raven iridescence.

Many cups of iridescence later, she was beginning to feel better, though she seemed to have developed tunnel vision. A hand at the next table cried out, "Hey, Ess! Join us!" and though she had no idea who they were, she decided to find them fascinating. Especially one of them, a short woman with shapely hips and large breasts but a thin waist, so that Essa imagined she was all made of spheres. Essa wondered what it might be like to bury her face in that orrery.

Nobody seemed to mind her flirting, so she expanded her interest to the man in the spectacles beside the shapely woman. She shared her black wine with the two of them, turn and turn about from one goblet.

"What did you do back home?" said the man. "Were you a trader there?"

"No," said Essa, "I was a sex therapist."

"A what?"

"If someone had sexual problems, I helped them. It was a paraprofessional job. Experiential."

She was making it up: she had had one job before she left the Fjord of Tears, working in a café until she saved the money to travel to the sea. But the woman was nodding seriously, "Ah, yes, a sensate focus specialist. My cousin does that work. It is very difficult. You must be a very sensitive person."

"I am," said Essa. "Why, I'm so sensitive that if there's a peapod under the mattress I get a bruise."

"A peapod?"

"Like a little banana."

"Who would put a banana under the mattress?"

"People with serious sexual problems have many strange habits. I, however, have no serious sexual problems."

"I can attest to that," said Lowlyn from beside her, suddenly. "What are you drinking, kid?"

She grabbed the flagon, hugged it to her chest, but it was suspiciously light. Turned it over. Empty, not even a stray drop to stain the white tablecloth.

"I'm drinking what you have," she said, taking his tankard from him. It was full of the malted wheat drink, whiskey they called it here.

The shouting in the other end of the room was requests for the singer, and soon everyone was bellowing along with the lugubrious, palindromic popular song:

> *no-one remembers the dead*
> *except the dead*
> *no-one remembers me*
> *I walk the long road to the sea*
> *I leave my mountain home*
> *my soul is sore*

Essa's new friends were leaving, though she draped herself around them and tried to convince them otherwise. Gata was at the other side of the room, making some kind of speech, introducing Lowlyn. When her belly began to rebel, Essa had barely time to stumble outdoors before she vomited unpleasantly behind some bushes. When she returned to the hall, Lowlyn had just finished speaking, and the staff of the pottery were cheering. Essa made her unsteady way to that end of the hall, and Gata saw her and pulled her up onto the little riser where they stood. They stood arms around waists, and Essa hoped with the small part of her mind left functioning that it wasn't too obvious that without those linking arms she'd fall.

The rest of the evening was a blessed blur. She spent it mostly in a chair alone, near the door, waiting, drinking the red wine and trying to forget the taste of the black mixed with whiskey coming back up. At home, she fell into bed and passed out immediately. She wakened with a headache, hours into the next day, angry with herself for her sullen behavior the night before. But her hand hadn't noticed, and although their headaches were as bad as hers they bore them cheerfully: the price, said Gata, of a good party.

Everything seems to have a price, thought Essa, and I seem to be broke all the time.

Essa knew that soon she would be leaving Sailor Town to go on the next part of her quest. She had dreamed of staying in Sailor Town: this was the dream at the end of the voyage, the dream she must eventually forsake to follow her questions further. Maybe she would return to Gata and Lowlyn, or maybe she had to mourn losing them even as she stood on the cliff looking over their hometown.

Or maybe she still expected to get back here, call it home, to the white town with the red roofs, to an indigo-stained house, the blue house by the blue sea where a sailor and an artisan waited for her to come back. Maybe she still imagined she could take them to the Fjord of Tears, a long journey on a Black Ship to show them where she was born. Maybe there were still dreams, dreams she would take with her, and though a storyteller might know they would not likely come true—too much happens, too much time goes by, and from all the old stories everyone knows by now you can't ever go home—still she preferred to dream them rather than to forsake dreaming.

She went up on the cliffs every day to eat her lunch. She was tired of the tavern lunches with everyone else drinking their noon beer, or worse, pouring from a flagon of black wine into one of the transparent goblets—glasses—which showed her every iridescent gleam, tempting, nostalgic and bitter. Having decided to quit drinking, she went upcliffs.

There she reviewed her trade deals, rehashed her day's confrontations and victories, and rehearsed what she must sometime say to Gata and Lowlyn. But it didn't help when the time came.

She was alone with Lowlyn in their bedroom. She was folding

laundry and he was putting it away. She turned to him and said, simply: "I thought I could stay here. I thought loving you was enough. I've made a mistake. I'm sorry." He began to cry.

She put her hands on him, feeling the pain like darkness flow between them. She cried too, so he touched her cheek and neck; they stood there, separate but joined by their hands, the tears slipping down their faces silently. Then he said, very quietly, "Yes, I know. I know you're sorry." And he went away into his studio. She didn't follow him; she finished putting away the clothes and sat in the dusky bedroom until full dark, then went out before Gata could arrive home.

Sitting on the cliffs, she watched the lights of the town change, move, open and close. Sometimes they blurred behind her tears, but most of the time she sat there uncrying, trying not to think. Finally it was time for supper. She was too exhausted to light her own way, and she fell once, scraping a knee and the palm of one hand and bringing a more elemental sort of tears. Home, the lamps were bright and a quiet Lowlyn, smiling slightly, served their favorite fish dish to a sulky Gata and a tired, silent, deeply grateful Essa.

The next day she packed her bundle and left. She stopped to tear the one-page note to her from the trader's notebook, then wrapped the book in a brief letter and entrusted it to a captain of a west-soaring ship. She had made deals with this woman; she and the rest of her hand were trustworthy.

"Won't you come with?" she said generously, as she tucked the notebook into her turban-end.

"Not this time," said Essa. "If you take the notebook to the trader at the address I have given you, he will read it and honor our agreements. You will have the commission I have promised, plus a percentage of new east-west trade. What is not recorded in the notebook is in this letter I have sent, so please keep them together."

"I will keep them safe." The captain repeated the legal promise. "I will take on this commission. I thank you."

"I welcome you to our family of trade," concluded Essa formally, and took her leave.

And walked down the dock until she stood under the shadow of the Black Ship.

Negotiations with the captains were tricky. Two of the hand disliked her intensely, one—Cabroca—was impartial, and two wanted the south-north trade she could promise with the Fjord of Tears. Finally Cabroca decided in favor of trade. She spoke sternly to Naio and Pewhim.

"You are hand of my hand," she said, "but honor is above love in this case. This hand has promised safety to this woman. She is not responsible for her mother's presence here three hands of years ago, nor is she to be blamed for her mother's enemies. She will sail on our ship as our passenger. This is our honor. She will return with us alive, and she will honor her trade agreements. As we will ours."

Sullenly, the two men agreed. The other men, the ones who supported Essa's trade mission, divided: one chatted with Essa while the other consoled Naio and Pewhim.

"I am Mateus," said the one to Essa. "That is Angelo."

Essa was watching Naio and Pewhim, wondering if Cabroca's stern words would do any good.

"Don't worry about them," Mateus said. "They are young and headstrong, but they see sense eventually."

Young? They were almost twice Essa's age. Yet she saw that Mateus, Angelo and Cabroca were older yet, as old as her father had been when he died.

"They came to us after two of our hand were killed in the first ship," he said softly. "They were handless. Two alone can barely lift a cup, you know. It all comes down to that. We were lonely too, and they had been through what our partners had been through. So we handfasted the next year. They are much younger, and they spend much time away, but we get along well enough."

"You don't all sail together, then?"

"Sometimes. But Angelo and I have been staying home some turns, lately. We are feeling the northern cold too much, out there where you're from—too high. The air is thin, for us. And the south is too—active."

So that's why she didn't remember them from the trip here. She was about to ask him more about their route this time when Cabroca joined them.

"Why didn't you stay home?" she said bluntly to Essa.

Taken aback, Essa managed: "I have work to do. There is obligation—honor—a promise to my employer."

"And there is this matter of your mother."

"Yes."

"Don't let it get in the way of your work. We want those southern percentages."

"I won't. I want the trade to go back to my employer."

"You think she will be alive?"

Her employer? How did Cabroca know that the trader's patron was a woman? Oh, her mother: Cabroca meant Essa's mother. "I have no idea."

"I hope she is, for your sake," said Cabroca. "But if you find her, she can't sail on this ship. So keep your ears open for land routes. And don't insult any merchanters."

She walked away as abruptly as she had come. Essa looked at Mateus, stunned. He made a droll face, but it didn't make her laugh.

"Oh, goodness," he said, "we've hurt your feelings."

"No," said Essa. "That is not an issue."

She shrugged, and he shrugged, and she went to find the cabin they had assigned her. It was Gata's cabin, which meant that someone on the ship was thinking kindly of her: this somewhat surprised her. The real surprise was that Gata was in it.

"What are you doing here?" They both spoke at once.

"Dammit, you can still make me laugh," Gata said.

"Running away from home," Essa said.

"Lowlyn will be angry that you didn't say goodbye to him."

"I did. Just not to you. You were out. As usual." Essa said the last satirically, copying Gata's style.

Gata sighed, a deep breath which lowered her tense shoulders. She shook her head. "What fools we are," she said. "I was going instead of you."

"I was going in secret so you wouldn't follow me. Did you tell Lowlyn too?"

"He packed my bag," Gata said.

"Mine too," said Essa. They laughed until they were wiping away tears.

"Welcome to the ship of fools," Gata finally choked out.

"Thanks so much," said Essa. "It's my pleasure."

They felt the jolt of the gangplank coming up, and jumped up to rush out on deck. On the dock, at the far end, Lowlyn was standing, waving. He had worn his red turban so they could see him. They stood by the rail together, waving at him with their free hands and the hands they'd clasped with each other. They must look like champion skiers after winning, thought Essa, then thought, there is no such championship here, in this land of heat and sun.

The deck crew cast off. The ship rose. Essa remembered her

first departure. This one was the opposite in every way but one: she was running away again, toward her answers, away from her questions, as always caught between consummation and desire.

If it had only been the other way around, she would have been happy. As it was, she was traveling again.

And Gata was with her. She couldn't help but be glad, though Lowlyn stood alone, dwindling into a small red spot at the sea-edge of a white town with red roofs. The sun penetrated the sea, making the surface negligible and lighting the sea bottom as if it were a new, shining, fluid kind of land. It hurt Essa's eyes to watch and cry at the same time. She turned away from the rail and Gata, and went back down to the cabin.

Gata came to the foredeck where Essa sat cross-legged. Trying to remember her meditation disciplines after months away was irritating: she was glad to consider Gata's presence an interruption.

"What's up, love?" she said, answering Gata's expression.

"I haven't menstruated yet," said Gata.

"Since when?"

"Home. Three weeks before we left."

That made seven weeks. A bit long even for an irregular schedule. Essa began to smile, then laughed aloud.

Gata was scowling.

"Didn't you want to be pregnant?"

"I'm afraid." Gata began to toss her worry-coin in her hand, the coin with Essa's face on it.

"Of being pregnant?" But that was not it. "Of what, then?" Silence from her partner.

"The sailors won't talk to me," said Gata after a while. "They clam up when I pass. Something is going on."

"What? Why wouldn't they—?"

"Hands may entwine but each finger knows which palm it belongs to."

"Their leading hand has guaranteed my safety. Stop worrying."

Gata was silent again, and her restless coin-tossing stopped with a sudden snap of her fingers. When Essa looked at her, Gata was crying, almost stealthily, tears slipping down her cheeks silently.

Essa, shocked, moved to put her arm around Gata. For all the months, the moments of love, the arguments, the fear, she had never seen Gata weep—unlike herself, who cried for everything from anger to orgasm.

"Gata, Gata love, what is it?" she said, feeling ineffectual.

Gata simply wept, slipping down until her head was cradled in Essa's lap. Essa could only stroke her hair back from her teary face and murmur endearments. In the back of her mind, she hoped practically that none of the sailors would come near here. Gata would be angry enough that Essa had seen her like this.

Finally she sat up, sniffed, wiped her face on her sleeve. As Essa had predicted, she sounded almost grim when she spoke.

"I don't want to lose you," she said. "Or this child to lose a mother. Three conceived her, at least three should nourish her."

"You warned me once before, and nothing happened."

"Then we came home. Even those two would not shit in their own nest. Now, they are far from home, getting further every day, and they are going to be harder for Cabroca to control." Essa couldn't think of anything comforting or negating to say. She knew the thin line she was walking. Gata went on. "There are lots of crew who could agree with them. Mostly they don't want bad luck. They haven't decided which way the luck lies. If they decide against you, they'll see you thrown off no matter how high we are. If they decide against Pee and Nai, those two may act alone out of frustration. Either way—"

"Tell me about it!" said Essa, also grim.

"I just have been," said Gata crossly, then, "Oh. Right. Another idiom?"

"Yes."

They sat silently, arms about each other. The sun beat down on them, warming the high, cold air. There was nothing much to say.

That night Essa put her hands on Gata's naked belly. "Think of it. A child!" she said.

"Yes, imagine that," said Gata grumpily, but her smile broke out despite herself. "It is yours and mine, you know. It is still as hard for many to truly conceive as it is for many to kiss at once. Not that it doesn't happen, but—"

"But this one is ours? How can it be?"

"I know it. Don't you know sailor folk can do this?"

"I didn't really believe it until now." They smiled at each other in amazement.

"I love you, Gata," said Essa.

"I love you too," said Gata. Essa hugged her, feeling the constriction of her throat. Gata said, muffled, "Hey, hey! What?"

"You never say that," said Essa. "Well, hardly ever."

"You already know. What's to say?" Gata was truly puzzled. Essa laughed, dizzy at the speed of her changing moods, despair to joy only an instant's travel. She feared she would never see this child. Yet she felt so full of love and joy that she could hardly speak. It has been, she thought, the strangest time: certainly the strangest voyage of my life.

Even though Gata had warned her—an ironic echo of the last voyage, but a new-minted danger—she couldn't look out for everything, and the murderous attack when it came was almost totally a surprise.

Her arms were lashed to her sides and a heavy cloth wrapped around her head. Cliché, she thought, then had to fight for breath. A great deal of shouting was going on, one loud voice by her ear crying, "Lower, lower!" Gata's voice and Mateus's farther away, calling confusedly about *the pilothouse, help her, he's got a knife, look out*. The voice beside her was Naio's. She kicked and heard him yelp, felt him shove her against some wall and swear. Her adrenaline started to catch up. She tried to kick him again, but he tripped her and she fell heavily on her back.

Again she had to gasp for air. The folds of the burlap heavy, as her sucking pulled it into her mouth. She spit it out, panicked, pulled her head back and it hit the deck. Now everything was swaying, but then she figured out that it was the ship, swooping enough to make her queasy.

More shouting—*we'll crash, get him out of there, Pewhim's at the wheel*—and then Naio shouted, "Do you think we care? We were on the Black Ship when it went down. We threw the women to him, but he killed the ship anyway. Have to give him this one before it's too late."

He was dragging her along. She struggled but didn't know which way was safe to go. He stopped and rolled her; she resisted, and he put a toe into her gut, hard. She went limp for only a moment, but it was enough for his last push, and when she began to struggle again it was in air. The cloth fell free, but her arms were still half-held by a trailing rope.

She could see the ground—trees and some sparkling water— too close. Her involuntary attempt to bring her hands up flipped her around. The last thing she saw was the silver ship above her, Naio struggling crazy-faced in the grasp of other sailors, trying to throw himself off, it seemed, and being held back. She had a moment to wonder why before she hit the first branches and crashed through them. Her head hit the ground a split second before her broken body.

The Remarkable Mountains (4)

Annalise has gone down Hasfeld way with her family for the year, and her absence is hard to bear. Sometimes I lie awake beside this sleeping man and I want her so badly: I don't think for sex but for talk in the language of my youth. Yet the barbarities it is possible to say in that language that this one won't encompass are abhorrent to me. This language has its own problems, though. Finally I have decided to teach all the languages I know to my daughter, but wait on the home tongue until she is five and can defend herself.

Once I heard my grandmother say: give me a child until he is five and I will have him for the rest of his life. It was certainly true of my husband: she hand-fed him and he was her creature.

I imagine that little Essa (as they—as we all—call her here) will grow up someday and go face him down. Perhaps she will kill him. Wouldn't that be fun. My child doing what I could not do. But she will be a child of the Range, of these Remarkable Mountains: it is possible she will not be able to lift her hand.

Not that that makes her any different from me; just we would do the same things for different reasons.

Shame on me. She is four years old. She is not my instrument of revenge. I have lived here and spoken this gentle tongue for five years and still I am no closer, I sometimes think, to salvation—at my own hands or theirs. The Fjord of Tears indeed. I have shed enough.

Half the village has been away tree planting and today we came to join them. The journey took half a day and when we came over the edge of the valley it was a strange and amazing sight. A line of people moving across the clear area of the valley, they pace ahead slowly, then stop, their planting staves rise and fall, and they pace again. Collectively, they make a raggedly ponderous forward motion, as if an army were trying to waltz across the field.

After only half a day along that line, though, I do not feel I have been waltzing, or if so, waltzing in the Underworld. F. had enough energy left to rub my shoulders a little before falling asleep. I stay awake as usual to finish this note. Essa is staying with Annalise and her family while we spend a few weeks on this task. At the moment the thought of rising to it tomorrow is hell, but that is my muscles speaking for me.

There is lots of logging west of my hometown. But they don't reforest on this scale. I know there were some projects with slave and convict labor and even some idea of using dirigibles to drop seedlings (after the first Black Ship everyone had dirigible projects— none of them were done, of course) but mostly the valleys are converted to farming and if they have problems with erosion, that's seen as a separate issue. As usual F. was scornful: "Their grandchildren will have no paper to write on and no grain to eat," he said.

They have elected me to the elders. And talked me into it. After I agreed I went down the Fjord to Annalise and sat with her for hours, doubting myself. Her children ran in and out. For a while after the last miscarriage I didn't come here: I couldn't bear the contrast, couldn't bear being jealous of sweet Annalise. But that was only a month or so, before I longed for her too much to keep up such irrational behavior.

Now I take her children on my lap as if they are my own. They are my nieces and nephews, and family ties are warm here in the Fjord. I've sent Essa to F.'s sister and her brood; they take her in as if she always lived there.

And now I'm to be an elder—not just part of the net, but one of the ones who weaves it and keeps it strong.

It is a long way from the Land of the Dark Isles. I hope it is long enough.

I took a stone back home from the creek. I put it on the table and said to F.: "Look. I am this stone. I have been tumbled and moved, and it has all shaped me. I am a decent shape now, but it was long and painful to get that way and I lost a lot."

"What you didn't need you lost," he said. "What you needed, you kept in your core. You are the child who refused to beat your servants. You had the decent shape when you began." He picked up the stone. "See how it keeps its shape through the journey? Its essence remains the same even if it is ground down to sand."

I laughed. "Won't let me be morbid, will you?"

"No need," he said, tossing the rock out the open window into the rock garden. "You have a different life now. You have me, and we have a child, and you live in the mountains, which I say is the best place to live, though I've never tried elsewhere. And the garden is ripe, and the sun is bright, and tonight there's a storytelling and dance."

"Indeed," I said, "it does sound like the best of all possible worlds." He smiled and went back to his jam-making, and I went out to pick peas. Of course, I shelled and ate the first few, standing by the edge of the garden and dropping the pods into the compost. Thinking of metaphors. F. does not like me to think of the past and be sad, but while I am happy here, people are dying in the south. People are being enslaved. It isn't possible to think it all away on a fine day in late mountain summer.

The peas are sweet and green-tasting. They are like so many other things: they make me glad I am alive, here not there, and going on. But. But. But.

I left him in the tumbled bed, the light turned low to shine a reddish glow on his face made placid by sleep. His hair was graying now, and hairline receding. Living with me had been no easier than the rest of his life.

Sitting on the side of the bed, I felt my body drawn against my will into two or three harsh, silent sobs of pure despair: aging, I resisted the idea that I would have to return to the life I had led since I became legally a woman and thus my first husband's prey. Bait, I thought of it by then, though at first, I might merely have thought that my grandmother had made a mistake. By this time I had realized that the old woman knew exactly what she was doing: was pulling the teeth of the tiger with a tool made of the prospect she least respected. She had liked her nephew because he was dangerous; all she had wanted to do was make sure if he harmed anyone it was not her, but in consequence she had given him a gift: my life, to manipulate as he chose.

And thus she had taken away everything I ever wanted, and was doing it again.

It was my parents who had made the mistake, abandoning me

to her machinations although they had not realized it at first. I could not blame them: they had thought they were doing something which would be good for me—and in the end, also, they had paid for their mistake with their lives, too high a price. But I was determined that my daughter would never be drawn into the same net, would never pay the same kind of price.

I looked back at him under the light, then I climbed down the steep stairway to the central room, put two more logs in the stove, and sat naked in the sphere of its warmth, thinking of him, thinking of young Essa, asleep in her own loft on the other side of the house. Finally I took the book in my hand and began to write on its blank foreleaf, a message to my daughter. I left the book under my counter, on the table, under a slip of paper with her name on it. Then I went to pack my old knapsack, taking only what would be useful.

At times I could hardly see for the tears streaming out of my uncooperative eyes. Sometime during it he woke up, went yawning and scratching to the toilet, then came back and without speaking put his arms around me. That made me cry in earnest, and he comforted me. Afterward we talked a little: not much; we never talked much. Until now we hadn't needed to talk much.

"Do you have to go?"

"If I draw the spy on before he knows I have a daughter, she will be safe, and you with her. If she had been a son, perhaps we would all have been all right. But we can't take the risk."

"I will miss you, and so will she."

"Tell her stories. Make me bigger than life."

"You already are."

"Nonsense!"

"Why did I bring you home, then, when I was never content with any ordinary woman?"

"Oh, the usual reasons, I suppose."

"Think as you like."

The litany was a familiar comfort. We could even smile at the end.

"You are exceptional too," I said, meaning it perhaps a little less than he, but not much. He had lived with me for eight years, after all, when no-one but Annalise before that could seem to manage not to try to kill me long before that many years had passed—that too was a joke between us; but this night it was no longer a joke. And in fact, he had always made me happy and though I would not be able to do any wailing once I left the house, that didn't mean I wouldn't grieve him full sore.

"Go pack the food you want," he said. "I'll finish here." And he stroked my face.

He brought the pack down from the loft and put more things in it: when he reached for the counter and book I said, "No. That's for Essa. I want to leave her something special."

"This has blood on it," he said distastefully, flicking the counter with his nail.

"If you don't tell her, she won't know," I said. "Its beads shine in the sun so beautifully. And it is the only thing I have from before, something special to leave her from my life."

"You are leaving her her own life; you made her and you're saving her."

"She is seven; the subtleties may escape her. This way she has something real. And an explanation."

"Not the book too! But you love it!"

It was true that the book my parents had given me to record my travels was the only other beautiful thing I had, handmade and decorated and with its own stylus and tiny tightly-capped inkpot along the edge, for convenient writing in the field. "I want her to understand, too. If not now, then later."

"I don't want you to have to leave everything . . . "

I went to him and kissed him, pulling his hand away from the book to hold me instead. He stood with his arms around me. "I have the memory of you," I said, "and of her, and that is more than a trinket and a book. Let me leave with only what I need, and what is safe."

He had a stubborn look about him, but it turned out that it was only to stop himself from crying, which as soon as he began so did I, and we had to stop for a while to comfort each other into calmness again.

"I am too old for this," I said then. "I am exhausted already, and I haven't even gone."

He chuckled a little. "Well, my dear one, that is the life of an adventurer: what you told me you were, long years ago."

"I told you the truth later!" I was still capable of indignation, even in this extremity. He chuckled a little more. I put the pack by the door and went to get a few last-minute provisions. Essa came out to go to the toilet then, child-somnolent and sweet, and I had to disguise my intent and hug her good night and tuck her back in with a smile I didn't feel, so wrought I was with the sight of her, her perfect childlike anonymity. Then it was time to finish dressing and go, pulling quickly away from him and from home, before the enormity of it overwhelmed me and robbed me of purpose.

I met Annalise at the inn and we were well away toward Hasfeld by sunrise.

"If this is not necessary," she said, "I will have your heart for supper."

"If this is not necessary," I said, "we will come home and live happily ever after, the way they do in all those fantastic tales in the books I read to Essa."

But I didn't think we would ever see Eslyn again, and so it proved; and that is how I left the Remarkable Mountains, carrying less than what I came with, and leaving behind all that I loved except that one stalwart companion, to go back into the darkness I thought I had escaped forever, that I could never escape.

Life in the zone of control (3)

After that they fuck ferociously at every opportunity. And it is, as well as lovemaking, fucking. Even the waif with her limited experience recognizes it, and it troubles Escape-from-bondage greatly.

It doesn't stop either of them, however. They hide in broom closets and wine cellars for a fast encounter; they play sexual games in the kitchen at midnight when he's on night duty; they even fuck once in the great hall, under the portrait of the matriarch, to show their disdain. They stand up in stairwells, him lifting her to enter her. They go down on each other in corridors. It's a clandestine and forbidden feast.

Still, he worries a great deal about how similar their diligent and sweaty congress can be to the services he has performed over the years for various members of the household and their guests. Finally she says, impatiently, "Well, there isn't anything they haven't thought of. There isn't anything new to do."

=Doesn't help.=

"And we are doing the things for different reasons."

=I suppose.= He isn't convinced, but they don't stop being "lovers," a word in the sign language that they invent, making a noun out of the verb form of his entwined fingers.

"Languages!" she says suddenly, one day, in the midst of sex.

He raises his head from her, looks his question without stopping the motions of his hands.

"In all languages the sounds are pretty much the same," she says. "Except in the secret language there are some funny clicks and things. But they make completely different words. One language people don't understand another language people. And there are secret languages like yours, and those can say all sorts of secret things. So it isn't what noises you make, it's what they go together to mean. Like spelling. The same letters make up all different words, bad and good. And if you can't read it, it's a secret."

He has been teaching her to improve her spelling, somehow sidestepping the headaches to instill an awareness of how letters work. She has not forgotten the horror with which she saw the pages of the madwoman's book and realized she could understand that sneaky language of blood marks. But this is something different enough to cause him to free his hands and put them around her face. Then, of course, he has to sign, and she laughs as she feels his invisible handprints drying on her face.

=All right,= he says. =That will calm me down nicely!= Then they laugh and roll together on the bed and growl and bite like puppies, rough until he grabs her hair and pulls her head away from his nipple.

"Did I hurt you?" she says, aghast: their greatest sin.

=It's all right. You haven't bitten me to the bone yet!= He laughs.

"I will," she says, "but don't worry, it won't hurt."

Not knowing where that comes from, she has to go to sleep then suddenly, but that's all right: they were pretty much finished for that night anyway.

The child was wakened in the middle of the night by her mother.

"Come outside," her mother said, "and see something wonderful!"

This happened with full moons, spectacular views of the Spine of Night, comets, anything sweet and nocturnal.

The child was having a particularly sweet dream, though, and she said, "Oh, mama . . . "

"Shhh, shhh," said her mother. "Just come."

The child pulled her warm trousers and jacket on, socks, shoes.

"Hurry!" said her mother. "I don't know how long it will go on."

The child saw sleepily that her father was up too, outside, his head tilted back, looking up. Her mother pulled the quilts from her parents' bed and they went out.

The air was cool and dewy and the sky was burning. The darkness was lit with a cold, pale flame. The child made a light around them but her mother smothered her hand, said, "No, no, let the sky light us."

The dark, starry sky was full of misty-pale light, flickering so fast that the stars seemed to ripple. Flickering like the hearth fire but it was cold outside. The dark shadows of trees were outlined against the leaping rays.

"What is it?" said the child at the same time her father said, "I've never seen it move so fast."

The child was used to the stories of wonder coming from her mother, but her mother too said, "What is it, then?"

"They say it's because of sunspots. They flare all the way here, and light up the sky somehow. Probably the same way you light us with your hands, little one. By vibrating the air."

"What is its name?" her mother said. She was spreading a quilt on the meadow grass. The child lay down, and her parents settled, one on either side, and pulled the other quilt over them all. They lay there a long time, quiet.

"I'm so glad we live far from town, to see this," said her father. The child felt the cold on her nose, but she was warm between her parents. Watching the sky gave her the same feeling watching the fire did. Only now, she felt she was lying below the center of the cold fire, looking into its depths. The earth flipped around and vertigo overtook her. She swung free for a panicky moment, until she was anchored by her mother's voice.

"Isn't it amazing, little one? Was it worth waking up for?"

The child took her mother's hand beneath the quilt and squeezed; she was too buoyant to talk. She could rise up, and feel she was falling, into the silent, benevolent maelstrom of the sky. She could go anywhere. She remembered a dream of running down a mountain. Now she was running in air. She took her father's hand too, for safety, and fell asleep inside the warmth and wonder.

Her parents must have carried her to bed, for it was there she awoke in daylight. She ran outside to see whether the sky was still there, still blue, still intact. It was clear and sunny, and small white clouds spotted the blue in the most normal way imaginable.

"Look, mama," she said. "It's the same!"

"Nothing is ever quite the same, daughter," her mother said. "Every moment is different. And memory changes

*things, too. Now you know the tricks the sky can do, will you
ever see it the same?"*

*The child would have liked to insist it was still her fa-
vorite blue sky but she had to admit that her mother might
be right. Might be. She went to eat her morning bowl of raspberries silently, thinking. Remembering a blue-blackness
shining with mysterious luminosity. Aurora, her father had
called it. There was a little boy in the village named that, the
son of her mother's friend Annalise. That the sky-fire had a
name, and that a person may be named it, meant they, last
night, weren't the first to see it. That seemed pretty strange
too, when she thought about it. She ate her raspberries very,
very slowly.*

A dream fading, and Fierce-frightened shivering in her solitary, wide
bed. She goes to the window, tries to find the stars, but they are a
different shape, and fear strikes the knife into her head again, so that
she almost falls against the stone sill. But she manages to stagger back
to bed, sleeps precipitously, forgets on awakening that she dreamed
at all.

Escape-from-bondage has to pull them apart and shake them to stop
the fighting. Fierce-frightened is hissing at the boy like an animal,
and he is cursing her in his high voice. Escape-from-bondage grunts
angrily at both of them, shakes them again, and drops them at his
arm's-length apart. They crouch, tense and ready to spring into battle again. The waif notices with satisfaction that the boy's face is
scratched and bleeding. That should make him popular upstairs for
a while, she gloats.

Escape-from-bondage rounds on her. =What's this about?=
"He told me he gives better blow jobs!"
=Maybe he does.=
"He said you told him so!" She is starting to cry now, with fury.
=Ah.= and he laughs. =That's it!=
He goes over to the boy, who has turned now and is backing
away from him and into the corner of the kitchen.
=You told her you gave me a blow job?=
He has to raise his hand before the boy answers, terrified, "Yes."

=You had better give me a blow job then. And I will say who does best, not you.=

"Now?" he squeaks.

Fierce-frightened watches in anger and fascination. Escape-from-bondage has never used his size against her but he looms over the boy with a menacing, violent air she has never seen.

"All right," says the boy.

Escape-from-bondage makes a disgusted "tscha" sound, pulls the boy up roughly and stands him on unsteady feet. The boy is thin, short, trembling; he shrinks from the big hand which pushes him against the wall. He reaches toward Escape-from-bondage's loin-cloth but the big man slaps his hands away.

=Listen to me,= he signs with his free hand. =These things we do for them. Them. It is not good to get caught ourselves in the process.=

The boy shakes his head in confusion. Escape-from-bondage drops the thin shoulder so the boy slumps against the wall, still paralyzed and fascinated like a snake. What is a snake, thinks the waif, and almost smiles to herself, but she too is fascinated.

=Listen,= says Escape-from-bondage. =It is not a waterfall, or a stone stair, everything the same from the top to the bottom. We are more than that.= His hands spread wide and the boy looks from hand to hand desperately. =We are not like them. We do not have to pretend to be them to make ourselves big.=

"You are already big," says Fierce-frightened impertinently, smirking a little at the boy.

=You are just as bad. Fighting in the hall over gossip and boasting. Why didn't you ask me?=

"I got angry."

=So what? And you . . . = he looms at the boy again = . . . someday I will test your technique. If you want a proper lesson. Come and ask me. Your choice. Do you understand?=

The boy nods. Escape-from-bondage grabs him again, shakes him harder this time, until his head snaps back and forth once, then drops him again.

=I thought you figured out it was stupid to lie. Every time I catch you lying I'll shake you harder. Either your neck will break or the habit. I think you like your neck better. Then when we've got the lying taken care of, we'll work on the blow job. Right?=

The boy backs away, and Escape-from-bondage lets him go.

When he is out of arm's reach, he spits dry in the waif's direction, flips his fingers at Escape-from-bondage, and runs.

The rough shout is laughter, the waif knows. She smiles in relief, but the face he turns to her is angry. =You were jealous.=

=Jealous?= She doesn't know how to say it, so she signs. He spells it, and through her headache she sounds out the letters, him prompting her with words it sounds like until she has it about right. =Yes. Jealous. Stupid. Ownership. Like slaves. I hate that. Who cares about blow jobs? Is it a trophy? Am I your trophy?=

He starts to walk away. "You're the only thing I've ever had!" she shouts at his back. "Not even a name of my own! No body! Nothing! And then, you here. Giving me something. He wanted to take that away, say it was just fucking!"

=Clever Fierce-frightened,= he says. =Fast-thinking Fierce-frightened.=

"Don't pretend to be such a boss. You aren't so perfect yourself, to pretend to be so good."

He comes and takes her by the shoulders and she thinks he will shake her too. But instead he lets her go with an impatient gesture and that "tscha!" and signs, =If you are so concerned about the quality of your blow jobs go give one to the regent. You'll find out soon enough if he thinks yours are as good as his favorite fancy boy's.=

"You are 'jealous' too!" she says, amazed, then backs away from his furious face. "But not of me, right? You were the fancy boy once, weren't you? You want to be him, with your tongue back so you can give good head. Don't you? Don't you?"

The growl low in his throat is a voice she has never heard from him, but the sign is clear enough. =You are a pain in the ass,= he says with one harsh sharp chop of a hand, and stalks off. Fierce-frightened stands looking after him. She doesn't know what to think, so, economically, she doesn't. She goes into the lavatory to wash the blood out from under her nails and off her arms and face. She can't do much about the mess on her tunic. Then she goes back to work.

Life in the zone of control (4)

This day the regent wants to go out. She helps him dress and then he insists she come up with him. He makes her take off the simple tunic she wears and dress in the complex bodysuit of a court attendant. Seeing her in the form-fitting scarlet-and-gray seems to amuse him. His smile is three-cornered and unpleasant. She doesn't want anything to do with it. She looks away into the mirror, to see what she has done wrong to make him smile, but nothing looks awry.

She does not like the implications of this new gear—despite her ambition, she knows how promotions in this place come with their disadvantages—but she likes the suit. It covers her up, and is hard to get into from the outside.

In the bar, the seats are comfortable crescents facing wide vistas of the sea, the sky, the landscape, all screen copies of reality. Why didn't they just make holes in the walls and look at the real thing? She must ask Escape-from-bondage, she thinks. The bar is full of courtiers, laughing and betting on some slave game going on behind one of the screens.

Recognizing him, the men leave their seats and urge him to sit. She is seated too, beside him, despite the fact that she is a slave. He insists on it. He smiles at some of the young men with that barbed grin that implies they have failed tests they didn't know they were being given. They jump to get him a drink, counters for the game, a sweet snack, as if they were slaves themselves.

And she supposes they are, at that. She has never thought of such a thing before.

She looks at the urbane, smoothly-clad prince beside her and wonders what has become of the palsied, urine-smelling, attenuated weakling of time before. He does not have the strength of Escape-from-bondage, she thinks, but he has much more power. Don't fuck the regent, the madwoman said, but she lives in a cage. And Escape-from-bondage has no tongue. This man plays these others like counters on that slavegame board, and disdains to look sidelong at the screens while he does so.

Eventually, however, he turns directly to the ocean scene spread across three or more meters of wall and says:

"Look. Look at that sea. I grew up by that sea, they're playing this particular coastline just for me," and he puts his arm about her shoulders and draws her close to his side. She is terrified, looking into the great eye sloshing with surf, knowing it looks back at them. She cannot speak to him, dares not move in case she draws the screens' attention. He is the despot. It all belongs to him. But she has to go back below-stairs when he is done with her, and answer to the jealousies and hierarchies there. She will be punished tonight unless she can find Escape-from-bondage and hide behind him.

"Let's go outside," he says, and standing, keeping her clamped to his side with one strong arm, walks toward the blackness between the seacoast screen and the prairie with the blue sky full of clouds. She is brave enough to look unconcerned although one hand clenches the inside of her pocket with sweaty desperation. Behind the bar, the young catamite is polishing glasses. She straightens a little, contrives to look content, thinking, this must mean I win. With him, anyway.

In the darkness a door. He punches the escape bar, the latch springs, and they walk out into the light. She blinks furiously in the unexpected glare, brighter by far than the screens' rendition of nature which had seemed vivid but hardly cast light into that dark club. Here she is blinded. He walks surely toward what seems to be the glowing edge of the world, drawing her with him. She sees nothing, is sure she is walking into death. She is sure she will die. She even thinks perhaps she will not mind: it had not been so bad the last time. On the other hand, there is Escape-from-bondage—she doesn't want to lose that.

But she can't stop; he puts his hand into the middle of her back and pushes her ahead.

Shockingly, she feels cold flatness against her belly. She recoils and looks down. They have come to a railing which fences what she sees, now her eyes are starting to adjust, is a terrace. He smiles coolly and gives her his sunglasses. She puts them on and sees first, directly ahead of her with no indication of distance, the true horizon. It is when she tries to understand the distance that she looks down and sees the sheer jumble of rocks end at the sea fifty meters below. The sea breaking on a rocky shore with a few sandy crescents strewn with drift. The sea stretching to the horizon, spotted with a few sailing vessels and above one ship a mirage—he points to it without speaking; it is the same ship sailing upside down. To the left the cliff curves into a headland, to the right she can see islands in the distance.

Ahead, for the first time in her short life, nothing but air until the earth curve makes a horizon. Clouds above, great cumulonimbus towers with the sun shining them to whiteness that glares even more into her eyes. The distance is awesome. And it is real.

She looks covertly at him. He sees her look, and laughs; he laughs and he lifts her chin with his hand, and holds her head while he kisses her. He squeezes her cheeks roughly until she opens her mouth. She hopes he does not hear the working of the machinery of her thoughts. He lets her go and laughs again.

"You will learn," he says. "And maybe you will even learn to like it. I can teach you to ask for it, like it or not." She can't understand why he would want her, the slaves' rags-to-catamite story coming true around her if she could believe it. She looks at him with a mixture of calculation and terror.

"It's all right," he says inexplicably, "we'll use each other." And there they stand at the edge of the world, regent she is not supposed to fuck, but supposes she will have to, like it or not, and frightened, power-hungry waif from the south. It is rather peaceful, really. She has no experience of peace, nor of how to stand in the same relationship to sky and sea as the most powerful being in her world. But she has gotten used to other terrors in her short life. She expects she can get used to this too. She will never mistake it, though they stand thus side by side, for anything safe. They stand side by side, yes, and watch the waves crash on the rocks far below; then they lift their eyes in eerie, accidental unison to the decorated sky above the far flat horizon.

As they look, she becomes Essa all in a great wash, a tsunami, Essa who remembers that first day she came down to the shore, down from the Remarkable Mountains her home—all the memory comes then, and washes away almost all traces of the last two years of truncated life. There is hardly any waif left when that wave recedes. She does not know any more exactly why she stands, wearing odd clothing, on this puny cliff with this strange and unpleasant man beside her, but she remembers just enough to get by on.

She laughs aloud, and turns to the autocrat beside her.

"I am from the Fjord of Tears," she says, "and I think you are my mother's husband."

"Too bad you remembered," he says. "I was looking forward to kissing you again."

To be a slave who becomes the princess is another cliché of fantasy stories which are told to keep teenagers happy in the Fjord of Tears. Or anywhere, Essa supposes, that teenagers want more than just the life their parents show them every day. When Essa remembers, she takes the calculator out of her turban, remembering how to use it now, and begins to count what they say is hers. All of it from her mysterious mother who here, like in the mountains of home, had lived, made a home, had a family—only here, it was her birth-family, they called it a dynasty, and it was already corrupt.

Essa stops counting when she realizes she is going to keep very little of this wealth, and starts a new counting, a list of what she can safely carry away.

Life as an aristocrat is as truncated as life as a slave, but her pockets are smaller and she no longer thinks that her mother's husband is a god. She still wonders, however, about her mother.

To celebrate the return of the heir to the throne, though apparently not to invest her with the actual title of queen—there seems to be no hint of that, which makes Essa laugh to herself—the prince is throwing a party.

I suppose they don't "throw" parties here, thinks Essa. Probably they proclaim their intentions or something. The invitation she has received is certainly a masterwork of diplomatic language.

The regent has been planning the event for some time, which Essa, invested as she is with only the haziest of memories of her amnesiac self, thinks rather odd: if he knew that the slave was Essa, why had he not had her examined by doctors, helped? Yet she can't remember this having happened—and when the regent with his oily good manners talks of the party, he says, "But my dear, you were always the guest of honor. It was only a matter of time before you caught on."

Essa then begins to make a point of telling everyone she meets how amazing it is to regain one's memory and discover one is not a servant but in fact part of the family. "What a pity," she says, "that after all this I did not find my mother here to welcome me." The listeners hear her with a variety of reactions from controlled outrage to amusement. She keeps track of who says what. No-one, of course, says anything useful; they are all still alive after twenty-five or more years with the prince, after all.

After she has been doing this for a while, the regent comes to her with a rather set smile and begins one of his flowery speeches.

"I am looking forward to introducing you to the company," says the regent. "I wonder how many of them will have noticed by now that you are the same waif I brought from the south?"

"Probably they will not have to notice," says Essa, "since I have told a great many of them the circumstances in which you, shall we say, rescued me." She wonders if he wears make-up, to make himself look younger, or if it is an odd gift, like the gift of light she had inherited in so much greater strength (until her injury, that is) from her mother.

"They will, of course, see my great pleasure in having you here," he continues, irritated, "and wish to celebrate with us the existence of a direct heir, for which possibility I have acted as regent for so long."

"And for which, I am sure, my mother will be grateful. When I find her."

"We will have the celebration at the full of the moon . . . "

"Convenient for romantic trysts on the balcony among lesser lights of the nobility."

" . . . entirely suitable to the solemnity of the occasion."

"You were much more fun when I didn't know who I was."

He glares at her, and she laughs. It takes an effort, but she has decided that whatever age she is, she is too old to be cowed.

The memories of the waif from the south are struggling to get out. Essa has nightmares every night. She understands the hand signs of the servants and slaves who clean the fireplaces and the corridors. She stops the big, kindly-looking mute one and says, in the hand language, help me. Help me.

He tilts his head to the left and looks at her, his hand on his throat. She thinks he might mean, why don't you speak?

=Help me,= she signs. =I have been someone else and I don't know who. Please. I don't know the rules.=

=You're not supposed to know this language, either,= he signs, hands close to his chest, his back to the screen at the end of the corridor. Are they surveillance screens? It has not occurred to her until this moment, though now it seems it should have been obvious. She moves closer to him so that the screen cannot see her hands either.

=Why not?=

=It is the secret talk of slaves,= he replies.

=I understand why you need a secret talk in this bizarre place,= she says, making up a sign for "bizarre." Still, he looks quizzical at it.

"Bizarre place," she says.

He makes a tiny grunt of laughter. His voice sounds pitiful to her.

=What made you mute?= she says.

He opens his mouth to show her the scar where his tongue has been cut out. She feels her gorge rise, has to cover her own mouth and gulp to prevent herself from vomiting.

=I liked you better before,= he signs.

=I'm sorry,= she says. =I don't know who I was.=

=You were my friend,= he replies. She feels tears start, and brushes them away angrily.

=I could be your friend now,= she signs back. =Maybe,= he says, with a sign that assumes the negative, and laughs shortly again.

=I can't help it!= she says, her hands chopping the air.

=I know,= he says. =But it doesn't help to know things, sometimes.= His hands, making the equivocal sign for "sometimes," hang in the air. They are big and she feels like she wants to hold them.

=You remind me of my father,= she signs.

He glares, and now it is time for his hands to shout. =I was your lover,= he storms at her, =and you liked it.= Then he pushes past her and, grabbing the ash bucket and the broom, runs away down the long corridor, his great form light on soft-shod feet, and silent.

She looks after him, crying for memory she doesn't have, angry and hurt and sad. And, she realizes, very lonely.

*   *   *

She can't leave it—him—alone. She calls him into her room, where she has now hung an embroidered bedspread over the wall with the screens, shuts the door behind him, and comes at him with hands flying. He grabs her wrists gently, but his face is angry.

"Uh!" he shouts, his harsh voice like a crow's.

He lets go and =Talk!= his hands push at her. =You can talk. She could talk. Talk. Don't patronize me.=

"Patronize" is a sign from top down, and his face imitates the regent's.

"I'm sorry," she says. "You are my only friend here."

=If I'm your friend, what's my name?= he says angrily.

She closes her eyes in despair. Her hands come up, and move, but she can't look to see what they say or she will stop it coming. She feels his hands take hers. She opens her eyes.

"What did I say?" she says up to him, where he stands so close he casts a shadow over her.

"Lowlyn," she says. "You're not like my father at all. You're as big as Lowlyn." His question. "A lover I was handfasted to in Sailor Town. What did I say?"

He lets go and makes a sign. Fist opens, flies up.

"Fly up from captivity," she says. He laughs again, that bitter sound. =You used different words before,= he says, and spells them out.

"Escape . . . from . . . bondage?"

=That's what you said. You couldn't spell very well, though. That's new. You can call me whatever you like, now. You're the princess.=

She begins to shake her head and the motion becomes violent, her head exploding with pain, the world streaking by until she closes her eyes. "No! No!" she says, her voice rising. "I am not the princess. No! I am Essa!" His hands imprisoning her head firmly wake her from what has seemed, suddenly, like a terrible dream.

"What was that?" she says, weakly, her own hands coming up to clutch her temples where a ferocious headache rages, trying to gnaw its way out.

=She used to get bad dreams,= he signs. =Her head would split like that, suddenly.=

"She?"

=You, but she wasn't you and you aren't her. Maybe you will join her someday.= She gets the impression he thinks that will be an improvement.

"Can you help me? I am her, whatever you think."

=I'm not sure. You have a name. She didn't.=

"She didn't? But you do, and you are a slave too."

=I gave myself a name from my dreams. She was afraid of her dreams. She was afraid of everything, but she lived anyway. I used to call her Fierce-frightened.=

"Adjectives? Names are nouns."

=She might have given herself a noun= he spells it =eventually. A name= he spells that too, for emphasis. =But I was just teaching her what she already knew. Spelling. Lovemaking. She had always been . . . = His sign is for "sex," but it has a violence in it.

"Raped?"

But the word is from her home language. He doesn't know it. She tries to explain forced sex but that seems to be a slave's life here. She goes back to his sign for "lovemaking," and contrasts it with the "fucking" sign. He nods.

=I can imagine, just barely, a place where 'forced-sex'= (he exaggerates the sign, for irony) =is wrong. But we don't live there. We live here. She lived here.=

"She had a short life," Essa says.

He nods, pretends to wipe away a tear. It is a melodrama-actor's gesture but it moves her deeply.

"You miss her."

He nods, and she sees that there are real tears in his eyes too.

"Please," she says. "Find her in me. A little bit. Let us be lonely together a little bit."

=I have been a slave all my life= he says. =I had forced-sex with the regent's aunt. Your great-grandmother. Fierce-frightened used to look at the old bitch's picture and shiver. The one in the Great Hall?= Essa nods. =She saw something. She didn't know it was the shadow of her own face. Your face.=

=But you loved her, me,= Essa says with her hands. She doesn't know the words for it in the regent's language, doesn't know if there even are words for the tender emotions.

=Yes,= he says. =And I still do. But now I am afraid of you.= He is sweating. Why would it take such effort to say?

"But I don't belong here," she says. "Every day I feel like throwing up. Where I come from 'rape' is a word. People take care of each other. People touch. People are kind. Everyone here so far tells lies. Except you, I guess, but I can hardly believe it any more.

I have become like that dog of his who has been kicked and beaten too many times. I expect another blow."

=Not like she did,= he signs. =The first day she was here, I told her about the deaf and the mute slaves. The second day I saw her, she asked me when her tongue was to be cut out. When I told her he wanted her intact, she fell down. I thought she had fainted, but she was staring. Staring. She had learned to do everything quietly.=

=Even make love?= Essa asks.

=Yes,= he signs. =Yes.= He grabs her hands and looks as if he will try to speak, then shakes his head in frustration.

=I still forget I can't,= he says. =There are words out loud for it. There must be.=

=I don't know them.=

=Learn them. Or teach me the ones in your language. Then maybe I can love you a little like I love her.=

And he leaves, leaves her standing there.

An angry ennui still surrounds Essa. Her two lives are like two quarreling voices in her head. The party seems only an external manifestation.

The crowd swirls around her, all the court but the most loyal of the despot's followers, who are probably searching the rooms of those who have ever expressed sympathy for the heir. For Essa.

Faces seem to streak toward her out of the gloom, ogle her, make some comment, and dwindle away. She would have suspected the buffet fare to be spiked with intoxicants, but she realizes that all the strangeness is outside herself. Even before she ate the sliced meats which had made her mouth numb, the spiky vegetables which had restored her taste, the smooth fruit libation poured by the mute slave who had once helped a waif from the south adjust to coastal servant life, even before this Essa had known the night would befuddle her. Just when she needs wit, too.

But it is too soon since she has had the tribal mind of the amnesiac. She can't detach from the magics, take them for granted as a civilized person always should. She has forgotten her sophisticated manners. Everything presses on her senses as if her nerves have been abraded, all the nerve endings exposed to air and light and danger. It's not unreasonable, she supposes, considering where I am. But she hates it nonetheless.

Across the room a woman is watching her. By her black attire she establishes herself in high society; by her wild black hair she shows her disdain for smoothness. Every time Essa looks at her, she is looking back, her eyes knowing Essa more than is comfortable. Essa forces herself time and time again to break the eye contact, to glance away as if casually.

The woman has wide, comfortable hips, a shapely body, and small hands and feet. From the distance across the hall, and in the dim light, her breasts, exposed by the fashionable dress, seem decorated. Is that a new fashion too? Essa glances down involuntarily. She has chosen the most dramatic of the attire presented to her, a form-fitting net of black knit fabric decorated with iridescent overlay like the wings of that saucy bird which scavenges in mountain towns. Her own breasts are bare but for the slight shadow of makeup the dresser applied. She looks up again. The woman is grinning as if she has understood Essa's sudden fashion problem. Essa has to laugh herself, which makes the nobleman close to her turn with a politely questioning look.

"Nothing. I saw something funny," she says.

"You had better not tell me," he says with what she supposes he thinks is wit. "This crowd is partisan. I am too. We defend our friends from even an imagined slight."

"Or even an imagined threat?" Essa is working the crowd automatically, probing for supporters and enemies.

"Most certainly. Have you seen the blooming trees in the garden? My mother told me that your mother particularly loved the garden."

"Yes, so the slaves say."

"Say?"

"They have ways of telling me." She emphasizes the "me" to emphasize her command of the magics necessary to her cause. Though really, the slaves communicate by that fluid and beautiful sign language she has found she knows, and the blow on the head has long since removed her magics. She doesn't know if she'll ever get them back; she doubts it after the years which have apparently passed since she was thrown out of the Black Ship. It was, the returned Essa realizes, the reason for the slave girl's vaguely-remembered terror of the darkness, which the mute slave has confirmed: for the first time in her life she had been unable to call a light at need.

They walk in the garden, and the woman is there. Closer up,

Essa can see that she is definitely not a Land of the Dark Isles person, though where that exotic wild beauty originates she would not be able to say. She walks up to the pair, but speaks not to Essa but to the young man: "Go back into the hall!" He looks at her in startlement.

"You just want to be seen with the princess. Don't be stupid. She doesn't know you and she doesn't care."

It is the first clear speech Essa has heard from any of these people, and she expects the young man to bridle at it, but instead he makes the woman a deep courtesy and without a word turns and strides back through the open doors of the hall.

"You should show me how you do that!" Essa says, but the woman is briskly turning away.

"You, Essa, come with me." It is also the first time anyone has used her name. Essa isn't sure any of them even know it. Surprised, she follows.

They walk through to the other side of the garden, in silence and at a stiff pace. They come to a bower against the wall.

"This was where Annalise came with your mother every day," says the woman, turning. Though they are far from the party, Essa still hears shrill voices, as if she overhears a quarrel at a distance. The woman's breasts are rippling. Essa glances down and sees that each breast holds a woman's face, and they are turned to each other, quarreling in a language she doesn't know.

"Pay them no mind," says the woman. "They have been quarreling for generations, in a way. They are the chieftains of their villages. They are imprisoned there until they make peace."

Essa laughs. "It looks like you will be burdened with them for some time!"

"Yes," says the woman. "I am like you, in a way. For you, two women ride your skull. The woman you were, the woman you weren't. Now, you must become another woman: both, neither, all, any. How will you do it?"

"I don't know," says Essa.

"Nor do I," says the woman, and gestures across her breasts, "any more than I know when these tiresome hags will resolve their battles. But I know it must be soon."

Essa is silent.

"Will you be queen of this country?" says the woman. "And put the despot to death, and free the slaves?"

"Don't think I haven't thought of that," says Essa.

"But . . . ?"

"Would it work?"

"You tell me."

Essa looks around. "This is a beautiful place."

"It was their secret, their hideaway."

"How then do you know of it?"

"I am the Carrier of Spirits. I know what the dead know."

She has heard of this figure of whom the nobles speak with an odd mixture of scorn and fear, of whom the servants sign with awe. She has not expected the Carrier to be so beautiful, so earthy, so . . . human.

"My mother—"

"No, she lives yet; I know her not. Annalise, though, is dead. Long dead. I can hardly remember her memories any more. So many have died since then."

"Did she know where my mother is?"

"They were together when she died. The last thing Annalise heard was your mother's voice."

"Where is she, my mother?"

"It was a long time ago. They were in the south, near a walled village. Annalise never knew the name."

"I will go to find her."

"It was a long time ago. Three hands of years, at least, by the way the sailor folk measure time."

"Do you also hear their dead?"

"Yes, all."

"Is Gata among them, or Lowlyn? Is the daughter there that Gata would bear?"

"No. None of them. Gata's bitter other-mother left a bad taste some two years ago."

"A bad taste?"

"They do taste bad, those. I don't have to like all I remember."

"Do you know all of history then?"

"I know what has happened to all of the dead, and I know what was remembered by the dead Carriers who go before me. I do not know what came before the time of the first Carrier. There was time before then. They had Sin-Eaters then, but the sins were not remembered, and there was nothing for joy. I am glad I don't remember those twisted times."

"The times are pretty twisted here," says Essa, looking around at her mother's sanctuary.

"Yes, it has been even harder for me since I came myself to this land. In my body, I mean. When I lived across the sea, these were just memories. Now I walk among the living people who choose it, keep it going."

"What must I do? What must we do?"

"I can do nothing more than I already do. It is enough to collect the dead, that they may be remembered. Another task would burden me to my own death. As for what you must do—you must make your own life. I will look with interest on your second death when I receive it, to find the answer you found."

"What do you mean, my second death?"

"You are a rarity, Essa. You have already died once, and I have your memories until that death. I have only known of a few twice-dead, and I have never met any of mine. When I was close by here, in the Dark Isles, I thought, I will come and find you. It wasn't easy. There is no ship which will admit to sailing between those Isles and this land which scorns them yet bears their name. Humans are so strange. Now I have seen you. It is odd. You do not look any different. Yet I know you must be. Dying changes a person."

She begins to walk away.

"Wait!" cries Essa.

The woman turns. "I am going to leave this place soon. I cannot wait."

"You have Annalise's memories of my mother," says Essa. "Can you tell me?"

"Perhaps some. I may see you in the palace for the next few days, until I go. But I may not."

She puts her hand up to one breast. The face in it tries to bite her finger, and she laughs. "They quarrel with everything," she says. "They will quarrel with Death herself."

"Are you Death?" says Essa.

"No, simply Memory," says the Carrier. "Death is more grand and beautiful, and her breasts are smooth. When you see her, you want her through your fear, because you know she will take you far and love you best. That is why orgasm is called the Little Death sometimes."

"I do not want her. I want all of life."

"I see that now. But should I meet you in a hundred years— and for your sake, beautiful Essa, I hope it is your full remaining hundred—I will find you changed. Life will have left you, and everyone hates the lover who betrays them." She looks at Essa's face, and laughs. "Your expression!" she says. "It's precious! You must forgive me, for I am too filled with memories of dying to have the same innocence with which the living are blessed. I envy you sometimes, but it is a long time since my own life and death were all I had to concern me."

"Are you the only Carrier?"

"Yes, that I know. If there are others, they carry people of whom I know nothing, people who have never met the lifeweb I record. It is an interesting philosophical question. Could another lifeweb exist, and never overlap? You have given me something with which to amuse myself for a long time. Thank you!"

She steps swiftly back and hugs Essa quickly, an unexpected touch and surprising after all this time of the limited touch of these repressed people. Perhaps for that reason, the touch seems to cut through Essa's protective, insulating cocoon. As the Carrier walks away, Essa watches her sensual, relaxed stride. Just before she turns a crook in the path, the woman throws her hair back from her face and shakes it down her back, then looks back to Essa and waves. Essa smiles and waves back and the woman disappears.

Annalise's life, all those memories of her mother. Suddenly Essa wants to run after the Carrier, hold her, make her tell Annalise's whole story. But it is too late. She can only hope she does indeed find the woman in the labyrinth of the palace before she goes away. Or maybe not, thinks Essa, and laughs. Then she sits down in her mother's sanctuary and falls asleep.

Escape-from-bondage suddenly pulls his hands away to sign. =Is it true I can ask for what I want?=

"Of course," says Essa.

=Then stop. Leave me alone.=

Bewildered, she sits up and looks down at him. He pulls back on the bed, looking surprisingly young for someone of his bulk and age.

"What's the matter?"

=You are not Fierce-frightened.=

"No, I am Essa. But that was not supposed to make a difference."

=It does.=

"I don't understand."

=You are someone who has everything. You can have me if you want. It's in the rules. I can't refuse.=

"Yes, you can. Of course you can."

=Not any more. You are the princess. Once you take your power, you will be the queen and you will own everything in this country. Including me.=

Horrified, Essa backs up even further. "But I am not—but it makes no difference to me!"

=It makes a difference to me.= He has slow tears rolling down his cheeks. He pulls one swift, almost furtive hand up to rub them away.

=I loved Fierce-frightened,= he says. =But she is gone.=

"I'm sorry too," says Essa. Unsure what else to do, she stands up and hands him his robe. "I didn't understand. I wanted a friend. I thought I knew how to do that. I used to know."

=It doesn't work here,= he says, then pulls his robe on.

"I guess not," she says.

=Different languages, she always said,= he signs slowly.

"What?"

=Different languages can't say the same things. Use the same sounds for different things. That kind of thought. She used to get lessons from an old woman who lived in a cage in the south. The old woman told her all about words. It used to make her head ache, you know.=

"You told me," says Essa. He is making an intense effort not to show her how upset he is, but his signs are sloppy, like slurred speech. Her heart is breaking for him, as she used to read in the old books, but it really feels like that. She reaches out, but realizes she should not touch him again.

"Could you maybe tell me about her, sometimes?" she asks. "You're the only one who really knew me when I was her. I can't remember. That's what makes my head hurt. So how can I know anything she knew?"

=You don't need to know the life of a slave. You need to learn new things, to be the queen.=

"I will never learn to be the queen," she says, and suddenly knows it is true. "I could never learn enough, and if I did, I would kill myself from shame. Look what I almost did to you, just from wanting something."

=Wanting is dangerous here,= he replies, as gentle with her, it seems to her, as she is feeling toward him.

"I'm sorry," she says again. "I am so lonely."

=Everyone is lonely,= he says. =It's the way things are.=

"You weren't lonely with her, were you?"

=Yes, certainly. Nothing changes that. That's not what we were doing it for.=

"What were you—no, I'm sorry, I shouldn't ask you that."

=No, I will tell you what she said. It was a slave rebellion,= he says.

"What?"

=It was a slave rebellion. That was what it was for.=

"And now," says Essa slowly, "you too are rebelling."

He looks at her, surprised and on guard.

"You are afraid, but you remain honest. That is against the rules too, isn't it?"

He nods, smiles slightly. =She was wise,= he signs regretfully, his hands still shaky.

"If she ever comes back in me," says Essa, "would you believe it? Would you be able to see it?"

He shrugs.

"If it happens, what will you do?" she presses him.

=If it happens,= he replies, but she can see that now he can hardly hold his hands steady enough to sign, =if it happens, I will think of something.=

"Please—" She turns away to the window, to give him privacy for his fear, then must turn back because she has to see him if he replies. "If I ever give you an order, don't obey it. For the sake of the slave rebellion."

=I think I can maybe do that,= he says, =but if I can't, you will have to forgive me.=

"As Fierce-frightened would have done."

=No. She would have understood by her nature. She lived her whole life in my world. You just got here.=

And he goes out, closing the door gently behind him. Then he opens it again. =Lock the door,= he signs. =The regent walks late.= And he is gone.

She locks her door and lies down, but she does not sleep, and dawn comes after a while.

Life in the zone of control (5)

She sees the Carrier in the garden. As she gets closer, she realizes that the big man with whom the Carrier talks is Escape-from-bondage. His hands are flying, but she can't read his conversation through the branches and the Carrier's shoulder. She feels a tension in her belly, moves closer quietly, thinking to eavesdrop, but before she can, she sees Escape-from-bondage lean over and kiss the Carrier on the lips. She hears the peal of laughter from the Carrier as the two draw apart. Essa feels a fistful of connectors pull and twist in her belly. It is envy, she realizes, but she does not know, she thinks with a start, which one she envies most. The Carrier pats Escape-from-bondage's face, her hands symmetrically arranged on either side of his cheeks, and he smiles, turns and slips away with that preternatural lightness which is to Essa the big man's chief identifying characteristic. When Essa comes down the path into the Carrier's view, the woman is sitting on the bench in the sunlight, the blue highlights in her raven hair gleaming almost like the sea, or like black wine in a clear Sailor Town goblet.

As Essa remembers that, and the ravens of home, without thinking she touches the Carrier's hair, then draws back, blushing. "I'm sorry! I wasn't thinking."

"Your head is slower than your hands, these days. I imagine it is because you have the injury," and the Carrier reverses Essa's gesture, one of those small hands touching Essa's head where the scars lie under her hair. Essa shivers in the sunlight, draws back surprised not at the touch but at the shiver.

As she moves away, the Carrier's hand drops, but the sensation of touch does not go away. It is as if the Carrier has attached one of those invisible strands such as Essa has just felt in her belly, this one to the point where the woman's hand made its contact, and as she moves away the connector stretches into something thin as a hair which binds Essa to the woman irrevocably.

Essa backs away, thinking in one part, I am being rude, but unable to do more than say, "Excuse me, I'll see you later, I hope, I must go, excuse me," before she is safely behind the screen of bushes. She brushes with her hand at her head, as if to dislodge a spiderweb with which she had collided on a run through the woods of home. The thread will not brush away. As she gets further away from the Carrier it is easier to ignore. But it is not gone.

Essa dreams of the Carrier of Spirits' breasts. She dreams she cups them in her hands, and the tiny women imprisoned there bite her fingers. That's what happens when you try to fuck the gods, she says to the Carrier, they fuck you a little too. The woman's laugh wakes her up into a pearlized pre-dawn, unable to sleep again. She gets up with that sense she has had all day of being tied to the Carrier with a thin silk thread, and goes looking for the woman's room, thinking she knows exactly where it is.

Escape-from-bondage is in the corridor outside her room. In this dreamy state, that doesn't seem strange. She uses the sign language to ask him where the Carrier lives, and he points up along the thread, as if he can see it. She feels still asleep. He makes a sign =Careful!= but she doesn't understand until she hears the footsteps and looks up to see the despot pacing ahead of her down the long, elaborately decorated corridor toward the east wing.

He has not heard her. She stops, and looks to either side for an escape, feeling like she is still inside the dream world where nightmare surfaces without warning. Why does she feel so frightened of this man? Don't fuck the despot, says a voice in her mind, in the mountain language, and she shivers. It is as if the shiver transmits itself down the stone floor of the corridor. The man stops, looks to either side, but not far enough back to see her. As he turns she steps into a doorway, in the umbral zone where he is out of sight and so must she be to him. She presses back against the door behind her, hearing his footsteps as he turns and begins to pace back toward her. The panic in her seems tangible now. If he catches her—what? She strains against the door, one hand behind her twisting the knob in desperate slow silence. But there is a bolt, it seems, which holds it locked. She feels the sweat stand out all over her body. The dream thread suddenly pulls her, the door opens, she is pulled inside and the door is quietly closed again, a bolt sliding home almost silently, with only the tiniest *snick* to her preternaturally stimulated hearing.

She stands in total darkness, then hands guide her to turn and go farther into the—room? Bedroom, she realizes, as she is stopped by the edge of a high bed. The hands are small which touch her. Then she is left without touch, and in a moment a dim light begins to glow. The Carrier of Spirits stands over the lamp, her face cast into dramatic shadow by the light from below.

The Carrier is still wearing her party gown—Essa supposes the woman attended the banquet Essa had avoided the night before—though she is barefoot, the high filigree-leather boots lying on the fur rug beside the bed, and she has brushed most of the glitter out of her hair. Essa looks involuntarily at the beautifully-shaped breasts—she has not seen them since the night of the party, in the garden. Tonight they are plain. The quarreling women are gone. The Carrier follows her glance, laughs.

"Oh yes. They go away. It would be too much otherwise. I'd never get a moment to myself."

Taken off guard, Essa giggles. She thinks of a strange thing: "you are crazy," she says almost unconsciously, "and I think you are the most frightening dream I have ever had, but I like you."

The Carrier laughs. "You are double-minded," she says. "And not like they mean in the southland. Your poor grandmother."

"Who?"

"Your mother's mother. She looked south all day."

"Why?"

"It was the only place she was ever happy. She was so damaged. People who exploit other people's bodies also steal their souls, in a way. I heard one of my dead say that, once, and I think it awful wise."

"Damaged?"

"The old woman whose portrait hangs in the hall made a collection of them, her relatives. In the end she had them killed. I have all the generations of them now, except your mother. And the beginning of you, of course, but you are not like them. It is hard sometimes."

"I don't understand what you are talking about."

The Carrier comes to her and takes her hand. "Sit down," she says. "Little one."

Considering that Essa could look down on the top of the woman's head, into the curiously vulnerable-seeming parting of the long dark hair, she thinks it rather presumptuous to be called little one.

"It's what your father called you," says the Carrier. "And your mother too, but I just have him."

"Do you read my mind?"

"No, only your face. You will have to learn to control your face in this place or you won't last long enough to do any good."

"I don't know what good I can do," says Essa. "I have been waiting to try to find out. It doesn't seem to be working. I just feel smaller every day."

"Well, that's a start," says the Carrier approvingly.

The face forms slowly, like a freeze-frame depiction of a boil growing. The skin over the Carrier's cheekbone points, swells, and then, as the nostrils and mouth open, breaks. The eyes are still unformed, giving the protoface a blind, mutant appearance. Essa finds the formation nauseous to watch. She looks away but it is worse not to watch, to imagine only. She turns her head back in time to see the eyelids drawn like a line, then the eyelashes spider out from that line, and finally the eyes open. They fix on Essa without surprise.

"Hello, child," the face says. "Are you one of mine?"

Essa flicks her gaze to the Carrier's eyes, violently out of scale above the face. The shift makes her even more queasy.

"What do I do?" she says, and swallows bile.

"Just talk to her. Ask her questions. She is dead, you know. She won't recognize you again. She never knew you."

"One of mine? What does that mean?" Essa asks the Carrier, but it is the strangely serene face which answers.

"You have the look of Eka, but more of her brat. But your hair color—that's not in our line. If I've missed one of mine I should be making plans for you."

"Doesn't she have any sense?" says Essa, rather wildly.

"No," says the Carrier. "She is transparent now. I told you to remember she is dead."

"Who is Eka?" says Essa.

"My daughter," says the face, and spits dry to the side. Essa sees the skin of the Carrier's cheek stretch on one side, wrinkle on the other as the face turns.

"And who is her brat?"

"Eka's whelp. With him."

"Him?"

"My son. The fool. I should have killed him at birth too, like the others."

"Tell me about your life," says Essa, shivering.

"What's to tell? It was a life. That nephew of mine finished me off too early. I had plans for that whelp. But I hadn't found her yet. Her and her slave sister. They would have made a nice matched pair once I broke them."

Essa thinks that the sweet, unlined face could have been the face of any of the old women who tell stories at the midsummer fest in the Fjord of Tears. The woman is smiling slightly, looking like she is entertaining visitors for an afternoon chat. Essa says, horrified, "Did you really talk like that when you were alive? Did you really say those things?"

"Who will stop me? I can do anything I want. My father taught me that. Not that he knew everything."

"Who was your father?"

"They said he was a Dark Isles man, but that was just the people trying to make trouble for him. We never let anybody through that blockade. He was from the south. He had scads of relatives down there.

"I remember they deposed his father-in-law for the slave training. He had sailor fertility tech and he started making slave triplets, male and female sets from the same sire and dam, for sex shows. The people were outraged. Only the royal family could fuck family. But after they killed him they put my zombie mother on the throne, and my father had been the king's catamite for years. That's how he earned my mother. So he turned around and killed the upstarts, hung them up to drip-dry themselves in the square. And he lobotomized the slave sets and put them in a compound to breed.

"It took me a while to get the throne. I had three sisters and two brothers before me, and they took a while to kill. By that time there were three generations in that compound. I think there were thirty-two graves and fifty-seven of them living, forty-one fertile and fourteen of those pregnant."

"What kind of story is this?" Essa asks the Carrier. She and the face reply almost in unison. "The kind of story I carry," says the Carrier, and the face says, "The kind of story that will teach you how to go on. Pay attention. All of mine have to learn the right way to go on."

"And what will I learn from this?"

"That the old man was a fool. I remember how I felt when I saw that compound full of mutants, misshapen, rolling around in their own shit, and fucking with those little mindless grunts and cries. Most of them had the scars on their foreheads, and I thought, yes, he was a fool, my father. I can make people with minds do this. I don't have to have them bred stupid and crazy and skewered if they're not. He was weak, but I won't be that weak. That was when I started training my own little stud. My nephew. He was a good learner."

"Good enough to kill you."

"Am I dead? I suppose I am. That's what you say. I can't seem to recall that. I can remember him killing me though. Fucking me to death. It was interesting, really. I'd done it to slaves, but it was the one thing I'd never felt myself, of course. I suppose you only get to feel it once. What happened then?"

"Where did you come from? Where did a creature like you come from?" cries Essa, repelled.

"Out of my brain-dead mother, of course. My grandfather had the idea my father used on the slaves. Stick that skewer in the brain. He didn't need her brain. Didn't I just show you that? It's better if they don't think. Look at Eka and that son, what thinking did for them. They called him 'Styn, can you imagine? Means 'fair' or 'even-handed' or some stupid thing, in south-talk. Imagine. Bloody fools. I did for them, though. I saw them burn. It was something, to see them burn."

"It was strange to burn," says another, a dreamy voice. Essa starts. Without her noticing, another face has formed, this one on the Carrier's smooth left shoulder. The eerie resemblance of the two faces to each other, and to Essa herself, terrifies Essa. She does not want to be of the line of this casual murderess who boasts of her crimes, and this new face has even more of the same strange detachment.

"It was the last thing I remember," says the face. "What happened then?"

"Never mind," says Essa, at the same time as the top face says, "I took the throne back, Eka, you fool. Did you think you could keep me away from it, with the child gone and my protégé made your heir? It was a mistake you made: you should have ruled, yourself."

"Yes, mother, it certainly was," says Eka. "But I didn't want to, and we were thinking that his greed would outweigh his loyalty."

"Well, you were wrong."

"I see that," says Eka, still sounding like she speaks from a drug dream. "The men came at sunset. I had been looking toward the south all day. It was one of my bad days. That means I'd been drink-

ing all day, you know," she says confidentially to Essa. "He understood, I know he understood. He was always very sweet. Of course,
I wasn't an obnoxious drunk. And he did have that woman if he
needed her. He could afford to be sweet.

"It feels strange to be telling it this way. I think I must be dead,
but it doesn't really show in my voice. Where am I? Let me stay dead.
I don't like it out here. It's small and crowded."

"Yes, you are dead, it's all right," says Essa, curiously moved to
comfort this frail-voiced shade.

"Yes, I think I like being dead. You never get hungry. I hated
eating. It made me real. 'Styn was always telling me I was too thin,
but it was hard enough to exist at all, even as a shadow. I don't know
how I managed to be pregnant, when I think of it. I was so gross.
Huge. Like his slave woman. I wanted to be dead, but I was afraid
to die. Isn't that silly? And in the end, when we did die, it wasn't so
bad. But I hadn't expected it to be by burning."

"You deserved it," says the upper face scornfully. "And I enjoyed watching. The only time I ever saw you on fire about anything—" she cackles, then sobers into disgust, "—except that over-
protected little wimp of a child of yours. I made you burn, all right!"

"It was strange to burn, mother. It was strange how when we
held each other, 'Styn and I, our bodies protected our hearts. We
lived a long time. Much longer than you thought, I believe. I saw
you turn away, you know. It was the last thing I saw. I opened my
eyes and of course the fire took them just after I looked at you going.
After you've burned a while," she said to Essa, "you don't feel
much. I guess the nerves just burn away."

"It's different, hanging," says a third voice. "Hanging hurts the
whole time."

"Who are you?" says Essa to the face that has replaced the Carrier's left nipple, but she knows the answer.

"Annalise. Who are you?"

"Essa."

"No, you aren't. Essa's a child, seven, eight. How old are you?"

"I grew up since you died."

But Annalise seems not to retain that, returns to what she can
remember. "The crows peck at you," she says. "Eyes they like particularly. Soft, I guess. They're very experienced, the crows in the
south. I had to keep blinking to keep them away. Not that I could
see much after a while. And your mother was chained up underneath, where I couldn't see her. I could hear her, though, talking

to me. She said she loved me. Isn't that odd? I knew it, but to hear her saying it, over and over, out in public like that, it wasn't like her."

"Perhaps," says Essa, her voice catching in her dry mouth, "she wasn't quite herself at the time. It must be a bit . . . upsetting . . . to see your friend hanged."

"Friend, lover, sister. All of them. Sometimes I wish F. had liked Jed. The sailors sleep all together in one bed, you know, like puppies."

"I know," says Eka, dreamily. "I heard about it from the genetics tech. She said they touched all the time. 'Styn and I slept in the same bed. Everyone thought we were perverts. And we are," she says proudly, "we are."

"They're perverts in the south," says Annalise. "Don't touch each other. Not even their babies."

"Perverts," says the cheekbone face. "Wouldn't beat their daughter, wouldn't fuck her. Didn't I teach them anything?"

"What's your name?" says Essa to the arrogant old woman.

"Eg-ha," she says.

"Eka," says the shoulder face at the same time. "Annalise," says the breast face, as if she doesn't remember having just said so. Essa supposes she doesn't. After all, it is life which creates memory. She will remember this night too long, she thinks then, looking at the faces. They are such parodies of life, real and unreal, that she is dizzy with disgust.

"Take them away!" she says to the Carrier, bending over the cramps in her belly. Suddenly, without warning, she is vomiting on the fur rug at her feet. She can't stand any more. She holds herself up against the high mattress on the bed, the acrid smell of bile making her retch again and again.

"Take them away," she gasps, spitting, nose running bile.

"Are you sure you want that?" says the Carrier.

"Can they . . . come back . . . any time?"

"It's hard work," says the Carrier.

"Can they?"

"If I call them. If I can find them."

"Then take them away, for the moon's sake. I can't . . . I can't . . . "

Blackness presses against her ears and cheekbones with a tangible, sickening pressure, and the room is reeling. Essa crawls blindly up onto the bed, curls around the pain in her belly. With her eyes closed the vertigo abates, but still she has to clutch her arms around herself in a tight hug to keep from vomiting again. She can dimly hear the Carrier folding up the rug and taking it through to the lavatory, hears the water running. The cold cloth on her forehead shocks her and she gives a little cry.

"Shhh, shh," says the Carrier, wiping her face and neck, leaving the cloth on the back of her neck for a moment. The chill steadies the room.

"The dead are stressful companions," says the Carrier, "for mortals."

"And for you?"

"I do not find them . . . particularly restful," says the Carrier. "Myself, I try not to talk with them at all."

"But you remember."

"Yes. That is what I do."

"How . . . can you?" Essa asks thickly. The woman holds a cup of icy water to Essa's lips and she sips, rinsing her mouth clean of bile, swallows with a grimace, sips a clean sip.

"It is what I do," says the Carrier. "I do it. It's not can or can't."

"Who elected you? What made you the lucky one?" whispers Essa hoarsely.

"I can't remember any more," says the woman. "It doesn't matter." She takes Essa's chin and turns her face up. Essa screws her eyes tighter shut. She is afraid that the faces are still there. The Carrier takes her hand and touches it to face, shoulder, breast. The skin is smooth.

Essa opens her eyes to the Carrier's smile. She looks like she cares. Essa finds that confusing, considering how relentless she must have to be.

Her hand still rests on the Carrier's breast. It is as soft to the touch as in her dream, but no faces to bite. She has already been bitten enough by the reconstructions of her aunt, grandmother, and great-grandmother. She is grateful the skin is unblemished again, and she surprises herself then as her hand begins tentatively to trace the deep curve under the breast, the gentle slope above the nipple, and then the nipple itself as it begins to rise.

She brings her other hand to the right breast, soft but for a slight grittiness which she realizes is a dusting of the cosmetic glitter brushed out of the Carrier's long hair. It glitters in the dim light, and clings, so her hand sparkles with tiny starpoints when she lifts it to look at it.

She seems the same, if the shape of her hand is any measurement. She touches the smooth breast again, feeling this nipple too rise under her palm. She is still shaken from the experience with the dead, but her hands are expressing a hunger for life—even in this primally reactive state she recognizes the mechanism. And in the same detached part of herself, she feels immensely presumptuous. But the small hand of the Carrier comes up to cup her face, and the woman bends to kiss her at the notch where neck meets shoulder.

"I have been waiting," she says, "for that. For this."

"Since the faces?"

"Since the garden."

Essa is glad she is sitting down already, for in the dizzy wave of desire she now feels, she would have surely fallen if she had to stand. The Carrier takes her hands away to undo the fastenings of the black gown. It falls away from her body. The skin is as smooth as on her breasts all along her body; how young her skin for one who must be so ancient, Essa thinks.

The small hands then reach for Essa's wrap and pull the belt undone. As it opens, the woman kisses her mouth, and pushes her back on the bed. Essa pulls her arms free of the sleeves and holds her hungrily.

"How old are you?" she says when her mouth is free. "What is your name? Are you a god?"

"I don't know," says the woman. "Older than you can imagine. I've forgotten my name. I've taken in so many names. What will you call me for the night? None of the names you know. Someone I have never been. That would be good."

All the time her insistent hands roving across Essa's shoulders, breasts, sides and belly, teasing at her, never going quite to the groin until Essa moans with frustration. Then the woman laughs.

"You are too fast, little one."

"Don't call me that," says Essa thickly. "You are the little one. Barely reach my chin."

"Except lying down," says the woman. "Everyone's the same height lying down."

Essa under the Carrier's hands is filled with an almost unbearable languor. But she thinks, with that tiny ironic corner of her mind still left functioning, that she will bear it. Oh yes. Indeed. She finds it, overall, quite bearable. She chuckles in her throat.

"Do your worst, little one," she says. "I am ready for you." Which, she suspects, is on some level she will find out later patently untrue. But never mind.

"I am ready for you too," says the woman, taking Essa's hand from her hip and pulling it to her vagina, to show her as proof the dense moisture there.

"You are a. Most. Interesting. Creature," says Essa carefully, at intervals.

"Yes, I suspect so. By now," says the Carrier, her voice sounding almost abstract. But under her fingers Essa feels a ripple through the woman's belly, strong and dark and deep. One makes a throaty sound of appreciation, and it is echoed by the other. Essa pulls the woman down to her, and rolls her over until Essa kneels above her, hands reaching into her, mouth on her breast. If one of those faces comes out, she thinks, it will be a powerful strange thing. But nothing happens except another rise of that inexplicable dizziness, like no sexual response Essa remembers ever feeling. The Carrier laughs again, and pulls Essa down, rolls again until she is above and Essa lies spread across the bed. And after that she thinks nothing coherent for quite a long time.

Essa wakes frightened and gasping from a dream of faces. "What did my mother look like?" she was screaming in the dream.

"Shh, shhh," says the Carrier's accented voice, and she sits up abruptly.

"What was I doing?" she says. "Fucking you like that. What on earth?"

"You are a passionate woman," says the Carrier. "Death takes you that way. You wanted to do the same thing with Gata, didn't you, after the day in the square? And you'd just met her."

"How did you kn—. Oh."

"Yes. When you died? You remember dying, don't you?"

"I think so."

"Yes. I remember your dying too."

"I don't want you to have my life!" says Essa with sudden anger, pulling the pillow from under her head and throwing it across the room. It knocks over a bottle of perfume on the dressing table shelf and a heavy musk flashes through the air around them.

"Very effective," says the Carrier. "Of course you don't. And I'm not sure I want it. But there it is. In with the rest."

"Another thing stolen," she says.

"Life is a thief," says the Carrier. "It's inevitable."

"Like this? Violence and perversity?" Essa means the palace around them.

"Sometimes. In my memory, violence and perversity more than you can imagine."

"I'm sure," says Essa, gloomily and sulkily. The Carrier laughs.

"Poor little mountain girl," she says throatily, and reaches out to run her hands down Essa's body. The same dizzying desire chokes Essa again. She shoves the hand away roughly.

"When you fuck with the gods," she says furiously, "they fuck with you too."

"I am not a god, little one," says the Carrier. "I am just Carrier."

"Little one," says Essa, and launches herself furiously at the tiny laughing figure, not sure what chokes her now: rage, impotence, desire, fear. The little woman is strong enough despite her size to match Essa.

"It will turn into sex whether you want it to be death or not," she says, grasping Essa's wrists firmly, hardly sounding stressed.

"How could I want it to be death?" says Essa, still fighting.

"You can't kill your past," says the Carrier, holding Essa's hands aside easily.

"I can't fuck it into oblivion either," says Essa, and throws herself backward, away from the contact. The Carrier comes after her gently, takes her hands, and strokes the red marks on the wrists with her thumbs. The heat spreads.

"You can love where you want," she says, "with permission. That's all you need."

"Do you know about Escape-from-bondage?" says Essa, surprised. The Carrier looks vaguely puzzled. "What?" she says, and runs her hands up Essa's arms to stroke the inside of her elbows. Her touch is absolutely symmetrical. Then she sits, her hands still on Essa's forearms, and waits.

Essa has to clear her throat to speak. As if the heavy musk which now permeates the air of the room is smothering her. "What do you want?"

"Permission," says the Carrier.

"Yes," says Essa, opening. "For this time."

"Enough to get on with," says the Carrier, and pulls Essa off balance, so she falls against the woman's body—and the tide takes her. Long afterward, hours later, when her orgasm knifes through her like an electric current, and she feels the violent ejaculatory gush spurt against the Carrier's hand, she cries out, "What do you want? Are you trying to get the rest of me now too?"

"Shhh, shhh," the Carrier says against her hair, holding her as she sobs. "You are safe, little one. I will have that soon enough. I am not interested in that. This is real. This is safe."

"And you read my mind," Essa says, "along with everything else." Her head aches suddenly, a pang as sharp as the orgasm had been.

"No," says the Carrier, "I read your body." Her small hands, stroking, take the pain, then calm her, and Essa, drifting, chooses sleep over fear.

"No relationship in this place is completely safe," says the Carrier. "I am the best for which you can hope."

Essa laughs. "What am I to do, then?"

The Carrier shows her characteristic boredom at such a question. "Whatever you want," she says, and walks ahead of Essa through the door, leaving Essa speechless and still standing, thinking, it's that simple, is it? And realizing that yes, it is that simple.

"But you haven't shown me any more of Annalise, or of my grandmother, or of the old woman!"

"I couldn't do that now," says the Carrier. "It would be . . . unprofessional."

Essa begins to laugh, an edge of hysteria in it, and her head hurting more.

"I can't believe you said that," she says. "Unprofessional?"

"Certainly," says the woman seriously. "I can't use it as part of a personal relationship, it would be—"

"Don't give me that," says Essa angrily. "You didn't give me the choice of sex or reruns. You took me when I was exhausted from watching my history all over your body. Do you think it's professional to entice with it, to capture a partner, but once you have her you deny her what everyone else is given freely? If you'd given me the choice, I'd have chosen my history."

"You think so?" asks the Carrier, and Essa can't read whether the tone is arrogant or ingenuous. Whatever, Essa feels an edge of the powerful darkness which always engulfs her with the Carrier's touch. Angrily, she turns away, but she is still conscious of the woman like a retinal afterimage. After all, now Essa is linked in that strange way she has been since the night she first went to the Carrier's room—no, before that, since the touch in the garden—and now knows where the Carrier is wherever Essa is.

"I think so," says Essa, "no matter what this magic is you have, no matter what you've done to me."

"What do you mean? I have done nothing," says the Carrier.

"Except bind me to you," says Essa bitterly.

There is a long silence. Essa feels the Carrier move toward her, and braces herself to resist touch. But the woman only walks around her to stand in front and look into Essa's face. She looks, and Essa looks away, until finally she can't bear it and turns her eyes back to meet the Carrier's gaze. Immediately she is drowning again.

"It's not magic," says the Carrier. "It's love."

"I loved other people," says Essa, preventing herself from saying instead, how would you know? "It wasn't like this."

"They were convenient," says the Carrier. "I saw you, remember? They were way stations."

Essa opens her mouth to protest, then stops. She looks down and knows she is blushing. She sees the Carrier nod, and looks back again, compelled to danger.

"But I'm a way station for you," she says. "You are leaving without a glance back."

"I will look back," says the Carrier. "But."

"But?"

The Carrier shrugs with a strange resignation Essa would almost call despairing if she were in the mood to concede anything. "I am old," the woman says finally. "You are young, and will die sooner. It may as well be now as later."

"I could die of this," Essa says.

"Of course you could," says the woman. "The best do. We should all hope for it."

"For what?"

"To die of love. But not for a long time."

At her words Essa imagines a long lifetime of loving, filling up her skin until she can hold no more, lying down old, full and content when her next century is over. The Carrier smiles, and Essa's heart turns over.

"I always thought that was a cliché," she says. "You know, 'his heart moved within him at the sight of his lover's face.' But it isn't."

"None of them are, if you say them right," says the Carrier. "And you will remember that long after you have forgotten me."

"How could I forget you?"

"I have to go east next," says the Carrier. "East and north. Have you any messages for your kin in the sailor town?"

"I still can't believe it. Leaving? After getting me into this?"

"This?"

"This. This! Don't play stupid."

"I will find them if you like, and tell them you are not dead. What else would you like me to tell them?"

"Oh, you can't, not now," says Essa, finally crying. "Not just now." She sinks down to the floor, sobbing. The woman leans over and, finally, touches her. "Little one."

Essa can't speak.

"Little one, I must. You know I must. It is only for a while. I will receive you when you die, with special love."

"That won't do me any good." Essa struggles through sobs, finds speech, bends it until she can keep hold of it. "It won't be a little while for me. It'll be my life. And when you receive me, I'll be dead. I won't be there to enjoy you in turn. You'll just have a record, you won't have sentience within you. I saw that with those women you showed me. They were just automata, puppets of their own old lives."

"Yes. But I will take you in with sweetness, little one."

"Don't call me that!"

The Carrier laughs and Essa tries to laugh too, but only begins to cry again. The Carrier kneels down beside her, pulls her up and they stand. Unsteadily the woman leads her to the bed, and pushes her down gently. Essa will not let go of her hands, pulls her down alongside. "Lie with me here a while," she says, between escaping hiccups of sobs. "And I will . . . I will tell you what to tell my old family."

"Are you going back?" says the Carrier.

"I think not," says Essa. "I don't think so. I am not any more the one who was their handfast partner."

The Carrier smiles, and Essa looks at her beloved face, so close, so deep, to fall into forever, and says, "Did they feel like this?"

"I don't know," says the Carrier. "They aren't dead yet."

Life in the zone of control (6)

The room is very hot and stuffy and Essa feels inclined to doze off. She shakes herself awake unobtrusively, shifts in her seat. She sits beside the languid nobleman from the party in the garden, at what is clearly the fulcrum of the circle of chairs. If that's the way to describe it, she thinks sleepily; though it is a circle there is a definite focus point and she is almost in it.

Almost. The talking is being done by the two people on Essa's other side, the saturnine woman with the light hair and heavy expression, and the thin, intense, hollow-faced man beside her. The nobleman at her right hand seems proud to have her there, but when he tries to speak he is cut off by one of the controlling two with a kindness bordering on the patronizing. Deflated, he sits back in his chair with a sulky attempt to look like he doesn't mind. Essa grins, and he interprets her grin as support and puffs himself up again. She stops smiling immediately, with a horrified pang of understanding. Everything she does in this company has more power than she thought. Everything she does in this country.

It is because she is the heir. Her headaches keep her forgetting that, for her own safety, but it is not safe to forget it either.

The princess. The thought of course makes her head hurt, and the heat and pain make her dizzy. The room begins to spin, and suddenly a cold sweat stands out over her whole body, fighting with the heat-responsive perspiration already soaking her underarms, back, and the fold under her breasts. She leans forward with her forearms resting along her thighs, and puts her forehead into her hands. Her hands are clammy and sweating and there is no relief in their pressure against her equally-clammy forehead.

The thin man looks at her. "Are you all right?"

"No," says Essa, mountain manners, automatic truth, then shakes her head slowly and sits up. "I'll be fine," she says. "It's hot. When does the discussion start?"

"Discussion?"

"You invited me to a discussion group. It's very interesting, what you two have said, but I'm interested in the others too." She turns to the circle. "Who you are, you know. What you think."

"Yes, yes, all in good time," says the woman.

The young nobleman is sitting up straighter. "Yes, I've prepared some remarks," he says.

The woman speaks over his voice. "All in good time. First, we establish the theoretical base. There is no sense in getting ahead of ourselves."

"I'm not sure I understand just what this theoretical base is for," says Essa. She sees that the woman is impatient whenever she talks, but doesn't want to interrupt her. Across the circle, another woman speaks shyly.

"I think it's more a matter of exploration," she says. "Nobody wants to commit themselves until they know what they're committing to."

"Committing to?" Essa says. "What exactly is it you are discussing, then?"

The faces in the circle have, for a moment, a comically similar expression, as if they are all in a lookalike game. Finally the thin man says, "It's hardly a matter of commitment. Just theoretical discussion. You know, options, hypothetical models, projections, applications. A way of generating ideas. Simply put, a way of conceptualizing alternative modal response."

Essa manages not to grin again. "And what do you want from me?"

"Oh, if you support us . . . " says the hapless nobleman, even as the man and woman on her left, in eerie unison, say, "Nothing really. Nothing."

"Just to be part of the discussion," says the conciliatory woman across the circle.

Essa's head begins to throb again. "I suppose," she says, slowly, "having a princess in the room is useful. Unfortunately, you have come to the wrong princess. It's hot in here, and I haven't a clue what you're all talking about. Those of you who talk. And my head hurts, and I'm afraid I'll have to be going now."

And picking her way over feet and around chairs, the pain narrowing her vision to a clumsy tunnel, Essa pushes her way out of the circle and to the door. As she opens it she looks back. The thin man is looking at the young noble, and jerking his head toward Essa in an unmistakable command to follow and sheepdog her. The blond, heavy-faced woman grabs his arm as he starts to follow, whispers, "And shut your big mouth." The nobleman's face is sulky.

Essa slips through the door and pulls it shut behind her. The throbbing in her head will not abate. As she runs down the stone-floored corridor, the pounding rhythm alters to keep time with the jarring of her footsteps. She hears the young noble's voice calling her, but hears it through a haze of pain. The last thing she wants is his solicitous sycophancy. She chooses a side corridor at random, and dekes sideways into a servants' stair. It takes her down into a level she doesn't remember, but seems to be able to negotiate as long as the pain clouds her vision and she doesn't think too much. Finally, however, it hurts too much to keep running, and she stops, sinks down, and rests. She discovers as she wipes her wet face that she has been weeping too, as well as sobbing for breath. Her vision begins to clear, and she realizes she has no idea where she is. She is alone in some sub-corridor, lost, and shivering with the evaporation of sweat into the cool underground air.

A woman, a slave, is walking by. She stares at Essa with—is it fear? "I'm sick," says Essa, half-standing, reaching out. "I need help." She signs Escape-from-bondage's name. The woman's eyes widen and she runs away. Essa sinks back down, and fatigue and post-pain exhaustion descend on her.

Is it soon, or half an hour, before Escape-from-bondage comes to get her? She can't tell. She follows his gentle-handed guidance back to her suite, where he tucks her into bed. Almost before he has gone out, leaving the door locked behind him, she has fallen asleep.

=But you are my friend. She is my friend,= says Essa in the hand language.

=She is your lover. She is a carrier of souls. I am your slave. You have no friends here in the Land of the Dark Isles.= Escape-from-bondage is impatient, angry—and curiously formal.

=You keep telling me that,= Essa replies.

=Until you listen,= he says, using the sign which also means =pay attention.=

=You have my attention,= she says. =I have paid. What more tests?=

=There is something left,= he answers. =Don't ask me. Ask the old man. Ask the nobles. You know the one you like? The shy one?= He doesn't wait for her nod. =He likes to beat me, and he likes to suck me. A strange combination. I hardly ever get that, any more especially.= He grins, a grin she doesn't like, and bulks up his adult body a little, a kind of all-over expansion she has seen in animals facing off at the edge of their adjoining territories, in the mountains. He is not doing it at her, however, merely amusing himself: he gives a sharp bark: his laughter, that repulsive and eviscerating sound. She shudders.

"Maybe," she says, "I have never had any friends."

=That is likely,= he signs, =from my experience in the world. But you would know best. You are the one who has lived your life.=

"Some of it," she says.

He laughs again.

He has such good manners, she thinks, that I forget. I forget that he has been alive in a different world than the one in which I grew up. And I forget everything about how it was when I was alive in his world.

I forget everything he tries to teach me.

She shakes her head in wonder. It has begun to ache, of course, but that isn't the point.

=The universe,= he signs, as if reading her mind, =has treated me much differently than it has treated you.=

She can't decide whether anger, grief or irony fuels this comment. Whichever, it is the deepest thing she has ever seen him say.

The deepest thing, anyway, that Essa has seen him say, she revises herself.

"Tell me how I can find that kid. That young noble we were talking about," she asks Escape-from-bondage.

=The one from the meeting yesterday?=

"Yes," she says, though she knows he knows perfectly well.

=He's with—= the sharp sign which means the despot.

Essa does not like to spend any more time with the despot than she has to, but she has the courage of the Carrier's touch in her belly now, for all the Carrier has sailed away, and she goes down the corridors to the offices, thinking that she can probably wait outside until the lad is done. The lad? He must be her age, chronologically, yet she feels like his grandmother in some weary way she can hardly quantify. He seems—naïve, yes, but also unformed.

She thinks of what Escape-from-bondage had said about the kid—she realizes wryly that provisionally, until she knows his name, she'll carry on thinking of him that way—that he likes to beat the slave, and go down on him. That doesn't make the lad seem less naïve, maybe even more so. It proves that he believes in privilege, believes what he has been told is his. Has never asked questions, even in the circuitous way of the people at yesterday's "discussion group."

Remembering their circumlocutions, Essa snorts. A startled slave shies back against the wall. Essa feels the stab of pain through her temple that she always feels, along with the gut-level distress, at the servants' fear. The juxtaposition of her previous thoughts with this confrontation with fear is suddenly sensible: Essa realizes that the nobles have the same set of reflexes, but theirs are verbal and mannerly. She walks faster. She has not been sure until this moment, but now she knows she will try to help the group in their "questioning." Maybe it can make a difference, make a stand against the despot and the generational evil he represents.

Finding the lad becomes more urgent, and indeed, she sees him leaving the regent's suite of offices. She hurries to catch up with him. He is smiling slightly.

"Hello," she says. "I wanted to talk with you."

"We'll go get some wine," he says. "I want to celebrate."

"Celebrate what?"

"I got something out of the old man that I've wanted for a long time," he says smugly. "Finally I gave him satisfaction."

"Satisfaction?"

"You know!" he says, and wipes his middle finger around his wet lower lip suggestively. "Satisfaction. I'm pretty good, I guess."

"Well," she says, surprising herself with her acerbity, "you've been practicing on the servants. You should have learned something."

"Oh, that," he says. "I don't mean that. I always do that to him. I mean the meeting."

"The meeting?"

"The people yesterday. It was the first time I'd been invited. They have it where there are no screens, you know. Halfway to the slave pit. But I finally got in."

"Finally?" She feels like one of those small mammals the sailors keep on their ships, which learn to echo human words and repeat everything you say in their presence. The lad talks on, unaware of her perturbation.

"Well, it took a year, but you helped, you know, talking with me at the party like that, out in the garden. They wanted you on their side. And I must admit, I wondered which way you wanted it, yourself. After all, if you win you'll be the one to please, and he won't be around to give me a reference!" and he laughs loudly, and repeats the gesture with finger and lip, a particularly repulsive little mannerism, Essa thinks.

"So I helped you, by talking with you, and then what happened?"

"Well, when you left the room in the middle, I knew what you must mean, so I went to the old man first thing. And this morning, here we are."

"—Eh?—"

"And there they are," and he gestures to his right, to a solid stone wall. She shakes her head. "I forget," he says. "You're new here." He makes some contact with the wall and it shifts—eerie, like the Carrier's skin when a face is coming out—to a view of the balcony where she regained her memory. Another touch, and they walk through the wall onto that balcony.

Her eyes dazzle. She takes the dark glasses out of her pouch and puts them on, hoping the stab of light will not bring pain with it for the rest of the day, as glare so often did. She follows the lad to the edge of the balcony, and they lean against the rail.

"There," he says, and gestures down.

She squints at him, still not understanding.

"There they are," he says impatiently. "I told you."

At the foot of the cliff, great gray-brown birds soar on wide wings above, and swoop down on, some bundles of material. Above, on the rocks, servants pick their way down the cliff. The scale suddenly comes into focus for her, and she realizes that the bundles must be bodies. She looks back at the young noble. He is looking down, and smiling.

"He let me help," he says. "It was the only time he has ever let me help with anything like this."

"Maybe he's getting weaker," she says stupidly, "and needed strong hands to do his dirty work."

"You think so?" says the kid brightly. "That would be great! What an opportunity!"

"Get away from me," she says.

"What's the matter? Are you really against the old man after all? He won't want to hear that."

"Those people did nothing to you," she says, still stupid.

"No," he says, "but they would have." He grins complacently. "And now they won't."

She turns back to the bodies, small and unreal with the sea starting to rise around them. The servants—but they are slaves, she thinks furiously; tell the truth!—the slaves have reached one of the bodies and are tugging it out of the water, pulling it roughly up the tumbled rocks. It unfolds to a somewhat human shape, head down, bumping lifelessly. And it is, she thinks. It is. She begins mechanically to count the bodies, her fingers on the abacus in her pocket, stroking the beads.

"What will you give me not to tell him?" the young noble is saying, his immature voice taking on an echo of the despot's insinuating tone.

"But you don't do it as well," says Essa slowly, consideringly. "You really don't have the polish, the years of practice. He was better than you before we were born, I'm sure."

The lad looks at her uncertainly.

"And," Essa says, "you can tell him anything you please. If you can talk with your mouth full," and she makes the obscene gesture she'd learned from Escape-from-bondage in the very conversation where she learned about this one's sexual habits. The young noble starts toward her, then moves away unwillingly, remembering, she supposes, that she is still the princess. Fear still has dominion, she thinks.

"You'll be sorry," he says. Essa hasn't heard that childish taunt since her aunt's house in the mountains, and she laughs aloud. The lad bolts through the wall, and Essa's laughter veers from hysterical mirth to a great retching sob, which hurts her throat. Only one, and then she stands still.

She is already sorry: sorry for being stupid, and ignorant, and alone. Sorry there are no friends to have told her, and no-one to blame. Surprised her head is not aching, given how much her heart is, she stands and watches until one by one the bodies—she verifies her count: twenty-three, the same number as at the meeting yesterday, she thinks, less of course herself and the lad—are retrieved, roughly bundled up the cliff and into a cavelike doorway at the foot of the sheer rise. There must be tunnels all through this rock, she thinks. Fierce-frightened would have known.

Fierce-frightened would have known all of it. Essa can see why Escape-from-bondage thinks the replacement of his brave and savvy lover with Essa has been a poor exchange.

She stands at the wall where she regained her memory, leaning on the metal rail and feeling its cold through the layers of clothing. The day is heavy and gray and the sea is turning from its crest, high against the now-empty shore. The breakers crash against the stones as the tide backs reluctantly off the pebble beach.

The islands out to her right look like layers of torn mist, dark gray shadows against a lighter shadow.

She imagines her mother once stood stunned like this on this terrace, and looked at the sea and the Dark Isles. Yet she left home long before her parents' house had been burned to make a pyre for her murdered family. Why? She was the heir to all this privilege, and she had left it to her husband.

She had known how evil he was.

Why would she leave the people in his hands?

The wind is cold, off the gray ocean, and the clouds are low and moving fast toward her, like armies of the heart massed to strike and strike again, until she is defeated for good. Why was her mother always leaving, leaving the worthy and virtuous to their fate at the hands of tyranny?

Why is Essa leaving, when she is now heir in her turn, and could fight for what she believes? It is an illuminating question in more than one way: until this moment she has not realized that despite self-delusions of incipient heroism, all this time she has thought only of leaving.

She holds in her hand the abacus, its beads dull in the dull, cold light. Yet where her fingers clench on them they warm secretly, like all the secrets she holds that she can never tell, like all the secrets of her mother's that she will never know, hidden, burning a hole in the icy days, making a path through the grayness.

Out of the door behind her comes the regent prince. She has long since stopped thinking of him as her mother's husband, seeing him with his concubines and catamites, and remembering her own father loving with her mother in the firelight of home. She has simply thought of him as sleazy—a mistake of underestimation. But today she remembers, remembers him as if with her mother's body, feels the fear and the resistance as he bends his magnetic meanness on her.

She remembers the first day he brought her here, and kissed her, not expecting the sight of the sea to bring her memory back, expecting that he could overpower her and make her his, and thus lay claim to her mother's heritage, the credit of which had bought him all the power in his life, and which had been about to run out when he saw her in the southern slave market and recognized her mother's face.

She thinks, if he comes near me I will kill myself; then, suddenly, if he comes near me I will kill *him*. She has never had such thoughts, even after she left the trader town. Thoughts enough to make her hate him even more, for showing her the part of her she thought could never exist. He stays near the building today, though, protecting himself from the wind, and she turns again to the view, protecting him from herself.

"Did you kill my mother?" she says.

"I wish," he says.

"Did you find her?"

"I only found you. So far. If I had found her—"

"It is too late to threaten," she says, and turning again to him she sees the wind tangling his hair and revealing his balding temples. His face is spotted, and his hands mottled and gnarled. He is as old as when she had nursed him as a slave, she remembers with a disconnected flash.

"How did you do the magic?" she asks idly, knowing he is safe from her and she from herself.

"Magic?"

"To seem young, old man," she says impatiently.

"It is not magic," he says. "It is sufficient to want enough. Then it comes as one wants it."

"But only for a time," she says, and knows by his face that she has guessed right. She almost tells him then that she is going away but she knows it would not be wise to do so, so close to the cliffs where twenty-three people have just met death. She holds the abacus tighter.

"What's that you have?" he says.

"Oh, a counter," she says, though the adrenaline flood almost closes her throat.

"Oh? Let me see it."

Her hesitation is telling. He leaves the shadow of the building, and the wind catches his robes, makes him huge as he tacks toward her against the wall of air.

"Let me see it."

"I don't want you near me," she says, putting her hands in her shallow pockets, the abacus catching the silk.

"You opened your mouth to me," he says, "once."

It is enough. She doubles up and vomits across his shoes, his hem. He screams like a salted slug, and grabs—her hair with one hand, the hand holding the abacus with the other. He bends her back across the rail, bends her hand back and up, bends over her. She thinks crazily of vampires as his mouth comes down on her wrist and he bites. She screams too as the pain flares, the blood flows, and his fingers grope for the abacus, slippery with blood and sweat, which her relaxing fingers are loosing.

She brings up a knee into his groin or belly, some place soft anyway, and when his teeth relax she pulls her hand half-free with the last of her strength and throws the abacus backward into the sea. He releases her to lunge for the rail, and she turns more slowly, to watch the small rectangle turn and fall, turn and fall the long, slow hundred meters in an arc so beautiful, so wrenching she moans aloud. The clouds are parting and the abacus falls through a shaft of sunlight so that the beads gleam one last time for her, and then falls more, until with a tiny, almost invisible splash, a tiny shining dot disappears into a glowing tumble of surf.

He draws himself up. "Well," he says breathlessly, but no less softly than usual, "you have lost your mother's only gift."

"The sea is clean," she says.

He turns to her, eyes burning, and raises his hands again, claws reaching for her. She rises up into his threat, and stares him down.

"I have everything of my mother that I need," she says. "I could kill you if I wanted."

"I see," he says evenly. "And—" scornfully "—you choose not?"

"Yes," she says, and she stands even straighter. "I choose not." And she walks past him across the terrace, opens the door, and walks into the welcome darkness, leaving him behind.

Hearing him follow her, not caring, she goes to make a bundle, and setting the strap across her shoulder she goes down the stairs to the palace door.

"I lied," he says behind her. "I knew where she was all the time. I could have killed her anytime. I just . . . chose not."

She closes the door between them, and, like her mother, walks away.

Women who transgress

Log. Annalise writing. Dumped yesterday afternoon like sacks of potatoes out of the black sail-ship. Why when we trusted them? Two inanimate bundles, two animate, treated the same. I am only bruised but she has a broken leg and her arm and face badly lacerated. My bottle of spirits broken but I've wrung out sodden shirts across her wounds, hope it will still serve to sterilize them. Best I could do, we both stink like a still-house. She's delirious. The young man, Naio or was it Pewhim, the two of them like bookends, whispered to me, don't trust the south: obligation is slavery here. So I do no begging. The forest has half-killed us but maybe can cure. If she doesn't die. I never seem to die or even risk it. Ideal helpmeet. If only I didn't miss my family so. Seven years, almost eight, really, is a long time to be left with nothing but what we started with. A pack each, and each other. Older, much older than we want to be. Her pack is light enough but most of it taken up with a sweater she made herself, and wrapped in it this book. I read the log before I started this one. Can't help reading, always did it, got me in trouble in her parents' house. Well, long ago now. So I know what's in here. Sorry she has it and so will she be, but maybe can write a bit, keep herself busy while the bones knit. If the rest of it doesn't kill her.

DAY 2

Don't think I got the leg straight enough, or she has bent it thrashing around these last two nights. Wish this country weren't full of primitives waiting to pounce. Need a doctor but no such animal here, not like at the coast or across the water. Besides, nothing to trade. She left her jewel abacus for the kid. We could be eating better if she hadn't but can't do much about it now. I left some things too that I'd rather have here now. And the people who kept me warm at night, even more. She's no help. Fever and chills and shouting in the night. Yesterday I tied her to a tree when I had to go looking for food. I'm acting like the queen's taster, testing stuff I think is all right. Feel like a fool but I don't know the livestock or the plants in these southern woods.

DAY 3

Saw my first southerner, from afar. Already dead, hanging outside a town wall, her feet still kicking. A crowd turning away. If I understand their shouts and gossiping, she fucked a commoner. Or went into business with one? Stupid language they have, full of possessives. I crept back into deeper trees and gave up idea of passing for one of them, going to market.

They're a mean people and build everything inside walls. Farms as well as towns. No way to steal eggs or milk for her. Like a fox I've become. What fools we were to come here. Just because we thought he's found us, wanted to lay a false trail. Here they kill people as casually as that, and we're too close to his borders. He trades down into here. Her face is probably still on his coins, even. Fool she is and fool I am but I follow. She's quieter today and slept a while without sweat. Ate some tubers and mushrooms cooked into broth until mushy. Tasted not bad, considering. She didn't really wake though. Wish we could talk, I miss it. Talk to myself. Writing's not satisfying. I'm not made for it, much as I like a good read. Night coming. Must kill the fire. I can hide small smoke, not light. Clever women. Not the kind they like around here. Women seem to get it in particular, from what I spied.

Lean-to finished before supper. Not too bad in spite of everything.

DAY 4

Bruises look worse today but they'll fade. Her face a mess. Cleaned out pus, sewed some of it, pulling together skin over raw flesh. Grisly. She woke up. Didn't scream only because I gagged her with a stick. She bit half through. Things I've had to do for this difficult friend. Her hand and arm bad. Streaky. Soaked in hot water, ⅛ of the last salt. Nasty forest, no moss, no medicinal bark, that I recognize. Lots of trees I don't know. Years to know what they're for.

I'm spying on a kind of farm. They never touch the children even when they fall and cry. Saw a parent—a woman, men seem to parent only the animals—hold her broom out to the kid so it could help itself up. Then she turned away as if ashamed. Kid toddled off. Weird. And they hanged a woman for some transgression I still can't translate. I thought at first congress. But maybe commerce? Unlawful commerce? Unlawful congress? But it didn't sound sexy, sounded more like revolution to me. I should know. But everyone in the crowd very complacent about it. Like merchants, petty-minded and smug.

Why did they dump us off that black explorer ship? Treachery. All fine until the night before, then something happened and by breakfast we were suddenly strangers. To be disposed of. Like baggage. Why, why?

DAY 5

Tomorrow I'll give her the book. Her log, after all. Today she talked all day, or we did. I had to tell all my news. Was afraid to tell the hanging but after lunch she seemed strong enough. Anyway I am supposed to be the sidekick, though goodness knows it's been years since I remembered how. Or her, for that matter. She is still beautiful. Maybe I shouldn't have written that. She can read. Well, she knows how I feel. Should know. Why I bother keeping her alive.

Path through woods quite near here as things go. A worry when we talk. Can she move soon? I'd hate to lose the shelter of the big rock. Makes a good heat sink too, for the cold nights. Now I have to keep her warm. No room for cold feet here, though at home I was famous for them. It gets damp at night. The sweater helps, and I have a sheet of plastic foil which keeps in heat, though it's old and pretty torn up. Taped it together before we left but it's too old to last well and she lashed it around a bit those first nights. Oh well. All things wear out. Even we will and if we succeed in dying of old age I will be very happy; it'll mean he hasn't found us, or these southerners taken advantage of our weakness. I am tired of it but would rather die of old age than politics anyway, even so.

DAY 6

When she saw the book she cried. Hard put to quiet her in case of woodcutters, hunters, etc. on the path. Not sure I should give it to her—she talks of burning—I can't bear to see books burnt. Saw too much of it when we were home. But must do some hunting of my own and it is hers after all. I've done my best. Her turn now.

I've been feeding a crow which comes around the camp. The crows here are all black, not hooded with gray like in the north. I remember how they used to cluster on the walls above the hanging bodies of the punished criminals. It seems, according to Annalise, that they do the same here. She saw a woman hanged for some kind of crime and the crows were waiting. She says that I shouldn't encourage this bird, that someone might notice it is always in the same place, at the same time, cawing for food. But I cannot give up mountain ways that easily. There is nothing to do, lying here, but think. And write, if I choose to write, but I am sick of myself. This book will never get back to F. and my daughter, and if I write what I want to write, and it is found, I will lead them straight to her. So. What is there to say?

I had a few moments, it seems, to learn that there is another kind of life than the life we led in the tower. The shadow of the Dark Isles does not fall on the horizon of everyone. When the Carrier receives my memories there will be that bright time when I believed I could escape the curse of being born into my family. There must be a tale for that; Annalise will know. A tale which explains why one cannot be happy. Because for a while there, in the Range, I thought I could have a happy life. I thought it was possible to be absolved from the stain of one's origins. To be free of history.

Next Day

Annalise says that I am being morbid. She says there is no fate, there is only life. Life justifies itself, she says.

And did you learn that from books? I ask her.

I do not like this new bitterness, she says. Have you forgotten it was your own choice to leave the Range, bring yourself back into the danger zone? We had a choice at Nagroma. We could have gone farther down, past Hasfeld, where the Black Ships don't go. We could have gone back to Avanue where nobody has a name and all the spies would ever have found was Minh, Minh, Minh living happily ever after. We could have taken the children and the lovers. We could have made a trader family there. We could have gone to Sailor Town and made a hand.

All right! All right, I shouted to her. I made a mistake. And now it is too late. What do you think I am angry about? And who do you think I blame? I was made an elder! I should be able to think better now. But I made a mistake and here we are and here we stay.

And like a fool I began to cry. I couldn't stop, though we should have been back on tower rules: no crying, no breaking down. But I have lived too long in the Range.

And so has Annalise. She sat down and soothed me back into my bed, smoothing the clothes around me, and she was crying too. I should have thought, she said. I didn't think at all. At least you thought.

Not well.

I was so frightened, she said. They reach past the adult in us, these memories, and down to the frightened children. And we ran back into their web. Is that all life's for, to be stupid in the end?

I don't know, I said, but if I'd had a way I would have killed myself today.

I know, she said. Why do you think your bed's here and I cook there?

What will you do when I'm strong enough to move? I said.

Trust you, she said, and then I could not stop weeping, though I tried at least to be quiet, and we lay there together holding each other, sobbing.

If it is possible to die of this, said Annalise finally, maybe we both should.

Then I had to comfort us both, for her sake. We did our best, I said. We did what we thought would work. The skyship was there. It went a long way very fast. That seemed to make sense. We did it. And it was wrong. And here we are. That's all.

Take your own words to heart, she said, bitterly.

I will eventually, I think, I said. It will take a while. I have too much time to think, all day.

I told Annalise I would carve a game for us if she would give me a knife. That mountain game of letters making words which intersect. She looked at me carefully but she gave me the knife, and though I admit I was tempted, even once pressed the point against the outside of my wrist, I could not break her trust. Where life exists, hope exists, she said as she went to find some food. I have carved a number of the little blocks, but I forget how many of each letter there are, so I have not started writing the letters on. We would have to play in the language of the Range, because every tongue uses its letters differently, and I have no idea at all how many I would make for trader talk, or sailor talk, or the Dark Isles' dark language, or the southern dialect. And how would I make the different intonations of trader talk—would they be different blocks, with the letter and the tone mark? It would take some thinking. Not that I don't have the time for it. But I'll start with Range talk, and Annalise will remember, when she comes back tonight, how many of each. She always remembers things like that.

In the Fjord of Tears they say a task like this is like pulling cows' teeth, but when I was a farmer for a while I noticed that the cows up there stay put for almost anything you care to do to them, so the fault for all the difficulty must be the dentist's. Does that mean if I approached my task another way it would be any better? Looking back on things that happened more than twenty years ago and that hurt now almost as much as they did then, I often want to stop, but I can't think of any other way to tell my story, or talk to my daughter if she ever finds my life of interest. If she is ever given the chance. Will she ever reach me?

Most of the time, putting aside fantasies of dramatic rescue, I, with all my remaining being, hope not.

Blood is good to write with. It dries fast, though. I am writing with Annalise's blood. She hangs above me from a gibbet, and they have chained me underneath. They didn't hang her well—she was alive and struggling. Someone thrust a knife at her hoping to kill her but the blood fell on me for a long time: the cut didn't kill her quickly. For a while people walked by and looked and laughed, but night came and then day again and it was market day. Now everyone is going into the town. It's quiet here outside the walls.

I don't know how I will go on. I decided to catch the last few drops of Annalise's blood and write her a eulogy. Now I am determined to send this book to my daughter, to keep her away from the southern lands.

I don't even think this foul land has a name. The south. My name's lost too, now, and Annalise, of course, Annalise is lost forever, name and body and mind.

I was a little crazy for a while, screaming and so on, but I'm fine now. Blood has a nice texture for writing; I think I'll use it from now on. I won't be needing as much of mine. What I can give to my daughter I've given. Annalise was the last of my blood here. I left, they left, she left. Right, left. Like a marching army away from me. Self-pity stupid in this circumstance. I will probably die too and what happens to the book then?

Women who transgress. Who won't take from others and be slaves for it. Who stand up and say no. Annalise did it and she died. I have done it and I am dead enough that the difference makes no difference.

I'll be fine. Just as soon as I wash all this blood and pain off. Or maybe keep it. Have nothing else now.

Some of the people throw a little at me. Acting ashamed. I didn't eat, thinking they were trying to obligate me, but then I realized it was night and they were gone and they couldn't see me or what I ate or whether it was theirs. Annalise was still dying then. I thought about it. Should I eat for her or not eat for her? What does a hanged woman want from a chained woman? Oh, this is too much. Really. People have gone too far. This will have to be stopped. Like the sailor song: if I had my way I would tear this building down. I used to think about that a lot when I was telling F. about my childhood. Tear it all down.

One woman in chains, who can't walk straight anyway, will tear it down? If I could walk straight, would Annalise be dead now? No sense thinking about it, that way madness. Did she stay and fight for me, or because she was angry? I heard her yelling No! No! No more! as she fought them. Screaming as she swung her knife and the brand from the fire at them. She got one in the eyes, I know, but soon after that they dragged her down and one kicked her in the throat. No more talking then. I was already a prisoner. My leg had crumbled under me and I had no weapon. This book tucked in my turban, that's all. Thank goodness for sailor fashions. But too far to reach when I thought of putting out eyes with the pen. So they held me and made me watch them kick Annalise half to death. Drag her behind their cart to the town walls. Hoist her clumsily up with a rope around her neck. But no kind garrote, just a slip-knot choking but not killing her. She kicked some. One of them stabbed her with her own knife. She began to drip on me. Messy. She's usually so neat. Lost the kicking ability quick, though. Struggled a little. Her eyes were wide, terrified. She tried to reach out to me when she saw me dragged up, but then she saw I was not her rescuer and she closed her eyes. I saw the rope had looped around her sweaters and scarves. No wonder she wasn't dead. Then they chained me underneath where I couldn't see much any more. Her feet, her foreshortened torso.

She swings a lot in the hot wind. I can't count on her for shade. I'm getting pretty dry. Face peeling from sunburn. Lips chapped. Maybe use the pen to kill myself. Somehow think though that Annalise expects something of me still. Her caking blood protected my face from more burning. And let me write this. And I licked it up and am not so thirsty. I could drink my own too, if I had to. That would be all right. Blood sisters again.

We did make love menstruating, just to play, drew pictures all over each other. That was better than this.

In fact, I can't think of a thing good about this. Except that a cloud is going across the sun now. And maybe

I am going a little crazy, which will make it all so much, so very much easier to bear.

Messages from Annalise in the sky. Well, that's all right. She says I'm not going crazy, only a little mad for good reason. Stay awake, she says. I won't be around to watch your back. I love you, she says. I love you too, Annalise. Even if you are dead.

A lot of flies. I would try them but I don't want the diseases they carry. They are more interested in Annalise than me. She was always generous with small beings. Flies. Me. Children.

Yesterday I didn't write. I'd used all of Annalise's liquid blood and the rest was dried. So this time I've had to pierce my arm and use my own. Am not catching it in the little inkwell, just dipping the nib in the bubble coming from the nib-puncture. There are a lot of nibs left, but still, I must be careful with them. They have to last my whole life.

My blood will last. No worry about that. There is a lot of blood in a woman. It will be enough for the rest of my life.

Which may not be long, though Annalise says if I am careful I can live forever. Who would want that? I tell her. Live like this? I am still chained up. People still drop food, but precious little fluids until I sucked a little blood from my arm and croaked, I'm so thirsty! I didn't ask for anything, I was very careful, but these people can be manipulated. Someone dropped a water-skin, looking away as he did so, and someone else kicked it into my reach. Now I have plenty of water, anytime I want. I don't hunger and thirst after anything now, except righteousness. Isn't that what that mountain cult says is good? Don't they say I shall be released?

Annalise says she will be rotting soon, and falling down, and I should try to get them to take me away before that happens. But I'm just not eager to leave her, until I absolutely have to. She's all I've got left, after all. She smells a bit, but I'm sure I do too, though I've tried to keep a place at the very edge of my radius of chain where I shit and piss. Hard to avoid it though, with the chain so short. And the flies. I pour sand over the shit to seal it, then kick it away as far as I can. But a certain foulness results nevertheless. I suppose I'll have to give up being finicky. I got into a bad habit in the mountains, caring about things.

The one putting the rope around Annalise's neck couldn't get the knot right. It wouldn't slide. I'll remember that until I die. You were white with terror, you'd pissed yourself, and I don't know if you shit too, I know I did. You get that scared before you die, that's all. Don't you? Blood was running out of your mouth and nose, and tears out of your eyes, and you were looking at me with that beseeching look, like I could do something, but I couldn't even walk, when they kicked me around they did a thorough job, I was gasping and puking when they were done, and if one hadn't turned me over with the last kick, I'd have drowned in it, because I couldn't move. I spit my mouth free and I kept looking back at you. The least I could do was watch. My sister, my lover, my friend. The day you were going to die, and we both knew it.

And the fool couldn't get the knot right. He pulled at your neck until you gagged, and sagged down in the grip of the two who held you upright. And he fumbled and fumbled at the rope until I was almost ready to do it myself, if I could have, just to have the terrible sickness of it over, and the answer given.

I could see you felt the same, and suddenly I saw your damaged mouth twitch in a familiar way, and through the rush of tears into my nose I laughed at the same time you did. Our laughter was hysterical, wild, shrieking, but it was laughter, not screaming, and I said in the mountain tongue, If you want something done right . . . ! and a soldier kicked me in the face, which shut me up, and when I saw you again you were still grinning, though now you were holding your belly with the arm the guard had let go so he could slug you in the gut, grab your hair and yank your head up into the noose again.

Piss on it, said the one at the knot. It's good enough. Hoist her.

You cried out my name, and I remember I thought how you did that the same way once when we were making love, with the same anguished love. The little death, they call it in Trader Town; this would be the real thing. They tied me under the gallows with the other end of the long rope, another one of those fixed loops around my neck, and then they pulled you up above me, and blood from your wounds dripped down.

So that's how they hung you, Annalise: with a noose that wouldn't slip, and it took you a long time to die. It took the blood a long time to stop. I talked to you: no answer except the answer I knew was coming: no answer.

I stayed with you all the time, Annalise. What choice did I have? I remember it still. I will always remember.

Now I hear your voice, you talk to me, yes, certainly I'm mad, you're dead, sister. If I had any voice left from screaming, I would scream some more. If I could open my veins wider with this pen—but it's too delicate. So I'll bleed the story out, anyway, and my eternal shame, because I didn't save you, Annalise. I didn't rise up and cut you down.

It took the crows a long time to take your face away, and your lovely competent little hands. It took you a long time to fall.

Something happened today worth piercing a vein for. F. died. I felt the pain strike his heart. I felt it before, never bad enough; then, I thought it was me not him. But this was him. And I felt him go out. Like a candle, out. Like my heart, which went out a little when my parents were murdered and I felt them burn; went out a little when I felt with joy my grandmother's death; went out for I thought the last time when Annalise hung above me and ebbed away. But there was some left, more than I thought, because some of it died today with him, and some is holding onto my daughter's life, the only thread left. No, be honest, there are two, the other a greasy string running to the foul life of my cousin husband. If I could only snip that string myself. There was never a day since my parents were killed that I wouldn't have done it in a moment, if I could have. Annalise cried and cried, moral woman that she always was, about the death of one spy. I wouldn't have shed a tear. Maybe I am my grandmother's after all, the darkness in the heart, the maggots eating the evil, and swelling. But there is a bright thread which is my daughter's life. She hangs in the air above me like an angel. I will have to stay alive, to keep that thread from breaking. It is so beautiful.

Woke in the darkness so racked with desire it felt like pain. Alone and old and mad: I know what I am. Locked in a cage I'm sometimes tempted to think I made myself, until I realize that thought would be further madness. I was dreaming of Annalise but in the way of dreams she turned into F. Since they're both dead I've precious little chance of release. Oh yes, Annalise taught me to bring myself off, but release is more than a perfunctory orgasm in the darkness. Release is the turn of intimacy into itself: intimacy separated into two people and then joined again. Sometimes I have a nightmare and it is this: what if my father had not brought his other daughter into the hall? What if Annalise had never looked at me from her seat on the library table and recognized me as her twin despite my age? Then I truly wake screaming. I can't go mad again—goodness knows I've tried. I've tried to lose these thoughts, these loves, these tears. But now I only have this angry, thwarted eccentricity to sustain me. I'm aware I've lost my courage. What was left after Annalise's blood dripped over me? F. died, I felt him, and my daughter was better off left alone. Ironic that I'm safer from my husband's spies, here in the middle of his vassal south, than I ever was before. They think here that they cage me to contain my danger-

ousness. If they but knew, the danger's all outside the bars.
I'm tranquil here most times; I didn't choose my bars but
I remember now, I don't choose to break them. I'd ape
the poet and say they make me free, but that's not true any
more either. I'm afraid to be free. I used up my freedom,
up there in the Remarkable Mountains.

Sometimes I wake up with a weight on me so heavy I
think someone got into the cage and smothered me. I'm
almost relieved until I realize that I'm still alive and the
weight is the past. I can't forget it. I've tried. People think
I don't know I'm mad. I've tried my best to be. I did it
on purpose, for a while, when I felt like I was starting to
get sane again. Then where would I have been? Sane,
locked up in a cage, alone, stuck with it. That's no life.
Seemed more logical the other way.

But I wonder about it, times like now. When I feel the
weight of my past so strong that I know the world isn't
done with me. Who have I been? Did I run away, or did I
really have a life? Was Annalise right, or my grandmother?
Was my mother the escapee or was I? I can't make up nor
down of the questions, but they drive me to draw blood
again, to scrawl them here. As least my daughter will know
I asked them, even if I didn't have any answers.

Lately I've started meditating on the nature of power.
I told that poor fool of a girl that I am the most powerful
person she knows. She wasn't surprised because she thinks
I send her dreams, just because she knew the same languages as I before her head injury. But I was surprised to
realize I believed it. I've held to it all these years as my only
strategy, when I've lost everything else from manners to a
straight back. But I didn't know I believed it. With that
kind of attitude, I could actually get out of here.

She'll be sold away south soon. I'll stay until then.
And after, where would I go? I'd better not get too sane.
I'm almost blind now; I know what cataracts are well
enough to recognize them from within. And I have a
mostly-warm place with enough food, even though I can't

stand up in it. Maybe the tradeoffs are enough for now. I can't expect, the way I am, to circle the whole world and come home. And if I do? F. is dead these five years, I knew that the night it happened, I felt the pain in my heart. And could I rely on that sense of family I always had to find my daughter? I get no idea of her in the north at all, though in the last year or so her thread has seemed to thicken and brighten. But that's all I know. I cannot feel anything proper from her but the knowledge she's alive.

I am feeling a little connexion to the girl. Foolish of me to let it happen. What if I start feeling her life too? I can't afford it. I'm sure she will die young—younger than me. I have a protected, safe life here in my little cage. I've lived here for years. She is a slave, and they don't last long. Someone will buy her and use her up.

Ee-yah! Annalise says. Protect yourself! Beware! But it is not really her this time, though often enough in the night she comes. It is my own face behind a mask, speaking in her voice, saying, Be careful! You know what you know about loving. It hasn't been good for your health, so far.

My health isn't too bad. It's my situation could use some improvement, sister of mine.

The book of Ea

Before Essa can leave the city she has one commission to perform, something she has put off guiltily since she regained her Essa memory and lost most of her amnesiac self: to mail the book of the old madwoman to the trader town, to be sent on as the old woman had requested of the waif. Down in the dispatch office, she unwinds it from the silk scarf she has wound around it, the same scarf she used to use to wrap her mother's abacus.

She has a piece of oilcloth to package it in, and a marking pencil to mark the destination, but when she opens the book to find the name and place to which it is addressed, she reads:

ESSA
Daughter of Fynagra and of a Land of the Dark Isles woman
Eslyn Town, above Hasfeld
Fjord of Tears
Western Continent

It is her name. It is her book. The woman in the cage was her mother. Then, in a bizarre reprise of the day on the wall, the waif rushes back complete, and the dreams become real.

She must have made some sound as she swayed and shook.

"Are you all right?" says the dispatcher. Essa sees recognition in the canny, concerned face. She is dizzy, but she too recognizes. The woman and her man had intervened when the slave Essa once was stood confused, baited in the marketplace by soldiers of Essa's mother's husband. Later, when Essa was in the castle, she'd seen the man throw a rock through the carriage door, and signaled to him that she would keep silent; she had thought that favors were exchanged and done, but suddenly she knows she is where she needs to be.

"The despot!" Essa says suddenly. The woman looks nervously about them. "Oh, sorry," Essa says, quieter. "It's just, prince he's not, my mother's husband he hasn't been for five handsful of years, and I've hated him so for chasing her down, but now I know he didn't murder her. He knew nothing, whatever he said. Isn't it amazing! Really."

The woman is alarmed, hurries Essa through under the counter, through the door into the back of the depot, and up some stairs to their private quarters. All the time Essa is talking. Finally, the woman shakes her: "Hst! Hst! are you mad? Are you mad? Quiet!"

Essa is brought about by the shock of the woman's cold-water tone, and she sinks into the soft chair by the stove, the book still in her hands. "My pack . . . " she says.

"I'll get it."

Essa feels like a clock winding down backward. She is suddenly slumping, unable to sit straight. She opens the book again and reads her name, then closes her eyes, lays her head back and remembers the madwoman's blind eyes, her warm hard grasp, her rasping voice. She remembers as if it were a dream the first time they spoke together, when Essa the naïf begged the woman to take away her bad dreams. The waif was remembering, even then.

The tears hurt her eyes, and she wants to scream. Leaving the palace today, she had been running away though she carried it off with an air of victory. The loss of her mother's counter had hurt so much more than she wanted to acknowledge, even to herself, but she had felt at least that she had reduced the despot—yes, it was a fine conceit at the time—to powerlessness.

When all she did, she realizes, was get away from him, like her mother—and to what? The same mad, trapped end, eventually? Here she sits, with only a twenty-pound packsack of clothes and a waist-pack of valuables and money to buy her way around the world; an hour ago, she would have had the power to send for her mother, even hire an airship to fleet down south and collect her in style, put her mother on the throne or take them both back to Sailor Town. Now, having dramatically relinquished her birthright, she has nothing.

Except a book she sits holding in clenched hands, a book written in her mother's blood.

The dispatcher and her man are called Ynra and Hoj. Hoj works in the recycling plant below the tower, and Ynra keeps the dispatch office and a small store beside it. They shelter Essa on the second floor of their house, which is two stories built above the office and store, in a tiny dim room with a small window looking out on a wall ten feet away. The areaway runs below but Essa can't see the noisy people passing through to the alley, and they can't see her. The window is too small to lean out. It is nailed shut anyway, except for a tiny air vent which slides aside a few inches. Essa realizes that other fugitives must have been lodged here, but she doesn't care. She draws the curtain, lights the lamp, and reads her mother's journal.

> *This is the book of Ea, which I have written in tears and blood.*
> *I give it to my daughter, who bears my name.*

Essa can hardly read the last line for her tears. She runs her fingers along the lines as if they were raised like the Range alphabet for the blind. Ea. Her mother's name, that she never knew. She remembers Annalise saying "Ee-yah!" She had thought it some kind of exclamation. Her father had called her nothing but "your mother" in stories. Essa had called her "mother" and "mommy."

Her name! That Essa bore? But Essa's name hissed where her mother's did not—ah, but Essa speaks more languages now, and suddenly she understands the differences in pronunciation: Essa, Eh-ah, Ee-ah, Ee-yah, Ea. And Eg-ha—Ega—and Eka too. Yes. She bears her mother's name as her mother bore hers. She begins to laugh.

Ynra, coming in, finds her laughing and smiling through tears. She looks at Essa, questioning.

"I have just found out my mother's name," says Essa.

"Ea," says Ynra, pronouncing it differently than in any of Essa's theories, and much the way she pronounces Essa's name. "Of course. The queen name. What do you mean, you didn't know it?"

"No. No-one ever said, in all this time. She told me herself, in the book."

"It is the same as your name."

"Well, now I know that."

"We don't use names much, here."

"Yes, I know." She laughs again, but the laugh catches on a sob, and she turns away to the window.

Hornets keep getting in the room through a crack between wall and ceiling. Essa is reading her mother's journal over and over, but interrupts her reading often to catch the buzzing little brutes in a glass and guide them out the sliding panel of the window. But soon she realizes that even when there is no insect in the room with her, she can hear a low angry-sounding hum all the time. She listens at the walls and sloping ceiling. The nest is behind there, under the roof. With toilet paper from the little lavatory, she blocks the cracks between ceiling and wall as best she can; the number of hornets reduces but she still must evict three or four every day. She feels like a bouncer at a Trader Town drinking-house.

From the sublime to the ridiculous: weeping over her mother's words, then getting up to capture hornets for export. Every day she has been in the room, either Ynra or Hoj has brought her delicious meals morning and noon and smuggled her down to eat evening meal with them after the early sunset.

Essa remembers wistfully the long temperate summer days in the Fjord of Tears, but it is much closer to the equator here, and even though the weather is hot and the under-eaves room beginning to overheat in the afternoon, the night falls early. Essa has never liked this early darkness, even when she was amnesiac, and she is grateful for the evening descent into a cool lamplit lower room, where Ynra and Hoj slowly move from awkward guardians with an agenda of their own to potential friends. Essa misses the Carrier fiercely, and sleeps poorly.

The third day a butterfly happens in through the open airhole, and Essa is so grateful for its non-lethal beauty that she lets it stay for a while. She lies down on the bed with the cool-feeling cotton cover and leans her cheek on her hand, watching. Perhaps the butterfly will find the exit again by itself; she fears her rough method of eviction will hurt its dusty wings.

It is yellow, with a maze of tiny lines she thinks are black until it rests for a moment and she realizes they are a deep blue, like the sky at midnight on the spring solstice in the Fjord of Tears. She reaches up a finger and lays it in front of the insect. After a moment's hesitation, it walks onto her fingertip—just as Ynra knocks and calls Essa's name.

"Come in slowly," says Essa, "I'm catching a butterfly." Even the whisper of air from the opening door alarms the creature, but only enough that it beats its wings heavily for a moment. Slowly, Essa lifts it and moves her hand through the airhole. Outside, she moves her finger to dislodge the bright flier gently, but it clings for a moment, beating its vellum wings, before it flies free. As it flies up, the sunlight which doesn't reach this window catches its wings and they glint golden, like a royal coin.

When she turns to Ynra, she sees the woman is crying.

"What is it?" Essa jumps up and steps across to her, but the woman shakes her head. Essa leads her to the little bed and they sit down together, Essa's arm around Ynra's shoulders.

"It's just like us," Ynra says when she finally calms enough to talk. "Is it your hand will free us? What is in the book?"

What *is* in the book? Essa has been in the room for days, long enough for the despot's toothmarks on her wrist to scab over and begin to heal, and she still has no better answer. The narrative is cool at times, even when the woman has written about death and grief; the stories of youth particularly seem footnoted with an adult cynicism which Essa is old enough to realize is the only defense her mother could have had. It is astonishing to Essa, especially since she is steeped in the Range theory that abused people become abusers, how much hope and gentleness survived in her mother.

Essa remembers her mother's unfailing patience and her soothing touch. How did she learn, and how did Annalise learn, the soft and kind things they knew?

Annalise. The thread which ran through the years, Annalise and her mother, their love, something Essa had never thought about or suspected. And the horrible end of Annalise's life, and her mother's mad recording of it with her own blood. Blood service, all the years. Half-sisters, lovers, adventurers, survivors.

Yes, thinks Essa, survivors even if Annalise is dead now. Even if my mother has died since I was there. Survivors in their words and in the love they left us. If I ever get back to Eslyn, I will show the book to Annalise's children, and they can show it to their children. That is the only thing I can think of to do with the book.

How can it bring the despot down?

When Ynra comes that night Essa stops her. "I need to talk with you." Ynra sits down on the bed.

"I can't find anything," says Essa, "except life. And death, of course. But no state secrets, nothing. I don't know how to help you."

Ynra bites a fingernail. "Maybe," she says, "maybe . . . "

"Hmm?"

"Maybe you could read it to me?"

"Or you could read it." Essa pushes it into her hands. Ynra leafs it open, shakes her head. "I can't read that language," she says. "You have to read it, and translate."

Then Essa thinks for the first time of language. The diary is in three languages, actually, but the pages Ynra has opened are in the tongue of the Range. There are other sections in sailor talk and the local language—but none in the southern tongue. Even at the end.

Between them, they read the book, Ynra when it is Dark Isles talk, Essa translating the others. Sometimes that means such a need for precise and tedious explanations as Essa has not felt since her handfasting—and since she was amnesiac and an old madwoman gave her impatient, frightening lessons in a courtyard.

When it is done Ynra is silent. Tears are still drying on her cheeks. "Yes," she says, "we must do something."

"But what? A woman's story. Just that. A footnote on history, she said in that one entry. What?"

Ynra gets up. "Come down," she says, but they don't stop in the eating room. They descend cellar stairs and then, below the cellar, clamber down through a well-hidden trapdoor into a sub-basement.

There, lurking like a monster crouching in darkness, is a printing press.

They have to thread their way through stacks of boxed paper, and rolls standing on their ends, to reach the cone of light above the press. Hoj is there, wiping his fingers on a rag, his small stature even more dwarfed by the web of another larger press behind him in the dark. It is a factory for subversion, Essa thinks delightedly. She laughs. Hoj looks up in startlement.

"Ynra," he says, warily.

"It's fine," says Ynra. "I've brought the princess down."

"Oh, mother, don't call me that!" says Essa, horrified. Now it is Ynra who laughs. "But you are," she says. "You are the queen, in fact, if the despot would admit it. Pointing that out could bring him to his knees."

Essa hasn't thought of that. By leaving the palace she thought she renounced everything, but the people may not agree. Who gets to determine her fate? She clutches her fingers around the book.

"I know what must be done," says Ynra, her face looking feral in the single-source light. "We will publish it all. We can use the pantograph to make perfect copies of the pages, and you can translate on the facing page. We'll set that text in type, of course, but they must see how she wrote it. I wish we could show the blood."

"Blood?" says Hoj, disoriented. Essa opens the book and shows him.

"It is my mother's blood," she says. "She wrote it with her blood. To me."

"Rust ink," he says, sniffing. "We could do it. What's in there?"

"Her life," says Essa.

"Yes," says Ynra with enormous satisfaction. "Her whole life."

"But is one life enough?" says Essa.

"If it isn't," says Hoj, "we'll publish yours."

So her mother will have her book, the book Annalise always wanted written. It will be published on whatever paper they can get, and it will go around the country like a plague. A virus, incurable. And, Essa hopes, fatal. Maybe it will make a story one day. "And Essa walked down to the sea, looking for her mother, and this is the way she found her, and this is who she found."

She hopes it will be enough. Because she has decided there will be no princess, no new queen, to go with it. "You don't need another despot," she says to Ynra and Hoj and seven friends who cluster into the printing chamber. "You will just end up the same again in a few generations. You need the butterfly's life, the government of freedom. You must think something up. Publish that in the next book."

"Oh, no," says Ynra. "The next book is the book of Essa."

And so it will be.

But afterward, Essa hopes they take some time off to think of a governing system. They will need something.

She has no doubt now the despot will fall, and helping push him will be her mother's mad hand. The words written in blood damn him more than the tales of his deeds. That their queen should have come to that will enrage the people. Essa needs do little more, except tell her story to Ynra's recording device, and hope Ynra is a good shadow-author.

Because Essa cannot stay to write it herself. Her mother may still live, and Essa is still determined to find her. She has wasted too much time already, helping start a revolution.

*   *   *

Essa tells her story to Ynra in ragged hours every morning, and in the afternoons, alone in the room, or at night after she returns there from dinner and the evening below, she writes bits of it down herself, though she finds that much harder. Ynra likes the scribe role best but she is a good editor too, asks questions which make Essa think, remember, and sometimes cry or laugh. When she comes to their departure from Sailor Town on the Black Ship south, Ynra laughs with her about how Gata and Essa met in the cabin, each having tried to spare the other.

"I was younger then," says Essa. "Of course, it feels more recent because there was all that time when I couldn't remember who I was. I wonder what my . . . " but she broke off abruptly, rubbing the itching scar on her wrist.

"Your what?" Ynra prompts.

Essa looks at Ynra's eager, sharp face. This woman is, perhaps, her friend now. But she needs these books for her revolution. Which would be more important to her?

It seems, Essa thinks, that I learned well some of those hard lessons in the tower. Escape-from-bondage would be proud of me.

"I think that's all for today," Essa says finally. "I have to think. I'll see you at supper."

"You all right?" says Ynra, as she always does after these sessions. Sometimes Essa is not, and Ynra comes back throughout the afternoon, to check on her or give her a cheerful word.

"I just have to think," says Essa. "There's something . . . I'll talk with you about it later, all right?"

Ynra hugs her, and then reaches for the writing tablet, looking quizzically at Essa. After a moment, Essa shakes her head, so Ynra leaves the tablet and stylus and goes off downstairs.

But Essa cannot write after all, of course. Because what she had been about to blurt out was the existence of her daughter. If nothing had gone wrong in the pregnancy or delivery, Gata had borne their daughter, and since the Carrier had received no such child, she was growing up now in the sailor town with Gata and Lowlyn. Looking like Lowlyn's child too, because Gata has a pair of blankies, so there would be no danger of the Naio-Pewhim feud continuing.

Essa wonders if there is a cord connecting her to her unknown daughter, like the cords her mother wrote about, which Essa cannot see for the same reason she cannot make light. The gossamer fiber of her invisible connexion to the Carrier she has begun to take for granted, but now she questions again, with a new question: not why, but why only one when her mother was linked to all her kin? She wishes she had the connexion, to give her the illusion at least that she has given something to her daughter beyond just life.

Life, and danger: because now here is Essa writing her book, telling her life in such a way that her path could be traced across the face of the world. There is only one town which sends Black Ships west and south. There would be only one pale potter there married—handfasted, rather—to a sailor and a woman from across the sea. If they want to find her daughter, they can.

Yet if the revolution succeeds, her daughter might read the book someday, and how would she feel that her mother had left her out? Like her mother leaving the Fjord of Tears, and Essa the child never understanding the reason. And despite her intellectual awareness now, she still feels the loss, the absence of the love and presence she could have had. The lessons of a madwoman to an amnesiac do not substitute for those lost years.

Essa lies on the bed for most of the afternoon, staring at the ceiling and the blank window. The scab on her wrist itches until she impatiently tears it off, revealing the angry reddish skin beneath. At one point, the arc of toothmarks has not healed enough, and a tiny line of blood-beads swells. A book written in blood? Life was written in blood. Occasionally tears leak silently from her eyes, and she blots them on the pillowslip and fights for control. Finally she gets up and takes up the stylus.

"Foreword or Introduction or Preface," she writes, not knowing the difference. She will ask Ynra. She stares out the window for a few more minutes at the wall an arm's length away, then continues.

> *The Book of Essa* is different from the life of Essa. I am telling my life into this book to show the reader the world, and the possible futures beyond the way people now live in the Land of the Dark Isles and the southern reaches beyond that land.
>
> There is danger in telling my story, danger not only to me but to those who shelter me, those who know me, those who love me.
>
> For that reason I am leaving out those of my loved ones who cannot take care of themselves. It is an arbitrary choice, reader, and if I had not told you, you would never have known.

But then someday maybe someone who is not in the book would come forward, and say, I knew Essa, or, I loved Essa, or, I played with Essa in the Fjord of Tears, and so on. You would look in the book. You would not find such a person. You would think, if Essa could lie about this, perhaps the rest of her story is a lie. It would become a fantasy to read to children.

So I will tell you. There are a few people in my life who are not in *The Book of Essa*. This does not mean I love the book less, but only that I love them more. If someday I can tell you about them, I will know that a new world has come into being, the world we dream could set us all free of tyranny, lies, injustice, prejudice, fear and sorrow.

When truth triumphs over all secrecy, we will all sail the silver ships, we will all know the joyful beauty of the Fjord of Tears in autumn, we will choose our families and loves and friends and no evil but only natural process will sunder us. Until then I give you my mother's life in her book, my life in mine, to show you that we can know one another. The secrets I have kept from you I wish I need not keep. Someday I will tell you the rest.

She signs her name, then lies back on the bed and almost immediately falls asleep. When Ynra comes to get her for supper it is after sunset, and the room is dusky.

Essa, waking slowly, looks up at the smiling shadowy face, then reaches up and hugs her. If she were at home in the Fjord of Tears, or in Sailor Town, she would have kissed her, she feels such sudden tenderness of shared purpose, but she knows what ordinary people of the Dark Isles think of such freedom. To talk, however, is within Ynra's freedoms.

"If we were in Eslyn, or the sailor town, we would be kissing now, not talking," she says drowsily.

Ynra does not draw away, but Essa feels her become tense and still. "Maybe in the Dark Isles there are some women who know how to kiss you," she says. "I am not one."

"Never mind. To make contact is enough. I have had—" and Essa thinks of the Carrier, gone from the Dark Isles on a bright Black Ship, and shivers slightly "—enough of the other for now."

Ynra hugs back, then straightens up briskly. "Come to supper," she says. "What's this?" She picks up the tablet and reaches for the lamp.

"Read it downstairs," says Essa. "I'm hungry."

Essa wakens from the dream sweating. In the dream, Gata and Lowlyn were looking for her, Gata swollen with pregnancy, and a window in her belly where a little Essa looked out, screaming in rage; the two of them trudged down dusty roads, bedraggled, and festooned with the usual irrelevancies of dreams—pottery wheels, books, ribbons, and a tribe of cats getting underfoot and wailing for food. All of them, humans and cats, starving and weeping and footsore. Essa saw that they all left bloody footprints. In the dream, she thought: how dare they follow me? Then she was terrified they would catch up to her. Then, ashamed and horrified with herself. She may have cried out, because when she finds herself wide-eyed and shaking, it seems the echo of a shout of rage hangs in the room.

"What is it?" says Ynra, sitting in the dark by the window. Essa is still too confused to question this presence. "A dream. A dream," she says thickly, and begins to cry silently. Sniff. "Just a dream."

Then she wakes more and the tears stop. "What are you doing here in the middle of the night?"

"You were sick, sweating. Then I heard you moaning in your sleep. I thought I'd keep an eye on you."

"Moaning? I have to go to the bathroom." She gets up, swaying, and pads down the little hallway to the water closet. Coming back, she walks into a candlelit room.

"You'd better stay awake for a while until the dream goes away."

"You do that too?"

"Yes, sure do. I don't want to go back to some of those places! Want to talk about it?"

"I dreamed about the people I handfasted with. They were obsessed with me the same way I have been with Ea. They were wearing out their feet looking for me."

"What do you want it to mean?"

"Want it to mean? I thought it already meant."

"It means, yes. But you can make it mean more."

Essa shivers. "It means enough."

*   *   *

One morning Essa reassembles her travel pack, and when Hoj comes in to see her he finds her tying the flap down.

His hands are full. "Don't go anywhere until you read these page proofs," he says, grinning.

"Page proofs! Already? Wonderful!" Essa grabs them from him, laughing. He grins even more widely. Essa looks at the title page: *The Book of Ea*. "I guess I can stay long enough to proof that."

"I can hardly wait for the reviews," Hoj says.

" 'This slim volume . . . ' " Essa says in a solemn, book-reviewer voice, then looks at the proofs. "This is beautiful."

"The cover's not ready yet."

She hugs him. "You do good work in your cave, Hoj the subterranean."

He leans back, still hugging, to look at her. "So do you, Essa, daughter of Fynagra and of a Land of the Dark Isles woman."

Ynra at the door says sharply, "What's going on?"

"Page proofs!" says Essa. "Look!" and she goes to hug Ynra in turn. "Look how beautiful it is. I've never helped make a book before."

"What's this?" Ynra is looking at the pack.

"I didn't know it would be so exciting. I'm glad they were ready before I went. We'll have to check them quickly."

"Where are you going?"

"Where I was always going. To find my mother."

"But there's so much to do here!"

"You don't need me. I've done my bit."

"What do you mean?"

"The books, of course."

"But it's just the beginning," protested Ynra.

"My mother is the beginning," says Essa, still gentle through her surprise.

"Yes," says Hoj. "But I think Ynra feels focus will slip without you here to keep people aware."

"No," says Ynra. "Just, there is so much to do . . . "

"This always waited to be done," says Essa, "and I can't wait any longer. My mother can't wait any longer in a cage in the slave south."

Ynra looks at her with a look so blank and surprised that for a second Essa almost expects her to say that Ea is more use in a cage in the slave south, making a symbol for the revolution. But Ynra says with slight shock, "You know, I almost forget she is real. Me! And I am supposed to be the change agent."

Essa relaxes. "Page proofs, then? And then I'll be off."

Ynra, still shaking her head slightly, takes the manuscript Hoj is still holding, nods to the sheaf of paper in Essa's hands. "I'll read," she says. "You check. Do you have a pen?"

It is a companionable task, which takes several hours over two days. So in the end Essa sets out for the south late in the day, walking out of the city with the market gardeners who daily bring their produce to the central square. The evening shadow of the tower lies long across the town. Not for long, Essa thinks. Not for long. She hopes—she has grown to believe, while in Ynra and Hoj's passionately insistent presence—that what they have done will banish shadows.

Essa has noticed that in the stories about quests against fate, towns are always lousy with guards looking for the fugitives, inns fraught with people who recognize them, and roads mined with experiences which add up to the answer to all their problems. Whereas Essa, walking south, taking the occasional odd job to earn food and shelter, is invisible, or might as well be. There are no coincidences. Nobody remarks on her resemblance to the face on the news broadsheets, let alone on the money she is earning. To be the queen of an ancient kingdom, even the abdicated queen, apparently counts for nothing in the universal scheme of things.

This is much as Essa, steeped in the mountain tradition of equality, has believed, but she has been in the Land of the Dark Isles long enough for some of the assumptions to rub off on her surface, and she finds herself ridiculously piqued. For so long, her life has been bound up in that identity: in finding it, in remembering it, in resisting it. Now she has stepped outside it again, but she finds herself with the impulse to confess her life story to total strangers.

In a medium-sized market town on the Wayle River she sees the finished books for the first time. *The Book of Queen Ea,* they have expanded the title to read, and *The Book of Essa.* On the cheap one-color covers, Hoj has woodcut-printed a decoration in the shape of a medallion, like the coins everyone uses every day, but subtly different. On her mother's book, the face is old, twisted, changed in the ways Essa had described to Hoj. On her book, the coin face has

a mountain hairstyle and a scarf tied around the hair in a way that
suggests a sailor's turban. Both are effective and evocative.

Around the market booth a crowd clusters, buying either one
or both of the books until the vendor has only a few left. Only then,
after the crowd has abated, does Essa quietly approach.

The vendor is a small, swarthy woman who reminds Essa of
Gata. She looks at Essa sharply, then says over the heads of the few
remaining people, "Oh, hello. Ynra said you would pick up your
order." And she wraps and hands Essa the two books. The other people, leafing curiously through sample copies, do not even look up.
The vendor is a true southerner; she doesn't smile, though Essa involuntarily does.

Essa retreats to her camp in an overgrown coppice outside
town. She has camped where obviously woodcutters had come on
their recurring visits, taking some comfort in the resulting sense of
history.

Thank goodness, the days are longer down here. After she has
cooked her meal, she sits in the golden evening light and leafs
through the books. At first she can hardly bear to linger on the pages,
but soon she is caught by the familiar words, and before long she
has read her mother's journal again, cover to cover. It seems subtly
different bound in covers, more unified, with more authority of voice
even than when she had first seen it transformed into type, while she
was checking the proofs. Again Essa shares Ynra's and Hoj's vision
of the power this narrative might have to move the people. Even if
this had not been her own mother's story, Essa would have been
moved.

As for her own story, which she has not seen in print before at
all, she cannot approach it this evening. She stays in the camp an
extra day, tidying the hearth area, napping in the shade, and busy-
ing herself with sorting her pack and doing small repairs: anything
to give her an excuse for her immobility, when in fact the presence
of the books has enervated her beyond her understanding.

The second evening she steels herself to read *The Book of Essa*.
It is a curious document, all headings and episodes, with some en-
gravings for illustration—a Black Ship; Essa with her family, though
Hoj's rendering of Gata and Lowlyn was far from the mark; the
Fjord of Tears; Trader Town; Sailor Town. All seem highly roman-
ticized. Essa cannot criticize any episode for factual errors, exactly.
All are as she dictated them to Ynra. But the result is somehow far

from her memories. Even Essa's own words have taken on a greater gloss, and the Essa of the book seems to have more profile, more strength, more focus. She has a goal.

Essa reflects that this must be true for all the heroes of books; all the history books which are supposed to be about real people and events must have the same effect on the people who were there, if they are able to read them. The same unfamiliarity, the same curious way of throwing life into stronger relief.

With her detachment, Essa can also see that the book is well-written. This too surprises her. Ynra's written voice does not evoke her actual self to Essa's mental vision; rather, there seems to be a calm, detached other person there, one who tells the story with a sense of justice and a desire for beauty, which gives the lie to the cool tone, so strongly passionate it cumulatively becomes.

Surfacing from the story of her own life, Essa shakes her head with astonished admiration, and puts the books away in her pack.

At the next town she sends a letter to Ynra, complimenting her on the work, couching her praise in roundabout terms so that should the letter be intercepted, a reader, even one suspicious of Ynra, would have no clue to the actual subject.

Essa is proud of herself. Her friend may be a biographer of genius, but she writes a mean circumlocution herself. Must be all those languages. Nuances. She walks on, her pack two books heavier.

A miserable day, and nothing Essa can think of to explain why. No unquenchably painful memories—or, in fact, a steady stream of them, as usual, but now so commonplace that tedium, not pain, results—nor portents of future doom. The weather is sunny and pleasant, the forest is beautiful, and the intense physical pain of the first strenuous days has abated long since into a frustratingly healthy fitness for travel. Essa has even, in days past, noticed a joyous lifting of spirits not at all commensurate with the grief, mourning, departures and losses she has been counting over like phantom beads on the long-gone counter.

In fact, Essa thinks wryly, she should welcome this melancholy as a familiar friend, since she indulged herself in miseries of various sorts for some years, coming out of her adolescence and making her first questing travels into the world. Only when she was amnesiac and uncivilized did she have surcease. Then her terrors were both more tangible and more basic: the lovely metaphysical terrors of tribal life, which when she returned to her anthropologist self she had had to renounce in favor of the logical and ephemeral anguishes of the more high-minded.

Now her mind has woven a lovely scheme of rationalizations around all of it, while fresh air, nature, and fitness have conspired to imitate for her a happy ending wherein she walks confidently and cheerfully into the future, without a backward glance.

How convenient.

Finally after two warm hours of striding along at the prescribed adventurer pace, Essa is furious. She flings her pack and staff down beside a picturesque stream, kicks her boots into a nearby thorny bush, and wades fully-clad into the water. There are bruising yet slippery rocks beneath her stockinged feet; she tugs off first one sodden sock then the other, throwing them back toward her pack. One snags on the high branch of a conifer; the other falls into a patch of mud near the bank. Just the sort of thing her mood expects.

There is a relatively flat rock in the center of the stream. She sits down on it, feeling the water shock cold against her genitals, and hunkers down as far as she can. She feels the push of the current against her back, and it tugs her pantlegs and trailing fingers. She stands up in a great swoosh of flying silver water drops, and birds fly up from the bank, scolding. She wades to shore, wrapping her bare toes around smooth stones and avoiding the sharp ones. On the bank, where fallen conifer needles and bark and humus particles cling immediately to her feet, water streams away and she shakes herself like a wet cat.

There is a jumble of big smooth rocks at the bend in the stream, and she crawls up on the biggest to lay herself out like a wet shirt to dry in the sun. So much sopping laundry, she thinks, with a reflex of self-disgust.

She falls lightly asleep, wakes once hearing wind creak branches one against another, and again to turn away from sun as it overheats her. It is only when she hears the birds go up again in startlement that she sits up from a dream, blinking at inchoate reality, to see an old woman with a staff walking down the stream.

The old woman's eyes are cloudy with cataracts and she is dressed in wrinkled, tattered clothes, wet at the hem, splashed with water at middle, and with a kind of stream-washed griminess overall. The woman is Essa's mother.

* * *

Essa has reached the point in her own story where she understands she has no time to fool around.

"Mother?" she says, disbelievingly. Her voice doesn't penetrate the sound of the water; the blind old woman doesn't notice her yet.

"Mother!" she calls then, loudly.

The old woman turns to her as she sits tensely on the rock.

"Who is it?" she says. Only then Essa remembers that in some languages this is a polite form of address, but she forgets whether this is one. She changes to her home language—not her mother's tongue, her mother tongue: that one she reflexively spoke first.

"My mother, it is Essa," she cries as she scrambles down the rock. "I remember you now. Do you remember me?"

She is pulling the old woman bodily out of the stream in the guise of helping her out. The woman is half assisting, half resisting.

"Girl, I remember your voice," she says. "Didn't I give you lessons?"

"Yes, but I had been hurt then, I didn't remember you. Don't you remember how I spoke Fjord tongue? This tongue? I was the only one who knew how. But you never recognized me either. I was grown up."

"I remember a girl brings me sweets. Doesn't she . . . ?"

"Yes," says Essa, "I did."

"She went away with my book. To mail it to my daughter. The bloody Fjord of Tears; wish I'd never gone there or never left, one or the other."

"What are you doing in the water?"

"Eh? Huh?"

"Walking in the stream."

"Going to the ocean."

Essa's turn to shake her head, then, realizing her mother can't see her, to say, "What?"

"Going to the ocean. Water all goes to the ocean. Got no money, you see. Can't see much. Don't dare ask anyone, years in a cage, got to go before she leaves home and I lose her. Going to the ocean. To cross on Black Ships, sailing. They should take me. To find my daughter."

"What's her name?"

"What's your name?" asks the old woman, slyly as if she were tremendously wise.

"You must tell me now, mother, what is her name. Because maybe you have found her, and you won't have to wade in any more streams. Wouldn't that be nice?"

"Won't you say? Strange thing to say. You are a strange pup, you always were . . . Essa?" And the woman's face changes some, undoes its concentrated strangeness and turns for a moment comprehensible.

And then it is easy.

" . . . then when I met you I'd had a knock on the head . . . " Essa finishes, but trailing away; her mother trails away too, a lot, too much really, but Essa doesn't care, so glad she is that they have so strangely found each other.

"And what the hell were you doing in a sail-ship? Didn't I tell you how they threw us out, right in the south where it would do the most harm?"

"No, that was in the book. I didn't have the book when we left home. I didn't have it until I left the despot's palace. Your husband."

"I suppose he was that, once, though thank Annalise I never did have to sleep with him."

"Annalise?" Though she knows the story, still visions of some strange rite of substitution come to Essa, and her voice is shocked. The old woman laughs a crude, caged laugh.

"She got me out of there in time. She'd read all the books, you see. I didn't. Didn't have the patience. So I didn't know anything. Doesn't matter now. She's dead. They hanged her. Didn't I tell you?"

Essa sighs. "Yes, you told me," she says, though like everything else it was in the book, in the crabbed hand of the madwoman who latterly used her own blood for ink.

"Went crazier then than anytime," says her mother. "Couldn't quite make it back. Like all the other journeys. Always going in circles." And immediately, there in the sun, leaning on the rock, she falls asleep.

"You left me. What did you leave me for?"

"To protect you."

"From what? From what?"

"Everything I had brought with me. The past."

"Didn't it ever occur to you that I wanted your past? That I needed your past? That it was my past too?"

"But it was shit. Shit!"

"It was life. You made something out of it. Then you deprived me of it."

"I left the book. It was your father who put it in my pack. He made sure I took everything painful. He tried to protect you too."

"Yes, and he went away when you did, in all but his body. Until he died he was like a ghost. What do parents think they are doing? You think you owned my young life, that you could do whatever you wanted with it? You think it was yours? Look how much time I spent looking for you. Look how much it cost. All because you *protected* me."

"Ungrateful brat. Crying and yelling. What do you think it cost me? Annalise, my life, my vision, my man, my home—for you, ego brat. Self-centered. Just to keep you alive so you could have a daughter and leave her."

"How do you know about her?"

"I can feel her. You know I can feel everyone in my family."

"Oh, that's from you too? Linked to the Carrier like a fish on a hook? That's from you too?"

"Don't complain to me about it. I felt you all the time. I felt everyone I loved and everyone in my family. And when you threw that thread of yourself off I felt her too. And I knew it was a daughter. The line runs so strong through the cunt."

"So?"

"So are you going back to give her our precious past? Or what's your rationalization? Going to *protect* her?"

"Quit distracting me. You want to blame me to get the heat off you."

"Yep. And you want to blame me. What's the difference?"

"I don't know. I don't know."

"And what's the point?"

"I don't know."

And after that, they did not speak for a while.

"My whole life was a waste," she says. Her mother doesn't argue. She is making some kind of cat's cradle out of the wool Essa bought her in town. She has two sticks and is jabbing at the wool and it is growing a kind of shape.

"What's that?" says Essa, interested despite herself.

"Knitting," says Ea. "Haven't you ever seen it? No, I forgot, you never lived in Dark Isles."

The work is intricate and yet simple. It's a lot like crochet work, thought Essa, but had a more logical, linear flow. It doesn't seem at all the sort of thing her mother would enjoy, and she says so.

"Tranquillity of mind," says Ea. "Very important. Years in that cage I thought I'd go mad for something to do."

A giggle escapes Essa, then she claps her hand over her mouth in Fierce-frightened's gesture of shock. Her mother looks up. "Oh, I know, I was mad I suppose, but you know exactly what I mean, you young minx. Now, if my daughter were here too, she'd tell you—"

"I am here," says Essa, angry again.

"That's what you think," says Ea craftily. "That's what you think."

She goes off to sit on the bank with her knitting and Essa is left to fold the sleeping bags and tent by herself. She notices her hands are shaking as they used to do in the palace when Fierce-frightened changed the sheets of the sick despot, or cleaned his room when he wasn't there. When he was there, of course, she had not dared shake. She looks at the hands of Fierce-frightened working mechanically and in terror and she thinks, how did her hands get on the ends of my arms? and her head begins to ache. She is developing a strategy for that now: she sits down and begins to think very slowly, and the aching abates. My mother is right, she thinks. Her daughter is no longer here.

She wonders if the Carrier of Spirits will be able to tell them apart when the time comes: Essa and the waif, now that they are both in her. Or will they somehow be united by then? Their lives had been so different: one long, naïve and ingenuous, one short, knowing and savage. Now Essa calls herself by her old name and nothing in either life comes when she needs it.

She falls asleep in the sun: she can't always control the aching enough. When she wakes the side of her face is sunburned and her mother is measuring her arm with a piece of string. It is the waif who leaps away with a start.

"Oh, calm down," says Ea, irritated. "I'm trying to get your measurements for this sweater."

"What?" says Essa stupidly.

"Sweater. I always thought I'd knit you a sweater. So here we go. Sit up, I need your back waist length."

Essa sits obediently. She feels her mother's capable hands along her backbone, measuring her. Does she measure up? She begins to cry, silently, as the waif had learned to do.

"Crocodile tears," says Ea matter-of-factly.

"What?"

"Crocodile. A sort of predator. Said to cry before it eats its prey. Tears which don't mean anything."

Furious, Essa turns, but her mother faces her with such a calculating gaze that her own drops.

"I shouldn't feel sorry for myself, is that what you're saying? I should shape up?"

"It would be an idea," says Ea. "You'd be a lot easier to travel with."

"Me? I'd be easier? I can't believe you're saying that! You're crazy as a crow, you cost all I had and all I can earn, and you do nothing but—knit."

"Consider the poppies," says Ea. "They do no work, nor do they knit."

"Cute," says Essa. "Should be a proverb."

"Already is," says Ea.

"Says you," says Essa.

Ea laughs. "How old are you again?" she says.

"Seven," says Essa. "The age I was last time I was your daughter. And two. The age Fierce-frightened was when she lost her mind to me. And twenty-two, the age I was when I fell out of a cloud. And twenty-five. How old are you, mother?"

"As old as I have to be on any given day," says Ea. "Ask me again tomorrow. I'll be younger then."

"Will you get young enough to forget the cage?" asks Essa, meaning it.

"You must be crazy," says her mother, "taking me seriously like that." She stomps off theatrically to knit. Essa goes to town to work at her part-time job, and brings home some sweet dumplings for dinner.

"You look a lot like the queen," says the baker, now that it doesn't matter.

"Everyone says that," says Essa. "You should see my mother now; she really has the nose. And the hairline too. I don't have the hairline."

"No-o," says the woman, comparing a coin with Essa's face, laughing.

"I always thought I could pass myself off as the long-lost," says Essa, and the woman laughs.

"Wouldn't have done much good, from what those books say," she says, tossing the coin back into the cash basket. "Might as well stay here and keep working for me as go be a slave in the tower."

"I suppose so," says Essa. "Can I have one of these crescent rolls?" At the baker's nod, she takes the curved sliver of thousand-layer pastry and bites in all the way to the fruit filling. It is raspberry, and suddenly the taste of her mother's sunny garden is in her mouth. She remembers the kind voice of the quiet woman who had been her mother then. She remembers eating the berries warm from the brambly bushes. She thinks of the mad old woman who is her mother now, waiting in the woods, knitting her a sweater to keep her warm, though around them they are tormented by the eternal summer of this damnable land. Tears suddenly stand in her eyes.

"Here, here," says the baker, "what is it? Are they too tart?"

Essa laughs shortly. "No, not tart. My mother used to make these for me. I miss her."

The baker nods. "Yes, I know how it is. I lost my mother two years ago. When did you lose yours?"

Essa has never heard the idiom. Lost her mother. Yes, that's been the whole thing: she has lost her mother, and she will never find what she lost.

"Last year," she says, thinking of the moment when she discovered that the mad old creature in the cage was her mother, the heir-apparent of the Dark Isles. Suddenly she realizes that with the shock had come an astonishing grief, a sense of loss which has been overshadowed by the lightning-flash of discovery, but has remained there to confuse her memory until this moment.

She picks up the tray of crescent rolls and carries them into the showroom. As she arranges them in rows in the display case, she thinks about the grief, the loss. The moment when, irrevocably, she understood that the quiet, gentle, loving mother of her childhood would never be found, that she would have to make do with madness, eccentricity at best, flashes of brilliance from behind a mask of cunning—and above all, absence. Essa's mother would never come home. Essa had lost the past along with the dream. In that moment, finally, her denial was over and she accepted her bereavement: and that was the moment when she discovered that her mother lived, that she was not dead, that she could be found, something Essa had not known through any part of her search.

Understanding this again, she feels a stabbing sense of shame. To grieve that her mother was not dead, after her greatest fear had been to find that she was, seemed the ultimate betrayal. All the other angers—that her mother had left, that her mother had deceived her—paled beside this anger; none of the loves—the love of child Essa for her young mother, the love of adult Essa for her mother's memory, the hope she had loved through her journey, the love of the waif for the madwoman—none of these loves seemed enough to cancel that shameful moment of embarrassment. And now, months later, Essa burns with the same blush: she does not like the woman who would resent such an outcome, yet she cannot escape herself.

That afternoon Essa watches Ea as her mother knits beside the fire. Ea insists on a fire though the weather is warm enough that they have never moved from camping-out into lodgings in any town near which they have tarried. Essa is sick of the everlasting temperate weather, wishes for a good Range snowstorm. She is sensible enough to realize that it is winter there and it must be her body in its seasonal rhythms asserting its desires, so she manages not to get too irritated at Ea. It would be unfair to blame her for the weather. Too.

Essa grins at that thought, and watches her mother's face. Ea is intent on her knitting, staring off upward with her nearly-sightless eyes while her fingers swoop and the needles click. The late afternoon light makes her skin more golden, and an occasional flare from the fire flashes a reddish glow into the shadows of her cheeks and eye sockets, but the flattering light cannot hide the wrinkles, the scars, and the twists of fate reflected in the drooping eyelids, the crooked lips. Ea's hair is white and thinning, and she combs it straight back, but it still curls into untidy ringlets and softens around her face, giving her a curiously fashionable look: Essa's hair, the same as her mother's but for color, was very popular in the Tower of the Dark Isles during the season she spent as princess there, because it did naturally what all the beauties, men and women, were trying for: hung tangled and wild, like a feral child's, around her face and down her back. And Ea's is the same. But Ea, thought Essa, is truly feral, a feral child grown old.

It is the ravished face of a woman at the end of her time, though Essa knows her mother is only twenty-five years her senior, and Essa must be not more than twenty-five herself now. One fifth of Essa's natural span gone—but "natural" means nothing now: her mother will not have half what the people of the Remarkable Mountains expect for a lifespan. At that thought she sighs involuntarily.

"What is it, love?" her mother says, her voice as warm as any caress Essa remembers from her childhood.

"I am thinking about our birthday," says Essa, for they have the same natal day, the first full moon after the autumnal equinox.

"Must be coming soon," says Ea. "Or, no, it's passed, hasn't it? Last night must have been the second full moon. It's so hard to keep track down here. I haven't been in the Range for years but I still expect it to be winter."

"Are you reading my mind?"

"It's not my gift," says Ea offhandedly, and rummages in her knitting bag for another skein of wool. She finds the end unerringly by touch, begins to knit it into the row of stitches. Essa thinks of the raised secondary alphabet of the Range, which the blind use there and in Trader Town.

She thinks, I could teach languages. We could teach languages.

"Old mother, how crazy are you?" she says.

"Oh, the wind's not blowing today at all," says Ea.

"Would you like to start a school of languages when we get back home? The Range will need more trained travelers."

"It's an idea. It's a sound idea."

Essa giggles. "Sound, except for the slave language. That has no sound."

Ea's hands stop. Her face is shocked. She opens her lips to speak, closes them, opens them. "I was more of a princess than I thought," she says. "I never realized it." Tears start to roll from her eyes, though she sits motionless.

"Ee-yah! Mother! What is it?"

"Ways I was a fool," her mother says. "Just another way I was a fool. I have a whole list of them. Some people hold grudges. Not me. Just lists of failures."

"No, not!"

"Oh, yes. Here I missed a language under my nose. And now it's too late. I can't see it."

"I can show you with your hands on mine."

"Too late. I am too old. I am too blind. There is no room for vision any more."

"You taught vision to a frightened girl with no memory. You must have had it."

"Oh, I had it. I gave it away."

"It's not like that. You can't lose it."

"You hope. Look at me. Can't walk, can't see, and crazy on top of all that. And I'll die soon, you know—I'm used up. School or no school, I don't have much more to do."

"But I just found you!"

"For what I'm worth. Annalise's mother, you know, she was a slave until my father freed her, she used to move her hands so beautifully. I remember how I tried to imitate her when I was young, but my mother stopped me. She said, 'You must leave to others what belongs to them. You have your own.' She must have known. Why didn't she tell me straight out?"

"You knew Annalise's mother? I never knew that."

"Oh, yes. She was such a lovely woman, with a classic face of the east coast, out of sight of the Dark Isles. Except for the scar, of course. And she was so big. My mother was thin, thinner than I am now. She couldn't eat too much without throwing up. But Annalise's mother was fat and strong. I remember I wondered if Annalise would grow fat when she grew old. I imagined one day I could nibble on one of those great scones!" And her mother laughed an open, ribald laugh. Essa laughed too, in surprise.

"I love you, Mother," she said.

"And I love you, my Essa," said her mother. "I'm sorry I'm crazy. I really can't help it."

"Don't worry about it," said Essa. "I think we'll manage to work around it."

The book of Essa

It is the old despot, and with him is Escape-from-bondage, carrying his bundle.

Essa stands stunned.

"What is it?" Ea says querulously. "Why have we stopped?"

"Your—" but Essa's throat closes and she has to cough before she can speak. "It's your husband. He's standing on the road in front of us. He's with someone I know. A friend."

She speaks in the secret language with her mother all the time now, she realizes when both the old man and the bulky, mute one look at her in surprise.

She raises her hands. They feel heavy as lead. =It's my mother,= she signs. =Don't tell him.=

=He knows,= signs Escape-from-bondage. =What do you think we are doing here? Are you Fierce-frightened yet?=

=We're both in here.=

"What's going on?" says the despot, and he sounds as querulous as Ea. "What are you saying, you women? Are you plotting? You might as well not. I don't have anything left but him and you don't need to take him. Do you?" he adds craftily.

"You were deposed," says Essa.

"Yes, for now," he says, "but when I get back there with you two, they'll soon step into line. There are factions of the army with me, you know, around here somewhere." And he looks around vaguely.

"He's crazy, isn't he?" Essa says to Escape-from-bondage.

=Total nut case,= he signs.

"No use talking to him," says the old man. "He's no use. Can't talk, you see. Useless for carrying messages. Cooks all right, though. Cooks all right. Not as good as the palace, but we're on a campaign."

Ea stands swaying. "What on earth am I going to do with him?" she says. "You'd better get rid of him like you did before."

"We should make a camp here," says Essa to Escape-from-bondage. =What are we going to do with the two of them?= she adds in sign.

He shrugs.

"Make camp," says the old man. "Good idea. You surrender, then?"

"Quite out of place," says Ea. "Quite out of place. I've done with him. Make him go away."

Essa and Escape-from-bondage get the two settled on opposite sides of the clearing, then begin to make camp. They are smooth as teamwork together, but Essa hardly notices, preoccupied with the two ancient mad beings dividing the camp between them. Until Escape-from-bondage touches her and signs, =So you are back together.=

=I am both of us, anyway,= she signs, =since I left the palace. The old woman in the cage? She was my mother. I found her. Or she found me. And we've been traveling north, back home.=

=Home?=

"The Fjord of Tears in the Remarkable Mountains," she says, and the words soothed her tongue.

"And you, Escape-from-bondage," she says. "Why did you come with him? You have surely lived up to your name now."

=I thought he might actually find you,= the big man signs. Tears come to her eyes. After a moment he carries on. =And I don't have that name any more.=

"What is your name now?"

=You will find it.= And he goes back to the tent he is pitching.

Finally Essa lies in the arms of the mute man, still with no name for him to replace the one she'd called him when she was Fierce-frightened, long ago now.

"Did you read the books?" she asks.

He nods and smiles.

"Did you like my life? I put you in."

His smile a little wry. His arms are around her so he can't talk. He kisses her forehead. That used to mean *be quiet*—but she can't.

"It's just, to find you, so strange. For you to find us. How did you?" He jerks his head backwards. *Think about what you just said.* "Oh, the books, of course. The madwoman in the cage. Where I was bought. I guess it's not so weird." He shakes his head, smiles.

"That's how you found out she was in me." Nod. "And so you

wanted to see me again." A little shrug, then he kisses her on the mouth, chastely but firmly. Shut up, shut up, his two kisses say. She laughs. "Are we going to make love? Or for that matter, fuck?"

He smiles at the reference to the time with Fierce-frightened, shakes his head.

"Fine," she says. "Go to sleep."

She puts her head down on his shoulder, he tightens his arms around her, and they drift. Just before she drops off, she says drowsily, "Good night." His hand presses her shoulder. "Friend," she says, even more indistinctly, but he hears, and his hand squeezes twice. Sleep takes them then.

"They're crazy, aren't they?"

=Oh yes.=

"Not us. Sometimes I think it's me. I get used to them. They seem like the world sometimes. Traveling in secret like this. Never seeing anyone else real but you."

=And you admit I'm not very real either. Outside the palace.=

"Oh, you're real." She takes his arm, squeezes. "But them. Where are we going?"

=The coast,= he replies. =To get a ship. A merchanter to take you to the trader town.=

"Oh, I suppose," she says, "but what will we do with them?"

=We will take him to the provisional government,= he signs, and his face is grim, =and they will put him in jail, or they will string him up, I don't care.=

"He thinks he is taking us to prison," she says, laughing a little in panic; she tends to forget this side of him now that she is mostly Essa.

=Well, he is wrong.=

"He seems so harmless now," she says, looking at the old man bathing in the stream below them. "Such a pitiful thing he has become."

=You think that absolves him?= and his look is so grim she steps back.

"Don't turn that wolverine face on me," she says. "I know he is a monster. Don't you think I know? Don't you think I remember?"

=Not like I remember,= signs XX (as she has come to think of him), and turns away, back to the camp, leaving Essa watching the scrawny old body drying himself on the streambank, and reflecting on the nature of hate.

"Leave him alone! He caused all this!" Essa storms at Ea.

"It's my life, I can talk to whoever I want. He's the only one who understands what it was like."

"He loved it, you hated it. It wasn't the same for both of you."

"Never mind. He knew them all. You didn't."

"I've met them all," says Essa. "But not alive, I'll grant you that. You didn't give me a chance."

"You wouldn't have wanted the chance."

Though she knows Ea is right, she pushes it anyway, out of anger. "You never asked me."

"That's as it should be. I was your mother."

"Was. Was?"

"Am. Am."

"Yes, you are."

A moment for their thoughts to change and range, and Ea surprises Essa as usual: "What would I have been like if I had been born in the mountains?"

"Boring!"

They laugh. Essa loves that: she remembers—faintly, but still remembers—a time when that was what everyone did.

"Where is she?" Essa is shaking the old man, screaming at him. "Where is she? What have you done with her?" She pushes him to the ground and sits over him, pounding his head on the ground.

XX has to drag her off him, toss her away. The old man hikes back toward a tree, hissing. She remembers, crazily, in a flash, a fight with a catamite in the lower kitchen hall of the palace, when she wasn't Essa.

XX has to make a ragged shout to distract her from her enraged stare at the old man. =What? What?= he signs impatiently.

"My mother is gone. He must have done something."

=Maybe she just wandered off. Have you looked?=

"Yes, I've looked, curse it, I've spent half the day looking. Do you think I'm stupid? But her little bundle is gone, her staff. The last time I saw her they were going off together. *He* did something, I know it, I know it."

"She just left," says the old man, his tone a sly reminder that he was once the despot, used to manipulation. She lurches to her feet, advances on him again, but XX blocks her.

=Sit down. Calm down. He's not strong enough any more to do much.=

"You don't have to be strong to kill a blind woman," she says wildly. "You don't have to be strong to tell her the wrong direction, to tell her lies." And Essa begins to cry again, sobbing with fury and frustration. XX puts a hand on her arm but she paces away, refusing to look at him. "Don't be so reasonable!" she shouts. "Don't be so fucking nice. He did it. He's a monster, don't you remember? You said so yourself."

"She just went," says the old man. "Really. It wouldn't be appropriate for me to dispose of her, this close to getting my regency back. She was going to support me, we'd talked about it. She didn't want the throne, really. She was going to tell them."

"There is no throne, you foul old fart!" Essa screams. "There is no fucking throne. There is no palace, no slaves, no wealth, no army, no chance. Don't you know that, you old fool? You are out of your twisted little mind, you evil thing, and you're too stupid to know it." She rounds on XX. "Are you going to help me look?"

=Of course.= His infuriating calmness remains. She shakes her head, which is beginning to ache.

=She may have indeed gone on her own,= he signs. =You two had been fighting. She was pretty strange herself, you know, even before that. She might have just taken a notion.=

They search until dark, but find not even a trail. There is no sign that she has passed by way of the water, and the creek develops a rapids a mile downstream. None of the travelers on the market road have seen a dotty old woman. The woods reveal no trace.

Ea is gone.

The next day the search is equally fruitless, and even Essa has to admit there is little chance to find a person if she doesn't want to be found. Especially as neither Essa nor XX are experts at this kind of outdoor search. Essa sits by the fire that night, her shoulders slumped with exhaustion. Finally she speaks dully.

"I shouted at you; I'm sorry," she says. "I was upset, but that's no excuse."

Her head is bent so she can't see XX's hands, though she sees by the motion of shadows that he must be trying to talk to her. She is too tired to watch.

She lies down where she sits, pulling her coat around her shoulders more tightly, and sleeps instantly, crumpled in a tense, curled-up heap there. She wakes briefly to see that XX has covered her with her sleepsack, and has tended the fire so that it is still strong; he lies across the fire under his blanket, and the old man sits wrapped in his, back against a tree. Both of them are awake. Essa sits up.

"I don't suppose I ever found her, really," she says. "Not really." She turns over so her back is to both of them, lies down and wraps herself tightly in the quilted sack. This time, it takes some time to get back to sleep, and even after she sleeps, she searches nightmare woods until dawn.

She tries to sign, so the old man won't hear, but XX has turned to look off into the distance. Into the trees. Essa feels like she has been surrounded by trees for a long time.

The old man is watching her, though, and he laughs. "So," he says. "It's a way of talking to each other. It's the same moves every time. Why didn't I think of that? And watching the screens all my life, and the slaves."

"Because you are essentially stupid," she says. "Gluttony is essentially stupid."

She finishes rolling up her mother's bedroll, then her own. All the things Essa bought Ea—the sleepgear, the changes of clothes, the big light pack—are still here, and Essa is trying to decide what to do with them.

"Get your things together," she says, "or when we go, we'll leave them here, and you with them."

"Don't talk to me that way," he says. "I'll have you flogged. The army—"

"Old man," she says, "you are a fool and a pain in the ass. And I'll talk to you any way I please, now. I have no one to protect."

"Your mother is alive somewhere," he says. She grabs him by the shirtfront and lifts him off the log where he has been sitting. "Talk to me again about my mother," she says, "and I'll turn you over to him. He would kill you in an instant."

But XX pulls her away, and pushes the old man roughly back to his seat. Essa shrugs away from him and throws the last of the gear into the packs. In the end she leaves her mother's pack, with half Ea's things in it, leaning against a tree, but stuffs one change of clothing and a heavy sweater for Ea into her own pack. If they find Ea, she will have them; if Ea comes back here, she will have her pack. If she can see well enough to find it. Essa cannot do any more.

They start out trekking that day in silence. After a while Essa says, "I want to catch transport. I don't care if we're recognized now."

=There's a village ahead with a terminus,= XX signs. =We came down there.=

"Fine."

No more talk all day.

In the evening they line up for the transport. "If you want to get us back to your tower," says Essa craftily, but with the same angry threat in her voice, "you will shut up and shuffle. Otherwise, we leave you here and your precious invisible army will not find us again."

And he does keep silent and shuffle, pulling around himself the mantle of old, harmless man, shaking a little. Essa is reminded of the sick man Fierce-frightened had nursed, and her skin crawls, sitting beside him on the transport, looking out the sealed windows at the landscape blur by. And after all that walking, she thinks. They are in the capital by midnight.

The fall of the tower

Essa wakes in the wide bed with the kind of languid pleasure she realizes she has not felt for years. She is completely clean for a change, and she is not in a bedroll on the ground. Those underpads for sleepsacks were not as miraculous, after months, as they were cracked up to be: nothing like a good mattress—and this was a good one—under a good comforter.

The bed is also big. XX lies with her, but far enough away that in sleep they have both been able to spread out without crowding each other. It is amazing. Not since Trader Town has she had this much room to sleep, and that was—how many years ago? Her two recent lives tend to overlap like stacked phototransparencies, but if she sorts them out they make over three years back to back. Maybe close to four? How long had she lain recovering when she fell out of the cloud—the dirigible? She has no way of knowing exactly. Here, south of the equator, the seasons are different and come at different times than in the northern hemisphere. And Sailor Town had been somewhere in between, more tropical. She sighs.

At the sound, XX rolls over and looks around with feral, instantly-alert eyes. He will, she imagines, never lose that habit of the palace slave. When he sees her, he smiles and makes a little sign with his head: *hello, how are you?*

She tilts her own head back and forth and smiles, then realizes that she is acting for the screens. But the cameras are no longer set up in the corners of the room, the spyholes are plastered over, it seems, and paintings hung over them. Ynra had showed her that with pride, the night before.

The run up the stairs to the battlements left her sweating and Essa shivers in the wind from the Dark Isles. She looks out at the familiar view, ghosted with the falling gleam of her mother's abacus, the broken bodies on the shore, the rush of memory, fear and pain. She rubs the scar on her left wrist.

Curious, she thinks. It is the only scar which shows. Except, as she saw in the mirror yesterday, a streak where the hair grows white from the scar on her head, where she fell out of a cloud.

A few days in residence here have her troubled. She doesn't know what she expected to have come of the brave plans of the revolutionaries, but she did not expect the provisional government's self-righteous, ecstatic dogmatism. She had been astonished when she saw the excerpted sayings from her mother's and her books on big posters in the squares. It put her in mind of "Climb the Remarkable Mountains" and "Sail and soar" in a square a quarter of the way around the world from here.

When she had said some of this to XX, he replied, ='Change of rulers is a joy of fools,' they say.= Later she saw the same slogan scrawled on the bottom of one of the posters, and other defacements had happened overnight.

She wonders if the screens have been turned off after all. It would be useful to have such a system if unsure of power.

Her sweat has dried and she is beginning to feel a little warmer. She suddenly thinks wryly: once upon a time, thoughts like that would make me shiver. I am getting as cynical in my old age as XX.

But she cannot help her thoughts running onward. Change of rulers is a joy also to the new rulers, she thinks. Too much joy.

If she were to doubt her insight, the fierce and protective joy she sees in Ynra's face is ample proof of its accuracy. She has heard that power attracts corruptibility. It's such a pity, she thinks, looking at the relentless bright horizon, that we are not pure. Or at least, that we don't treat each other better.

It used to be reflex with Essa to think of the Range with nostalgia when she did these political musings, but now, carrying Fierce-frightened, and after many talks with XX, she wonders, what would a person of the Range do in Ynra's shoes?

Essa had the chance to be in Ynra's place, as head of the new government, and she gave it up. This thought makes her uncomfortable, but despite her useful double mind, she does not quite perceive that in remembering that fact, she may have answered her own question.

Ynra sits by the window. They have been discussing the counter-revolutionaries who have been defacing the posters, putting up their own, and scrawling the apt, Essa thinks, graffiti on posters and walls. Ynra has just ordered a wave of arrests. Essa can hardly believe this is a woman she had once considered having sex with.

"You can't just lock them up!" she says.

"Why not? They'd do the same to us in a minute. You can't reason with them."

"You sound just like him." Essa doesn't stop to think; she is reacting as she had in the debates in the upper room.

"I should have expected this," says Ynra. "After all, whatever else you did, you are the princess."

The familiar ache begins in Essa's skull, but she has learned to ignore the ominous pressure. "I am Essa, a woman of the northwest," she says. "And that is all I am."

"You are a woman," says Hoj unexpectedly, "after whom the Carrier of Spirits inquires."

"Was she here?" asks Essa with a pang.

"Here and gone last month," says Hoj.

"Upper-class superstition," sneers Ynra. "Just the sort of thing to flatter the queen's daughter."

"You were my friend," says Essa helplessly.

"Were? Was?" Ynra is sharp. "Are we not still friends?"

"Look at you," Essa says. "You are playing with me. You used to love me."

"What do you mean by that?" Ynra says. "What kind of foreign talk is that? What kind of foreign perversion did you expect of me, coming back here?"

Essa turns to Hoj, but he shrugs. "Ynra has thought a lot about this," he says. "After you left the cause."

"Left the cause? I went to find my mother, the woman whose book rallied you. And where is it, by the way, the original? It belongs to me and I want it back."

"It belongs to the people," says Ynra. "To the revolution."

"You sound like a romance novel," says Essa disgustedly. "But you can have your clichés if you want. I just want my mother's book, and the royalties on mine, and I'll go home. To the Range. And leave you with your revolution."

"What about the old man?" says Hoj unexpectedly. "You have been pleading his case."

"No, I haven't," says Essa carefully. "Now please listen to me, because this is for the record, and it is important. The old man is a monster, and he deserves to be accountable for it. But his monstrosity doesn't allow you an equivalent barbarity. Adding a wrong does not erase the first. You will fall the same way he fell if you rule the same way he ruled."

"Yes, yes," says Ynra impatiently. "Living and perishing by the same words, or whatever it is you say in the Range."

"The Remarkable Mountains to you," says Essa, sharply.

While they have been speaking, Hoj has gone to the glass case on the far wall, opened it, and rummaged about in what seemed to be a pile of cloth. "Here is your mother's book," he now says.

Ynra turns on him. "You have no right!" she says.

He walks across, gives Essa the cloth-wrapped book, then turns to Ynra. "You have no right," he says. "There are some things which do not belong to everyone, and there are some things that must. Essa is right. We have put off establishing an independent judiciary for too long. It will soon be too late."

"We have that in our long-term plan," says Ynra defensively, then turns to Essa. "A long-term plan which doesn't need you!" she continues explosively.

"And a good thing too," says Essa tartly. "I'm getting out of this country while I'm still alive. I've lost enough here."

"What do you mean by that?" Ynra asks, furious, her face whitening.

"Just that life is short," says Essa, "and I have spent too much of mine in the Land of the Dark Isles and its foul southern satellite. I will be leaving as soon as I can find a merchanter to take me."

"But you have no money," says Hoj, but he speaks not toward her but toward Ynra.

"Very well, you can have the royalties too," she snaps. She strides to her desk, dashes off a note. "Give this to the paymaster."

"Thank you," says Essa. "Thank you," she says again in a different tone to Hoj. She walks to the door, pauses with her hand on the push-plate. "Listen to yourself," she says. "You have masters again already. Paymaster! Humph." And she goes to find XX, to say goodbye.

But he too surprises her, though in a different way. =What would you say if I came with you?=

"But I thought you—"

=I brought the old man back. That was my job. Now I have no job.=

"I'm sure they offered you one."

His gesture is a rude and scatological one. She laughs with relief and pleasure. "Well, friend, if we travel on, where do we go?"

=It doesn't matter,= he replies, =as long as it is away from here. It will be interesting,= he adds.

"Yes," she said. "They have a curse in Sailor Town: may you be alive in interesting times." His bark of laughter triggers her giggles. She realizes suddenly that she is close to losing control. She sobers, puts a hand on his shoulder.

"I didn't expect to get out of this place at one point, today," she says, and tells him about her argument with Ynra, and Hoj's unexpected change of allegiance.

=She'll hate you more,= he signs seriously. =We're not gone yet. We had better be careful.=

She has not, however, expected him to be right. "Dammit," she says the next day as they shrink back into a narrow alley, waiting for still more of the provisional police to march by, "I am getting tired of being warned about impending doom. My life has been full of warnings." He signals her to be quiet, but instead she leads the way across the square under the noses of yet another group of armed guards, talking animatedly as she does in a loud, complaining voice about how he was always nagging her about something, telling her it was for her own good, how she was sick of the sound of his voice, how he was to be quiet and leave this to her, everyone knew that merchanter traders could charm the pants off small-town boys like him, but she was born in the shadow of the tower and knew what was what, no matter what he said.

The guards pay them only a casual notice. "Don't sign," she whispers before they step onto the gangplank of the merchanter ship. "Act like I told you." Then they are being met by the merchanter deckhand, and she begins speaking yet another new language.

There is no sailing until the end of the week, the barquentine captain's agent tells her, and they do not take passengers—but they will be able to join the crew for a small fee. The fee takes half of Essa's royalties, the gold coins with her mother's face on them which the paymaster has given her. The ship sails at full moon—but there is one catch. They cannot stay on the ship until then. The harbor troops will search it for contraband and fugitives several times before sailing. They will have to find a place in town to hole up safely.

The agent helps to the extent of smuggling them off the boat and into the shadows after dark, and XX says he knows a place, so they dart up the hill, dodging guards again, until they come to a narrow lane where a gate is opened by a silent, scarred old woman leaning on a stick.

=She is from the castle, long ago,= he signs. =She was a wet-nurse there.= Essa did not dare ask if this was her mother's nurse, who had been beaten in defiance of a promise by Ea's mother. Broken promises everywhere.

For the next three days they lie low in the rabbit-warren where the old woman and several other ex-slaves live like fugitives themselves. "What are they hiding from?" Essa asks. "Life outside the palace?" XX nods. Essa had been joking, but he isn't, and she knows her joke was sheer nerves. Life outside the palace is not much better these days than life inside had been before. Food is getting more and more scarce in the town, and on the second day the old woman brings them two pieces of paper.

"Read," she says to XX in a hoarse voice. Essa, who has thought her mute, is startled. She takes up the pages to read them aloud but the old woman snatches them and pushes them at XX, grunting.

=It's all right,= he says. =This is the one whose life the Carrier remembers. It is enough.= And he hands one of the pages to Essa. It is a handbill from the provisionals, torn from a post or notice board. The provisionals announce, it says, that the former despot has been rehabilitated and will be appearing in the public square two days hence to repent of his crimes against the land and to swear allegiance to the new government that will be proclaimed at the same ceremony. Essa sees Ynra's mark in more than the signature: in the clever wording and the rust-colored ink which has ceased to represent Ea's blood and now has become the symbol of the new leaders. But the handbill has not been printed on Hoj's old press but on the high-speed printers of the palace, and very high-tech and glossy it looks too.

The other handbill is printed on rough paper and with an even shakier press than the one on which Hoj once printed *The Book of Ea* and *The Book of Essa*. It is a call to boycott the ceremony and a demand for the resignation of the provisionals in favor of a true committee of the people's representatives, to be chosen by acclaim the night before the official ceremony and in the same square.

XX hands the poster to Essa so he can sign it to the old woman. Essa reads the words again, and shivers. This is the way it all began, half her world away. The old woman has begun to cry, and XX is comforting her. Essa goes away down the winding corridor to the room where she and XX sleep. He will be some time, she knows, before he has finished comforting the woman, discussing the developments with the rest of the ex-slaves, and tiring himself out. He believes she can take care of herself. Someday, she thinks, I would like to be fragile and ordinary again. But she goes to sleep soon enough, though not before she finds the blank record book she has brought from the palace, and within its ornate cover begins to write a few notes of the day's events. She still has the two handbills, which she folds small and tucks into the envelope that forms the inside front cover of the book. When she has slid the stylus (so much more modern than her mother's, with its enclosed refillable ink capsule in the handle instead of an inkwell and metal nib—but try siphoning a drop of blood into that, she thinks; I'd better not get into serious trouble) back into the edge of the binding and latched the cover shut, she sits with the book in her hands for several long, blank moments before she recalls herself and lies down to sleep.

The next night is the night of the demonstration—and the night they are to board the barquentine at midnight. XX wants to go to the square, but they know his height, and her recognizable face would be too conspicuous, so they stay within the labyrinth while the others go.

After the old woman is gone, they converse spasmodically. At one point XX tells her about how fat the old woman used to be when she was young, and Essa remembers her mother's description of Annalise's mother, but XX never knew who was Annalise's mother. Essa thinks, I must ask her when she gets back, then realizes that they will be gone before then. Another silence falls between them, quietly companionable despite outer tensions.

The shelling starts a couple of hours later, just after the last flare of sunset has died. There has already been some small-arms fire from the direction of the square, and they have just gone out on the roof to see if they can see or hear anything else when the first shells light up the sky. Her first reaction is to the beauty of the flashes against the deep blue of the sky. Then she shudders with guilt; these are deadly fireworks. That is beauty, that is death, thinks Essa.

There seem to be two sources of shelling: one to the south and outside the town, with the shells bursting behind the tower of the palace, and one closer and further down, with the shells landing nearby, perhaps in the square. At least in Trader Town they did the dirty work up close, Essa thinks irrationally, angrily. Then she remembers the tanks. Neither she nor XX thinks to take shelter. They stand on the roof for an hour, shielding their ears against the louder explosions, and huddling together when the shells seem too close.

When the moon rises above the tower, blood-red from the debris in the air, it is time to go to the barquentine. Wordless, they gather their bundles. XX takes his pocket knife and pricks his palm until blood runs, smears the blood over his left palm and Essa's, and they leave their handprints, with fingertips pointing to the harbor, on the inside of the gate.

Then they go out to make their way down to the waterfront.

She can hear explosions down by the harbor wall as she runs through the twisted alleyways. She doesn't know the way but she keeps running downhill, knowing that eventually all roads led to the water. The rule of all coastal towns. Another explosion, closer this time. She only hopes the barquentine is still there and that they can reach it before they are killed by a random shell—or worse, are caught.

XX runs behind her. She hears the soft pad of his feet and the slight grunting of his tortured breath. She is gasping herself, a higher, more desperate sound, but they dare not stop running. She only wishes she could stop her mind. Leaving this land like this, she knows, is leaving everything she has lived her adult life to do—and everything which has kept her from a life of her own. If her mother by any chance lives on, she will never know it now. It will never matter again. But she has no choice, and so they run and run, and her thoughts run and run like some poor rodent in a cage runs its wheel, always downhill, always down.

The harbor wall looms up so suddenly that she almost falls over it into the sea, would have starfished over if she had been any taller, whirls around to stop XX before he can run the same risk and lose. They glance around wildly to get their bearings: XX grunts and pulls her to the right, the east, along the slippery cobbles. The tables of a harborfront café, tumbled about and interstrewn with broken chairs, suddenly bar their way, and this time she does fall, thinking "black wine" suddenly and inexplicably. He pulls her up and through, not over, the barrier, and on. They run through the darkness which now begins to be sliced with fiery flickering between the flashes of exploding shells.

The town below the tower is burning. The shells have taken

down several of the smaller towers and the bombings have blocked the streets up from the harbor and scattered rubble across the wide harborfront road. The stones are slippery here too, sometimes—she realizes suddenly, from the smell, that it is with blood. Some of the rubble is human bodies, or shattered parts of bodies, cast like leaking garbage across the ruts. She jumps across the head of a man—she knows it was a man because she can see it all fringed 'round with hair—which sits like an upturned vase directly in her path. She feels her leg brush the severed neck and after that her pant leg clings wetly.

It is a little quieter where the barquentines are anchored. The ships look strange compared with the graceful dirigibles she remembers. Merchanters. Don't offend any merchanters. The vessel they want to join is there—the middle of the three. She pulls her backpack around and clutches it to her chest as they pelt up the gangplank, losing momentum until they stop on their first step onto the deck, gasping for breath and fighting for equilibrium as the boat sways notice of their arrival. The two burly merchanters who greet them emerge from the shadows, pull them into shadow, and say nothing.

"I'm Essa," she says, not recognizing them. "I paid—"

"Shhh," hisses one. Essa and XX are pulled down a steep stair or ladder—it is dark here—and with a boom a trapdoor—hatch?—shuts above them. The lights flare. Essa stands with her hand above her, realizing that this is of course not her light, but disoriented nevertheless, and her head begins to throb.

Around her the crew is grim. "We were about to give up," says one of the two escorts.

"No we weren't," says a more cheerful voice. "Had to stay to see what happens. Curious, we are. Gets us in much trouble." The accent would have been charming in other circumstances.

Essa sways and falls to her knees with a bruising jolt. "Take her in there, make her rest," says the voice—the captain? she thinks foggily. But she is too dizzy to look. XX helps get her to her feet and into a little alcove where they sit huddled together watching the activity.

"To the deeps with sail at a time like this," says the disgusted voice. "I'm firing the engines." The deep throb of the rotary soon drowns the other noises. Essa's eyes are only half-focused, so she sees only in silhouette that a human figure stands up to a contraption in the far corner—no, in the apex of the sloe-shaped room—and begins to steer by turning a large wheel with fast, dramatic hand-over-hand sweeps. She feels the motion of the ship begin before she sinks down, her head in XX's lap, and loses consciousness.

She is shaken awake by rough hands into shouting and confusion. She scrambles with the others up the ladder, no care taken about the light this time. The boat stands out in the harbor, near the mouth of that vast oily expanse of water, which reflects blackly the chaos on land. The town burns like a torch, and above it, the tower trembles. As they watch, another explosion cracks the parapets, the noise coming across the water to them a moment later. Then, slowly, and in silence because the great clap of sound has yet to reach them, the tower splits like the mirror of the Picksey Woman, and with a ponderous, graceful progress through a perfect arc which burns itself into the air, it falls on the town. The gout of flame which bursts above it mounts three times the height it used to occupy. Now, the cliff-top is empty of everything but fire.

Essa and XX stand clutching the rail. The motion of the ship is nauseous to Essa, who huddles against the high rail with miserable and exalted horror. XX has raised his head and is screaming on a high, eerie note, his face a rictus of glee and hate.

"Ynra," says Essa. "The old man. Hoj."

He does not hear her. He raises his hands. =The evil place has been taken by flame,= he signs economically, in three brutal motions. =We will never come back here.=

"There is nowhere to come," says Essa. "Nothing could survive there."

"You be surprised," says the cheery accented voice. "Takes a lot to destroy everything. I've seen it. Sack a town, next year it's grown back and ready to sack again. Like an orchard, really." And the booming laugh rings out over the water. Essa turns her head to look at the pirate.

Out of the fire and into—what? A cooking pot? she thinks. But she is too tired to care. She slumps against XX, who leans down on her shoulder heavily, and they go back down into the crowded cabin, find their pinched alcove, cramp themselves into it, and try to shut out all noise and motion. After some hours, Essa falls into a fitful sleep to the accompaniment of XX's snores. *And so they were, and so they lay. And sailed in a barquentine away.* The nonsense rhyme from the old book accompanies her back into sleep.

At Avanue

A dream:

The child's father was going away somewhere, and her mother was doing something very busy and important, so the child had been sent in country to visit her auntie. She went exploring every day in the unfamiliar trees and countryside, so different from the many tumbled-together houses to which she was accustomed.

The wind was different here. It made a high, pure note unlike the gusty huffing of home. It was the sound of trees, the child decided. There were other notes too in the dappled music of woods and clearings: buzzing in two sets of tones from fat bumblebees and tiny round utilitarian honeybees; birds she didn't recognize singing in tumbling families of notes, around and around; squeaks of mice and chatters of squirrels; drumming from far away the source of which she could not find, for it ran away whenever she chased it; creaking trees trying not to bend in the wind; a little flexible rodent, like a ferret but with catlike ears, whose feet made tiny percussion on fallen branches and leaves; and a flat, hot note from crickets in the grass. She caught some of these dusty grasshoppers and took them home in a pocket, but they stopped making the noise then.

"Mercy," said her aunt. "Mercy on the poor creatures. They're born to grass, and in grass they should remain!"

Can you be born to a certain place where you should stay? This is something the child had never considered. She had a mother who traveled far. The traveling was like a song the child could hum if she knew the tune. Was it a song which should never have been sung?

She asked her aunt over and over. "Where is my mother born? Where am I born? Where is my father born? Where are travelers born? My traveling mother, where?"

Finally the woman took her on a long walk. The child was tired by the time they had climbed up and up a high hill. They stood on a promontory and looked out on a puffy sea of trees, and, far and away down a slash in the green fur covering all the world, a gleam of water with sunlight striking off it. The woman pointed.

"There is where you were born."

"But where am I born? I am here, and that is there. Where am I supposed to be?"

"Supposed to be?"

"Like the grasshoppers are supposed to be in the grass, not my pocket."

Her auntie laughed. The child liked that laugh. There was a high, cool music on this hill, made of that laugh, a silent wind past her ears, and the sound of far sunlight glancing off a silver-black mirror.

"You can be anywhere you want," said her auntie. "As long as no-one picks you up and puts you in their pocket, and keeps you in darkness without anything to eat."

"They stopped singing."

"They couldn't move. Grasshoppers sing with their legs and wings. If you were a prisoner, you might not be able to sing either."

The child looked up and around. The sky was clear and its blue was so pale it was almost white. It was a very hissing sky. "Is there anyone big enough to put me in their pocket?"

"Not in the real world. It happens in stories and songs."

"In songs?"

Her aunt turned so her back was to the breeze, and began to sing. She had a low, throaty voice, with a little rasp in it, so that the child thought maybe her auntie was a grasshopper too, though she looked more like the neat little rodent, with her pointy face, small hands and sleek pulled-back brown hair.

Afterward the child couldn't remember the words. The story was about some giant who drank up the sea and all the dolphins flopped and floundered so they cried out to have their water back. So the giant peed until the ocean was full again. But some of the dolphins liked dry land so they cried out again, so the giant shit some land and they went to live on it and that was where people came from.

Mostly the child remembered the way the song made gluggling sounds as the giant drank the sea, and little crying noises for the dolphin voices, and then a rushing line when the giant peed. It's why she remembered the story, later. Because it was one of the times when people music actually made sense.

"But what about my mother?" she said, persistently, after she had thanked her aunt for the song. "What about her? Where is she born?"

"I don't know, darlin'," said her aunt. "I don't think we'll ever know."

There was a song missing there. The child heard it in her voice. But her auntie's tone was so definite and so sad that the child knew it was a song her auntie could not sing even if asked. This was different from all those songs adults would not sing to you just because they wanted to keep them to themselves.

The child decided then that she could have a secret song too, like everything else in the world, a song she imagined without telling it, and it would be the song of where her traveling mother was born to. If it was not the world the child knew, then there must be another world, and there must be music in it.

A window, with dawn light starting to pearlize the sky. That pinkish-blue light unbearably beautiful through the rippled windowpane. A dream fading: a child, a childhood different from hers: Essa stirs and makes a small noise. The trader stands up and comes across the room to look down into her opening eyes.

"Minh," she says, unsurprised; then, "what am I doing here?"

"And for that matter," he says, pressing the button on the end of the cord near her face, "where is here?"

She laughs a little but stops at the ferocious pain in her head. Tries to put her hand up but can't move. Tries to lift her head and the pain almost knocks her out.

"Shhh, shhh," he says, meaning, don't move. Then he says it: "Lie still." She remembers the whisper from her recent dreams.

"My hands," she says. She feels a hard binding around her wrists, pulls a little.

"Shh, shhh, I'll get it. You were tied while you were unconscious," he says. "You kept pulling out the intravenous. And ripping at the bandages." He works away until she feels her left wrist come free, but even then her arm is too weak to do more than lift and let fall.

"Am I at Avanue?" she says.

"Further south," he says, "nearer Trader Town. We had to bring you where there was sailor medicine."

Sailor medicine. For some reason the thought panics her, and she remembers, as if through a dark fog, Gata and Lowlyn. For a confused moment she thinks she has a daughter to protect, then her head clears.

"They'll take the word home," she says. "They'll tell everyone about the woman who fell out of a cloud onto her head." She realizes she doesn't want this.

"What?" says the trader. "You came in a merchanter. With the big silent guy."

=XX,= she signs with her left hand, automatically.

"Is that his name? I thought XY. He seemed to think that would do. It's hard to understand him, you know. His language is full of names. Not easy for me."

"You were good at names when I worked for you. And the notebook was full of names for me to follow."

"Thank you for that," he says. "I trade on my own now, thanks to that notebook. She, my mother, you remember—" and he waits for her blink "—she was impressed with the net we made but she didn't want one that big. She was getting old, she said. So she gave the eastern net to me, and whatever came later from the south. I gave part of it away to a dark-skinned man . . . " Here Essa feels like laughing again, but she stops before she's done more than twitch, for the pain, and he stops.

"Listen to me babble on. They'll be here with a painkiller soon. They told me to ring when you woke up."

But it is not the medical staff who come in first, it is XX. She thinks he and the trader circle each other like dogs in the street. The trader is much shorter, and much more pale-skinned, and gentler-looking, but the big mute is sizing him up as if they were going to fight a slave battle.

"What's going on here?" she says, sharply, then "Oh!" and they both turn to her, concern cutting through whatever ritual they'd been starting.

"What's that dance all about?" she says, then has to stop. This time she's managed to bring her hand up to shield her eyes from the light a little, a bright light above her head, she realizes. The trader presses another button, above and behind her head on the wall she can't see, and the light goes off. In the comforting dawn light from the window she reads XX's familiar signs.

=We carried you off the ship south of Avenau,= he says, spelling Avanue wrong. =You were raving and pounding your head against the bulkheads. It was frightening. Most of the time you were some-one else, not Essa, not Fierce-frightened, not the in-between Essa. You tried to bite me. They sedated you and said it was some kind of intercerebral bleed—" he spells that too, she had little idea if wrong or right "—and you had to have surgery. You talked in your sleep all the time. They brought you here by—=

"Air ambulance, in a sail-ship," says the trader, and XX gives him a hostile look.

"Names," says Essa.

=—and cut your hair. I tried to stop them cutting your hair so they sedated me too. In your sleep you recited something you re-membered about where to find someone around here, so I told them. It was him—= a flip of the thumb =—so then he came and learned some hand words. Not the language, really. He makes signs like a duck.=

"Ducks have no hands—oh!" says Essa. She has learned about laughing though. Besides, she feels it's more like hysteria—absur-dist, frightened hysteria, succumbing to which would not come amiss, she thinks, coolly. But she won't. "So why shouldn't they cut my hair? It's not a big deal, to fight over."

He looks shocked. =You are a fertile woman,= he says, =of course they shouldn't cut your hair.=

She spreads her hands in confusion. There is nothing in her memory about such a taboo.

=It is wrong,= he signs.

"It was necessary," says the trader. It is obviously an argument they'd had. "Would you rather she died?"

It is XX now who spreads his hands in that equivocal gesture which means everything it has to. The trader turns away with a snort. "Dodge the important moral questions," he says. "Never mind. It was them who cut her hair. Blame them, not Essa."

"Did you blame me?" she asks.

XX shakes his head, then drops down in the chair beside the bed and takes the hand so recently freed. The trader moves to the other side and works the other wrist free, but doesn't let go of the hand once he has untied it.

"Stop it," she says. "You two are making backwash all through me. Stop being fools about each other." She turns her head back and forth, despite the pain. The window has brightened behind XX's head and the light is shining on the trader's long pale face.

"About me," she adds. And falls back down into the nothing.

"Here's the imaging of your head," says the medecin. "See where the dark patches are? That's scar tissue. Then these places here are the recent surgery."

"Trepanned," says Essa.

"That's the old name," says the medecin, "but we don't do it with an auger any more. Brace and bit. Barbaric." She doesn't look at Essa, only at the image she holds up against the sunny window. "Then, here's the area of healing. Your brain has established these alternate pathways, here, see? We didn't disturb that area much."

Essa is too polite to say she can't see at all why those yellow areas are any different from the other yellow areas which are, it seems, healthy tissue. She is much more concerned with this word "much." "Much?" She knows that specialists get overzealous and narrow-minded. Or at least, get narrow-field vision.

"Not at all, we think, but of course we can't say unequivocally." Ah. Just being careful. Though she looks more shifty, as if she has a political problem with Essa but has too much control to behave unethically.

"Will I be able to play the piano again?" Essa says, desperate for even a momentary contact.

The medecin, unexpectedly, laughs creakily. "I've heard that one a lot," she says. "But I still get a chuckle out of it." A dry chuckle, Essa thinks. A rusty chuckle. Never mind. She'd saved Essa's life, or at least her sanity. She isn't required to have a sense of humor, for that. Just steady hands in the surgical gloves, to make those microtools precise while they carved scar tissue and blood clots away from the zones which now show yellow on this transparent, vivid, multicolored image.

The medecin takes the transparency away from the windowpane. "There," she says. "I'll call the rehabilitation specialist. He'll talk with you about what happens next." Her eyes on the file where she's stowed Essa's brain image, she begins to leave.

"Wait," Essa says urgently. "What does happen next? What will it feel like? What can I expect to happen? Is this all the surgery I'll ever need? What about medical follow-up? What if I go away from here, what will I have to do?"

The medecin turns reluctantly. "It depends," she says, pursing her lips, unconsciously making a strange little fish-mouth which has Essa both giggly and despairing of any answers. Finally she speaks again.

"It depends on the next three weeks. If the clots are gone and don't re-form, you can go back north. They'll watch you at Avanue, but you will probably be fine." (Probably? Being careful again, Essa hopes.) "Then if they do re-form, or if problems show up later, we would look at another surgery, with laser this time, not as invasive, and see what then. You can look at getting back almost everything you lost—except the memory of course. Whatever was stored in the dead zone is irretrievable. No healthy tissue there at all. Necrotic. Unpleasant. Lucky you got back what you did."

"But what about this division, this sense of two people?"

"Common in amnesia. Don't let it bother you. Just have to live with it."

Discomfort makes her more brusque by the minute. Essa is beginning to rather like her, so, characteristically, wonders if she could make her blush, given the right circumstances. These are not the right circumstances.

"Enough?" says the medecin, and Essa realizes she has been staring at the woman silently.

"My light," she says, with difficulty. "What I do. My gift. It's gone."

"Might come, might not. How many years now? Three? Can't tell. Not likely. Gone too long. Sorry. I'll send Haldy in. Call if you get worse."

And she goes out. Essa does laugh, finally. Call if you get worse. Good advice!

That peculiar light just before sunset, before gloaming: it is then that Essa sees for the first time the famous dunes at Avanue, which roll like fat people in their sleep, and shift restlessly forever.

They cast long shadows, these sleeping giants, and Essa shivers. She has walked too far—after the trip north she was so grateful to be out of hospital—her hands and feet are cold, and she is dizzy with exhaustion. She sits down on the ragged grass at the edge of the bluff which overlooks the dunes, and tries not to hate them.

Her mother's words, remembered in a dream, sound like water flowing in her thoughts. There is no water here. The grasses under her are dry and stiff, and they grow in sand so fine it grits through her clothing against the skin of her ass. The sea is too far away to see or smell. But at least she is alone.

Though she is shivering, it is still a hot day, and the sun has warmed the sand. The ground radiates heat into her body. She lies down flat on her belly, her head to one side so that she can still see the dunes, and puts her hands beneath her; gradually they warm.

Gradually her body comes back into balance and she starts to see an eerie beauty before her. The sun is fully down when she sits up, brushes the sand away as well as she can, and hugs her knees to her chest. She puts her chin on her knees and watches darkness descend over the low rolling landscape.

This is unlike any cliff on which she has rested yet. It is low and gives no perspective. The dunes come up almost to her feet. Yet the demarcation is quite abrupt: there is no grass growing anywhere after this brief crumbling drop-off, and she can see as the land-breeze begins to quicken that ahead of her the sand is moving. In fact, she realizes, she can hear it, a low sweeping sound which has mounted from inaudibility until it inexorably backs every other sound: sounds of grasses moving, insects scraping, birds calling from the invisible sea far beyond her viewpoint are all subsumed in one great sand-song.

It is a sound so relentlessly sad that Essa can hardly bear to listen, but so persistent that she cannot ignore it now that she has become aware of its susurration. She pulls her sweater—the one her mother made by her knitting—around her and waits.

When it is fully dark and the wind has died again, she rises and begins the long walk back to town in the dim light of stars and crescent moon.

There is no harmonious moment. Essa knows this and yet she waits for one. The moment when she could turn and what she wants would be there, and she would recognize it. But there is never a moment like that, like there is in the romance novels, when everyone takes a break in their adventure and the protagonists come suddenly face-to-face, with no distractions, and really see each other for the first time.

It often happens at the river, Essa has noticed in her reading. They are bathing in some remote river and they stand suddenly naked together and recognize something—and not the obvious, either, she thinks wryly, not the obvious that their nipples are puckered with desire, and if one or both have cocks they are visibly erect. No, it is some essence they see, so that their real nakedness becomes a symbol of an openness of spirit. The thought of it makes her laugh—but it also makes her hungry. Hungry for that to happen to her again, that openness—though she wonders if it ever has. Maybe with the trader, almost—but he put her on the Black Ship years ago and that was that. And maybe Fierce-frightened felt something like that with Escape-from-bondage, but Fierce-frightened is half-gone now and though Essa now remembers, she does not feel what she remembers the waif felt.

And maybe, with the Carrier of Spirits, that terrifying joy she felt opened her, but that was more like being torn widespread, barely giving permission, for her own good and the sake of passion but hardly restful to the spirit.

And there is never, Essa thinks, the clarity of feeling those stories have, those stories where there are never any loose ends. There is never a past which still ties the heroes, never two irritable men circling them, never a family left behind which they remember—as Essa does Gata and Lowlyn and the nameless daughter she has decided never to know—in a cloud of guilt, never a thin silver cord binding them to a mysterious and painful brilliance. Never any impediment to the heroes moving together, their hands raising in unison to touch: touch hands, touch faces, touch the other's breast slowly, with wonder. Never, in real life, the freedom and warm weather which allow them, in the books, to move together to the bank, never the smooth sward beside the river on which the heroes lie down, slowly, to explore each other with awe and without thistles or mosquitoes.

Essa is so hungry that if she closes her eyes she feels a kiss, some strange idealized kiss, descend on her gently. This is not immanence, not at all. It is the crystallization of a desire she cannot name.

She lies beside XX nights, she loves the trader without lying with him, though she wonders now and again if they ever will keep the promise that once existed between them, and she knows she could go on forever like this. The kiss would live on her shoulder, ready to engulf her whenever she was at rest. In the bath, now, she sees her belly muscles flutter with the tension needed to keep her breath from pounding out of her in that hunger, needed to keep her from relaxing into that kiss which does not exist.

Why a kiss? There is nothing much about kissing in the romantic adventures. They are all about doing, so it is hands, always hands, hands which are loved, hands which touch, hands which explore, hands which go deep into another lover in the most intimate of caresses—the things, she thinks, that Annalise learned to do to Ea from books, from books. *creating own identity—pulling away from cliché*

→ But Essa thinks of mouths. Of kisses. Of mouths exploring each other, of mouths exploring bodies, mouths engulfing hands— a fingertip, a thumb caressed by a tongue—or mouths encouraging the swelling power of genitals. She dreams while awake and the dream is of the power of mouths and tongues: kisses, caresses, flesh, words.

different kind of story

Words. She knows so many. She knows seven languages, and all of them different, and in all of them she is hungry. She has no idea what to do next, and there is no-one she could ask. She is an adult now. Her father is dead. Her mother is gone. She has no brother or sister. Her friend Minh? She does not know what to ask his self-contained calmness. And XX, her lover? How does she ask a lover where to find the satisfaction she is not getting from him? It is not good manners.

The silver thread, narrower than a hair, only the thickness of an imaginary cell, still binds Essa to the Carrier, but in a frustratingly ephemeral way: it is there, but it tells her nothing: it is not a conduit, only a connexion. Essa feels none of the connexions her mother felt: to her mother should she live, to the partners she left in the sailor town, to XX or the trader here, and—especially missed—to her daughter.

Why Essa should be bound to the Carrier she cannot guess, unless it is a new gift brought out by the head injury, as her light seems to have been snuffed the same way. She remembers the Carrier with love, but the thread is an artifact of a longing she cannot fill and has had to put behind her. She would rather know if her child is living.

She says as much to XX and Minh one night as they sit relaxing in an Avanue eatery, a comfortable, cave-like cellar where they go often.

=Why?= says XX. =You have decided not to go to her.=

"That doesn't mean I don't love her."

=Yes it does. You may feel some atavistic sort of ownership, but love comes of knowledge.=

"No, it doesn't! What about love of the universe? One doesn't have to know every human and every organism and every rock—"

=All right, all right. But for what you meant—=

"Fine. I agree. I don't love her that way. But I regret not knowing her. Even though—" and she forestalls his rising hands with a touch "—even though I decided not to go back, and I think I decided well, I have doubts."

=Doubt is useless,= he replies. He may be right, but that doesn't help much.

"Minh," she says then to the trader, who is watching the conversation and shuffling his new cards, "should I have gone back?"

"It's unlike you to ask any such question," he says. "Are you ill?"

She snorts. "Oh, no. Just alive and stuck with it, as your poet said."

"Then isn't that your answer?"

"Not yet," she said. "I can't rest easy on that part of the decision, though I lose no sleep about the rest."

=You don't regret not going back to Lowlyn and Gata, do you?=

Essa ignores for the moment the possible edge to XX's question. "No, not at all, but I think it's because they are adults. They can fend for themselves. But it seems unfair to give a child my absence for a natal gift. She'll know: they'll tell her. I know them. They're honest as mountaineers, for all they would like me to believe you never trust a sailor."

"Whatever we might say you have said to yourself," Minh says thoughtfully, laying cards in a pattern and starting a game of solitaire with them.

"Indeed."

"So when will you listen to your own answer?"

"I want to know that. I am tired of lying awake with the hamsters running on their wheels in my head."

"Hamsters?"

"Little pet rodents they keep in Sailor Town. Children keep them. They are nocturnal, and they run all night on these little wheels in their cages. The cages are cheap and the wheels squeak. It's astonishingly irritating."

"I can imagine having a cageful in your thoughts is equally precious."

She laughs. "Indeed."

=It's no joy to sleep with either,= puts in XX. =Squeaking all night, and grumpy all day. I'm just as glad I have no family to consider.= And he invents a rude sign for "hamsters"; the trader chuckles silently into his cards, and Essa spares his hands a theatrically exasperated look.

"Who were your family?" says Essa. "I never knew."

=Slaves are moved away from family as soon as possible. That old woman we stayed with?= Essa nods. =She was my wet-nurse. Nearest thing I had to family. But she left the palace early.=

"Weren't you close to anyone?" Minh asks.

=Not if I could help it. It wasn't safe.=

"It doesn't seem easy either," Minh says. "I find your old world hard to understand."

=This is clear,= XX signs with that arrogance with which he is always too ready to engage with Minh. But they are all getting used to this: as Essa begins to bristle, XX makes a conciliatory softening of his hands, and the trader quietly gathers up the cards and shuffles them.

"My family are all weavers," he says. "They have been weavers for generations. They have gotten used to me being a trader and a traveler, but they are still surprised by it. Even they are surprised, even these northerners. None of these things are simple." He makes a face at this last, and Essa grins.

"Oh, well, if I had expected such wisdom, I would have asked you sooner! I know about 'simple.' It's the same as 'fair'!"

"Yes, exactly the same."

=All of you are crazy,= signs XX. =You think the universe will make sense if you keep at it long enough.=

"Well, it does!" says Essa at the same time the trader says, "Ah, 'logical.' Why not?"

XX's bark of laughter is familiar now, so neither of the others understands at first why the server hurries over, says delicately, "Is everything all right, Minhs?" When they do, they look at each other, then the hapless young server, and they all guffaw at once, and have a hard time stopping.

Perhaps, as the server clearly thinks, they have had a little too much of the black wine. But it is such a fine vintage that they order more anyway, and, reassured that the others are laughing, the server forgets to fear the big mute with the harsh loud bark and goes to bring them another flagon. It's one night when the squeaking wheel is silenced, and Essa sleeps soundly between trader and lover.

It is a simple answer, really. It comes to Essa in the memory of XX's old name. A fist is tight and tense, then it opens, relaxes, turns and flies up. It could mean Escape-from-bondage, but it could also mean: let it go.

Let it go. Let the past transform as it will, let the future unfold. XX was right in a way about her expectations: she has taken to worrying at the world, trying to get it to make sense. It is time to let go, whatever that may mean: daughter, lover, friend, past and future.

Simply let it all go. It will fly up.

Over time she and XX have many late-night conversations about the politics of the Land of the Dark Isles. His hands become more and more vehement. Her answers become more and more distant. She knows he will never truly leave the land behind.

"Why don't you just go back?" she says one day, impatiently.

=Why don't you go back to the Range?= he counters.

She looks at the idea, beside her recent understandings—if such ambiguous and uneasy reconciliations with herself can be called understandings—and suddenly grins. "You know, I think I had already decided to do that. And you—"

=I have already decided I must go back,= he signs, =but I was waiting for a time.=

"A sign?"

He laughs. =A sign, yes; a time you were well enough that I could leave off taking care of you.=

Now it is her turn to laugh, so much that she holds her belly and rolls in her seat. "And here I thought," she gasps, "that I was taking care of you!"

=You are honest, Fierce Essa.= It is a new combination of signs.

"Am I that fierce?"

=Yes.= He chops the single sign in the air beside his smile, meaning, it is true, but I like it.

"When will you go?"

=There is a Black Ship downcoast. I heard word of it last week. It is going up to the Range, then back to Trader Town and south. It could take you up and me down.=

"No," says Essa, "I think I'll walk. Like my mother did from Avanue. And I walked out of the Range. It seems like a good idea to go back the way I came. Close the circle. Besides—"

=?=

"I have been thinking about the south too. And I miss—"

=Amazing! You miss something!=

"Shut up. I miss the walking. Those days with my mother, before we met you and your wicked man."

=My wicked man?=

"Wasn't he, by then? Yours?"

XX thinks. =I guess he was. By then.=

"Think about why you took him on."

=To get away from him.=

"A pretty strange choice of escape, don't you think, Escape-from-bondage? A strange way of earning a new name."

=A name you have never tried to guess. Why?=

"You really want to know, after all this time?"

=Yes.= No smile.

"Because you had not escaped. Perhaps not until now."

=That was my name,= he says. =You were kind not to say it.=

"Not kind," she says. "Cowardly. I'm sorry."

=And now?=

"Now you truly will have to have a new name."

=I suppose so.= He does not appear happy about this, and she grins. She wonders if the name will be the one she has learned from his old name: transforming the old sign into the new. But she will wait to see what he finds for himself. She is not responsible for naming him. She has had enough trouble naming herself lately.

"Maybe," she says, "you will travel south to Trader Town with my trader. Won't that be fun for you both?" and laughs raucously at his expression until finally he gives her a rueful return grin.

=Yes,= he signs. =I can hardly wait.=

* * *

"I thought it might someday be possible to have a happy life," says Essa, "but it seems I am mistaken."

=So far.=

"So far? As if you still have hope? How in the world do you still have hope? After what has happened to you?"

=I'm not sure I will ever be able to have a happy life. But I think it might, just might be possible for someone to have a happy life.=

"Like me?"

=Probably not you.=

Essa snorts. "Goodness, that's an indictment. Why not me?"

=You are too naïve.=

This time she shouts with laughter. "Naïve! Naïve?"

=Yes.=

"What in heaven's name do you mean?"

=Not the name of heaven. Just the place you come from.=

"You don't know anything about the place I come from."

=It is true I don't know the place. But I know a great deal about the place now, after learning to know you. I know what kind of stories—not the stories themselves, mind you, but the kind of stories—they tell their children. I know what the children are led to expect from the world. Fair treatment. A happy life. Even that question you ask comes out of the mountains.=

"Is there anything wrong with that? You make it look stupid."

=There is nothing wrong, and there is something wrong. There is nothing wrong with making a place where children can be safe. I can hardly imagine it myself, but it sits on the edge of my vision like a small sun. It's a blinding glimpse of something. Safety. So very odd. And I suppose there's nothing wrong with a modicum of safety, though I think my way one at least learns how to react quickly. But there is something wrong in the kind of complacency . . . = his sign is complicated: a cat after cream, a fat despot = . . . which lets you think you have a right to a happy life just because you can think of the idea.=

"I don't agree with you. Everyone should be able to be complacent in that way!" As she speaks she illustrates the way by repeating the cat-with-cream sign. "But that other, that arrogance, I don't think we are arrogant, in the mountains, like that—do you?"

=Arrogant? I don't know. Arrogant? A curious word. The arrogance of privilege. You had safety. That's a privilege.=

"That was a privilege in your society. But in ours, a right, and therefore not to be arrogant about. Rather to defend, to protect."

=But you lost sight of what you were protecting. Took it for granted. Look how you tried to bed me when you were in-between Essa. You took for granted that everyone had what you had, and just acted as if it were so. And it wasn't, and you were too blind to see.=

"That's not fair. I was also brain-injured and reacting to a horror I could hardly remember and certainly couldn't understand. Of course I wanted to think something was familiar. So I mistook one kind of familiarity for another. It didn't kill you. It didn't even hurt you. You grew from it. You learned a little trust, you stepped outside your bloody class-consciousness, and you didn't have to put out anything you didn't want to. And in the end, it probably had something to do with why you were wandering around the southland with a mad king in tow."

=Mad regent.=

"I'm using literary license. The mad king is a trope of literature and myth."

=But that mad king in the play we saw, the one with the daughters, he wasn't wicked, just betrayed.=

"There are wicked ones too. Let me . . . wait a minute. Expert deflection job! We weren't talking literature, we were talking about whether I did you any harm."

=No more harm than any other change in circumstance ever does for anyone. Every change is a violent revolution. Every growth in self kills the self before. Sometimes it's a self one doesn't want to lose. I didn't want to lose Escape-from-bondage. He had a good life. He was boss slave. He could afford to have dreams. And he had lovely little Fierce-frightened to fuck. She was a tasty thing and she fought enough to make her interesting. And she gave great blow jobs.=

"So do I."

=I suppose you do, but not great like hers were great. You think too much. You're always stopping to ask me how I am, whether I like it, what I want. Don't you know that what I want is not to want? Not to have to want anything? And she used to just take me up in her hands and on her tongue and pull me through want. I didn't have to answer any questions.=

"She forced you. It was rough, what she did. She didn't know any other way."

=That isn't rough. Rough is an old bitch with razor fingernails—remember the scars? Remember Ea's book? I was probably one of the boy slaves she watched. I was there. I remember her. That's rough. I used to think that her parents should have beat her.=

"The old woman?" says Essa, confused.

=No. Ea. She was a bit like the old Essa. She was arrogant with protection. I hate that. Annalise at least had bruises. But nobody, not even the old woman, could touch Ea. She went on and on about safety, from her heights in her parents' tower. What did she think it was like to be a slave? She didn't even figure out we had a language. She was stupid with power.=

"She didn't use it."

=Power withheld is still power. She was so proud she didn't beat us. It didn't do us any good all those years waiting for her to lose her resolve, or her temper. Didn't do any good to the ones she owned that she set free. What were they to do? They were born in the palace. And only slaves could serve there. A dubious benefit, freedom.=

"You may argue so, but you called yourself Escape-from-bondage."

=True. True.=

"And you didn't think your position through to this orgy of rejection until you had the freedom to do so."

This time it is him laughing, that hoarse bark which always startles the part of Essa which remains naïve, comforts the Fierce-frightened part still curled in a corner of her mind. =True!= he signs, and hugs her. =True, Fierce Essa, and very clever you are to notice!=

"Of course I'm clever," she says. "I got dropped on my head. It always takes us mountain people this way. Drop me again a couple of times and I'll be a genius. Could we maybe go to bed now, do you think?"

=I think so,= he signs magnanimously. =If you insist.=

Essa spreads her arms and hugs the light.

"It's so wonderful to be back where the days are properly long in the summer," she says.

"They are long in the south too, are they not?" says the trader.

"It's different there."

"Yes, I imagine it is," he says.

They walk along the edge of the cliff. On their left the dunes shift slowly in the late evening's light breeze. The sun is so low that it seems almost as if the golden radiance it sends slanting across the world is the force that pushes the grains of sand along and tumbles them over the edges of curling dune-edge waves. Essa sees little clumps of sand detach and scuttle down the unmarked inner curl of a dune, leaving a trail as if a small animal had leaped and zig-zagged across the pristine sand. She stands and watches until the shifting grains of the dune erase the marks. She feels that her life is like that surface, marked and then erased, and moving, always mov-ing. What has it been for? Has she found anything? Will anything endure?

Ea had come from Avanue to the mountains, trading the shift-ing sands for the solid rock base. Essa will have to go back to the mountains next, find out what was left there.

"You have to quit tugging at me, both of you," she says idly.

The trader—Minh, she thinks suddenly, looking at his long face with love—smiles. "You are not territory," he says.

"Yes, I know," she says. "We will never be lovers now, will we?"

"No," he says, "no. Sunset brings an end to many things." Beautiful Minh there in the evening sun. She feels a sudden sense of continuity.

"It goes on through us and beyond," she says. "I have a daugh-ter."

"Yes, I know."

"When I go on, will you find her?"

"Maybe. Where will you go?"

"I don't know. I expect a door will open in the world. It has always been that way."

"No," he says. "It has never been that way, for you. You walked along a road which began wide and obvious and narrowed until there was nowhere else to walk. So you walked there. But you have never looked for doors; you have never expected to transcend the landscape."

"Now is different," she says. "Minh."

They walk along the cliff, their feet scuffing up sand from among the grasses which held its edge firm.

"Look at that," he says.

"I am not ready for any more lessons today," she says. He laughs aloud, a great delighted shout of laughter which rings out across the dunes and the grasses like a shock wave. There has been a lot of that lately, she thinks; it's a pleasing thought.

"Very well," he says. "I will back off. I am getting a little foolish about it, I acknowledge."

"I should think so," she says, tartly. "The two of you give me no peace. He bristles and you endure. He circles and you crouch protectively. You would make a great study for animal behaviorists."

He laughs again, a chuckle this time. "You were very far gone," he says.

"Well, I'm back," she says. "Not to be ungrateful, but ease up. I'm back."

"I see that," he says. "Minh."

Black wine

The messenger came in the early morning, as Elta was getting ready to go to work. She read the note quickly and scribbled a reply before grabbing her veil and bag and hurrying down to the warehouse.

She met with the man after work, in a quayside café. When she first saw him, as she walked down the hill, he was sitting alone at a table, the only person there without a turban, sun on his foreign smooth hair making blue-black highlights. As she watched, the tavern cat leaped to the table, sat down facing him with tail curled around paws. As she approached, he was speaking to the cat, a single word, something strange. There was a curious similarity between them.

She introduced herself, sat down in the shade on the other side of the table. He ordered black wine, which she'd never tasted. In the sun its glitter matched his hair. She picked up the goblet, sipped, made a face.

"You don't like it?"

"It's strange. I'll try it."

"If you don't like it I can order you something else. Your mother liked it, so I thought you might."

"Do you know Gata? We never had it at home."

"I mean your other mother." He paused, then inflected the word strangely as he said it: "Essa."

Her gaze sharpened on him. "Essa?"

"I brought you some things from her."

"She is alive?"

"I don't know. I haven't seen her in a while. But I was coming here, and I had her things. She wanted you to know something about your other parent."

"Thank you," she said politely.

There was a silence. She sipped her black wine, found it no more interesting the second time. It had been a tiring day and she wanted beer. The man opposite her watched silently, then flagged the server. Elta shrugged in apology, ordered a flagon of beer. The man sat quietly with her, waiting for the order to arrive, seemingly not uncomfortable with the silence. He was a tall, well-proportioned man with graying streaks at the temples in the long, otherwise-dark hair which he wore pulled back and tied with a thong. He smiled easily at her as she scrutinized him; fortuitously, just then the server brought the beer. Elta took time to drink a great draft before she spoke again.

"I thought you meant Gata in your note. You didn't put her name."

"We don't use names much where I come from. It takes me a while to get used to it, every time I go out."

"Out?"

"Out from home."

"Are you a merchanter? A sailor?"

"A trader."

"What is your name?"

He looked at her.

"Oh," she said, embarrassed. "You don't use names."

"Minh," he said. "You can call me that."

"Minh?"

He corrected her, but she couldn't hear how his Minh differed from hers, except perhaps slightly in pitch. She tried it that way and he said, "Yes, better."

She could not think of anything more to say. Finally it seemed he took pity on her.

"Would you like to know about your mother? Have some of her things?"

"I think so," she said. "I never really think about her much. You know, I have a job, I live on my own now."

"What work do you do?"

"I work in a warehouse . . . "

His gaze sharpened. "A trader too?"

"No. I drive a forklift."

"Necessary work."

"Yes, I guess. Keeps me in beer. Pays the rent. You know."

"Yes."

"My other mother was a trader. Essa."

"Yes, I know. She worked for me, once, a long time ago. Four hands ago, then. Also I knew her later. She wasn't a trader then."

"Oh? She had another job?"

"She had another life. Or two."

"I don't know what you mean."

"It takes a while to explain."

"Have you talked to my mother? I mean, Gata? And Lowlyn, I think he's in town these days. Did you talk to him?"

"I have talked with Lowlyn. Gata has been too busy to come out to meet me."

She shouted with laughter. "Gata. That's what she always says. Since she took over the pottery. But it's not time—she has loads of time. She is such a pain."

"Pain?"

"Idiom. She gives me a pain, see?"

"Yes. I see. Other languages are sometimes a bit challenging."

"Oh, I know. I had to take them in school. I was terrible. I tried and tried to learn, because Lowlyn wanted me to travel with him, but I don't have a gift for languages at all. I just can't remember the difference, you know. Like Minh. You just have to take it the way I say it. They think I'm hopeless. At school."

"I thought Lowlyn was the potter."

"He was. But after Essa died—well, he thought . . . " she said, embarrassed.

"Go on."

"Gata came back and she wouldn't go out. She had a berth on a ship and the family needed the money. She was pregnant but that wasn't it. She couldn't go out. There's a name for it, I guess. Fear of markets. Something. Anyhow, Lowlyn took the berth instead. She ran the pottery. So she doesn't go out. If you want to see her, you have to go up to the house."

"She didn't invite me."

"She wouldn't. Who needs it? If you want to see someone, you go there. Your note was nice, but kind of strange, you know? My hand figured you must be a foreigner. Otherwise, you'd have just come."

She had polished off her beer, now stood. "Are you coming now?"

"Coming now?" He looked up at her. His stillness was un-nerving. She jittered a little. "Yeah. Coming to see Mom." She gestured up the hill.

"If I am invited."

"Sure. I invite you. Come on."

They walked up a steep, cobbled street among the plastered and painted houses. The trader was looking around with interest. Elta snapped her fingers, hummed a popular song.

"You are a musician?" he said.

"Sort of. I play in a pickup band some weekends. With my hand. Nothing fancy. Pop covers, that kind of thing."

"Covers?"

"Songs someone else wrote. We just sing 'em. Try to give them a twist sometimes, other times sing 'em even more like the originals than the originals, if you know what I mean."

"I think I know what you mean. Faithful yet sharp."

"Yeah, that's it exactly. Every note on, but if there was a mistake in the original, we take it out. No-one knows why we bother to sound so good, but it's a matter of pride, you know?"

She walked backward ahead of him, talking and snapping her fingers.

"For instance," she said, "when I'm driving the forklift, right? You have your stack of crates, high as two people. Two tall people. Right? So you have to align them just right, or they topple. Everybody knows that. But for me, I want them to have shape. Shape, you know, lined up just right with the one beside them. Shape. Like in the music. The others, some of them, they just cover the tune. Sloppy, to my mind. I want the tune to take a shape."

"It seems odd that you can hear the nuances of the notes and yet you have no ear for language."

"Well," she said, "you caught me there. I can make a tune of what you say, sing it back. Minh," she said, by way of explanation, and he nodded, smiling.

"But that's where it stops. What it means? So I can sing these sentences, right? But maybe they just sound okay from the outside, but they don't mean the right thing. It's like music. People keep talking about the words. The words, who cares? The words. They just put something in the singer's mouth for them to pack their note around. I play. I don't sing. I can't remember words. Still, we're working with, now . . . well, we don't even use the words, sometimes. Unless we can get a singer. It's a line, like the instrumental line. That's all. Words. Hmph."

She whirled around.

"Keep walking up there," she said. "I'm just running into the shops here. I'll catch up."

Moments later, she rushed back to him, her arms full of two

loaves of bread, some flowers with their stems wrapped in paper, and a string bag full of . . .

"Onions?" he said.

"Yeah, why?"

"Oh, just remembering the names. Names for me are like words for you. They run away like water. The names of things, now these are necessary, and in my language we have them, but even then they are misty, they can change as the thing changes. An onion, you see, one name when it is fresh, another when it has been cut open, another when it is cooked, another when peeled and eaten raw. They are similar, but they recognize that things change. Like the shifting sands of the dunes at—"

He said a word. "Humm?" she said.

"Avanue," he said again. "They shift, they change. Everything changes. Every thing changes. So, every name of things must have the potential and the actuality of change within it. But people other places, they can't hear it or say it. Their things have one name. I find it hard to learn."

"People are funny, aren't they?" Elta said confidentially. "I've never been able to figure them, to tell you the truth. It's just not my gift."

"Your mother had that gift. She didn't always know it, but she always saw a great deal."

"You liked her, I guess."

"Yes," he said. She wondered what that meant in his odd language. At least, it sounded odd to her, all those words for the same thing on a different day of the week.

"Could Essa speak your language?" she said.

"Yes," he said. "Very well. She spoke many languages and knew two others which were not spoken. I think she knew seven or nine languages by the end."

"The end?"

"Well, by the time I knew her last."

"When was that?"

"Oh, several years ago, I think."

"You think? Don't you know?"

"We count time somewhat differently at Avanue, too. I have translation problems."

"Don't I know what you mean," Elta said. "Sounds like me and my mom. Gata, I mean. Translation problems, I mean. Here we are."

She pressed a bellpush by the door vigorously several times, then without waiting opened the big gate and gestured him through impatiently. "Come on, come on."

He turned back to close the door she had left open. "Come on," she said, "someone will get that."

"Who?"

"Oh, someone," said Elta vaguely, and strode across the court-yard and into a dim foyer. The woman sitting there in the shade rose to greet them.

"Mama!" said Elta. "I've brought a guy called Minh who knew Essa."

"I know of him," said Gata. Her voice was low and measured and she sounded reluctant. The trader stopped in the sun, where he was clearly visible, and waited.

"Oh, for goodness's sake," said Elta. "You look like a pair of circling cats. I've got some bread. I'm taking it to the kitchen."

The door shut behind her. Gata laughed.

"Quite a whirlwind, isn't she?"

"Yes, indeed."

"I suppose she kept you entertained all the way up the hill. It's her gift. She's an entertainer."

"She makes shapes, she says," said the trader.

"Oh, yes. Of everything except her life. That lousy job, when she could have work with me that would lead to something . . . "

"Well, she is young."

"Not getting any younger."

"She is very different from Essa."

Gata sharpened her look on him. "Essa is alive, you say."

He smiled and made himself into a willing stone for her edge. "She was alive when I last saw her. Apparently there is a Carrier of Spirits. Only she would know."

"Oh, yes. That woman. She came here, years ago. We made her welcome." Gata's mouth curved—not quite a smile, but the blush on the edges of her ears was unmistakable. Minh, he thought, this is interesting. Gata saw him watching, said unnecessarily, "She brought a . . . message from Essa." The blush deepened, then swept away as Gata's mouth tightened—at the memory, he wondered, of the rest of that message?

"Are you angry with Essa?"

"What for?"

"Not returning?"

"Why be angry? She got thrown out of a ship. I thought she was dead. When I heard she wasn't, from the Carrier, I was just grateful. I didn't blame her for not coming back. Her mother, then her. The sailors didn't do her family any kindness."

"You handfasted her, and you had her daughter."

"Yes, I did. We did. And that was—interesting."

"Interesting?" said the trader.

"Oh, yes," said Gata. "If you think to keep your gone lover with you, have her child. That will shatter your illusions!"

The trader, unexpectedly, laughed. "Would you like to hear about your gone lover?"

"Yes, of course."

He took a small package from his vest, unwrapped cloth from around several cards. Coming into the shade, he counted them out into Gata's hand.

"The cloud, the hand, the pit, the tower, the mother, the heart, the new wood," he said.

"Humm?" she said, like Elta.

"That was her life," he said.

"Will you take tea?" she said, holding the cards against her chest.

"Yes, indeed," he said.

"And tell me what you mean?"

"It's what I came for," he said.

"In the back," said the warehouse chief. "On the . . . "

" . . . forklift. I know," said the trader. He walked back into the shadowy warehouse. The air was filled with the fibers of cotton kapok, just as his warehouses were. The sunlight through the skylights made shafts of light which seemed so solid he skirted them. He knew that what seems a certain way may be a certain way, but secretly, not in the manner one expects. If he walked through the light, what effort might be required of him?

Elta was singing lustily over the noise of the forklift and the cartons being shifted. He stood in the shadow of a pile of boxes and watched her for a few moments. He noticed with a private smile that she repeated the same words even when they were clearly inappropriate for the music, but that every note, despite the fact that she was bawling it over engine noise in a dusty warehouse, was carefully sounded. It was a wailing song in the popular music tradition of this sailor place. He wondered what she would make of the obscure tonal shifts of the dune music of Avanue, or the mountain music which always made him think of the ten-thousand-foot cliffs of the Fjord of Tears, with their dangerous winds over beautiful meadows ending abruptly above the sheer drop to the sea. What would she make of her mother's life? Music with no words? That would be ironic, for the daughter of Essa, the granddaughter of Ea and Annalise— three women whose lives were hung on languages.

Finally he came out of the shadows and attracted her attention. She pulled the forklift around with a flourish and squealed its tires as she braked to a dramatic halt beside him.

"Well done," he said, laughing.

"I practice," she said.

"I am sure you do," he said.

"I'm playing at the village teaclub tonight," she said. "Want to come along? Have to leave now: having a bite with my hand and then some of them are coming."

"You have a whole hand? You are young."

"Not so young as all that."

"You did not ask me, yesterday, about your mother's things. The things I brought for you and your other parents."

"The cloud, the hand, the pit, the tower, the mother, the heart, the new wood," she said, almost sang.

"I'm impressed. You remembered words."

"Gata told me the song. The tune. She said, it was her life. She said you told her how, that you would tell me."

"Yes, I will, if you like."

"Come to the gig. Then we can go drink some of that expensive wine and talk. You can talk. Right?"

"Certainly. And it will not be expensive. I brought a crate with me. It is all I drink, for wine."

"Oh, yeah? How come?"

"Because of Essa. Sentiment. Romantic reasons."

She laughed. "You, a romantic? Give me another story!"

He shook his head. "You overestimate me. I am just a trader."

"And you came all the way here to do trade deals, that's all. Right. What trader brings his own wine? Why did you come? To find us? Why, after all this time?"

"Your mother was angry at her mother, because her mother went and stayed away. Are you angry with Essa?"

"Nah. Don't have time. C'mon."

She tugged his arm, and pulled him past the forklift to a small door behind some stacked crates. They threaded down a narrow corridor where the noise of some kind of engine thumped so loudly he could hardly hear her saying, "Besides, I have Gata and Lowlyn. And the other parents, eventually. One less didn't matter much."

"Aren't you curious?"

"I guess so."

They emerged into eyeblinking sunlight. She pulled him along the side of the warehouse to another small door, ducked in and emerged with a bag, and a veil which she began to wind around her head as they walked.

"Even—" he paused "—cats are curious."

"If I'm anything, I'm some kind of dumb bird," she said. "Notes in my head. Not much else. What's the point? Play, work, eat, sleep, shit. Fuck comfortably at home. Who needs more?"

"Do you need your other mother? Your genatrix?"

"Suppose so. Why, though, really? I mean, not that I'm not grateful, now you're here and everything, but why?" She looked at him with blank eyes, then dropped the veil.

"What if you want to have children of your own? Know where they came from?"

"They'll come from me. And the others. That's all I need."

"What if they ask you questions you can't answer?"

She stopped, turned one complete turn on her toes, slowly, and ended facing him, lifting the veil and tossing it back over her turban to hang down behind. "That's a good point," she said. "Really. Finally."

"Finally?"

"Well, to tell you the truth, I couldn't really empathize with the rest. I mean, parents. Generators. So what? They do it. We come out later. It works. Thanks, and all that, and thanks for doing a decent job of taking care of the kids, but. Here I am. Responsible for myself. What does knowing my other mother have to do with it?"

"Methinks thou darling dost protest too much."

"What?"

"Oh, a quotation from literature. I'm not sure which country, who. I think you are saying what you want to believe. You are curious. I see it."

He stopped, reached into his vest for the cards. They were a different deck than the one he'd sacrificed to keep Essa's cards intact, but he had had these for almost twenty years and they had become as well-worn. He stopped at a niche in the street wall and hunkered down. He spread his scarf on the dusty pavement and on it he laid out seven cards.

"Minh, minh, minh, minh, minh, minh, minh," he said.

She looked over his shoulder. "What is that? Oh," she said, and sang the tune which made a sentence: the cloud the hand the pit the tower the mother the heart the new wood.

"Yes," he said. "But this is your life. I do not know your wish, and I ask, what say the cards?"

"Let's look," she said, not recognizing the ritual. She reached over his shoulder and turned over the center card.

"The bard," he said, and laughed.

"Certainly," she said, unsurprised.

"But a bard sings words!" he said, still chuckling. "If you want to be that card, you will have to learn some, and in the right order too!"

She pulled her hand back from the card as if burned. He turned over the far right card. "The past," he said. "Out of the mist. Interesting. Good."

"Why?"

"The past was not an easy place for your mother, or her mother, or her mother before her. Out of the mist. Maybe the chain is broken."

"Oh, I suppose," said Elta carelessly. "What next?" She turned the card second from the right. He winced as she creased the corner slightly, laying it down crooked. He reached to smooth and straighten it. "The wand reversed," he said. "Hidden gifts."

He turned the next card himself, forestalling her hasty, half-extended hand.

"The waste land," he said, "reversed. It means you have gifts you throw away. Hidden, now thrown away."

"That's what my parents are always saying. Well, my mother," she said, grumpily, and straightened up.

"Then the bard at the center, governing past and future. And what of the future?"

"Read it but don't tell me," she said, and walked off down the street. He turned the cards over. The mother, the journey, the new wood, he said to himself, troubled. He shuffled the cards away.

When he looked down the street, she had disappeared. He stood slowly, wrapping the cards away into his vest pocket. She stepped backward around a corner ahead, and beckoned to him impatiently. Children were shouting and playing in the street but he saw her lips say, "Come on!" and he shook his head and chuckled again as he followed up the steep street. A whirlwind, her bearing-mother had called her. What would her genatrix have thought? Minh, he said silently, you would have liked this child of yours. He thought of the cards: the mother, the journey, the new wood. The mother was clear: in his bag he had *The Book of Ea* and *The Book of Essa,* and the two journals Essa had left behind: Ea's, written in blood, and her own. They were Elta's by line of blood, and in the near future he would give them to her. She stood at the corner, jittering on tiptoes. When he caught up to her she was already talking.

"And of course it doesn't work that way," she said, "so we have to improvise. You'll hear what I mean. You do like music, don't you?" she said anxiously.

"Yes," he said. "At home, I sing for my people."

"Great!" she said. "You can do a guest set. We can back you up. What is it? Plainsong?"

"No. Plainsong is mountain. This is dune music. I will show you, perhaps. If the others want me to do it."

"Have to be invited, huh?" She said it with a peculiar air of triumph, as if she had guessed something rather hard. He smiled at her again. She was endearing, and though he tended to see her as a child, it was a common failing of people of more years. At fifty-two, he was just nearing middle age himself, really, while clearly, she thought herself old enough for anything.

What journey? What wood? The same outcome as Essa? If so, it lay in mystery for him.

Elta was humming and beating time against the long tinted-plaster wall beside which they walked. The stiff climb didn't seem to affect her breath in the slightest. When she began to add words, he realized she was singing her mother's cards. She started with the correct order but she had begun to vary them in a pattern which had to do with the note order, not the images. She kept the words with their notes, created variation loops. He nodded in appreciation, began to hum a counterpoint in mountain plainsong, then quickly realized it wouldn't work, and switched to dune music. It was an eerie collaboration. She stopped after a moment, twirled around one full revolution on tiptoe, then hopped ahead.

"I can work with that," she said. "In the studio. We can record some of it. Tomorrow? I'm off work."

"That would be interesting," he said.

"Here we are! Supper!" she said, and they turned into a tall archway through open gates made of stained glass. "You like these?" she said. "Gata designed them. Beautiful. Commission. She does commissions. She lets me eat off the credit she got here in exchange. She can be fine. Sometimes." Then she was waving, running ahead to greet a ragtag crew of people at a table in the courtyard they were entering. Of them all, she seemed the oldest. He was suddenly glad he was fit, but again aware of his whole life, and what he knew of Essa's. Minh, he thought, we are wiser than we want to be, sometimes, aren't we?

"Minh," she called, getting the right pitch but pronouncing it completely wrong, "come and meet the band! The band and the hand!" And she laughed.

He resigned himself to a different name every day, and went to meet the young ones, smiling.

The trader had brought, wrapped in cloth in his shoulder bag, a small stringed instrument. He played its seven strings with special plectrum devices which curved around his fingertips.

"Portable fingernails," Elta said, approvingly.

"Finger picks," he said.

"Right," she said, turning back to her keyboard, looking for a key to harmonize with him, but his scale was not an octave, and she had to program the synthesizer to a new scale.

"First time I've ever tuned to a stringed instrument." She laughed, and began to pick out a background to the melody he was starting to pick.

"This is mountain music," he said. "Dune music is a cappella."

"What?"

"Unaccompanied voice."

"Oh. Right. Words."

"No, actually," he said. "Just voice. The words are improvised, mostly. Because . . . "

" . . . everything changes, right? So words aren't solid. Is the tune solid?"

"There are—'solid' tunes, yes. Also there are themes. Then there are improvisations."

"Do you know," she said, "I met a troupe of musicians from that southern land below the Dark Isles. They don't even have a word there for 'improvise.' They thought we scored everything. It was really strange. They watched and watched and they still could hardly get it."

"Because they didn't have a word for it."

"Oh! I suppose so . . . " she said slowly. "It never occurred to me."

"That words are useful for something?"

"Yes."

He laughed. "You should have met your genatrix," he said. "You would have been an interesting pair."

"She went to that southern land."

"Below the Dark Isles. Yes."

"Tell me about it."

"Later. The audience is getting restless. Too much tuning."

The crowd had finished buying their wine, their tea and fruit juices, had settled again around the tables. She turned immediately to them, began to introduce the next set. He watched her easy-looking camaraderie with the audience, saw again, as he'd already observed in the first two sets, that she created a persona at once more serious and steady than her daytime persona, and yet with humor and irony to make the audience chuckle and look more closely at the process. A careful performer, and a good one.

She was, he thought, much more serious about this than Gata gave her credit for being. He supposed that if she never left the compound she would not have seen Elta perform. He wondered how much distress that caused Elta.

He was looking forward to the first music he'd performed since leaving Avanue on this trip. And he was looking forward to the heel of the night, when, here at one of the tables with their stained and crumpled tablecloths or back in the restaurant where they'd eaten supper, he would talk to Elta about her mother.

Minh, he thought, as he bowed to acknowledge the greeting applause of the capacity crowd, I'm sure you never thought it would come to this. He could imagine how Ea heard Annalise at times like this. He wanted to hear Essa's voice.

From beside him, Essa's voice said, "Yeah, right! Give us that tune, traveler!" and the synthesizer notes began to chime behind his. He missed a note and turned in surprise. It was Elta, of course, with her voice like her mother's. He caught the tune again, and none of them knew—it was mountain music, they'd never heard it; how would they know he'd dropped a note? But Elta was winking at him, and when the riff came around again, he noticed she played the harmony for the correct note as he played it. His eyes had filled with tears involuntarily when he heard the voice; now he laughed aloud and picked up the tempo. She laughed too, and the audience began to clap and then, on the next tempo change, to stamp their feet. A couple of young people were dancing in front of the stage. Kids, really, he thought, and such show-offs; there are always a few of them, aren't there?

It is her gift, he thought then as Elta took a solo and created a vivid echo of his melody. She probably knows every music, in her bones.

He wondered if that Carrier of Spirits of whom he had heard so much from Essa had all the music in her memory too, and could she bring it out? What was the point, he wondered, of storing memory if it was not available? Memory was necessary to build the future, but why save it in the locked warehouse of one woman's—one being's—uncommunicative mind?

He wondered if someday Avanue medicine could map memory like they imaged the brain. He remembered the vivid colors of the image of Essa's brain, with the dark scar tissue of the injury across it. Eventually they had grown some living cells from a microscopic scrap of tissue removed during the operation, and transplanted them to that area, but he did not know if the regeneration had been effective. They said it would take years to find out, and he had not had years with her.

He had slowed the melody now to a sad, reflective circle of notes. Behind this basic structure, Elta was piling an increasing weight of harmonies, circling again and again to augment them. He thought it was like the weight of the past, the weight of memory, building and building until it seemed almost unbearable, and yet there was always room for more: another repetition, another variation. The clapping had long since died away and the audience was rapt and silent. Suddenly a clutch of despair squeezed his heart. How would he survive the rest of his long life? He was not yet very old, and yet he felt old. Like the Essa with the gray-streaked hair who had been carried raving off the ship at Avanue, and whose limp and pallid shape he'd tended unconscious until the day she woke to say "Minh" to him in the same rich voice he remembered.

I feel so old, she had said to him once. How will I live the rest of my life? Then, he hadn't really known what she meant, though he had understood. Now, he both understood and knew.

He glanced at Elta. Her young face was intent over the keyboard. She did not have any shadow on her. He wondered when it would start to hurt her, when her gift would become too heavy. Maybe, he thought, it will be all right for her. Emerging from the fog.

But he thought of the cards from which she had walked away, and he knew life is never easy for anyone.

"Minh," he said to her, "change." And as she pulled away the synthesizer layers, leaving only one long, trembling background note, he took the melody into a wild, whirlwind dance. He was improvising now, taking Essa's tune, that he had written for her, and adding her peripatetic daughter's speech and walking rhythms. She was grinning now, trying to keep up with him. Could she know? He doubted it, yet there were stranger gifts. She threw him a riff to which he had to respond, and suddenly they were playing a game of—what? Netball? Or this kenip-kenap they played here with noisy little paddles and stiff balls—back and forth, trying to stump each other with harder and harder riffs. The audience was laughing and cheering.

He noticed that despite the increased complexity, she never took her challenges outside the range, or the scale, in which his instrument could respond. She is very good, he thought. I must tell Gata.

"She wasn't like I expected," said Elta, lining up the edges of the stack of books on the café table. They had met in the quayside outdoor café where they first drank black wine, only a week before.

The trader was looking at her silently, sympathetically. He saw that she had tied the silk scarf about her wrist, under the cuff of her work shirt.

She pushed the books toward him.

"No, they're yours by blood," he said, throwing up his hands as if to ward them off.

"They're yours by love," she said. "And love and blood must not compete."

"You sound like you speak from experience."

"Oh, yes," she said. "After my parents handfasted the others, things were different. I was fourteen. You can imagine. You have met Gata. You have met Lowlyn. And you have met my other mother, my genatrix you call her. Essa."

"Yes, Minh," he said. "This is true. And I have met you."

"Are you my friend?" she asked.

"I have always been," he said. "I told you my name."

"Minh," she repeated confirmingly, getting it right. Was that accidental? "Is that unusual?"

"We do not ask, or tell, until we love," he said.

"Oh," she said, blushing, "and I asked you first thing! I'm sorry. I'm such a fool. My mother always tells me I have my foot between my teeth half the time."

"I could have refused," he said. "But my gift is to see. I saw you. You—" he looked down into his goblet of black wine: bought in the café again, not his private stock, not this time "—you looked like you would well use a friend of the sort I am. And—" a further hesitation "—you are like her. You are like her in the oddest ways, nothing I could have predicted. A tone of voice, a shape of the thumb. A shadow coming out when you are most yourself."

Elta cleared her throat, sniffed, cleared her throat again. Pushed the books into the center of the table.

"Gata told me stories about her," she said. "It is strange to read the other side—"

"An other side," he interrupted.

"—another side here. It is strange to see how she lived, where she came from. Gata really didn't understand, did she?"

"No, I don't think she did."

"Did you?"

"A little more, perhaps. I had traded in the mountains. I sent her east."

"She loved you."

"At the start, and at the end, I suppose that is true."

"And you loved her."

"Oh, yes, that is true. But that's not the story."

"Oh, I know," said Elta. "Do you know what my name signifies?"

"Yes. First letter genatrix. Next letters hand parents. Last two letters birth parent. I know the rules of sailor names."

"But the rule of the women in this line," she tapped the books, "was a different rule, and yet my name follows their rule too."

"The same word can mean many different things. The same phoneme."

"So I begin to see. But I'll never have a gift for it."

"Yes, I know. Your gift is quite different."

"Yes, but at least I understand it now. Something drove her, the words, the places she went, the things she did. Something I don't understand. Where did she go, in the end? What happened to her?"

"I don't know where she went, what happened. I only know what she said." He paused.

"What did she say?"

"She said . . . she was going to the New Wood."

"Her cards had that at the end!"

"Yes. So did yours."

"I told you not to tell me!" She got up suddenly, walked to the sea wall, drained her goblet and threw it in the sea, came back to sit down.

"Gata said she did that once, got drunk and threw something from this café into the sea. She was brought home by the watch and had to pay a fine. I'll pay for the goblet."

"No, I will. I can afford it. And foreigners have strange customs." He stood and walked to the wall, drained his goblet too, and threw it high and glittering into the ocean. Elta began to laugh delightedly.

The server came running. The trader gave him coins. "Two more goblets, black wine in a flagon, and keep the rest for your trouble," he said grandly, and the boy ran away grinning.

Elta said, "You have style. What were the other cards for me?"

"The mother, the journey, the new wood."

"Well, the first two make sense. I heard about my mother and it taught me something. So I went back to the college and signed up to finish my thesis."

"College? Thesis?" he said, taken aback. Wasn't this a forklift driver whose mother despaired of her accomplishing anything, who played nights with a jam band in a teaclub, who took pride in her image as a thoughtless, flighty pop culturist?

"Yeah, I went four years, but Gata wouldn't pay any more unless it was useful, and I was back to jobs and night clubs. Fine by me, really. I was sick of it. But the thesis I wanted to do was the music of all the places my mother lived and went. I wanted it from a kid, really. Listening to everything. Wanted to find her secret songs. Rationalized a thesis out of it, one night up late, horny and drunk and alone. I never actually told anybody—"

"Until now."

"Until yesterday. I went back up to my music teacher and told her about it. Must have made it sound all right—she said they'd give me half scholarship and my master's degree if I pull it off. Master's of music is the last degree, not like science or medicine where you go to the doctorate. Doctor of music, can you imagine? Surgery on a riff?"

She laughed, mimed a scalpel. The server brought new goblets and a flagon of wine.

"So I could teach if I wanted. But I'd probably only play. Still, if I want to do the tour, I might as well have something to show. And maybe Gata—" she paused, cleared her throat again "—maybe Gata will take a master's degree as enough. Leave me alone a bit."

"She's a difficult parent, but she loves you," he said, pouring the wine.

"I suppose she does."

"What about your hand?"

"I just live there," she said. "We're not really handfasted. They'll be fine with it. It makes the music grow, you know. That's really what we're together for. Not for—" she hesitated "—love."

"Yes. You said fuck comfortably at home. I never saw your home. And I'm leaving soon."

"Are you? Shall I come with you, come your direction first?"

"If you like. It's on the way to the mountains."

"I want you to be clear," she said. "I'm not looking for my mother—" she tapped her finger on the stack of books again "—like she did for hers. I'm not obsessed like she was. I don't even know if I want to meet her, you know. When I get to this last place, the New Wood, if she's there, I suppose I'll meet her, but it wouldn't be like meeting a mother. Gata and Lowlyn are my parents, for whatever pain I cause them and they cause me. That's how it works, isn't it? But she, Essa, she—"

"Minh," he said softly, naming Essa.

"—she is just a person in the world."

"Are you sure?"

"No. No. Of course I'm not sure. It's like those dunes of yours in that place. Anahue."

"Avanue."

"They shift. They move. I like what she wrote. Fat people sleeping. I could make their song—" and she hummed a rolling riff; he saw the dunes shift, and he shivered.

"See? But after I saw the places, heard other dune music besides yours, I could write it better. So I thought, I'll save from the job, butter up Gata and Lowlyn until they maybe give me some tuition, maybe even get a grant from the town. I'll record the music I hear in my head after reading these. Then I'll go see the places, and I'll write what I see there. It won't have any words. Unless I meet her. She can write the words."

"You can take the words out of here," he said, tapping the stack of books in his turn. "You can use their words."

She nodded, pulled the books back toward her. "I'd better keep them for a while, then," she said. "But I warn you. After the project's done you get them back. I travel light through life."

He laughed. "It's a deal," he said. "And I have another deal for you. I have a mind to help you with the trip. I have money. I will pay for your traveling, some of it, what makes sense."

She blushed again, and looked down at the books she now clutched to her chest. "I wasn't asking," she mumbled.

"I know," he said. "I was giving."

"What do I do now?" she said.

"Do now?"

"In your customs. I always get it wrong. I'm going to be such a stupid traveler. So what do I do back to you?"

"Accept," he said gently. "That's all."

"Accept with thanks," she said.

"No," he said. "Your thanks is the work."

"Oh, the work!" she said, forgetting her embarrassment. "It's going to be so great. I can hear it now . . . "

He raised a warding hand. "Shhh," he said. "You'll use it up. I know that never happened before, but this is bigger than you've done before, and more fragile."

"Oh!" she said. "Yes! That makes sense. I'll remember." And she folded her mouth shut with comic intensity.

He laughed. "You don't have to keep it a secret!" he said. "Just be careful. Do it, don't talk it."

"Were you her lover?" she said.

"No," he said. "Not quite, at the start; not at all, at the last. Her friend, then."

"I'm glad," she said. "Some say the generations can share all right, but I don't like it. I didn't like that Carrier woman smiling at me the way she did, while she was giving Gata my mother's message. I wouldn't want you to have been her lover too."

She meant Essa. He looked at her, sitting in the sun, smiling blandly, her eyes squinted a little against the strong reflection off the sparkling sea, and coughed a little, and smiled.

"You are going to be very interesting," he said, and she shouted with laughter. He smiled, and leaned back in his chair, settling himself a little. They both knew enough of what was to come to make them content as cats.

"Do you know where the New Wood is?" she said.

"No," he said, "and neither did she. But she said she had to find a place to live the rest of her life. And she set out."

"Well," said Elta serenely, "I'll find it."

And looking at her grinning and raising her goblet so that the black wine glinted its iridescent midnight-blue, he thought that if anyone could follow Essa, could find the New Wood, this singer could. He shivered in the warm sunlight, the same shiver he had felt beside the wall on that dusty street when the cards turned over.

The mother, the journey, the new wood. He raised his own glass and smiled at Elta.

"To the book of Elta," he said.

"The song of Elta," she said.

She put the books down in her lap, and smiled back at him, and they drank their black wine together in the sunlight.

The new wood

She awoke into darkness, and for a moment she did not know where or when she was at all; she almost raised her hand to make light before she remembered. She felt light somewhere though; she slipped out from under the arm around her without waking the sleeper. Following the pull, she stepped outside, the grass cool under her feet, and saw the path the forest had opened for her. Beside the opening stood the old man: thin, twisted, angry—waiting for her.

The moon had not yet risen but its light shone on the clouds above, so a little of its promise was diffused across the land.

She went toward the path, unafraid of him. She had grown so used to his malevolent, distant presence that she almost ignored him; her habit of putting out his food and milk had become as automatic as feeding the cats.

There was a moment, when she walked into the shade of the trees, when the memory of fear and silence came to her like a shadow, a rush of dark brilliance through her mind. She laughed. It was dark in the forest, and leafy branches slapped against her face and body; Essa put up her hand automatically, that gesture intact from childhood, to make a light.

And made a light.

The old man shrieked in fear. "What is that?"

"Light, at last," she said, still laughing. "And that has given me my answer. You will never have my soul in despair. I will possess myself in light."

Then in front of her she saw the doorway in the wood. Her light had lit it, though it was a hundred yards away through the trees. It shone toward her. She found that the path was easy, after all. The tearing branches of darkness were, in the soft globe she pulled around herself, the kindly shapes of trees again.

She began to run. The old man scurried behind her like a mouse, squeaking, but she could not hear his words for the clean sound of her feet on the wide, open path.

Would it be death? If so, she did not fear it, for she knew that her life would flow down the silver thread which always trailed her, to the Carrier of Spirits who would gather the rest of her in that vast sea of memory. Would she find her mother? She had found her mother. Would she go home? Where was home, anyway?

The trees were full of fireflies, and suddenly, as if a new goddess came to meet her, the moon, a vast-seeming golden sphere of light, softened at the edges by the thickness of the air, rose and came toward her. She ran in her own globe of golden radiance until she felt that like Skaalya in the legend she could learn to fly. She would fly up, she would dive into the Moon, she would know what this goddess knew, she would give herself to the light which had at long last returned itself to her.

She chased the moon toward her until they met at the doorway, the moon diving into the portal before Essa arrived. It was there, she knew, on the other side. Would she too pass through?

She stood in wonder before the doorway: was this what "wondering" truly meant? She could spend her life wondering.

The old man caught up to her, his face bleeding from the slap of thin whip branches in the dark. She had run too fast to leave the light for his passage. She turned almost in apology, but said nothing, for his face was pinched and cruel, and she remembered a cliff, and a falling star of stones, and she drew herself back and up.

Ahead of her was the bright doorway: green, iridescent, swirling, oval under the trees, lit from behind by the full moon.

She walked up to the swirling light of the wood. Her heart was beating rapidly as the heart of the kitten she had held in her hand only that morning. She remembered its wild-eyed, hastening gaze, full of anger and frustrated wanting. Then, she had laughed at it, laughed at the heart which fluttered inside the frail ribcage. Now she regretted the laugh. She had become young herself, and frightened. She hesitated.

"You will find your mother," he said, "where she went away from you into the future."

"I found my mother," she said.

"And lost her. And lost everything. Where did it go?"

Colder yet, at the bone. She stared back at him over her left shoulder. His face was sly, canny.

"You think it makes a difference now?" she said. "You think I need to know more? I don't."

"Here, you will die," he said. He was trying so clumsily to manipulate her that she laughed out loud at it.

"You are an old man," she said, "and jealous." She turned her face away from him, and toward the opaque chlorophyll storm.

The old woman had stepped out of the trees, walking along the scarlet thread binding them, and stood backlit by the moon, the thread looking black in this light, and solid.

"Yes, go through," said the old woman; "if you do not, there will be no silence for you ever. If you do not, the stories will rage in you, angry that you have not lived them. Go through and find the heart of the stories." The old woman pulled the string away, and handed her the heart at the end of it.

The heart of the world, she thought, waiting for me.

She put out her hand, palm forward and vertical, and slowly moved it toward the opal green fire. She felt the coldness grip her finger joints for a second, like the cramps she felt on damp days from the arthritis which would plague her old age. Through the cold, her hand stopped against the hard shell of the doorway. The softness of stone and the warmth of blood enfolded it.

She pushed.

The door opened.

"It is good. Go," said the old woman.

She put one foot up on the edge of the frame, began to climb through.

She heard the old man's voice behind her, crying, "Wait!"

She turned and looked again, this time over her right shoulder. His face was troubled, worried, doubting, without the sly grin with which he'd taunted her.

"It's too late to change your mind," she called. "You wanted me where I'm going; you lied; now I'm going. Be afraid, if you have to be. Or live a few more lifetimes, and follow."

The door was wide now. She turned her face into the storm of green, and swung her other foot up and through to complete the step forward. She felt the stone coalesce around her and the moonlight rush through with her.

Then she had slammed the door behind her and stood breathless in the New Wood.

It was the rush of joy she felt which woke her fully up.